Heart's Passage

Cate Swannell

Regal Crest Enterprises, LLC

Nederland, Texas

ISBN 1-932300-09-0

First Printing 2003

9 8 7 6 5 4 3 2 1

Cover design by Mary D. Brooks

Published by:

Regal Crest Enterprises, LLC
PMB 210, 8691 9th Avenue
Port Arthur, Texas 77642-8025

Find us on the World Wide Web at
http://www.regalcrest.biz

Printed in the United States of America

Acknowledgments

Heartfelt thanks to my partner for her undying love and support; to Beth Shaw, beta reader and late night gibberer extraordinaire; to Siggy for the snuggles; to Sue McCulloch for asking all the right questions; to all the folks at RAP, particularly Lori, Barb, Linda and MaryD; and finally to LL, ROC, RT and MG for the inspiration to battle on.

For my Lady Moonshadow, keeper of Steelwing's soul

"Being deeply loved by someone gives you strength; loving someone deeply gives you courage."

– Lao Tzu

Prologue

Somewhere, water was dripping. The sound echoed off the cold, rust-stained walls, deep in the bowels of Sydney's Central Criminal Courts. Down here, in the holding cells and interrogation rooms, the damp was rising. Everything smelled dank and wet and rotten.

The woman sat silently, her senses pounded into submission, all her energy focused on surviving minute to minute. Pale blue eyes flittered around the room, absorbing all the details. She sucked them in as if each piece of minutiae could somehow, at any moment, become a matter of life and death.

Hypersensitive, the dark-haired woman felt the hard edges of the bare wooden chair pressing against both the backs of her knees and her shoulder blades. The blue tank top and jeans she wore did little to stop the chill she felt deep in her bones. She blinked several times in the harshness of the bare bulb hanging a few feet above the scarred surface of the wooden table, and shivered, wishing she was anywhere but here.

Like a bad movie, she thought. *Like every bad gangster flick ever made. How the fuck did I get here? Seems like yesterday that I came to this city, full of piss and vinegar and big plans.*

Wearily she reached up and brushed her long hair out of her face, willing the throbbing headache behind her eyes to dissipate. No such luck.

A movement just beyond the arc of light drew her attention and she watched warily as the man moved forward out of the shadows.

Detective Ken Harding was a typical specimen of middle-aged Australian manhood—bald, 50-ish, with a beer belly that looked almost painfully swollen, and a drinker's nose that spoke volumes about his off-duty hours. Harding was a sweating, cigarette-smoking, walking heart-attack-in-waiting. The woman tried hard not to smell him; tried hard not to notice the perspiration rings on the cheap, polyester shirt straining across the expanse of his pot gut.

Harding was having his moment in the sun. Six months' hard work had led him to the woman, who looked up at him now through half-lidded, disinterested eyes.

Those eyes. He dragged his own away from her hypnotic blue gaze with an effort, and reached for his smokes. *Only one left. Fuck.* He shook the last cigarette out of the packet and propped it in the corner of his mouth, searching his pockets for his lighter.

Those baby blues had seen a lot, witnessed the last moments of many poor souls, some deserving of the woman's harsh brand of justice, some not so much.

But Harding had lucked out. *No doubt about it,* he thought as he flicked his thumb across the striker and lit his last cigarette. Around the time he had started tightening the net he had thrown around her, Sydney's No.1 underworld assassin had decided she'd had enough. *No way would she be sitting here now if that hadn't been her choice.*

He knew of at least six executions for which she was personally responsible, and God only knew how many others he didn't know about. An anachronism in a country where organized crime was still in its infancy, she was almost other-worldly, a legendary figure he had half-believed didn't exist, until the moment he heard her voice on the other end of the phone line, turning herself in.

One of the coldest killers ever known to the Vice Squad had become the super-grass to top all super-grasses. And as ruthless as she had been on the streets and back alleys of Sydney's underbelly, she had been equally so in the courtroom. Three of the biggest drug lords in the country were behind bars now as a result of her testimony.

And now she would get her reward. Immunity from prosecution, provided she kept her nose clean in the future, and a new identity.

Oh yeah, Detective Ken Harding—soon to be Detective Superintendent Ken Harding—was one lucky son of a bitch. The cop dragged deep on his cigarette and watched the woman warily.

Jo Madison was certainly worth watching. Six feet tall, with legs that went on for hours and a body...well, even Harding's long-dead libido and alcohol-pickled gonads felt a twinge as he took in her long, athletic frame.

A body made for sin, but she's colder than a witch's tit, he thought. Five weeks he had spent with the woman, and he knew less about her now than when he first got the phone call from her that had begun this process. She came from nowhere and now she would disappear into thin air again. A phantom.

Jo sat across from him, silent as a rock, giving nothing away in her face or body language.

He took another drag.

"So," he said. She raised one eyebrow slightly in response. "We need to talk about the protection program we're gonna put you in," he continued. Silence and a cold blue gaze were his only reply. "It's late. Tomorrow morning you'll get your new life. New papers, new identity, a job. We'll even buy you some new..."

"No."

"...clothes, and wipe off your record. What did you say?"

"No."

"Whaddaya mean, no?"

She just stared back at him.

"You don't mean no, Madison. Look, trust me, okay, we'll see you right."

"No."

"Fuck me," said Harding under his breath. "Look, I hate to remind you of this, but you just made a shitload of enemies. You need protection."

"Nobody looks out for me, but me," she said sharply. "And I know all about making enemies."

"Don't be bloody stupid, girl."

Madison slammed her hand down flat on the tabletop.

"Call me that again, fat boy, and I'll take out your voice box with that pen of yours before you even remember you've got a gun, let alone pull it," she snarled, her eyes perceptibly darkening in anger.

Harding raised his hands and backed up a step, cigarette smoke curling around him from the butt wedged between his fingers. "Okay, okay, no need to get bent out of shape. Jesus."

Madison sank back into the chair, content to let the cop sweat.

"Don't you realize that without the Witness Protection Program you're completely on your own?" Harding asked, flicking his butt into the corner. "They'll come after you, Madison, and there won't be a damn thing we can do about it. Except tag your toe and slam the fridge door behind you. You can't survive out there without our protection."

"What the fuck do you think I've been doing for the past 10 years, Harding?" replied the assassin. "I haven't exactly been running for Miss Congeniality. I've survived in this business without any help from you or your cronies, or anyone else for that matter. I've dodged more bullets than you've had cold beers."

Harding snorted. "And trust me, that's a shitload of bullets," he muttered.

Not even a hint of a smile touched Madison's lips. "Cut me loose, Harding. Wipe off my record and cut me loose."

"Jesus Christ..." Harding ran a meaty hand through what was left of his hair. "Where will you go? How will you get there?"

Again, the eyebrow.

"Telling you any of that would rather defeat the purpose, wouldn't it, Harding?" she growled, pushing herself up from the chair with a scrape of wood on concrete. At her full height she bested him by a good five or six inches. Her face was now in shadow but what light there was glinted off pale blue eyes.

"You can trust me," the cop said quietly.

Madison snorted. "Right," she said curtly. "Just give me my jacket and I'll be out of your life for good."

And there's a big part of me that doesn't want that, Harding caught himself thinking. Instead of saying anything he turned around, flicking the woman's leather jacket off the hook behind the door. He held it out to her and a long-fingered hand reached out to take it from him.

"There's nothing I can do to change your mind?" He had to give it one last shot.

She shrugged the jacket on quickly, sparing him a quick glance. "No."

He sighed. "Fine. Sign this." He pushed a piece of paper towards her then tossed his pen on top of it.

She grunted. "What's this?"

"A waiver," he answered curtly. "It just says you refused our protection."

She snorted her derision. "Covering your arse, Harding?" She leaned down and scribbled her signature on the bottom of the form before she flicked the pen back at him.

"Where you're concerned? Always. Come on then." He led the way through the labyrinth of corridors and stairways until they came to a heavy fire door. "Back entrance," he muttered, pushing down on the release and shoving the door outwards. Madison brushed past him and he followed her, leaning on the door to keep it open.

The night was cool and damp, streetlamp light shining off the wet sidewalks. Occasional flashes of lightning lit the alleyway like daylight.

Madison walked away without a word or a backward glance, hands buried deep in the jacket's pockets, collar turned up against the chill wind. Harding watched her retreating back, surprised to find himself quietly concerned about the woman's future well-being.

For Christ's sake, Harding, he chastised himself. *She can kill a man with a flick of her finger. She sure as shit doesn't need you worrying about her.* A flash of lightning cast everything in an eerie blue glow and Harding blinked against the sudden glare. When he blinked again the assassin was gone, melting into the night as quietly and as quickly as she emerged.

Harding blinked again, hearing only the drip of rain in puddles, seeing only a scurrying rat.

I hope she makes it.

Chapter
One

Arcadia Jones was bored. She had no business being bored, of course. *After all, isn't this every girl's dream?* she thought wryly to herself. She was dressed to kill, squired by one of the most powerful women in the Midwest—or so people kept telling her—and she was currently sitting on a barstool in the middle of one of the year's swankiest cocktail parties. *What is there to be bored about?*

She sighed, and took another sip from the exceptionally dry martini she was nursing. *Well, at least the venue for this schmooze fest is a little different than the norm,* she thought. Over 200 of Chicago's well-heeled men and women were currently kissing butt on the observation deck of the Sears Tower—1373 feet high, according to the natty little fact box on the gold-inscribed invitation. Not that Arcadia had received her own invitation. This was, after all, her partner's party.

She placed her martini glass carefully back on the bar top before she gazed around the room. It was set up as essentially a square doughnut, with the central core of escalators and bathrooms surrounded by a seething mass of partygoers, wet bars, and waiters. It was New Year's Eve and the observation deck was packed. Balloons, mirror balls, champagne, and caviar provided the ambience, but Cadie had no taste for any of it. She slid off her stool and wandered over to the floor-to-ceiling windows on the eastern side of the building. As she made her way through the crowd it didn't surprise her that nobody greeted her or stopped her for a conversation. This wasn't her scene after all.

It never had been.

At last she reached the window and, with a feeling of tired relief, leaned against the large pay telescope as she stared out at the spectacular view. It was a clear night and if it was possible for deep cold to look like anything, the crystal-sharp twinkling of the city lights and the few boats out on Lake Michigan were it. Snow didn't stay long on the ground in downtown Chicago, but the lights caught the swirling drift of a fresh fall being blown between the skyscrapers.

Cadie knew it was freezing outside and part of her longed to be out there, away from the pressing heat of the crowd behind her. She sighed again and turned back to face the masses. She closed her eyes, trying to tune out the loud conversations going on all around her. The talk was loud, the drinking excessive, and the politics fierce and, as usual, underhanded.

Here I am again, thought Cadie. *Alone on New Year's Eve, despite the crowd and the presence of the one person who's supposed to make me feel—* She opened her eyes again. *What? Something.* An ironic chuckle escaped her lips as it occurred to Cadie that feeling something—anything—would be better than this...loneliness.

She gazed across the room and caught sight of her lover...if that was the right word for what they were anymore. Cadie swore some days she felt more like an unpaid secretary and ego-masseur than a partner. Certainly there hadn't been much in the way of loving lately. *Actually there hasn't even been much civility,* she realized glumly.

The Republican senator from Illinois was doing what she did best, talking up a storm, pressing the flesh, and making nice with the powerbrokers of Chicago. She was surrounded by bankers, newspaper editors, and those quieter men, the ones in the expensive Italian suits who listed their occupation in their passports as "importer." Cadie watched, as she always did, with a kind of disquieted fascination as her partner moved easily from one group to the next, slipping comfortably into the rhythms of political maneuvering.

Senator Naomi Silverberg had come a long way from the bright-eyed college student with whom Cadie had fallen in love. Re-election in November had been almost a given, but, if anything, that had only increased Cadie's growing feeling of impending doom about their relationship. Power had, as always, come at a price. In this case, it was Silverberg's ideals and their partnership.

Where has it all gone? Twelve years of togetherness can't have been a waste of time, can it? That idealistic and principled, fun-loving woman she had fallen in love with back in college had long ago disappeared, it seemed, buried under a ton of compromise, lobbying, fund-raisers, and filibustering.

Cadie snagged a passing waiter by the elbow, picking up a very full glass of tequila sunrise from his tray.

When in doubt, she sighed, *opt for oblivion. Or at least a slightly blurred perspective.* She turned back to the view over the Chicago skyline.

It wasn't long before she felt an all too familiar presence beside her. The stocky, well-tailored senator leaned back against the railing and gazed back at the crowd. Cadie glanced at the familiar profile briefly, taking in the rounded features, deep-set brown eyes, and salt-and-pepper hair cut in a severely short style.

"You could at least try and look like you're having a good time," Silverberg growled as she pasted a smile on her face and raised her hand to a passing socialite.

"I am having a good time. The view is lovely," said Cadie. "I'd rather enjoy myself over here on my own, than pretend to care what these people think." *Oooo, grumpy Arcadia.*

"Give me a break, will you?" her partner hissed. "This is payback for support through the re-election campaign. You know that. What is your goddamned problem?" Silverberg shifted gears quickly at the approach of a suit. "Jack! How are you? Thanks for coming." She shook the man's hand and pointed him in the direction of the buffet. "Help yourself, please. I'll be with you directly."

Cadie held her tongue until the local government official was out of earshot.

"My problem, Naomi, is that half the people in this room are of the '112 indictments, no convictions' philosophy of life and the other half are butt-kissing, lobbyist-schmoozing, semi-corrupt politicians. And that paints you with the same brush," she snapped.

"Keep your voice down, Arcadia," muttered Silverberg. "When the hell did you get so holier than thou? You know this is how the game is played. You can't get anywhere in politics without these people, and more importantly, without their money." She glanced at her partner. "It's been like that since well before you and I got into it, and it will always be that way. You knew what you were buying into, so don't try and tell me it's come as a shock."

Cadie scrubbed her hand wearily across her eyes, aware belatedly that she probably wasn't doing much for her mascara.

"Look, I'm sorry, okay," she offered, tired of the squabbling. "It's been a long day and you know I've never enjoyed these things." She tucked her hand into Naomi's elbow and looked up at her. "It's just that you and I haven't had time for each other in...well, in years, Nay. I'm tired of feeling like I'm alone in this marriage."

But the senator was in no mood for that particular conversation and she impatiently shrugged Cadie's hand free as another lobbyist caught her eye from across the room.

"We're going on vacation soon, aren't we?" she grumbled even as she flashed a brilliant smile at the man. "What more do you want? Now, come on, let's for God's sake try and look like we're together and happy or the goddamned GLAAD representative is going to get on my case."

The senator moved off, intercepting the lobbyist, and steering him towards a group of local Chicago councilors near the wet bar. Cadie sighed and drained her glass again, grateful for the tiny buzz and blurred edges the tequila afforded. The mascara on her fingertips told her some repair work was in order, so she headed for the nearest restroom, working her way through the crowd and into the starkly lit bathroom.

Her reflection didn't do much for her mood. Her strawberry blonde hair was piled high in a loose bun, softly curling tendrils framing her face. She had never considered herself anything more than nice-looking, but Arcadia Jones had a gently beautiful face that was open and appealing. She was wearing an off-the-shoulder green cocktail dress which was stunning on her compact, athletic frame. Normally the dress would have emphasized her seagreen eyes, but right now the smudged mascara made her look like...

"Like an overdressed badger," she muttered to herself.

Just then a tall redhead staggered out of one of the cubicles, sniffing and wiping her nose suspiciously. The light sheen of sweat on her forehead spoke volumes for the effect of whichever illicit substance she had just stuffed into her nasal passages. Cadie dodged out of the woman's way as she struggled to keep herself upright on her stilettos.

"Looking for a little blow, sweetie?" slurred the redhead. "It's quality shit, I promise." She held out a small cigarette paper of white powder to Cadie. "C'mon babe, it's free and it's flowing like water here tonight."

"No. Thanks. Really," said Cadie, fighting down a wave of nausea. The woman reeked of alcohol and puke. Cadie turned to get as far away from her as possible.

"Suit yourself, cupcake," shrugged the taller woman. "But you don't know what you're missing."

Cadie's curiosity warred with the sick feeling in her guts. "You said it was freely available here tonight," she ventured. "Uh...where did you get it from, exactly?"

The woman laughed drunkenly and swayed a little as she tried haphazardly to reapply some lipstick. "Well, you're here so you must be a friend of Naomi's. So I guess that means I can trust you," the redhead said, turning to face Cadie. "Have you noticed the waiters in each corner, not doing much, just standing there?"

Cadie nodded. She had thought they were security guards blending in with the staff.

"Just say the word and they'll get you what you need. It's all been taken care of."

"By whom?"

The woman laughed, leaning in unsteadily and blasting Cadie with her rancid breath. "Well, whose party is it, sweetie?" She laughed again and stumbled out of the restroom into the midst of the crowd, a wave of party noise taking her place as the door swung shut.

For a stunned minute Cadie tried to get a grip on what she'd just been told. What she knew about who Naomi was—*or rather, who she used to be,* Cadie corrected herself—ran headlong into a battle with the information she'd just been handed on a platter. Another wave of nausea gripped her guts and suddenly she knew she was going to throw up. She made a dive for the nearest cubicle and emptied her stomach in a series of wracking spasms that left her clammy and sore.

"Oh God," she muttered. "I haven't eaten that much in a month."

She stood up slowly and flushed, leaning against the wall as she waited to make sure she'd cleaned up all the mess. When she looked down into the bowl she almost lost it again. The water sloshed back and forth of its own accord, testament to the wind's effect on one of the world's tallest buildings. Cadie groaned.

"That's just not right. I am *so* out of here."

She quickly cleaned herself up and left the bathroom, looking left and right for the senator. Cadie spotted her, finally, tucked in a corner with a group of be-suited men who seemed to be hanging on her every word.

Good. She's not going to miss me any time soon, thought Cadie as she turned towards the hatcheck room beside the bank of elevators.

"Leaving so soon, miss?" the attendant asked as he handed over her coat. "It's not even close to midnight yet."

"I'm not feeling too well," Cadie replied. "Thought I'd be better off with a cup of hot chocolate and a warm fire."

"Ah well. Happy New Year, miss."

"Thanks. You too." Cadie pushed the button for the express lift. The ride down was swift, but did nothing for the equanimity of her stomach. She was more than grateful for the shock of the

cold winter's air as she emerged on to South Wacker Drive. Snow
swirled around her as she looked left and right along the busy
thoroughfare. It was just occurring to her that finding a taxi on
New Year's Eve would not necessarily be easy when one magically
appeared at the curb next to her.

"Something had to go right tonight," she murmured as she
clambered gratefully into the back. "Indian Hill Road, Kenil-
worth, please," she quietly told the driver as she settled into the
seat, pulling the faux fur coat around her.

Happy New Year, Arcadia.

The dream plummeted her into a maelstrom of confusing
images and emotions. Everyone she knew was there somewhere.
Her parents. Naomi. Sebastian, still radiantly handsome, forever
18.

*There were plenty of nameless faces as well but Cadie felt
overwhelmed as they paraded past her. She realized suddenly that
she was on a carousel, clinging to a painted pony. Her own hands
swam in front of her as they clutched the gilded pole that impaled
her horse to the carousel's deck. A wave of nausea flip-flopped
her stomach as she spun, faster and faster, the faces of those she
loved flying past.*

*The carousel's music machine cranked out a tinkling melody
that sped up with the ponies, taking on an hysterical quality that
grated against Cadie's sensibilities.*

*Again nausea washed over her and she wrapped her arms
more tightly around the pole, fearful of losing her balance as the
pony's up and down motion warred with the centrifugal force of
the carousel.*

*The swirling faces closed in around her and now Cadie could
hear voices. Naomi's sarcasm, her father's constant urging to do
better, and her mother's tears. The nameless faces talked too—
about elections and fund-raising, lobbying, and drug deals. The
voices battered her, melting into a cacophony that pounded
against her. Cadie could taste the bile in the back of her throat,
could smell her own fear.*

*And then she felt another presence, this one behind her in the
pony's saddle, a warm, solid body behind hers. Strong arms
wrapped around her waist and pulled her closer still. The hands
that held her safe were long-fingered and elegant, but there was no
mistaking the steel in their sinews.*

*"Don't listen to them," came a low rumble against her ear.
The voice was distinctive; a rich alto that sent shivers down*

Cadie's spine. She tried to turn in the woman's arms but the arms held her firm. Instead, she turned her head, looking back over her shoulder into a pair of the bluest eyes she had ever seen. Nobody has eyes that color, she thought. Not possible.

The dream's landscape changed, the carousel fading away, replaced by a swirling, damp fog. The arms around her waist relaxed and withdrew, allowing Cadie to turn around. But all she could see were the eyes. Even as she watched they began to fade, the fog closing in around them. Irrationally, the fear rose again as the reassuring presence retreated and Cadie found herself wanting to ask her to stay.

Before she could voice her request, though, that voice came again in her head.

"I'll always be here."

And then, the eyes were gone and the fog closed around her...

Cadie snapped out of her dream-troubled sleep when she felt the bed move as Naomi slid in. She flicked her eyes to the alarm clock on her bedside table, unsurprised to see its red glare proclaiming 3.44am. *I guess I should be grateful it's not dawn.*

She held her breath, praying Naomi wouldn't attempt one of her infamous late-night displays of so-called affection. Thankfully she felt her partner settle into the bedclothes and heard her breathing slow into a sleepy, snoring rhythm. She closed her own eyes and tried desperately to still her mind enough to fall asleep again.

Disjointed memories of the dream floated back to her but Cadie couldn't get a grip on the details. *I felt so safe. And that voice...* She sighed. *I wonder who that was. Probably somebody I ran into during the campaign, I guess.* She put the dream out of her mind and closed her eyes again. *Sleep, Cadie, sleep.*

A few minutes later she blinked again.

No such luck. Cadie resigned herself to a restless night and gently rolled out of bed. Naomi snuffled and mumbled senselessly in her sleep.

"Hot chocolate," Cadie muttered, "a girl's best friend." She pulled on a thick pair of wool socks and her robe and padded down to the kitchen. As she moved about fixing her favorite winter beverage, she hummed quietly. Then she tucked herself into a corner of the bay window seat, her legs curled under her, and watched the moonlight reflecting off the snow in her backyard.

Her brain was still spinning from the evening's revelations. She didn't want to believe Naomi was capable of using drugs to get what she wanted out of her political career. But it did make some things start to make sense. Whispered phone calls, late-night meetings that were never explained, and a sudden decision two years ago to split their financial records after a decade of joint accounting, all bubbled up in Cadie's memory.

Privately she had believed the senator was having an affair. The scary thing was she hadn't been all that upset at the prospect. God knows it took the pressure off her in the bedroom, and that was more a relief than anything. There was something very unsexy about a politician on the make, Cadie had discovered. *But this...*

Cocaine. Cadie shuddered. She'd lost her older brother, Sebastian, to a drug overdose when she was eight years old. The trauma had led to a deep-seated distaste for any illegal substances. She had thought her partner had shared that conviction, had been certain of it. *Until recently.*

So I guess now we have to have a conversation, Cadie thought as she cupped her hands around the warm mug of chocolate. Quickly she lifted the mug to her lips and drained the last of the sweet liquid, replacing the mug on the table. She sighed and leaned her head back against the cushions of the seat. *Great. And we all know I do so well with confrontation.* She let her mind drift, and it wasn't long before sleep claimed her.

She was still there when Naomi came down for breakfast at 7am, clunking around the kitchen grumpily, banging pots onto the stovetop and cursing.

"Morning," Cadie said quietly from the bay window.

"Where the fuck is Consuela? I've got a 9am meeting downtown and I'm desperate for some breakfast," replied Naomi, looking decidedly unsenatorial in rumpled pajamas buttoned unevenly, her hair sticking out at all angles.

"It's New Year's Day, Naomi. I gave her the day off. There are eggs and bacon in the fridge though. That shouldn't take too long."

"Right. I'll have coffee too. M'gonna grab a shower."

And with that she was gone, harrumphing back upstairs.

"No, no, please allow me to cook your breakfast, Your Highness," Cadie muttered as she reluctantly uncurled herself from her nook. She opened the fridge and pulled out bacon, eggs, and orange juice, then put the coffee on as she heated up the frying pan. Three slices of bacon and two eggs over easy soon slid their way onto a plate, a steaming mug of coffee sitting next to it. Cadie walked back to the window seat, munching on the plate of buttered toast she had made for herself.

Twenty minutes later the senator re-emerged, buttoning herself into a tailored power suit. She put her briefcase on the counter and flopped down onto a stool, attacking the plate of food.

"Everything to your liking, Senator?" Cadie asked, trying hard to keep the sarcasm and weariness out of her voice.

Naomi glanced up and grunted. "S'not hot enough," she muttered.

"Doesn't seem to be slowing you down any."

Naomi threw her knife and fork down onto the plate. "What's your problem now, Cadie?" she growled. "And by the way, where the fuck did you get to last night?"

"Oh, you did notice, then?"

"Jesus. What, Cadie?"

"We need to talk."

"Not now. I've got a full day."

"Damn it, Nay, you're not the only one, you know."

The senator snorted. "Come on, Cadie."

"Come on *what?*" Cadie exploded. "I can't possibly be as busy as you? And even if I was, it's just not as important as your work, right?" The blonde came out of her seat quickly, facing her partner across the kitchen island, green eyes blazing.

"Is that what this is about? You're jealous." Naomi leaned over, spitting the words out around a sneer.

"Yeah that's right, Naomi. I'm jealous of a woman who's sold out every principle she used to believe in and has sunk about as low as she can go. Including, apparently, providing drugs to her financiers in exchange for support. I am *so* jealous of the political whore you've become." The words poured out of Cadie in a surge of anger she hadn't known she was harboring. But one look at the senator's face made her bite back any further accusations.

Cold fury oozed out of the stocky woman's brown eyes and Cadie felt a chill. "Whoever you've been talking to, they've told you a pack of lies, Cadie," the senator hissed. "Who was it?"

Cadie hesitated, thrown by the icy stillness in her partner's attitude. "A...just a woman at the party last night," she stammered.

"Just a woman? A stoned, high, fucked-up woman, I presume?"

"Y-yes."

"So you'd take her word over mine? You'd take the word of a junkie who happened to have the bad taste to hit up in the middle of my cocktail party?"

Cadie stayed silent. She knew she was no match for Naomi in a debate so she opted not to continue this one. Besides she could feel her stomach wanting to rebel again, a sure sign she was out of her depth. She watched as the senator picked up her briefcase and came around the island towards her. She didn't move as Naomi brushed her cheek with an air kiss.

"I'm hurt, Cadie. Hurt and disappointed." Naomi smiled a smile that held utterly no warmth. "You're right. Apparently we do need to talk. But I think it's you that needs to do some deep thinking. An apology, perhaps? I'll see you tonight."

With that the senator stalked from the room, leaving Cadie standing stunned and bewildered in the middle of the kitchen, in her stockinged feet and robe, feeling as if her life had just slipped through her fingers.

How the hell did I end up here?

The nightmare wrenched Jo awake like a slap in the face. She choked back the cry on her lips and sat bolt upright, the sheets clinging uncomfortably to the light sheen of sweat on her body.

It took a moment to wake completely but once she shook off the last remnants of haze Jo slumped forward, her face in her hands, elbows on knees. A splash of moonlight fell across her, turning her tousled black hair silver.

"Jesus Christ," she muttered. She took several deep breaths in an effort to stop her heart from beating its way out of her chest. It took all her concentration to fight down the panic and rising bile in her throat. She groaned again as flashes of the recurring dream images burned across the back of her eyes. *Oh, that was a nasty one.*

Muffled incoherent noises to her right stopped her short and Jo cursed when she recognized the lump under the bedclothes next to her as the woman she'd met in JC's Bar and Grill on the main drag of Airlie Beach the night before. Several stubbies of cider and a bottle of red had apparently convinced Jo that some company was in order. She couldn't remember much about it, she admitted to herself guiltily. *Not even...*

God, what is her name? Jo shook her head at her own lack of good sense and clambered out of bed. *And more to the point, what the hell was I thinking bringing her back here? Now I'm stuck with her till at least breakfast,* she thought despondently as she silently padded across the polished wooden floor through to the living area. She muffled another curse as she stubbed her toe on the cat's water dish on the way to the fridge. She hopped the rest of the way and balanced on the appliance's open door as she surveyed the contents by the internal light.

One can of Coke left. Time to go grocery shopping.

Jo withdrew the remaining can and cracked the seal as she wandered to the glass wall overlooking her particular patch of paradise. She quietly slid open the glass door that led to the verandah and moved outside.

Jo had done all right for herself in the five years since the cold night she had snuck out of Sydney after her brief, but fiery argument with Det Harding. As she had walked away from him that night all she could think of was getting as far away from the city streets as she could. *Sunlight,* she had thought. *I want sunlight and warmth on my back.*

Peace and quiet had beckoned to her from far north Queensland and she had made her way to the Whitsundays, a long, idyllic group of islands just inside the Great Barrier Reef off Airlie Beach and Shute Harbor.

Here she'd found a community of like-minded folk. *Not that they're all ex-assassins,* she thought, smiling wryly. *Though I can think of a few who might qualify.* They let her be when she needed isolation, and made her welcome when she needed to feel a part of the human race again. Many of the people here were refugees from big-city life who came north to try a get-rich-quick scheme in the tourist mecca of the Whitsundays, or were just looking for a simpler life.

And cheaper dope, she reminded herself with a smile. She'd stayed clear of that scene though—too many bad memories. She wasn't averse to a party, the evidence of which was snoring softly in her bed, but an alcoholic haze was the only form of oblivion she felt safe with these days, and that pretty rarely.

The last five years have been good ones, she decided. *Lonely, yes, directionless, sure, but at least I can sleep at night.* She laughed at the memory of the nightmare. *Sort of. And I'm earning an honest living.* Not that she really needed to.

A decade spent in the darkness of Sydney's underworld had left Jo a rich woman thanks to a couple of wise offshore investments. She had since removed all her funds from anything illegal and now the cash burned a large hole in her legitimate bank account. Contrition had stopped her from touching those funds, except in one respect.

The house high on the hill above Shute Harbor had called to her like no other place she'd ever lived in. Nestled into a lush rainforest on the side of the slope, the house was built of jarrah logs and made the most of the sensational views of the islands by being almost all glass on its northeast-facing side. It had cost the earth, but Jo hadn't hesitated for a second, deciding the isolation and panorama were well worth it. There were no neighbors in either direction for over a mile, she was just a 10-minute drive from the dock itself, and the forest around her was laced with the narrow dirt tracks she used for running and getting up close and personal with the abundant wildlife in this part of the world.

And there are worse things than being hidden away in the jungle. Jo had never been overly concerned about her former bosses and adversaries coming after her following her disappearance from Sydney, even though they had every reason to hate her. She knew she could handle anyone who got close enough to be a threat to her. She'd invested in a top-drawer security system that she maintained meticulously with the kind of caution that had become ingrained in her over the years. Jo had made a concerted effort to get on with her life as if she'd never been a drug lord's hired killer.

Even now, the thought made her shake her head. *Another life. One I don't ever want to go back to or be reminded of.* Which was why the dreams were such a pain in the subconscious.

Jo settled into the rattan chair on the verandah and put her feet up on the top rail. It was hot as only a north Queensland January night could be, damp heat wrapping round her naked body like a wet blanket. There wasn't a zephyr of a breeze.

Gorgeous night. The sky was cloudless and the moon full, splashing a silver sheen across Whitsunday Passage and Shute Harbor, which shimmered like a mirror. It made her smile quietly. She'd never really known what peace was until she had come here. It was hard to be tense when surrounded by total beauty like this surreal landscape.

It hadn't stopped the nightmares though. Jo sighed as memories of the dream intruded again. It was pretty much as it had always been. Horrible images from the night that had changed her life forever. She closed her eyes and let them come again.

The girl had been different from her other marks. Younger, for a start, and not a competitor of Jo's boss. She was just immature and stupid and had made some poor decisions. Like badmouthing him to his employees, ragging on his lack of competence in bed. And skimming off the top of the few drug deals he'd been generous enough to let her organize. And then, fatally, she had whinged to the cops.

Jo had fielded the phone call from her boss at 1am on a cold, wet and unforgiving winter's night.

"I want the little bitch taken care of, Madison," he had

barked. "I want it public, I want it messy, I want it untraceable. You got me?"

"Trying to send a message, boss?" she'd asked dryly, making the most of his soft spot for her to get in a little dig at his macho posturing.

"Just do it. I'll make the usual arrangements for your payment. I want her gone, Jo."

She'd hung up and knocked back the last of the large glass of very expensive scotch she had been nursing all night.

So much for a relaxing night off, *she'd thought as she carefully placed the glass back on the marble-topped dining table. Jo had taken her time preparing for her task. She had collected the tools of her trade—a custom-handled silver Colt Commander tucked into a discreet holster on the back of her hip, a wicked, thin-bladed knife in her boot and a piano-wire garrote, her weapon of last resort, hung from her belt.*

It hadn't felt any different from the other times. As she stepped out from her warehouse apartment deep in the back alleys of King's Cross and walked off into the night, there had been no inkling that this would be the end of the line for Jo, the changing of her life.

Jo had found the girl, much as she'd expected, sitting on the pavement in front of one of the all-night coffee shops on Oxford Street, sharing a joint with a thin, beautiful gay boy, fresh from the dance clubs.

Too stupid to know she's in trouble, *Jo had thought as she stood across the street, watching from a darkened doorway.* Or too stoned. *She glanced impatiently at her watch.* Time to make this happen.

She had shrugged herself upright and stepped forward into the light, waiting for a break in the traffic and beginning to cross the road. The girl caught sight of her and Jo had stopped, letting the wind heighten what was already, she knew, an intimidating sight.

The girl had seen a tall, gothic figure dressed in black from head to foot, ice-cold blue eyes boring into her, hands slowly flexing into fists and opening again by her sides. The wind whipped Jo's long, black hair around her face, and her full-length black coat around her legs. The girl knew Jo, knew what she did, and had felt the chill as realization hit. Her male companion had been a beat ahead of her, and was already making a hasty retreat.

Jo had waited. She knew there was no rush and the ending was inevitable. She just had to let it happen in its own time. Slowly the girl stood, unsteady on her feet from the hash and the fear.

"W-what do you want?"

Jo had let a feral grin cross her face.

"You."

That did it. The adrenalin had finally kicked in for her quarry, who took off down Oxford Street towards the city centre. Jo didn't rush but followed at a light jog, knowing at this time of night there wasn't much of a crowd for the girl to lose herself in. She saw her prey duck into an alley and had almost laughed at the simplicity of it all. It was a dead-end with nowhere to go but oblivion.

Jo slowed to a walk as she entered the alley, ignoring the stench from the piles of garbage. One foot kicked aside a rat carcass, and ahead she could see the girl crossing the pale yellow pool of light thrown by the bare bulb above a doorway. Jo walked on through the light and into the murky depths of the end of the alleyway.

The girl shivered, her back pressed against the damp brick wall. The woman walking towards her never slowed for a moment and the girl had squeaked as a large, powerful hand wrapped itself around her throat, lifting her off the ground. She felt the pressure build in her head as she fought for breath, her own hands fluttering uselessly against Jo's.

"Stop fighting. I will make this quick if you just stop fighting," Jo had muttered harshly. The girl went limp and she dropped her, drawing out her gun as the junkie crumpled in a heap at the base of the wall. The assassin stepped back, cocked the Colt and took aim. Green eyes welling with tears stared back at her along the barrel.

Then the unthinkable had happened. For the first time in her career Jo had felt a trickle of sweat down the back of her neck. That awareness made her hesitate. The tear-stained, elfin face at her feet sensed the hesitation and took its chance.

"Why?" the girl had whispered.

"You know why. You don't fuck with Tony."

"N-no. I mean, why you? What did I ever do to you?"

The words had cut through Jo like a hot knife through butter.

"SHUT UP!" she'd screamed. Jo surged forward till she was crouching in front of the girl, the muzzle of the gun pressed hard against her cheek. Images of a time, years earlier, and another girl—darker, younger even than this one—and another killer's gun, flashed before her eyes. "Just shut up..."

Jo had fought for self-control, her finger pressuring the trigger slowly, her gaze full of her victim's imploring, tear-filled eyes.

She was dumbfounded by the uncertainty and—horror?—welling up inside her. Never before had she felt such doubt. She had always been the cold-eyed killer who felt nothing, had never batted an eye as she ended a life. But this waif had reached in and squeezed her heart, somehow.

Again Jo had hesitated, torn and bewildered by her own lack of resolve. But then the decision was made for her, as footsteps hurried up behind her and stopped.

"What the fuck are you waiting for?" She recognized the voice as her boss' top henchman. "Finish it, Madison, for Christ's sake."

"Get lost, Marco. I've got this," she threw back over her shoulder, the gun muzzle still pressed cruelly into the young girl's cheek, where a trickle of blood was showing.

"Doesn't look that way to me. Looks to me like you were about to let her go," the man had sneered as he moved closer.

She had rounded on him then, standing tall, besting him by a good few inches, as she pressed the gun into his gut. His breath reeked of garlic and stale beer.

"I said fuck off, Marco, this isn't your concern." Her voice was low and threatening. But for once, the thug wasn't intimidated. He had sensed her earlier hesitation, had heard the quaver in her tone and now he drove home his advantage, like a sword into an armor's chink.

He slammed her back against the alley's side wall, wrenching the gun from her hand before pistol-whipping her viciously with the butt of the grip. Her world went black.

She had come to slowly, achingly, with a mouth full of filthy street water from the puddle she had landed in. Hacking away the foul taste, Jo sat up groggily, grateful at least that Marco had disappeared. She sat back against the wall, rubbing her forehead ruefully, her fingers coming away red from the lump she found there. Then she had caught sight of her gun, and beyond that a crumpled, bloodied form, now unrecognizable as human.

"Oh no."

Jo stood up slowly, using the wall for support, as she waited for her stomach to stop its flip-flopping. Once she was sure she wasn't going to throw up or faint she had made her way over to the girl. There was no doubting she was dead. Her face was unrecognizable—a mess of destruction. Jo guessed Marco had emptied her gun into the girl and then inflicted his own signature brand of violence upon her, probably with his steel-capped boots, just for jollies. She turned aside and vomited convulsively, splattering the wall and her own shoes.

What happened here? *Jo had struggled to understand how the girl had reached into her psyche and woken her from a 10-year spell. Whatever happened next, Jo knew she couldn't keep doing this. There was nothing left inside her except pain and remorse and darkness. She wondered at the tears streaming silently down her cheeks, helpless to stop them.*

She'd wiped her mouth with the back of her sleeve and reached for her cell phone. No doubt Marco was already telling her boss the good news personally. She didn't have much time. She dialed a number from memory and waited for it to be answered. Eventually a sleepy, gruff voice had picked up.

"Harding."

Jo shook herself out of her reverie. Sometimes she found herself disbelieving that any of it had ever happened. Life here was so different.

When she arrived in the Whitsundays—after a tortuous two-week journey hitchhiking along back roads and byways—she'd found work as a deckhand with one of the bareboat charter yacht companies. The work was physical and demanding, but that was something she enjoyed. Even though the pay wasn't great and tourists could be a pain when they traveled in herds, she got to spend her days out on the ocean with the salt wind in her hair and her other life a million planets away.

Two years ago she had earned her Master's ticket and a promotion. Now she skippered a 50-foot yacht with one deckhand and a cook, hosting small groups of tourists interested in spending more than just a day exploring the islands of the Whitsunday Passage. Sometimes the crew outnumbered the passengers.

All in all, not a bad way to earn a living, Jo reflected. And more to the point, she wasn't hurting anyone. She never wanted to do that again.

Jo took a deep lungful of the warm night air and exhaled slowly. Which is why she didn't make a habit of bringing tall redheads back to the house.

Damn. She didn't want—no, she didn't need—anyone that close to her. Apart from anything else, she had no intention of putting anyone else in the firing line should her old life ever happen to catch up with her here in Paradise.

And besides, I'm poison. Right? There's so much blood on my hands; who would ever want to be with me once they know the truth? And the truth always comes out. It has to, doesn't it? That's what being close to someone means, doesn't it? Honesty? Trust?

Jo sighed again.

Ah well. It's a moot point anyway. The redhead on the other end of the not-so-soft snoring emanating from her bedroom sure as hell wasn't the one. She was just the one she'd have to let down gently in the morning and tell the inevitable white lies to. *Sure, I'll call you.*

No, love wasn't in Jo Madison's future. She was just grateful to be alive, to have a second chance at living life right. Anything else was a bonus she just wasn't going to let herself expect.

Right?

Chapter
Two

Cadie settled back into her economy-class seat and tried hard not to think about just how tired she was. No matter how luxurious the seat, or how good the airline food, 28 hours was a grueling amount of time to spend getting anywhere.

And it isn't over yet, she sighed. An interminable wait at Sydney International to get through customs and immigration was followed by a bus ride across the airport to the domestic terminal to board a plane so small it didn't have a first-class cabin.

Not that she cared about that. But Naomi had been a bear with a sore head almost from the moment they'd checked in at O'Hare what seemed like a week ago. And the lack of a glass of champagne and room to stretch out had turned her into the ogre from Hell.

"What kind of a rinky-dink operation is this?" she'd yelled at a passing flight attendant as they'd boarded the small plane to Hamilton Island.

"Nay, would you relax? You're not making this any easier," muttered Cadie. "We're not going to a big city, just a little island. I'm sure only the smaller planes can land there."

"I don't give a rat's ass. I just want to get to the hotel and get some goddamned sleep."

Fortunately for Cadie and the flight crew, sleep had claimed the senator not long after takeoff on the last leg of their journey. She slumped bonelessly in the seat next to Cadie, snoring huffily.

Cadie rubbed her bleary eyes, just thankful the trip was almost over. *Only an hour to go before we touch down on Hamilton Island.* She lifted the blind on the window to her right and gasped at the tableau below her. The plane was making its way up the east coast of Australia, heading north from Sydney. It was a blindingly clear day and the ocean was the most beautiful shade of blue-green Cadie had ever seen. They were already over the southern parts of the Great Barrier Reef and there were occasional islands, ringed by white sand, passing beneath them. She could see different depths of water in the varying shades of color where she presumed there were reefs and atolls and lagoons.

Cadie had tried to read as much as she could about their final destination—the Whitsunday Islands—and was excited at the thought of spending the next three weeks in a completely different world. Already Australia was far removed from the frigid environment she'd left behind in wintry Chicago.

Just walking off the plane in Sydney had been a shock. It had been hot, like walking into a wet blanket—almost as if someone had sucked the air out of her lungs as she walked up the ramp way into the terminal. The air conditioning in the terminal building had been a relief, but she would never forget that first taste of an Australian summer. One of the flight attendants on this plane had laughed, though not unkindly, when she'd mentioned it.

"Wait until we get to Hamilton Island," she'd said. "There's nothing quite like the tropics in January."

Cadie smiled quietly to herself. She was looking forward to it, though she knew Naomi would no doubt find plenty to grumble about. She glanced pensively at her partner, stifling a giggle at the dribble of drool strung out between the senator's mouth and the pillow tucked under her chin.

Things certainly hadn't worked out the way she thought they were going to after that New Year's morning in their kitchen.

She had been dreading the senator's homecoming that evening, given the venomous nature of the morning's discussion, but Naomi had swept in bearing flowers and chocolates and a sunny attitude. She had set about the task of charming Cadie almost as if...almost as if she really means it, Cadie had thought cynically as the performance unfolded.

"Hello, darling. I thought we'd celebrate the start of our vacation with a quiet night in. What do you say?" Naomi had smiled brilliantly and then leaned in for a long kiss.

Cadie had never considered herself naïve, nor did she think she was susceptible to being sweet-talked, but she had to admit it was tempting to give in to this charming version of Naomi. It was a reminder of how things used to be.

"Okay. That would be nice," she'd said cautiously. "But we do need to talk about last night, and this morning, Nay," she insisted.

"Honey, it was a misunderstanding. That woman was either lying to you or was misinformed. Or you just got the wrong end

of the stick somewhere. You know me, Cadie. You know I would never get involved with anything like that, don't you, sweetheart?" This last was whispered against her neck as the senator honed in on one of Cadie's most vulnerable points.

Cadie had turned her head and placed her fingers gently over the senator's mouth, putting off any contact. She was trying hard to resist, trying hard to stay angry with Naomi. The trouble was part of her wanted to believe the politician. That small part of Cadie had a hard time resisting the puppy-dog brown eyes that looked innocently at her. The Naomi she had known 12 years ago, and through the early years of their marriage—before the politics had become a career and not a passion—certainly would never have stooped to using drugs to get what she wanted.

In the end it had just been easier to put her doubts away for another day, so much simpler to accept the reassurances of the woman she had trusted for 12 years.

She hadn't been very proud of herself for that when she'd woken the next morning with Naomi sprawled across two-thirds of the bed. But Cadie also hoped the upcoming vacation would be an opportunity for them both to do some re-evaluating of their lives.

And yes, she was forced to admit, there was a tiny bit of her that was terrified of leaving Naomi, should it come to that. It had been the longest, most significant relationship of her life. She had never lived alone, had never not been part of a couple, at least, not as an adult. The thought of saying goodbye to 12 years of history, to Naomi's extended family...Cadie had shuddered as she'd lain in bed, listening to her partner snore.

There was Naomi's career to think of as well. They had worked hard for what they had achieved—and being an out couple had been a big part of that feeling of achievement. Though she had increasingly felt left out of the decision-making process, Cadie was still proud of what they'd accomplished, particularly in the early years of their relationship. No, for now at least it was better to make like Scarlett O'Hara and think about it another day. What could be better than three weeks alone on a yacht in a tropical paradise for focusing the mind on love?

That philosophy had worked pretty well for Cadie until the day of their departure, when the reality of Naomi's attitude to the vacation slapped her full in the face. They had arrived at the international check-in lounge of O'Hare airport to discover a group of Naomi's closest friends gathered there to meet them. All with their own luggage in tow.

"They're coming with us," the senator had said offhandedly

to Cadie's enquiry.

"To Australia?" she'd asked.

"Yeah to Australia, and to the island, and on the boat," Naomi said impatiently. "Three weeks on a boat with just us sounded pretty boring to me, so I thought we'd take along our own party. What's the problem?"

"Are you kidding me?" Cadie had exclaimed. "What happened to the romantic vacation for two we planned? And when was all this decided?"

"What's the big deal? They're good friends and it will add some variety. I thought you said you wanted to have fun."

"They're your good friends, Naomi, not mine. I don't see any of my friends over there," she had gestured towards the casually clumped group, which was watching the couple interestedly.

"Well, whose fault is that, Cadie?" The senator leaned in, lowering her voice. "You're the one who decided you were too good for my friends. It's not my fault if none of your buddies showed an interest in coming along."

"I'm sure if they'd known there was such an open invitation on offer they would have jumped at it," she had muttered. Christ. *She looked around the group and groaned inwardly.*

Therese and Sarah, a couple of corporate attorneys from Chicago who shared Naomi's bad taste in modern art. Jason and Toby, the senator's PR team, whom Cadie had long ago silently dubbed the "Queens of Spin." Larissa McNeil, Naomi's former college roommate, and...Cadie winced. Larissa had a tall redhead hanging off her arm. A very familiar, tall redhead.

Cadie pulled herself back to the present. The redhead's name had turned out to be Kelli and, mercifully, she had utterly no memory of her New Year's Eve encounter with Cadie. Or if she had, she'd so far had the sense to stay quiet about it.

A sense of dread balled up in the pit of Cadie's stomach for about the millionth time since they'd left Chicago. All she had wanted was a few weeks to themselves so she could come to some kind of conclusion about where the relationship was going. Not to mention getting some badly needed rest and relaxation for them both. Instead, she had nightmare visions of one long intoxicated party, with no prospect of getting any sense out of her partner. At least they'd had the sense not to try and bring a stash into the country with them. Or she assumed they hadn't. She shuddered at the thought of what those cute little drug-sniffing beagles at Sydney International would have made of that.

"Ladies and gentlemen, we have started our descent into

Hamilton Island. In preparation for landing the captain has switched on the seatbelt sign. Please fasten your seatbelts, make sure your tray table is properly stowed, and that your seat back is upright."

Cadie smiled at the gentle Australian accent of the flight attendant coming through the loudspeaker. Some things were so similar to home, but the accent was an enchanting reminder that she was in another world.

The thought restored some of her excitement about the trip.

Damn it, she decided. *I'm going to enjoy myself regardless. There's so much to see that's new and different and beautiful. I'm not going to let other people spoil this for me. Including Naomi.*

She looked down at the senator and nudged her awake none too gently.

"Ww-wwhat, whassamatter?" Naomi mumbled.

"We're almost there, Nay," Cadie said. "It's time to wake up and get organized."

"Jesus, it's about time," she grumbled.

Cadie sighed.

Yeah. Including Naomi.

Jo was running late. She roughly tucked her dark blue company polo shirt into her khaki shorts and dove down onto the floor to see if her deck shoes were under the bed.

Yep. She pulled them on, grabbed her overnight bag, and ran to answer the front door. A personable young man greeted her with a grin.

"Josh, hi! Thanks for coming over."

"No worries, Jo. You know I'm never gonna turn down the chance for time away from the wrinklies, unlimited Internet access and cable television." He grinned again.

Jo laughed. "Yeah, I figured you'd jump at it." She smiled back at the good-looking 18-year-old. Josh was the son of her nearest neighbors and he had been her regular house and cat-sitter since he'd been old enough to drive. She watched as he made himself at home, making for his regular berth. "How are your folks?"

"They're good, thanks," he replied from the second bedroom where he was stowing his belongings. He re-emerged with Mephisto sitting on his shoulder. "He was lying on the bed waiting for me. God, cats are scary sometimes." He laughed.

Jo grinned. "You're not wrong. Sometimes I swear he lives about 10 minutes in the future and just comes back to freak me out every now and then. Don't ya, big fella?" She scratched the large cat's chin as he perched on Josh's shoulder, purring like a Mack truck. "Do me a favor, Joshy? Feed him his breakfast for me. I've still got a few things missing that I need to find before we go."

"Sure."

Josh took Mephisto to the kitchen and proceeded to have a long conversation with the feline over a bowl of kibble. Jo smiled and began the search for her sunglasses, sunscreen, cap, and cell phone. Finally she rescued them all from their various hiding places and she was ready.

"Come on, Josh. Come with me down to the dock and then you can drive the Jeep back for me."

"Cool beans."

"No hooning around in it this time, okay?"

"Yes, ma'am. I mean, no ma'am."

Jo chuckled. "Mephisto!" she called. The cat leapt up onto the kitchen counter and sat on his haunches. Jo leaned in and butted heads with him. "Be good, boycat." He purred his reply loudly. "Okay, let's go." She followed Josh out of the house and locked the door behind her, resetting the security system. "You remember the code, Josh?"

"Yep, no worries. 3-2-2-1 right?"

Jo nodded as she climbed into her red Wrangler and fired it up. Josh clambered in beside her and she reversed till she could maneuver around his beat-up jalopy. They bounced down the dirt track that served as Jo's driveway and she took a moment to collect her somewhat scrambled thoughts.

It was a gorgeous day; not a cloud in the sky and, although it wasn't yet 8am, the temperature was already climbing into the high 90s, with the usual high humidity for the time of year. Jo couldn't wait to get out on the water and feel a bit of a breeze. For now she just took a deep breath and appreciated the cool patches generated by the canopy of trees meeting across the track.

Her first appointment was a meeting with her boss, Ron Cheswick, the owner of Cheswick Marine. He would fill her in on the details of the boatload of tourists she would be responsible for over the next—

"How long you gonna be gone this time, Jo?" Josh interrupted her thoughts with just the right question.

"To be honest I don't know yet, mate," she replied. "I'll give you a call as soon as I know what's what, okay? You don't have any big plans do you?"

"Nope," he said jovially. "I was just wondering which Saturday night to have the party." He grinned from ear to ear.

"You little bugger." She laughed, slapping him across the

shoulder.

"Just kidding. Just kidding," the teenager said.

They slid off the last of the dirt at the bottom of Jo's hill and onto the paved surface of Shute Harbor Road, winding around the coastline till they rounded one last corner and came upon the port. Although it was early, the dock was already a hive of activity. Jo dodged other cars vying for a spot in the parking lot and headed straight for the secondary pier which housed the Cheswick Marine office and those of its competitors.

Shute Harbor was the major access port for the Whitsunday Islands and as such was a big focus for tourists. The main pier was a square concrete building with a large kiosk, the Coast Guard office above it on the land side, and a series of moorings around the outside ring. All the large catamarans and motor cruisers from the major resorts on the islands called in twice daily, picking up and depositing passengers, mail, and stores. In addition it was the starting point for most of the day-trippers going out on the smaller yachts, cats, and game-fishing boats.

The north end of the parking lot led to the secondary pier, a long, narrow pontoon that snaked out into the bay. It was dotted with offices, dinghy moorings, and piles of provisions. Not many tourists came out here, just the boaties and office staff. Most of the time the tourists who wanted to do a bareboat charter were picked up from their island resort, as was the case with Jo's group today.

Jo pulled up just shy of the pontoon and hopped out of the Jeep, grabbing her bag from the back seat. She flipped the keys to Josh.

"Take it easy Joshy," she said. "And listen," she pointed a finger at him with mock severity, "any party is okay, you know that, right? Just don't traumatize the cat, do clean up afterwards—and you know my rules about booze and drugs." She walked around the back of the car and headed for the pontoon.

"You got it, Skipper," he called after her.

"I'll call and give you some warning when I'm coming back in—just so you can get it habitable in time," she shouted back with a wave.

He grinned and revved the engine, peeling out as he accelerated out of the lot.

"You bugger," she muttered. "There goes another set of tires." She found it pretty hard to get mad with Josh, though. He was a good kid and despite all his big talk of parties she'd always come home to an immaculate house, a happy cat, and no signs whatever of anything untoward.

Jo strode along the pontoon, happy at last to feel the sea breeze taking the edge off the humidity. She noted that it was the prevailing southeast breeze, normal for this part of the world most of the time. It would make the trip to Hamilton Island, which lay away to the southeast of Shute, a little longer and busier, but she could handle that.

She brushed her long black hair out of her eyes as she looked away to the right and spotted her yacht in the distance. Well, technically it wasn't "her" yacht, but for the time she was skippering it, it might as well be. She could see her two crewmembers, Paul and Jenny, already on board, readying the long boat for its three-week assignment. She waved and gestured towards the office when she got a response from Jenny.

"Hiya, Jo!" Doris, Cheswick's indispensable and long-suffering receptionist, greeted her warmly as she stepped through the door of the small floating office.

"Hey, Doris, how are you?" Jo returned with a smile. "Is the boss in yet?"

"Surely is. Go on in."

"Thanks." Jo left her gear stowed behind Doris' desk and walked through into Ron Cheswick's tiny office, knocking softly on the door as she did so.

"Hi, Jo, come on in. Take a seat." Ron waved her over and Jo slid into the seat on the other side of his desk. *He looks particularly harried this morning,* she thought. Running this kind of business had its fair of share of stress, she knew. And at 50-something and not exactly at his fighting weight, Ron looked like it was all catching up with him. She watched as he rooted around in a drawer for the file on the tourists she would be guiding around.

"How's business, Ronny? We making money for ya?"

"Oh that's funny, Jo. No, really," he snorted. "That group of Germans Frank took out last week? They ploughed into the jetty at South Molle yesterday. Can you believe it? The boat's going to be in dry dock at least a week."

Jo winced. Most of the business the company did was true bareboat charters in which the clients sailed the boat themselves after as little as a few hours' tuition from the company's skipper. Just how much tuition they received depended on how much sailing experience the client had. Of course, there was no way to make the client tell the absolute truth about how much experience they'd had. And there was no accounting for stupidity and the influence of alcohol. The company's insurance premiums were astronomical as a result.

Not to mention the clients who would arrive expecting to

spend their dream holiday on their dream yacht, only to find their dream yacht in dry dock being repaired, and a smaller, less luxurious yacht waiting for them. The holidays were expensive and clients rightly expected the best for their money.

Nope, Jo wouldn't have Ron's job for quids. *At least,* Jo smiled, *at least not the way this one was set up.* If it were her business she'd make it all crewed charters, very exclusive, very small. And she'd specialize in the gay and lesbian market. There was a huge niche there that was going largely untapped.

Ron interrupted her daydream by slapping a file down on the desk in front of her.

"There you go. Thank God, this mob you're picking up today is the exception to the rule; rich as stink, and not in the least bit interested in sailing their own boat. At least I know the *Seawolf's* in good hands this trip." He sat down heavily and folded his hands across his belly, watching as the blue-eyed woman across from him thumbed through the file.

Damn she's gorgeous, he thought for about the zillionth time since he'd first met her.

"How many?" she asked without looking up.

"Four couples, so it's gonna be a bit crowded. Make Paul sleep on deck." He grinned.

"Three weeks? Damn, they're keen," Jo said.

"And rich, don't forget that," Ron reminded her happily. "They won't spend all that time on the yacht. But Jo," he leaned forward to make his point, "they're paying premium dollar for full-time service. You and the crew are on call for the full three weeks. If they want to sail, sail. If they want to dive, organize the dive-master. If they want to party, show them the hot spots. If they want to stay at a resort, make the booking and stay close at hand."

Jo nodded. And then her eyes fell on the passenger list. "A US senator? Jesus, Ron, that's some circle we're sailing around in, huh?"

"Oh yeah. And what's more it's not just any senator. It's the first openly lesbian senator, her partner, and six of their rich gay friends. That boutique market you're so keen on cornering just landed in your lap, mate." He leaned forward again. "Do me a favor?"

Blue eyes held his own as an eyebrow rose in inquiry.

"Don't blow it. Make nice, give 'em everything they want and hopefully they'll go running home to tell their little queer buddies all about faaaaaaaabulous Australia."

Jo closed the file and looked at him sardonically. "Y'know

Ron, for a straight bloke, you sure talk a good game."

"Yeah, yeah. Flattery'll get you nowhere, Jo-Jo. You know that deep down you're just pining for a good-looking guy like me." He grinned. It was an old and familiar routine with them.

Jo stood, leaned across the desk, and chucked him under the chin. "In your dreams, Ronny boy. In your dreams." And with that she strode out of the room.

"You have no idea, gorgeous," her boss muttered under his breath.

Jo picked up her gear, said goodbye to Doris, and walked back out onto the pontoon. She flicked her cell phone on and speed-dialed Paul onboard the *Seawolf.*

"That you, Skipper?" his gruff baritone answered.

"Sure is. Did you guys take the dinghy out?"

"Nope, we left it for you. Ron dropped us off."

"We fully loaded?"

"Yes, boss. Except for one case of champagne which we left for you. Wouldn't want you to think we'd robbed you of the warm and fuzzy feeling of doing some manual labor." She could hear his grin through the phone.

"Smartarse. Anything else we need before we disappear for three weeks?"

A female voice yelled in the background. "Tell her to bring chocolate!"

Jo laughed. "Tell her it's all taken care of, Paul. I'll see you shortly."

"Aye aye, Captain," he said flippantly.

"Oh shut up." She hung up and went in search of the *Seawolf's* dinghy, finding it not far from the end of the pontoon, hitched to a spare mooring. The case of champagne was already in the bottom of the small tinny, so she tossed her bag in. She took a moment to fish in her pocket for a hair-band and pulled her long locks into a loose ponytail before she donned her cap and stepped into the boat.

Jo reached back and yanked the string on the small outboard motor, casting off before putting the motor in gear and swinging the dinghy in the direction of the *Seawolf,* some 100 yards away in deep water.

God, it's a glorious day. She closed her eyes and turned her face to the sun for a brief moment, reveling in the feeling of the heat and wind and small splashes of salt spray on her face. *A whole other planet from King's Cross,* she thought. As she opened her eyes again she tucked away that dark part of herself once more. Every now and then she had to pull it out, just as a reminder of how good life was now.

"Hey Jo!" Jenny's happy voice floated across the water to her as she pulled alongside the stern of the boat.

"G'day Jen. Here, catch hold." Jo flicked the dinghy's tethering rope up to the deckhand. She tossed her gear bag up onto the deck and carefully walked to the bow of the dinghy. She gingerly held her balance as she lifted up the case of champagne.

"Hang on, Jo, let me give you a hand," Jenny said hastily, tying off the rope and starting to climb over onto the yacht's flat transom.

"No, she's right, I've got it," Jo said casually, as with one fluid motion she stepped from the bobbing dinghy onto the transom without so much as looking like she was going to tip over.

"Geez, Jo. I'm beginning to believe the rumors. You really can walk on water," Jenny joked as she leaned over and took the case from her skipper.

Jo laughed as she climbed up over the taffrail. "I wish," she said. "How are you, Jen?" The athletic brunette grinned back at her.

"Couldn't be better, Skip. And we're just about ready to go. Provisions are stowed, except for this one case. I'm gonna break that open now and put a few bottles on ice, so we've got something to appease the masses with when they arrive. Other than that we're all set. Paul's down in the sail hold, sorting that out."

"He's not anymore." Jo's tall, blond deckhand appeared on deck and made his way aft towards the two women. "We're ready to go, boss."

Jo smiled at her two crewmembers. Paul was the stereotypical bronzed Aussie—tall, buff, brown, blond-haired, and laidback. He was also a damn good deckhand, fast and sure on his feet, and strong with it. Jenny was younger and less experienced. She'd come to the Whitsundays a couple of Christmases ago for a working summer holiday, and liked the life so much she had decided to stay. Apart from working on deck when required, she was also the best cook in the company and would be responsible for keeping their guests fed and watered. She and Paul worked with Jo as often as they could and the threesome formed a formidable team and usually picked up the best assignments.

"Okay then. Let's get the paperwork done and we can get moving here." Jo dropped down into the cockpit and slid down the companionway to the main cabin. She pulled the charts out from their drawer and flicked to the relevant page. "Any chance of some coffee, Jen?"

"Yep." The cook passed Jo and moved around the galley,

stowing the last of the provisions and firing up the coffee pot. Paul flopped down onto the small sofa and put his feet up for probably the first and only time this trip.

"Did Ron fill you guys in?" Jo asked as she plotted their basic course to Hamilton Island on the chart in front of her and got it ready to relay to the Coast Guard office back on the pier.

"Oh yeah," Paul replied. "Could be a long three weeks I'm thinking."

Jo grinned. "Well, at least we won't have to worry about going on any damn-fool rescue missions. Not like that last mob we had."

The trio laughed as they remembered the group of French businessmen and their wives who had careened around the Whitsunday Passage on their own like some kind of demented pinball until, finally, they'd run aground way out on Heart Reef. It had taken a full day to refloat the yacht, not to mention the 10 days' worth of repairs.

About half an hour later, Jo and her crew were ready to sail. She'd filed the course she planned to follow for the day, called the office to double-check for any last-minute changes, and checked all the safety equipment, including the radio and flares.

"All right," she said. "Let's go."

She fired up the engine while Paul and Jenny moved about on deck readying the mainsail and smaller foresail for the moment they hit open water. Paul pulled up the anchor and Jo slowly maneuvered the yacht under power into the channel leading out of Shute Harbor. The wind picked up a little as they rounded the small islet at the mouth of the port.

Ten minutes later Jo killed the engine and held the boat up into the wind as the two deckies manned the winches and hoisted the mainsail. She bore away slightly till the sails filled and they were off on the first of what would be at least three tacks— changes of direction in which the yacht sailed at an angle to the wind in order to progress upwind—before they could reach Hamilton Island. She settled back in the cockpit, her right foot steadying the wheel.

Paul's right, she thought, as she watched the crewman cleaning up the deck, stowing the sail covers and making fine adjustments to the sails. *This could either be the easiest of assignments or a real pain in the backside.*

She was due to meet the passengers at 1pm, more than enough time for them to reach the Hamilton marina and put the finishing touches on the *Seawolf.* For now she leaned back and just enjoyed the sailing. They were doing seven knots, about average for the boat.

Jo glanced around. It was a pretty smooth sailing, though once they were out of the shadow of Long Island the chop would pick up a bit.

Not a bad way to make a living, she grinned as she took in the idyllic surroundings. Not for the first time, she sent a silent blessing to the young girl in a damp alley who had changed her life. *Wherever your soul is now, kid, I hope it's at peace.*

"Ready to tack," she called about 20 minutes later. Jenny scurried up from below and joined Paul on the winches. "Tacking," Jo yelled as she swung the prow of the boat first into the breeze and then away again on the starboard side. The huge boom swung across the boat, both deckies ducking under it and working the winches hard to trim the mainsail as it refilled.

"Nice one, Skipper," grinned Paul at the smoothness of the tack. There was nothing more damaging to mast and rigging than a violent tack that slammed the heavy boom hard from side to side. Jo had always had a gentle touch.

She grinned back and settled in for a good morning's sail.

The view from Cadie's hotel room balcony was spectacular. From where she was she looked out over the crowded Hamilton Island marina and away to a perfect cloudless sky and blue-green ocean beyond the mouth of the small harbor. She inhaled deeply and savored the smell of the sea and the close heat of the day, listening to the sounds floating up from the boats and dockside stores.

For the past 24 hours, Cadie had absorbed her new surroundings like a sponge. While Naomi and the others had spent the time sleeping off their jetlag, she had found herself wandering the resort and its surrounds, talking to the hotel staff and finding her feet after the long journey. She felt wired.

Hamilton Island was one of the first major resorts built in the Whitsundays. Its high-rise hotel and sprawling dockside shopping and eating precinct were the exception in the islands. Most of the other resorts were low-rise affairs, blended into their tropical environments. But Hamilton was also the biggest and busiest, thanks to the area's only airport. It also boasted a large marina that hosted one of Australia's most popular yachting regattas each year.

Cadie gazed out over the forest of masts in front of her. One of them, she knew, was the boat on which she and the others would be spending the next three weeks. She tried to guess which one it would be.

One in particular caught her eye. It was just pulling into its berth. Long and sleek, the yacht seemed—to her unpracticed eye at least—to be about the right length. She watched the crew moving around, stowing sails and other equipment. A blond man leapt onto the pontoon and wrapped two mooring ropes around the bollards at each end of the berth.

A tall, dark-haired woman was at the helm. Even from this distance Cadie could see she was stunning. There was an aura of confidence about her as she shouted orders to the crew and deftly gentled the boat into place. Unexpectedly, the woman turned and stared up at the hotel, and for an instant Cadie thought she was looking straight at her.

But that can't be. Not from so far away, surely? Nevertheless she found herself staring back and wondering at the slight tingling sensation she could feel at the back of her neck. *Wow.*

The dark-haired woman on the yacht broke the connection first to answer a question from one of her deckhands, and Cadie found herself hoping that was indeed the Cheswick Marine boat.

Time would tell. She and the others were due to meet the crew of their yacht in just under an hour. She turned back into the hotel room, and the cool of the air conditioning. Naomi was repacking her luggage, which was already scattered after just one day in the hotel. Cadie flopped down into an armchair and watched with amusement.

"Aren't you going to pack?" Naomi asked.

"Already did," Cadie replied. "I only brought the one bag, remember?"

Naomi grunted and continued to try and wedge her clothes into the already bulging case.

"Why don't you leave some of that in storage here at the hotel, Nay?" Cadie suggested. "We're going sailing, not on a diplomatic mission."

"I'm not spending every night on a boat, Arcadia," Naomi grumbled, stuffing yet another pair of shoes in. "There are resorts and restaurants and hotels all over this area, aren't there?"

"Sure," Cadie replied.

"So, a girl needs something to wear." Naomi grunted as she finally managed to close the bag.

Boy, that was weird, Jo thought as she turned to help Paul tidy up the furled mainsail around the tied-down boom. She had had the uncanny feeling that someone was watching her as they'd berthed. A glance up to the hotel had revealed a woman staring down at her. Blonde, sweet figure, very cute as far as she could tell. But it was the eyes that had held her attention. She couldn't tell their color from this distance, but they had held her gaze almost hypnotically.

She shivered slightly at the memory.

She couldn't have been looking right at me, could she? Jo shook her head, trying to focus on what she was doing.

She stopped and took a look around the deck. The *Seawolf* was looking better than it would at any time over the next three weeks. Boaties, used to living and working in confined spaces, were expert at stowing their lives away. Tourists, on the other hand, were another kettle of fish.

"Are we ready to be boarded?"

Jenny stood at the top of the companionway, hands on hips. "Ready as we'll ever be at this end, Skipper," she said.

"Paul?"

"Bring on the loopies, Jo-Jo."

Jo rolled her eyes at his use of the local derogatory term for tourists. "Get it out of your system now, guys. It's customer service and tugging the forelock from now on in," she warned.

Both deckies snapped her a mock salute. "Aye aye, Captain," they chorused in unison.

"Oh, shut up."

Jo jumped deftly onto the pontoon and started the walk up to the hotel lobby where she was to meet the senator's party. Along the way she was greeted by several acquaintances and she answered them cheerily as she climbed the hill. By the time she reached the hotel she had her game face on. She'd learned over the years that, while Americans found the Aussie laidback style of doing things somewhat charming, they also expected the very best in service, and usually they wanted it yesterday. Finding the balance between the two had always been a bit of a battle for Jo. In her early days as a deckhand she'd told more than one customer just where they could shove their strawberry daiquiri.

She smiled at the memory. Ron had been very patient with her. *God knows why.*

Jo caught sight of the hotel's head concierge and walked in his direction.

"Miss Madison! So good to see you again." The top-hatted and tailed man took her hand in a double-handed shake and beamed at her.

"Hello, George. It's good to see you, too. How's business?"

"Always on the go, miss, you know how it is. What can we do

for you today?"

"I'm picking up a party of eight. I was hoping to borrow two of your bellhops and a couple of your jumbo golf carts."

"No problem, no problem at all. Now, what was the party's name?" George bustled around his desk and began issuing orders left and right.

"Senator Silverberg," Jo told him.

"Ah yes," he said. "I think you'll find they are already waiting for you in the lobby."

Jo groaned. She was 15 minutes early and still they were waiting for her. *I can't win. Ah well. Showtime.*

"Okay, George, thanks. Give me five minutes to get them organized and we'll be right out, yeah?"

"Consider it done, Miss Madison. See you shortly."

Jo straightened her shirt and took a deep breath, then stepped through the sliding glass doors into the spacious lobby of the hotel. The senator's group wasn't difficult to spot. The Americans were clustered around the bar, surrounded by a mountain of luggage.

Figures, thought Jo. *God forbid they should read the recommendations about what to bring on a sailing holiday.* She pressed on towards the group, counting only seven. The senator stuck out like a sore thumb. She was louder than the others and was clearly the center of the conversation. *Besides, she just looks...*Jo searched for the word...*political. Time to bite the bullet.*

"Senator Silverberg?"

The woman turned at the question. "That's me. What can I do for you?"

Jo stuck out a hand in greeting. "It's more a case of what I can do for you, Senator," she said, summoning her most winning and professional smile. "I'm Jo Madison from Cheswick Marine. I'm your sail guide for the next three weeks."

Naomi looked the taller woman up and down with obvious meaning and her face took on the kind of leer that made Jo's skin crawl. "Really? Well," the senator drawled, "things are looking up." She held on to Jo's hand just a little too long. "And I can certainly think of a few things you could do for me, Miss Madison."

Oh, I don't like her at all, Jo thought as she tried not to snap her hand back. "Please, call me Jo," she said instead. She looked around at the other members of the party. "If you're all ready, I have some transport waiting outside to take us down to the boat where we'll settle you into your berths and give you the tour before you decide where you'd like to go this afternoon."

"We're just waiting on my partner," Naomi said. "She's in the gift shop, picking up a newspaper or something."

"I'm here now," came a soft voice from behind Jo.

Jo turned and was immediately caught by the most beautiful pair of sea-green eyes she had ever seen. *Wow.*

Wow, Cadie thought. *Those are the bluest eyes I've ever seen.* Their gazes locked for long seconds and the world contracted around them. It was like she and the tall skipper were wrapped in insulation. Everything else seemed muffled and fuzzy and suddenly unimportant.

Jo realized she had taken the woman's hand to shake it and hadn't let go. The blonde's smaller hand just seemed to fit in hers and she found herself softly stroking the back of this complete stranger's hand with the pad of her thumb.

"Umm, h-hello," Jo said wittily.

Ohhh, gorgeous voice, thought Cadie. "Hello yourself," she replied, trying to ignore the tendrils of heat from whatever the woman was doing with her thumb. "I'm Cadie Jones."

The senator broke the spell by bustling over to Cadie and throwing her arm around her shorter partner's shoulders. "This is Jo, um, what was it? Madison?"

Jo nodded, still unable to tear her eyes away from Cadie's. *What the hell is going on here?*

"That ought to be easy to remember," smiled Cadie. "I was born in Madison, Wisconsin."

Jo grinned back, relaxing a little as she took in the magical way Cadie's nose wrinkled when she smiled. *How cute is that?* she thought.

God, she has a beautiful smile. Her whole face lights up, thought Cadie.

Jo regained her senses and set about organizing the bellhops to carry the luggage onto one of the golf carts she had requested from the concierge. She made sure everyone was seated comfortably in the other cart. Cadie took her place just behind the driver's seat, and not surprisingly, Naomi sat down next to her, putting her arm possessively around her shoulder.

Oh God, please don't let her be like this for the entire trip, the blonde silently implored the universe. *She's going to drive me nuts if she stays attached at the hip for three weeks.* Cadie watched as their intriguing sail guide slipped into the seat in front of her.

Jo finally had everyone settled. She couldn't help noticing the senator's firm hold on Miss Jones. *I wonder if I caused that, or is this just normal behavior for a senator?* She let out the hand brake and nudged the golf cart forward, towards the gentle slope that led to the marina. *It never ceases to amaze me how two people you would never guess were partners can end up together.* She glanced over her shoulder at the couple, and met a pair of distinctly unfriendly senatorial brown eyes. Jo took a deep breath. *Oh, this is going to be a hell of a boat ride.*

Chapter
Three

One hectic hour later everyone finally had a chance to relax. Luggage had been stowed, some had been sent back to the hotel for storage, much to the crew's amusement, and everyone had been assigned a berth. The senator and Miss Jones had taken one of the two aft double berths, while the two attorneys, Therese and Sarah, had grabbed the other. Toby and Jason, and Larissa and Kelli had been left with the two smaller doubles forward, leaving the two single berths in the forepeak for the three crewmembers to negotiate between them.

Jo watched quietly as the passengers made themselves comfortable around the cockpit and aft deck. Jenny handed around a tray loaded with glasses of ice-cold champagne and nibble-sized hors d'oevres of prawns and caviar.

It's been an interesting hour, Jo reflected as she sat herself down on the roof of the companionway, her legs dangling down into the cockpit. She could already tell who was going to have fun and who were going to be the wet blankets.

Miss Jones—she kept being drawn back to those wonderful green eyes—was clearly determined to have a great time, and Jo was sure she would be up for anything. The two men, earnest, bespectacled types who looked disconcertingly alike, were also going to be fine. They were already bouncing with excitement and enthusiasm.

The jury is still out on the two attorneys, Jo thought. *But the senator and the two other women are definitely the downers of the group.* So far nothing had been big enough, luxurious enough, or interesting enough for that trio. And the senator was still sticking to her partner like glue, casting Jo more than one suspicious glance since she'd picked them up from the hotel.

Jo sighed inwardly. *If she's going to be like this just over one little hello handshake then it's going to be a very long three weeks. Just because you could have fried an egg on that handshake...Jo* decided not to let her thoughts wander too far down that path.

She watched as everyone settled into their places.

"Okay, well, officially, welcome everyone to the *Seawolf.* You've all met me, but this," she indicated Paul who was standing just behind her left shoulder, leaning on the boom, "is Paul Burton, intrepid crewman, and this," she nodded at Jenny who was standing next to her feet, "is Jenny Gulliver, our hostess and chef."

She waited as the hellos and introductions made the rounds of the cockpit.

"I thought I'd tell you a little about the *Seawolf*—what she can and can't do—and then we can talk about the kinds of things you'd like to get up to over the next three weeks." She smiled.

General nods and murmurs of agreement greeted that.

"The *Seawolf* is a Beneteau 50. Beneteau 'cos that's who makes 'em and 50 because she's just over 50 feet long. She was designed as an all-conditions yacht and she's quite capable of sailing around the world, though she'd be a bit leaner below decks for that kind of trip," she said with a smile. "For our purposes though, she's more than adequate." She caught Cadie's eye again and grinned back at the blonde's infectiously encouraging smile.

"We've got enough provisions on board to last us a few days at a time, but reloading is just a matter of calling our office and having them deliver stores by motorboat, or alternatively, we can restock at the nearest resort.

"There isn't anywhere in this region of the Whitsundays that we can't get to within a day's sail, depending on the conditions. So there's no reason why we can't touch base with all the islands and reefs if you wish to. Or we can anchor off Whitehaven Beach for three weeks, if that's what you'd rather do."

"What about diving and snorkeling?" Cadie asked.

"We have snorkeling gear onboard for everyone," Jo replied. "As for diving, are any of you certified?"

Shaking heads all round.

"Okay then. If you want to learn the basics and get your certification, it's as easy as a phone call from me to one of the local dive masters who will come and spend the day, or longer, with us. He'll bring all the necessary equipment with him.

"If fishing is your thing, we have a few sets of light tackle on board, though if game-fishing is more to your taste, we can arrange with one of the resorts to take you out to the outside of the reef where the big fish are."

The two men liked that idea, she could tell, making a mental note to contact the Hayman Island charter company.

"Excuse me?" It was Sarah, the quieter one of the two attorneys. "I heard that it's hurricane season here. What happens in that case, or any bad weather?"

"You heard right, it is cyclone season—that's what we call hurricanes, by the way," Jo replied. "But the long-range forecast for the next few weeks is very good, so I'm not anticipating any problems, though we might get the odd tropical storm in the evenings. Nothing that should worry us, however. As I said, we're never going to be so far away from a good anchorage for us to run into any kind of trouble."

"Is it safe to swim here?" Cadie asked.

"If it's safe to snorkel and scuba dive, Cadie, it's a good bet it's safe to swim," the senator said, somewhat derisively.

"Actually it's a fair question," said Jo, earning a grateful smile from Cadie. "These are tropical waters. That means there's a lot of wildlife, and not all of it is friendly. But if you stick to a few simple rules then you're going to have no problems at all, and you're going to see some gorgeous things down there."

"So what are the rules?" That was Larissa.

"At this time of year, the main things to look out for are jellyfish. The box jelly has a big square bubble on top and very long, trailing tentacles. So does the Portuguese man-of-war, but its bubble looks like a fat cigar with a sail on top. If you see any, stay right out of their way. They're very nasty. But the best rule is, when in doubt, don't touch. Everything around here is a national park, by the way, so by law we're not allowed to remove anything from its natural habitat anyway."

"What about sharks?" Therese this time.

"I've never seen one here." She waited a beat. "At least not one that was hungry." Paul and Jenny laughed, and she could see Cadie grinning, but the rest of the passengers were still looking apprehensive. "Seriously, people, there is nothing to worry about if you act sensibly, don't touch and never swim, dive, or snorkel alone."

"What if we hit something and start sinking?" This was from Kelli, a long, tall redhead with a strangely distracted look that Jo was all too familiar with. She'd be keeping an eye on that one.

"It's not going to happen. But we have a dinghy, and life vests for everyone, plus we have the radio, and three cell phones between us. We file our position and course plan with both our office and the Coast Guard twice a day. Rescue is not far away, even if we're out on the reefs."

Finally everyone looked reassured.

"So where we do we go now?" Cadie asked.

Jo tapped Jenny on the shoulder. "Jen, can you get the map from the charts drawer, please?"

"Sure, Skip."

Jo waited till Jenny had unrolled the big map of the Whitsundays on the cockpit's central removable table.

"We're here." Jo pointed at Hamilton's marina. "It's," she glanced at her watch, "about 2pm. We could leave now and go anywhere amongst the islands and be there by dinnertime." She smiled. "My personal recommendation is, as it's a full moon and a clear night is forecast, it might be a nice way to start your vacation by making it right up to Blue Pearl Bay, here." She pointed. "On the opposite side of Hayman Island from the resort."

Toby grinned. "Sounds like a plan to me," he said. "Can we help, you know, drive?"

"Sure," she laughed. "The only other rule onboard is that when it comes to anything to do with this boat and its wellbeing, my word is absolute law." She smiled toothily. "That goes for Paul and Jenny, too. So, yes, please do pitch in, but my advice is that these two know how to make this boat run, so it's a good plan to listen to them."

Toby nodded enthusiastically.

"Hang on a minute."

Jo smiled quietly to herself. She had been waiting for the dissenting voice to pipe up. "Yes, Senator?"

"What if we want to go somewhere you don't want to go?"

Jo tilted her head quizzically. "You're the paying customers, Senator, so we always want to go where you want to go. The limits to that are that I won't put this boat anywhere it's not designed to go, nor will I put it, or you, anywhere that is dangerous."

"What if we insist?"

Then you're an idiot, the crewmembers thought. "Naomi..." Cadie tried to soothe her pugnacious partner.

There's always one, thought Jo. *Always one who wants to play the power game.* "Senator, we are here to make sure you have the vacation of a lifetime. We're experts in our field, just like you're an expert in your field. You wouldn't trust us to run the country, and with all due respect, we're the best qualified to make decisions about the boat and where to put it. And the bottom line is, when you signed your booking form and sent us the check, you effectively signed a contract agreeing to those conditions."

Jo held her breath. Some people accepted that part of her spiel, and some people didn't. To her eye the cantankerous senator looked like one who wouldn't. But she was saved from further negotiations, by of all things, an attorney.

Therese laughed and patted the politician on the thigh. "She's right y'know, Nay. You're just gonna have to lie back and enjoy it."

Jo had to give the senator credit. She recovered well.

"Pass me that bottle of champagne and I'll think about it," she replied grudgingly.

Jo grinned, winking at Cadie who had flashed her an apologetic look for her partner's stubborn streak. "Looks like it's Blue Pearl Bay then?" She waited as affirmatives came from around the cockpit. "Okay, let's go."

Paul and Jenny swung into action, asking for volunteers and giving quick tutorials to those willing to get involved in the action. Jo dropped down into the cockpit and made her way to the helm.

It didn't take long for them to be on the move, using the engine to maneuver the yacht out of the marina towards the harbor mouth and then through into open water. The breeze had picked up since the morning and Jo was sure she could coax the *Seawolf* up to nine or 10 knots for the fast run downwind to Hayman Island. Her passengers were in for a treat.

Cadie was exhilarated. She had volunteered immediately for crewing duties and had helped Jenny hoist the mainsail while Toby and Jason manned the big winch known as the coffee-grinder. Paul and Jo had shouted encouragement to the new recruits as the yacht had slipped through the narrow entrance into open water just as the mainsail was lifting and filling with wind.

It had been harder work physically than she was expecting but she certainly didn't mind that. She felt satisfied and intrigued by the feeling of the moving boat under her feet.

In some ways it's like riding a horse, she thought as she made her way forward, fighting to keep her balance without looking like too much of a landlubber. *Landlubber...is that really a word?* Cadie found herself giggling as she reached the prow of the yacht. She was pleased to find a waist-high rail around the point—she made a note to ask Jo what that was called—and she carefully wedged herself in.

She looked down and had to laugh at the sheer sense of freedom she felt. Clear blue-green ocean disappeared under her feet as the yacht cut through the water. Cadie felt like she was hanging in space above the waves. It was a smooth ride and she reveled in the feeling of the sun, wind, and occasional light spray of saltwater on her skin. She resisted the urge to have a Titanic moment for about five seconds.

Oh, what the hell, she thought, and threw her arms out wide, laughing at herself and generally feeling like she'd discovered the secret of life.

Back at the helm, Jo couldn't help grinning at the blonde woman's exuberance. It wasn't the first time the tall skipper had seen a passenger make exactly that gesture, but it was the first time she'd felt that joy right along with her client. For about the 50th time since meeting Cadie that morning, Jo wondered at the unreal sense of familiarity she felt around the attractive American. *Where the hell have I seen her before?*

The rest of the passengers were finding places to sit around the deck. A couple who were settling on the leeward side were in for a bit of a shock when they turned north and the boat really picked up speed, but Jo figured that was all part of the fun of learning how to sail.

Warily she watched as the senator approached and stood just behind her right shoulder as the skipper stood at the helm. Jo's hackles rose in an eerie echo from a darker time. She felt herself moving onto the balls of her feet reflexively. She hadn't felt that automatic response since...since Marco. *Down, girl. She's just a customer. Relax.*

The senator leaned forward so she didn't have to shout. "Don't think I didn't notice how you were looking at my partner back at the hotel, Miss Madison. Not to mention that charming little handshake."

Jo's senses tingled and she itched to retort. But her better instincts, the ones that had re-emerged in a back alley of King's Cross and the ones that owed Ron Cheswick more than a few favors, kept her silent. *The customer is always right, Jo-Jo,* she reminded herself sternly.

"Stay away from her. Or I will make sure you never set foot on a commercial vessel again," rasped the senator. The stocky woman took that moment to walk away, moving to sit next to the two attorneys up near the mast on the starboard side.

Jo took a long, shuddering, deep breath, fighting hard to still her nerves. She focused on the point on the horizon she was aiming the yacht for and tried not to lose her cool completely.

What the hell was that? She frowned, trying to concentrate on the sailing, rather than the urge to punch the senator's smug face. *One handshake and she's making threats.* Jo whistled quietly. *Woman's got a problem.* The back of her neck prickled disconcertingly.

An hour later the *Seawolf* was in top gear, nudging 10 knots and listing over at 45 degrees to port as she ploughed her way north through the heart of Whitsunday Passage. Those passengers on the lower side of the deck had learned pretty quickly how to stay dry, and had scrambled up onto the high side. The two men had their legs hanging over the side.

Cadie was soaked to the skin and loving every minute of it. She'd stayed at her spot at the prow and had been caught a couple of times as the nose had dipped down one of the larger waves. She looked down and was stunned to see a pod of dolphins racing along in front of the yacht's bow. She glanced back over her shoulder and yelled to Toby and Jason. "Guys! Check this out!"

The two men scrambled forward and Cadie frantically started clicking off photographs with her digital camera. Soon all the passengers were forward of the mast, leaning out to see the creatures in action. Paul joined them.

"Paul, how can they do that?" Cadie asked. "How can they go that fast?"

"Oh, they can go much faster than this," Paul said. "We're doing about 9-10 knots right now, but they can intercept boats doing up to 30 knots. And then they just surf."

"Surf? You mean on the bow wave?" Toby asked.

"Yeah, but not just that. See, as the boat moves forward it pushes water in front of it and that sets up a pressure wave. That's what they're riding. The bow wave is just the bit of that above the surface that we can see."

"They're playing with us." Cadie laughed as the dolphins leapt over each other, gamboling through the water.

"They sure are," Paul agreed with a smile. "But they're also being pretty smart. They're hitching a ride and saving themselves some energy."

"How cool is that?" Jason asked.

Meanwhile back at the helm, Jenny took the opportunity to talk to her boss. "How are we doing, Skipper?" she asked.

"Pretty good I think, mate," Jo replied. "We ought to be at Blue Pearl by 6.30, 7 o'clock."

"We're going to need some more liquid supplies in the morning, Jo-Jo, if they keep drinking like they have done this afternoon," Jenny said.

Jo frowned. "Yeah? How many cases have we got?"

"Still got two, but they've almost finished one and it's not 4pm yet. We've still got dinner to get through, and you know how the first evening is always a long one."

Bloody hell, Jo thought. "Okay. Give the office a buzz, Jen.

Order up whatever you think we're gonna need. I don't think
we'll be going too far from Blue Pearl for at least the next day."

"Okay, Skip."

As promised, the *Seawolf* slipped into Blue Pearl Bay just on
moonrise that evening. It was still light enough for Paul to be able
to direct them through the forest of bomboras—tall towers of coral
that rose from the sandy bottom up to just below the low tide
mark—to a safe anchorage.

Jo dropped the anchor and started helping him tie the boat
down for the night. Her guts were still roiling from her encounter
with the senator but she wasn't about to let that show, especially
since she could feel Cadie's eyes following her.

Jenny had been below preparing dinner. She started to bring
platters of food up for an al fresco meal out on deck. Plates full of
fresh seafood—prawns, Moreton Bay bugs, crabs, lobsters, oysters,
mussels, and bowls of salad, were passed around.

Jo wandered down into the main cabin and sat down on the
small sofa, escaping the laughter and chatter up on deck for a few
minutes.

Long day, she thought. *Long, weird day.* She'd stayed away
from both the senator and Cadie—something over which she felt a
pang of regret. The young blonde was clearly in seventh heaven
and there was something about that kind of enthusiasm that Jo
craved to be near.

But this wasn't her vacation. It was her job. She sighed and
moved across to the yacht's sound system. Running her finger
down the stack of CDs, she settled on an old favorite and pulled it
out.

That should soothe some nerves. Including mine. She flicked
the stereo on, settled the disk into its slot, and adjusted the volume.

Back on deck it was a perfect night. The full moon ascended
above the rise of Hayman Island like a huge silver dinner plate,
bouncing incandescent rays off the glass-smooth water.

Cadie sat with her legs dangling over the side, gazing down in
to deep dark depths that were so clear she was sure she could see
occasional flashes of phosphorescence as fishes darted past. She
couldn't wait to see this in the daylight, though the night view was
certainly enchanting. And romantic. She looked around and
noticed that the three other couples were sitting with each other,
talking and eating. Naomi was talking with Jenny, coaxing
another bottle of champagne out of the hostess.

She sighed. It had been such a strange, wonderful day. The highlights had been very high—being out here on the ocean, actively involved in sailing the yacht, surrounded by such beauty. It was a whole new world.

And then there was Jo.

All day long Cadie had felt the tall skipper like a presence in the back of her mind, constantly. From the moment their eyes had met as the *Seawolf* had pulled into her berth at Hamilton Island, to right now. It was like there was an already established connection between them. *Something so familiar. So...safe. Known.* All day they had caught each other's eye and exchanged smiles. She had noticed, with some disappointment, that the dark-haired woman was keeping her distance. And she was beginning to have a suspicion about why.

The lowlights had been not unexpected, but disappointing, and somewhat hurtful, nonetheless. As soon as she had seen the group of friends at O'Hare, Cadie had known that Naomi was either completely oblivious about the state of their relationship, or just unwilling to put herself in a position to have to discuss it. That said a lot. She suspected that her relationship with the senator had slipped so far down Naomi's list of priorities that it just hadn't occurred to the older woman that some work was needed.

And then there was that bizarre burst of possessiveness back at the hotel. Over a handshake.

We weren't that obvious, were we? Cadie smiled to herself. *Well, maybe we were. But it was a handshake, for God's sake. It's not like we dropped to the floor and went at it like animals.* She found that thought oddly distracting.

Just at that moment, hauntingly beautiful music began emanating from below decks.

Ohhh that's perfect, Cadie thought, as she leaned back, elbows on the deck, staring out across the bay at the full moon. *I'm beginning not to care about Naomi's moods. This place is too sublime to spoil with pettiness like that.* She closed her eyes and let her mind drift, with the yacht, on the tide.

Jo stepped back out onto the deck, grabbed a plate of food, and settled into an unoccupied corner of the cockpit.

It seems to be a pretty happy boatload so far, she thought. The passengers were chatting and laughing as they ate. She noticed Cadie was sprawled on her back on the deck, seemingly asleep, with a large tiger prawn, half-eaten, lying on her belly. Jo grinned at the picture, but her brain resisted the temptation to go where her baser instincts were leading.

Across from Cadie, Paul was balancing a fully loaded plate on one knee while he did some running repairs to a sail with an industrial-sized needle and thread. Jenny was still below decks, keeping the food and drink available.

"Jo?"

The dark-haired skipper raised her eyes and found a pair of sea-green ones gazing back at her. Jo lifted an eyebrow in response.

"Nice choice of music," the blonde said, liking the ethereal quality of the instrumental piece. "It's beautiful," she said noticing how the moonlight had turned Jo's blue eyes silvery.

"Sure is. Glad you like it."

There was a long pause. At least it felt that way to both of them. Other conversations went on, but Jo felt like she and Cadie were anchored together in a slowly circling eddy, the other voices swirling around them.

Jenny came up from below carrying a large tray of chocolate mousses and broke the moment. "Here, Skip, make yourself useful," the hostess said, thrusting the tray in Jo's direction.

Jo accepted it and pulled herself upright. She wandered around the deck passing out the rich desserts, coming to the still-prone Cadie last of all.

"Can I relieve you of that prawn, madam?" she asked playfully.

One green eye came open. "What prawn?"

Jo pointed silently at the large half-eaten crustacean on Cadie's stomach. "Ohhh. No fear. It's too good to waste." Cadie sat up quickly and popped the morsel in her mouth. "Mmmm nevegy wasde fommmvvd."

"I can see that," Jo said, handing her the bowl of mousse and a spoon. "Here you go. That'll top it off nicely."

"Ooo chocolate. Excellent. Thanks."

Cadie reached out to take the bowl, her fingers brushing Jo's accidentally. Both women gasped at the contact, letting it linger just a little before withdrawing. Blue eyes met green again in the moonlight.

"Sorry," Jo muttered. "Must have picked up some static."

"No problem," Cadie said quietly. "Must be all the, um, electricity, around here."

Jo grinned and moved away. *Whatever else, the next three weeks are not going to be boring.*

The next few hours were filled with laughter and music as the passengers and crew started to relax and get to know each other while the moon climbed higher in the sky. The champagne flowed and inhibitions dropped, leading to a round-robin karaoke session loud enough to scare away the fishes.

Jo chuckled. She had seen it a thousand times, but the sudden relaxation of a bunch of townies out on the sea for the first time never failed to make her smile. She tried to remember her life in the big city, but as was always the case when she was out here on the water, she found the details of those dark days hard to grasp.

She looked up and found Cadie's eyes on her, a raised eyebrow asking her a question.

I must have had the weirdest look on my face, Jo thought. She smiled back at the blonde, who grinned, reassured.

She just had the strangest look on her face, thought Cadie. *Like she was trying to remember something very sad and far away. I want to get to know her. I want to find out what makes her look so alone sometimes, when she thinks nobody is watching.* A surprisingly depressing thought hit her. *I wonder if three weeks will be enough?*

Jo struggled to keep her eyes open in the early morning heat. The tall skipper was perched on the rail at the stern of the *Seawolf* and about the only thing keeping her awake was the thought that if she dropped off she'd topple into the water. It had been a frantic few days since they'd picked up this new boatload of Americans. The novelty of being on a yacht had kept them on the move, sailing from anchorage to anchorage as the tourists got used to their new floating home.

Hopefully soon they'll figure out that they've got plenty of time to see everything and we can settle in one spot for a while, Jo thought wearily. She knew Paul and Jenny were feeling the pinch a little too. The three crewmembers were up earlier and sleeping less than the paying customers in a bid to keep the yacht stocked and in good running order. *At least when we stay in one place we can all chill out a bit.*

Jo glanced down at the chart in her hands. They were anchored off a tiny reef just east of the islands. The skipper carefully plotted their position and contemplated where they might reasonably head today.

It was early enough for most of the passengers to still be asleep below decks. The exception was Cadie, who had made a habit of rising early, long before her partner.

Don't blame her, Jo thought, casually watching the blonde as she made her way up the companionway and into the cockpit, stretching as she greeted the day. *It's about the only time that grouchy bitch let's her out of her sight.*

The senator had proven herself to be a curmudgeon of the highest order. Her animosity towards Jo hadn't diminished even though the skipper had been very careful to keep her contact with Cadie down to a minimum. Jo wasn't happy about that. She'd continued to find herself drawn to the woman and the last few days had been filled with soft smiles and looks that had left the Australian feeling discombobulated in the extreme.

"Good morning." Cadie smiled at her sunnily, her nose wrinkling in a way that made Jo weak at the knees.

Good thing I'm not standing. "Hello there," she answered out loud, unable to stop her own grin. "Sleep well?"

"Mmmm, like a baby, actually," Cadie replied. She stretched again, arching her back and reaching for the sky, her t-shirt lifting to reveal a toned set of abs. Jo tried hard not to look, but...*but she's gorgeous*, she finally admitted.

"I think sleeping on the water agrees with me," the blonde decided, oblivious to the effect she was having on Jo. She looked around. "Gosh, it's beautiful here." The tide was low and the reef was clearly visible. "I wonder if I can persuade the others to stay put for a day. Can we walk on the reef?"

Jo nodded. "Sure. You'll need a pair of sneakers you don't mind getting wet though. Coral is sharp and you can get a nasty infection from any cuts and scrapes."

Alert green eyes pinned her. "Come walking with me now?" Cadie asked. She looked around as if worried anyone else could hear their conversation. "Before..." She tilted her head in the direction of the companionway. *Come on, Jo. Apart from anything else I'm desperate to have an intelligent conversation with someone.* The blonde took in the long, athletic body in front of her. *Okay, so that's not my only motivation.* She smiled at the skipper again.

Jo blinked. *Before Naomi wakes up*, she finished the sentence in her head. "I'd love to," she replied, unsurprised by her own lack of hesitation.

Ten minutes, and a short dinghy ride, later they were on the reef, picking their way through the small pools formed when the tide uncovered the coral plateau. Both women were in shorts and t-shirts. Cadie had a small backpack on, containing sunscreen and her camera, while Jo carried a length of an old broomstick handle. She'd learned over the years that tourists were insatiably curious about what was under rocks and coral overhangs, and were not necessarily good at listening to warnings about touching things.

Cadie spied something in the pool she had just stepped into and bent over at the waist to get a closer look. "Jo," she called out. "I think I've found an octopus."

The skipper made her way over, pleased to see that Cadie, at least, had absorbed the warnings and hadn't tried to touch the creature. When she reached Cadie's side, Jo bent down as well. She didn't see it at first but then her eyes adjusted. One sandy-colored tentacle poked out from under a lip of coral.

"Well spotted," she murmured, smiling at Cadie.

"He was out in the open and then he scooted under there when he saw me," the American said. "Is he friendly?"

Jo crouched down for a closer look. "Not particularly," she replied. "He's a blue-ringed octopus. Small, but nasty. They bite and they can spit venom."

"Wow. Blue rings?" Cadie peered closer. "I don't see any."

Jo swung the stick around and shortened up her grip on it. "Not now," she said. "But if I do this..." Gently she slid the handle under the tentacle, probing back under the overhang. Abruptly the octopus shot out, wrapping itself around the wood. Brilliant fluorescent blue rings flashed and flared across the creature's pale yellow skin in an aggressive display of color.

"Ohhh," Cadie gasped. "Pretty. In a sneaky kind of way." She laughed and Jo joined in as she carefully unraveled the little animal from the stick. Quickly it scuttled back under the protective lip of coral. "Was that a young one? It was so small. I always pictured octopuses—octopi?—to be bigger than that."

Jo stood up to her full height again. "No, six inches is about as big as that species get," she explained. "Packs a punch though if he gets a good enough bite in."

They moved across to the next pool, stepping from one piece of clear sand to the next.

"It must be something, living here are all the time," Cadie said.

"It has its moments," Jo replied noncommittally. Something in her was reluctant to give away too much personal information. *I like how we get on right now,* she thought. *If she finds out too much about me, that'll change, for damn sure.*

Cadie opened her mouth to ask another question, her curiosity piqued by the tall skipper's reticence. But before she could form the words her foot slipped and she felt her weight sliding down and backwards.

Jo saw it coming but didn't have time to warn the blonde as her foot headed for the deceptively solid-looking rock. Instead she moved quickly to wrap a strong arm around the American's waist, catching her as she lost her balance. The movement brought them close together, close enough to feel the warmth from each other's bodies, and to breathe each other's air.

For long, golden seconds they hovered in that tingling limbo between restraint and recklessness, the attraction between them almost palpable.

"Um, thanks," Cadie whispered as Jo gently helped her regain her feet. She was lost in the wide blue gaze just inches from her.

"N-no worries," Jo murmured. They were close enough for Jo to feel Cadie's heartbeat, strong and fast under her fingertips. "S-sorry," she said, reluctantly letting the blonde go and backing off a little. *Damn, this feeling is so...strong.*

"No, it's...um...it's okay," Cadie replied hesitantly. Her own hand was still on Jo's forearm and she wondered at the steely strength under the warm skin. She let her fingers stroke gently against the fine hairs she found there. Cadie felt her mouth go dry. *Hoo boy.*

Somewhere a bell started ringing and the noise startled both women, bringing them back to reality as they stepped away from each other. Jo, who was facing the *Seawolf,* looked over Cadie's shoulder, her stomach lurching at what she saw there. It was the senator who had rung the bell that hung near the port helm station and now the stocky woman stood with her arms folded. She glared at them across the deep stretch of water between the yacht and the small reef.

"What is it?" Cadie asked, seeing the color drain out of Jo's face.

Jo sighed. "Trouble," she answered grimly. Cadie turned and looked back, her shoulders slumping at the sight of her angry partner.

"Shit," she muttered.

At that moment Jenny emerged from below decks and waved at them. "Breakfast's ready," she yelled across the water.

Jo waved back as they headed back towards the dinghy. "I'm sorry, Cadie," the skipper said as she pushed the small tender back into deep water, holding it as the blonde stepped aboard.

"Don't," Cadie replied, more sharply than she intended. She softened her attitude, mustering a weak smile. "Don't, Jo. It's not your fault, okay?"

Jo didn't say anything until she was settled in the stern of the dinghy and had the motor running. She swung the tiller and pointed them towards the *Seawolf.* "You're the client, Cadie, and I'm the employee," she said quietly. "I should know better." *How the hell do I stay away from her? Fuck.*

They pulled alongside the yacht and Jo held the dinghy steady as Cadie jumped easily up onto the transom. Naomi had watched them every second and she stepped forward, roughly grabbing her shorter partner's upper arm. Jo bit down on her tongue, hating the possessive way the politician treated Cadie.

Damn it, Jo, get a grip, she thought as she watched Naomi lead Cadie below decks. She shut down the engine, tethered the dinghy, and clambered aboard the yacht.

Jenny watched the interaction between the senator and Cadie, and was nonplussed to find her skipper scowling as Jo approached. "Trouble, Skip?" she asked.

"None of our business, Jen," Jo muttered, moving past the brunette and heading for the solitude at the bow.

Jo stayed out of the way for the rest of the day, busying herself with any little chore she could find in the bowels of the *Seawolf*. Thankfully, the Americans decided to stay by the little reef for the day and it was fairly easy to avoid contact. The skipper felt bad for Cadie, who bore the full brunt of the senator's bad temper, but there was nothing she could do that wouldn't worsen the situation.

Discretion is the better part of valor, and all that crap, she thought as she sat in the gloom of the sail hold, far forward and deep in the yacht's hull. Ostensibly she was checking the *Seawolf's* spinnaker, but instead she had flopped down in a foul-tempered heap and taken a long, badly-needed nap.

Jen knows where I am and she'll yell if I'm needed, she reasoned before she closed her eyes and let sleep overtake her.

Paul tapped her on the shoulder seconds later, it felt like.

"Hey, snoozy." He grinned at her as she shook the cobwebs out her head.

".What's up?" Jo eased the stiffness out of her long legs, wishing she'd found somewhere more comfortable to fall asleep.

"The loopies want to head back to Blue Pearl Bay for the night, Skip." The big man laughed at her befuddled expression. "You've slept the day away, mate. Dinner will be ready by the time we get there." He slapped her lightly on the thigh. "Come on."

"Wha-...bu-...Jesus." Jo rubbed her face as Paul pulled back out of the hatch. She hoisted herself up onto the deck after him, standing and stretching as she took in the late afternoon position of the sun. *Ah well, at least we got them to stay put for almost a*

whole day, she reasoned as she helped Paul haul the mainsail up
on deck and started rigging it for the trip back to Hayman Island.

Everyone was in or around the cockpit. The cheerful lights
from the cabin, and those strung up in the rigging, gave everything
a friendly glow. The sail back to Blue Pearl Bay had taken an hour
and a half and all on board were ready for the dinner Jenny had
prepared. Jo had been too busy to have to deal much with the passengers and it was only now that everyone was settling in for the
evening that she girded her loins for trouble. She warily walked
into the light, wondering just what kind of mood the prickly senator was in.

"Evening all," the skipper murmured, moving to her usual
spot just in front of the helm.

Jenny handed her a plateful of pasta and grinned down at the
skipper. "Get all your chores done, sleepy?" she asked cheekily.

"Oh shut up," Jo growled good-naturedly. "Or I shall have
you keel-hauled."

Jenny giggled and moved away, making sure the rest of the
passengers were getting their dinners organized. Jo glanced over
at Cadie, oddly gratified to find green eyes already fixed on her.
The blonde threw her a wavering smile and Jo felt a pang, knowing it had been a difficult day. She was about to smile back when
Naomi leaned forward, blocking her view of Cadie.

Jo sighed and returned her attention to her food. *Get your
mind back on the job, Madison,* she chastised herself. *You've got
no business causing this kind of trouble.*

Dinner went by pleasantly enough and soon Paul pulled out
his guitar, launching into a series of raunchy sea shanties designed
to loosen everyone up. The copious amounts of alcohol being
downed by most of the Americans did plenty to help that process
along as well. Jo noted that Cadie was keeping her wits about her,
though. *Interesting.*

Cadie watched as Naomi and her friends kept drinking as the
evening progressed. She felt oddly detached from the group and
she had her own reasons for wanting to stay alert and sober. It
had been a difficult day, with Naomi barely keeping her temper in
check for most of it. Cadie knew that chances were the alcohol
would make her partner less inclined to be polite as the night went
on. She wanted to make sure she was capable of dealing with anything the senator might throw at her, literally and figuratively,
when they were alone.

The good news was that as Naomi became more and more

intoxicated she was paying less and less attention to her. And that meant she could get away with watching Jo. The tall skipper was quietly sitting against the base of the portside wheel, one arm wrapped around her knee. She seemed lost in thought and Cadie drank in the planed features, the blue eyes turned dark in the half light. *I wish I knew what was going on behind those eyes,* the blonde pondered.

"C'mon, Skip. Your turn," Paul said, nudging Jo from her reverie.

"Aw, give me a break, mate. It's been a long day," Jo said reluctantly.

"And what better way to round it off than with a song or two from the Pied Piper of the Passage..."

"The Siren of the Seas," Jenny chimed in.

"The Mariner of Melody," Paul said.

"...Miss Jossandra Cristie Madison," they both chorused.

"Oh, shut up," Jo said good-naturedly. "All right, fire it up."

"Which one?" Paul asked.

Jo thought for a moment. "That new ballad we were practicing the other day."

"Rightio." He played the introduction and Jo began singing, her rich alto floating out across the bay.

Cadie felt the notes tingling up and down her spine. *Ohhh myyy...*

Jo shut away her natural self-consciousness and tried to pretend there was nobody listening. *Nobody, but Cadie.* She closed her eyes and gave her voice full rein as she weaved her way through the slow song.

The last notes faded away into the night air and Jo turned back to a boatload of wide-eyed tourists, one sea-green pair in particular. Applause broke out.

"What the hell are you doing here?" Therese asked bluntly. "You could be making real money."

"Nah," Jo said. "I only sing when I'm inspired. And money doesn't do it for me anymore." She smiled.

"So what inspired you tonight?" Cadie asked quietly. She tried to ignore the dark look she was getting from her partner.

Jo hesitated before answering. "Well, I make an exception when Paul and Jen gang up on me like that," she said, wishing she could say what she was really thinking.

"She knows we'll toss her overboard if she doesn't," Paul said. He and Jenny shared a laugh.

"It wouldn't be the first time." She nudged him with her shoulder.

"Well, I'm ready to call it a night," Naomi said, abruptly. "Coming, sweetheart?" She reached out a hand to pull Cadie up off the deck.

"Um, sure." Cadie stood and followed the senator down to their cabin. She turned back just before the companionway. "Goodnight, everyone. Thanks for a lovely day, guys." She beamed at the crewmembers.

"No worries, mate," Paul said.

Jo just nodded and smiled as each of the passengers made their way below decks.

"Boy, the senator's a real kill-joy, isn't she?" Paul asked quietly once everyone was below. Neither Jenny nor Jo saw any reason to contradict him. "Whose turn is it to sleep on deck?"

"Don't worry about it. You two take the cabin, I'll take the deck tonight," Jo said.

"You don't have to tell me twice, Skipper," he grinned. "Come on Jen, you know how you love being in a confined space with me." He waggled his eyebrows suggestively.

Jenny rolled her eyes. "One snore from you, bucko, and you're out on your bum."

"G'night, guys."

"'Night, Jo-Jo."

"'Night, Skipper."

Jo waited till all seemed settled below, and then she took a last stroll around the deck. It was a humid night, with the barest whisper of a relieving breeze. She made her way forward and double-checked the anchor line, then found a relatively flat piece of deck near the forepeak and stretched out. Most people found sleeping on deck a glamorous, even romantic thought. For about 10 minutes, until they discovered that not much of a boat's deck is flat or clear of fittings. But Jo had never minded it. She sat down and stretched out her long legs with a sigh.

An hour later she gave up any attempt at sleep. Her brain was running circles around itself and she was hot. The breeze had died down to nothing and all she could hear was the gentle lapping of the water against the boat's sides, and the soft hum of the generator pumping out just enough power to run the fridge, freezer, and air-conditioning units below deck.

Jo decided to break one of the rules she'd spelled out for the passengers. She stripped down to her underwear and padded over to the swimming ladder still hanging over the port side. Quietly she descended into the water that was, only now, hours after sundown, starting to cool below body temperature. The dark water enveloped her and she felt blessed relief from the humidity. Slowly she made her way to the anchor chain and with a deep breath she duck-dived, following it down.

The moonlight gave everything a surreal glow, and the water was so clear she had no trouble finding her way. The creatures of the night were out in force, including a moray eel she could spy, head sticking out of its cave, at the base of the bombora the *Seawolf* was anchored against.

Jo's lungs started to burn and her ears ached from the pressure as she cruised deeper, until finally, about 30 feet down, and still another 10 or so from the sandy bottom, she turned and headed back up. She broke the surface with a quiet exhalation, stroking slowly back to the ladder.

She froze when she heard movement up on deck, a tingling at the back of her neck making her suspect who it was. It was the same tingling she'd been feeling since a certain green-eyed blonde had gazed out from a hotel balcony at her four days earlier. Jo shook the water out of her ears and hung on the bottom rung of the ladder, listening.

Cadie was furious to the point of frustrated tears. After she and Naomi had shut themselves in the privacy of their cabin, the solidly drunk senator had been bitchy to the point of nastiness with her younger partner. "What the hell do you think you're doing, Arcadia?" she'd demanded.

"What are you talking about, Naomi?" Cadie had replied as she moved around the cabin, stowing some of their gear. She knew damn well where this was going, and wanted to stay as calm as possible. If she could let it play out with minimum fuss, she knew the senator would be out cold as soon as her head hit the pillow.

"We haven't even been here a week and you're hanging on that woman's every word. Could you get any more desperate?"

"I'm not doing anything except being pleasant to a pleasant woman, Nay. She also happens to be trying to give us the best possible vacation."

"You're flirting with her."

"She's attractive. And don't tell me you haven't noticed. Being married to me has never stopped you noticing attractive women."

"If she touches you again, I'll kill her," the senator threatened.

"And I'll just bet you made that perfectly clear to her, didn't you?" Cadie snapped. "I'll bet my last dollar that's why she's been keeping her distance."

"Oh, I'm sorry, did I spoil your little flirt-fest?" Naomi sneered.

"Jesus, Nay, listen to yourself."

The senator leaned in and gripped the smaller woman's shoulders, shaking her slightly. "You stay away from her."

"Get your hands off me," Cadie said quietly, with all the restraint she could muster. The senator backed off uncertainly. "Naomi, I don't know if you've noticed but we're living in a fairly confined space here. We're going to bump into each other."

"Damn you, Cadie."

"What is your problem?"

"You. You're my problem. You don't think I'm giving you enough attention so you've latched onto the nearest pair of long legs with pretty eyes."

"You're drunk."

"And you're a slut."

Cadie snorted in derision. "That's very funny, Naomi. Do you think I didn't hear the way *you* greeted Jo back at the hotel? 'I can certainly think of some things you can do for me, Miss Madison'," she retorted. "Very classy, Senator. And do you think I'm blind about the look you gave her before you thought I could see you? You hypocrite!"

Naomi struck out with her right arm, but she was already off-balance and sluggish. Cadie easily ducked the swing, even though it was the last thing she'd been expecting. Naomi had never raised a hand to her before, not even when she was a lot more out of it than she was now. Cadie was stunned.

The momentum took the senator on to the bed and she stayed there, mumbling more curses and epithets in Cadie's direction before, finally, she was dead to the world.

Cadie stood motionless for a few moments more, not quite believing what had happened. *I've got to get some fresh air.* She stumbled out of the cabin and up the companionway.

The deck was empty, thankfully, and Cadie carefully negotiated her way forward, blinded slightly by a sudden blurring of tears in her eyes. She slumped down, sitting on the front of the hatch cover near the prow, and let the tears flow freely, her face in her hands.

Shit, Jo thought. *She's crying.* The sound tugged at her

heartstrings unexpectedly and she fought the urge to leap onto the deck and go to the woman's aid. *Damn. And I bet I know why she's crying, too. Good one, Madison. Spend less than a week with the woman and reduce her marriage to a puddle of tears. Just great.*

Jo shivered in the steadily cooling water.

Well, this was a great idea, she thought desperately. *I'll scare the crap out of her if I come up out of the water like the creature from the Black Lagoon. Not to mention the fact I'm practically naked. Just what we need in this situation.*

She sighed. She couldn't stay where she was, that was certain.

Slowly she started climbing up the swimming ladder, hoping she was making enough noise to give Cadie some warning and not scare her out of 10 years.

Cadie looked around at the splashing sound coming from her left. She was treated to the sight of six feet of wet, half-naked womanhood, sporting lacy black lingerie, emerging over the side of the yacht. Jo's hair was slicked back and silvery in the moonlight. Seawater cascaded off her well-muscled, sleek arms and legs. Cadie felt like time had slowed to a crawl, and she was glad.

Jo couldn't help but smile at the woman's expression. "Miss Jones," she said quietly, "you're staring."

Cadie shook herself out of her daze. "God, I'm sorry," she said, more than a little flustered. "Jesus, no wonder Naomi is pissed. I really am losing it." She tore her eyes away from Jo, as the dark-haired woman picked up her pile of clothes and came and sat down next to her. "You're going to freeze. You've already got goose-bumps," she said, reaching out her hand to touch Jo's damp forearm.

They both stopped still at the contact, before Cadie pulled her hand away quickly and reburied her face in her hands, groaning.

"Hang on, let me get a towel," Jo said. She remembered her gear bag was stowed below decks, close to the hatch just behind them that opened onto the small cabin Paul and Jenny were sharing. She ducked under the hatch cover and hooked her foot around a deck fitting as she dangled half in and half out of the hatch, reaching for her towel. Paul was snoring softly and Jen had her mouth open, oblivious. Jo smiled as she hooked the towel with a fingertip and scrambled to pull herself back up and out of the hatchway.

"Could you lend a hand, Cadie?" she whispered loudly, trying not to waken the two sleeping crewmembers. She was struggling to get a purchase.

Cadie groaned again as she was confronted with a pair of long bare legs and a toned, damp backside. "To be honest I don't think there's anywhere I could grab on to that I couldn't be arrested for," she objected.

Jo stifled a laugh as she finally extracted herself from the hatch. She quickly dried off and threw her shirt and shorts back on.

They both sat on the deck, their backs against the hatch cover, Jo facing slightly to port and Cadie to starboard, their shoulders just touching each other.

"Are we likely to wake them up?" Cadie asked softly, indicating back over her shoulder to the small cabin.

"They're both sleeping through Paul's snoring, so I don't think we'll penetrate the haze." Jo smiled. "They've had a long day. And they didn't get to take a nap in the middle of it, like I did."

"Ah, is that where you got to?" Cadie asked, a small smile playing across her lips.

"Yeah. I thought it was a good idea to hide for a bit."

"Wish I could have," the blonde murmured.

"I bet."

There was a surprisingly comfortable silence as they both took in their surroundings. Cadie looked up and gave a little laugh of surprise. "Your stars are all different," she said, leaning her head back against the hatch cover and gazing at the thousands of glittering points of light. "Now, why didn't that ever occur to me?" she asked wonderingly.

"It's a pretty big concept, stars," Jo replied. "Just trying to figure out what that whole sky-full means," she swept her arm around, "is big enough, without trying to deal with a whole other hemisphere's worth."

"Show me your constellations?"

"Sure." Jo tilted her head back and was slightly unnerved to realize how close together their heads were in this position. "Um, see that kite-shaped one there, just above the horizon?"

"No," Cadie said. "Where?"

"Follow where I'm pointing." Cadie leaned closer still. "See that super bright one, and then those three others under it, making a kind of twisted square? And then there's another bright one between those bottom two?"

"Oh, yes," Cadie breathed, right next to Jo's ear, sending tingles down her spine.

God, how does she do that? Jo cleared her throat. "That's the Southern Cross. It's the one we have on our flag."

"Ah yes. That one up there looks like a bicycle to me." Cadie pointed out another cluster of stars.

"A bicycle?" Jo laughed softly. "How do you get a bicycle? It looks like a fish to me."

"A fish?"

They both turned their heads towards each other simultaneously and the world contracted sharply around them, their faces so close they could feel each other's breath on their skin.

"Jo—"

"Cadie—"

Slowly they backed away, holding gazes. Jo felt Cadie's hand slide into her own and she grasped it tightly.

So warm, Jo thought. *Everything about her is so warm.*

Cadie felt Jo take her hand firmly. *God, this thing between us is so strong,* the blonde acknowledged to herself. "It's like I've—"

"...known you forever," Jo finished.

"Yes," Cadie nodded, breathing deeply.

"Cadie...this is a really...really...bad idea," Jo whispered sadly.

"I know."

"Apart from the fact you're married...and you're a client...and you live half a planet away...well...even if those things didn't exist..."

"Don't tell me...you're an axe murderer, right?" Cadie joked weakly, her heart sinking at Jo's words, even though she knew them to be truth.

Jo closed her eyes, swamped by the irony of the blonde's joke, and an overwhelming loneliness that threatened her composure. *Get a grip.* She opened her eyes again. "Let's just say you don't want to get to know me too well," she muttered, still held by the sea-green eyes just inches from her own.

"But see, that's just it," Cadie replied softly. "Four days ago I didn't know you existed. Now all I want in the world is to know everything about you."

"Shhh." Jo placed her fingers over Cadie's mouth, wondering at the softness of those lips. *Wow.* "Cadie, it's not possible." Tears welled up in green eyes and Jo's heart broke at the sight. "I'm sorry," she said. "I've caused you so much trouble already. Four days in and you're already crying on deck."

"That wasn't your fault," Cadie objected. "It's not your fault I'm married to a paranoid, neurotic, jealous—"

Again Jo's fingers silenced her. "You can't deny that we've been bouncing sparks off each other from the moment we met, Cadie. She noticed, is all." She smiled quietly at the beautiful blonde. "If you were mine, I can't say I'd be happy about that either."

"You wouldn't threaten someone over it," Cadie muttered unhappily.

"I would have, once," Jo replied. Cadie looked at her quizzically, but Jo just shook her head slowly. "Don't be angry with her for feeling threatened. We both know she had every reason to be."

"Had?"

Jo nodded, trying to be resolute as she felt Cadie pull her hands closer, her tears returning. "Tomorrow, I'll call my boss. Get him to send a replacement skipper."

Cadie's hand flew to Jo's face, cupping her cheek. The skipper couldn't help but lean into the touch. "Please don't make that call, Jossandra."

Oh, God, don't say my name like that, sweetheart, Jo thought. *How can I leave you be, if you say it like that?*

"I have to, Cadie," she said out loud. "You and Naomi obviously have a lot of problems. But don't run from trying to fix them just because you think you've met your—"

This time it was Cadie's turn to silence Jo with gentle fingertips across her lips. "Don't say it," murmured Cadie, looking deep into Jo's silvery-blue eyes. "It's not possible is it? We don't even know each other. How can..."

Jo nodded silently in acknowledgement of the strength of the bond she felt with this sweet American she'd known only a few days. She reached forward and gently wiped the tear from Cadie's cheek. "Don't cry, Cadie," she whispered. "By the time you wake up tomorrow, you'll have a new skipper and it'll be like I was never here."

"Is that supposed to make me feel better?" Cadie asked plaintively. *God, why can't I think of another solution before she disappears from my life completely?*

"I'm sorry." Jo cocked her head to one side. "Is Cadie short for something?"

The blonde nodded. "Arcadia." Jo raised an eyebrow in enquiry. "My mother had a thing for Greek antiquity."

"And what is Arcadia the god of?" Jo asked.

Cadie shook her head. "It's not a who, it's a where. Arcady was a province in the middle of Greece. Pretty unromantic, huh?"

Smiling, Jo pulled Cadie's hand closer and softly kissed the back of it, taking in the blonde's clean, apricot-tinged essence that seemed so familiar to her. The aroma resonated somewhere in her memory. "You are even more beautiful than your name, Arcadia Jones," she whispered, taking one last long swim in those sea-green pools.

Cadie's throat ached from trying not to cry. "As are you Jossandra Madison."

Only the soft lapping of water, and the gentle stroking of Jo's thumb across the backs of Cadie's fingers broke a long, tearful silence.

"Goodnight," Cadie whispered.

And goodbye, sweetheart. "Goodnight," she whispered back, feeling a pair of warm fingers sliding from her hand.

Chapter
Four

Jo jogged steadily along the dirt track, letting the rhythm soothe her jangled nerves and tired mind. It was about 8am and she was crossing Hayman Island at its narrowest point, the well-used path from Blue Pearl Bay to the resort on the southeast side of the island. It was already stiflingly hot despite the early hour, and sweat caused Jo's grey t-shirt to cling to her back as she ran.

The tall skipper didn't mind. It was just a relief to be off the *Seawolf* and doing something physical. She had felt like death warmed over before she started and at least the run was getting her blood flowing.

Sleep had eluded Jo after Cadie had returned below decks. The skipper had been a basket case by the time the tendrils of dawn were curling their way around the mound of Hayman Island. Any small scraps of sleep she had caught were haunted by disjointed nightmare visions of that damned back alley in King's Cross and a certain pair of green eyes at the end of her gun barrel. Eventually she'd given up the quest and had just sat with her feet dangling over the side, thinking.

What the hell happened here? Four days ago this was just another boatload of tourists, and I was happy being alone and unattached and...untouchable.
And now? *Jo was irritated with herself.* Now what, Madison? *How did she let this happen? It was ridiculous, wasn't it? There was no way she could feel what she thought she was feeling for the blonde American, was there?* Less than a week, for God's sake. And now the senator is on high alert and is going to make it difficult no matter what the actual feelings are...no matter how far away from each other we stay...shit. *Jo felt ambushed by the whole experience, a sensation she was not in the least bit comfortable with.*

She had lain back on the deck, her arms folded across her eyes, growling softly to herself.

I've got to get out of here. *She had glanced at her watch.* Jesus, it's only just 6am. Ron is going to love this. *She sighed and reached for her cell phone, pulling up the Cheswick Marine boss' home number, and pushing dial.*

Three rings later a bleary voice had answered. "Yeah?"

"Ron, it's Jo."

"Jesus, Madison, have you looked at the time?" *came the grumpy response.* "Ohhh fuck, what did you hit?"

"Nothing, nothing, Ron, relax," *Jo said hurriedly.* "But...uh, there is a problem."

"Well, which is it, Jo-Jo, for Chrissakes? What's wrong?"

Jo took a deep breath. "Ronny, I need you to get a replacement skipper out here," *she said.*

"Wh-what? What's going on, Jo? Are you sick, or something?"

For a moment she contemplated telling him exactly that, but then honesty won out. "No. It's...it's just a personality clash, okay?"

Ron sighed. This wasn't the first time he'd bailed Jo out of a situation with a client because she'd been a little unwilling to believe in the "customer is always right" philosophy. But the last time had been three years ago, and he'd hoped those days were over. "What happened, Jo? Some American just get a bit too pushy? I mean, Jesus, it's only been a few days."

"No, nothing like that Ron. I know this isn't what you want to hear, but can you just take my word for it that it would be best for the clients and for the business if you just got another skipper to take over?"

Ron heard the worry and stress...and something else he couldn't quite put his finger on yet...in his favorite employee's voice. But he also knew he couldn't get her out of this one. "Jo, I can take your word for it. I trust you, you know that. But there's nothing I can do. There isn't anybody who can take over. Frank's out on the Beowulf with a bunch of Japanese who need babysitting every step of the way, and Jim's gone in for surgery on his knee. He's going to be out for a month. You're it, baby."

Awww shit, *Jo had thought.*

"What about you, Ron? Come on, mate, you're ticketed, and God knows you could use some time out on the water."

He laughed quietly. "No argument there, but it's not possible right now. I've got meetings down in Mackay over the next week for a start."

"Can't Frank and I swap over?" she asked desperately, grasping at one last straw.

"No, mate. You don't speak Japanese for one thing, and for another, you know how they feel about women. They asked specifically for a male skipper."

Well, *thought Jo,* that's me buggered.

"Jo-Jo, you still there?" Ron asked.

"Yeah, boss, m'here," she muttered.

"Look, I'm sorry, mate," he said. "I'd like nothing more than to help you out of whatever situation you've gotten yourself into, believe me. But I also trust that you can handle this, whatever it is."

Jo fought the urge to burst into tears and tell her boss everything. "Okay, Ron. Thanks anyway," she had said quietly instead.

"Jo." Ron wanted to take away the sadness he could hear in her voice. "Just try and take care of yourself, okay? I'm sorry, kiddo, I just can't think of anything else."

"It's okay. I'll talk to you in a few days. See ya." Jo hung up and tucked the cell phone back into its leather case clipped to her belt.

Just at that moment Jenny had emerged from the hatch over the small cabin in the forepeak, ready to start preparing breakfast for the passengers. "Hey, Skipper," she said quietly. "Jeez, you look like hell. Rough night on-deck?" She sat down next to the taller woman.

"Yeah, pretty much, Jen," Jo muttered, worrying away at her bottom lip. "You got that list of provisions you need? I'm going to take a run over to the resort and pick them up, maybe make some bookings for this mob for dinner tonight."

"Sure. Uh, I was going to do that after breakfast but I don't mind staying here. It'll give me a chance to get a jump on lunch." She paused, looking at her boss. "You okay, Jo-Jo?" she asked, puzzled by the faraway distracted look in her skipper's eyes.

"Yeah, I'm fine. Thanks for asking." Jo had smiled wanly and patted her crewmember on the thigh. "Just tired I think. Is Paul up yet?"

"He was in the head when I came up," Jen said.

"M'here now," the man in question said, sticking his head up through the hatchway. "What's up, Skip?"

"Hey, Paulie. Run me over to the beach? I'm going to head for the resort and pick up some supplies."

"Sure. You want me to call ahead, get them to meet you?"

Jo shook her head. "Nah, I'm going to jog over. I could use

the exercise," she said, standing up. "You two going to be right with this lot for the morning?"

"No worries, Skip," Jenny said. "The day looks clear, so we'll do the snorkeling thing."

"Okay. Let's go, Paul."

So here she was, pounding along the sandy track, her calves burning and the sweat pouring off her, trying to figure out just how she was going to survive another two and a half weeks in close proximity to Cadie Jones without either imploding, or turning the whole expedition into a floating disaster.

I've just got to avoid looking at those eyes, she thought. *And those legs. And...ohhh shit...*

It was long past dawn when Cadie finally awakened. Surprisingly, for once Naomi had beaten her out of bed, which considering the almost certain state of the senator's hangover, was amazing. Cadie took the opportunity to just lie on her back, listening to the sounds around her, savoring the gentle rocking motion of the yacht. She could hear people moving around the main cabin. Her watch told her it was well after 9am, so she guessed Jenny was serving breakfast to those who had emerged. She could hear Paul up on deck talking with Toby and Jason about the prospects for the day's activities. Therese and Sarah were giggling in the cabin next door.

She couldn't hear Jo, she realized. *I guess she's gone then. End of story.* Cadie rolled onto her stomach, resting her cheek on the backs of her hands. Unexpectedly she felt tears welling in her eyes and she rubbed at them angrily. *Like you don't have enough on your plate, for God's sake, Cadie*, she thought. She went over the previous night's conversation in her head again.

It's not possible to fall in love in four days. There, I said it. Love. Four days. Not possible. All in one sentence. Now get over it, Jones. You sound like a bad romance novel.

She rolled out of bed, grabbed a towel, and headed for the small shower tucked in the corner of the berth. The cool water cascaded over her as she tried to clear the fuzziness out of her head. Instead she felt hollow, an absence, and then the sting of tears again.

"God dammit!" she said aloud. "She's gone. Deal with it. Deal with Naomi. You're on a luxury yacht in the middle of a gorgeous chain of islands. Enjoy yourself, dammit."

Jo slowed to a walk with her hands on her hips as she came to the outskirts of the Hayman resort. The dirt track gave way to a paved pathway wending between carefully landscaped gardens, surrounded by luxury low-set hotel buildings blending into the environment.

Hayman Island was the top resort in the Whitsundays, rated a five-star hotel with good reason. Gold-plated bathroom fittings, top-ranked restaurants and entertainment facilities, black swans gliding around the pools—it all added up to a quietly elegant ambience that catered to the rich and famous. It also meant the resort was rarely crowded and Jo didn't see another human until she veered away from the hotel proper and headed for the shops and stores down along the marina's waterfront.

Down here there was more activity. Shop owners were already up and about filling the needs of the various boats and restaurants. Jo walked down to the end of the row and stepped into the small, well-stocked ships' store.

She loved this place. It served double duty as an outlet for luxury fittings for boats and yachts, as well as a retailer of the best in fine foods. Jo took a deep breath and savored the richly scented atmosphere. She could distinguish spices, rope, and fresh seafood.

"*Bella!* Bella Jossandra!" A large Italian woman sailed out of the back room of the store, wiping her hands on her apron and approaching the tall skipper enthusiastically. She cupped Jo's face in her hands and squeezed. "Where have you been, *dolce bambina?* It has been so long."

Jo laughed and accepted the woman's tight hug. "Hello, Rosa, how are you?" she asked once she could breathe again.

"I am well; I am well. Come, come and sit down." Rosa pulled Jo over to the counter and sat her down on a stool. "Now you tell me everything that has happened since we last saw you. What are you doing here? You have a boatload of the tourists, yes?"

Jo nodded. "Yep, sure do. We're over in Blue Pearl. We needed some supplies, so I thought I'd come on over and see my favorite Hayman Island resident." She grinned.

"Ah, you should have called, *cara,* I would have had Antonio drive across and meet you. Never mind; never mind. You will need him to help you take things back, yes?"

"Yes, definitely. Thanks Rosa."

She beamed. "For you, it is no trouble. Give me the list." Jo handed over Jenny's list of requirements and watched as Rosa disappeared out the back, bellowing at the top of her lungs for her son. "Antonio! Antonio!" There was much hurried chatter in Italian and then Rosa was back.

"He will load up the truck and come and get you when he is done, Jossandra," she said. "Now." She planted herself on a stool on the other side of the counter from Jo. "Tell me please, little one, why am I seeing such a lost look in those precious blue eyes of yours, eh?"

Jo looked up, startled. Rosa had always mothered her, from the moment they had met on her first trip to Hayman over five years ago. She wasn't sure why, but the gregarious Italian mama had taken a shine to Jo, and was constantly seeing to her wellbeing. She had always been pretty perceptive, but Jo hadn't been aware she was showing any outward signs of her preoccupation.

"I don't know, mamabear. Maybe you're just seeing the fact I slept on the deck last night. Only I didn't get much in the way of sleep."

Rosa squinted at Jo knowingly. "Mmmm, maybe. You do have the little black baggies under here," she said as she scuffed gently under Jo's left eye with her thumb. "But no. I am thinking there is something else going on. Maybe around this region, yes?" She tapped above Jo's left breast.

The tall skipper felt herself blushing. "Sometimes you think too much, mamabear," she muttered, lowering her eyes.

"Ahhhah! You see, I can always tell," laughed Rosa, tapping the side of her nose with her index finger. "Now, please tell me everything. Do not step over the good parts, *cara.*"

Jo sighed. "There are no good parts, Rosa."

The Italian woman frowned and took Jo's hand between her own two. "Jo-Jo. What is it with you and the women, eh? I see you looking, and I know you are lonely, but always you are backing away from them. What is it this time? Is she ugly?"

Jo laughed. "No, Rosa, she's definitely not ugly. Quite the opposite," she said somewhat wistfully.

"Ahhh you see, I was right, there is someone making your heart go pitty-pat." Rosa wagged her finger at Jo. "You cannot hide things from your mamabear, Jo-Jo."

She grinned. "I know. I don't know why I try really."

Rosa took Jo's face in her hands again and pulled her closer. "This face is so sweet, Jo-Jo. Why is it not happy? What is this beautiful mystery woman doing to make you look so sad?"

Jo sighed again. "She's belonging to somebody else, Rosa," she said quietly. "And she's sitting back on that yacht, paying me a lot of money to be her professional sail guide."

"Ahhh, *cara*. I am sorry. That is difficult." Rosa sighed. "And how does she feel about you, this woman?"

"It doesn't matter, Rosa. Nothing's going to happen."

"Tch, Jo-Jo, you know better than to be so black and white, always about the world. I have lived a lot longer than you, and one thing I know, nothing is so black and white. If you and this woman are meant to be together, you will be together. Maybe not today, maybe not tomorrow, but some time. That is how the universe works."

"No." Jo dropped her eyes as she felt Rosa's scrutiny intensify.

"Always with you, you are hiding something, *mia cara*. Keeping something close and deep." Rosa tilted Jo's head back to meet her gaze. "This woman is different I think. She will find out your secrets." She smiled softly.

"You're thinking too much again, Rosa." Jo smiled as she replied. Just then she was saved from further discomfort by the appearance of Antonio at the door.

"G'day, Jo!" She was swept off her feet by an all-encompassing hug from the brawny, good-looking young man. "How are you, digger?"

"I'm good, Tony," Jo laughed as he spun her around. "How are you? Still terrorizing all the female guests?" She grinned.

"Jo-Jo, I'm hurt," he said in mock pain, one hand over his heart. "You know you're the only woman for me."

"Boy, are you barking up the wrong tree," she retorted.

"A bloke can dream, can't he?" She laughed and sat back down on the stool. "The truck's all loaded, so just let me know when you want to head back, okay?"

She nodded.

"I've just got to make a phone call, mate. Then we can go."

"No worries." He headed out the back again, as Jo turned back to a beaming Rosa.

"He's a handful, Rosa," Jo said with a smile. Tony's mother nodded.

"Yes, but he is a good person. Like you, Jo-Jo. It will take quite a woman to keep you, I'm thinking."

Oh, let's get her off this subject, thought Jo. *She's already freaked me out enough for one day.* "Have you got La Scala's phone number, Rosa?" she asked, changing subjects quickly. "I need to make a booking for this boatload of tourists for tonight."

"Yes, yes. Here it is," Rosa replied, handing over a business card for the island's top restaurant. "Do you have Jenny and Paul with you this time, Jo?"

"Sure do," Jo replied, digging out her cell phone.

"You are in port tonight, *si?*" Jo nodded. "Then the three of you are coming to dinner, no arguments."

Jo grinned. Rosa's cooking was legendary. "No arguments here, Rosa. Thanks." She then paid attention to the phone as the restaurant answered.

Cadie was in the water, experiencing the full technicolor explosion that was the undersea world of Blue Pearl Bay. Jenny had suggested she take a swim before breakfast, as swimming for a while afterwards wasn't a good plan. So she was drifting across the top of a beautiful seascape. The surface of the water was smooth and glassy and with the sun blazing out of a cloudless sky, the visibility underwater was crystal clear and out to infinity.

She let herself float over the forest of bomboras, watching as a school of tiny fish flashed around the top of a coral outcrop, the sunlight bouncing off their scales like a million tiny mirrors. There was so much movement and color, she hardly knew where to look first.

She could sense Toby and Jason off to her left, doing pretty much as she was. Therese and Sarah were closer to shore, while Naomi, Larissa, and Kelli were still on the boat eating breakfast. She knew the chances of getting Naomi in the water were remote, but she'd tried anyway. The senator had avoided eye contact with her, and grumpily said no.

Cadie tried to let the gentle rippling of the ocean soothe away her stress. It wasn't difficult to get carried away into another world when a myriad of strange and fabulous creatures cavorted almost within arm's reach. At least that's how it felt.

She found it hard to judge distance in this strange environment. She took a deep breath and dove down as far as she could, surprised by how far away the white, sandy bottom really was. She couldn't get anywhere near it before her ears protested and her lungs screamed for another shot of oxygen. Cadie took a second to gaze with wonder at the wildlife swirling around her, including a beautiful blue, green and yellow fish gawking right at her, before she pushed back towards the surface.

She came up laughing, delighted by the discoveries of the morning, just in time for a ringing bell to draw her attention back to the *Seawolf.* Jenny was standing on-deck, waving and shouting. "Last chance for breakfast, guys! Come and get it," she yelled.

Cadie waved back as she trod water, pulling off the mask and snorkel. "On my way," she shouted back, kicking out and heading back for the swimming ladder hanging from the port side of the yacht. She clambered up onto the deck and looked back over her shoulder, grinning as Toby and Jason raced each other, splashing and wrestling as they did so. Therese and Sarah were making their way back as well, but were a little more leisurely, faces down, watching the wildlife below.

Cadie grabbed her towel and quickly dried off, pulling on a pair of shorts over her damp swimsuit. She noticed Naomi, Larissa, and Kelli were in the same positions as they'd been an hour ago, sprawled on the deck. The senator was watching her.

The blonde followed Jenny below decks, her rumbling stomach reminding her that dinner had been a long time ago.

"Smells good, Jenny," she commented, reaching for an empty plate and surveying the array of food. She selected some strips of bacon and a fried egg, mushrooms, and two tiny sausages.

Oooo, I love those, she thought, curling up in a corner of the sofa. *I want Jo here*, she wished, nibbling on a strip of bacon. She shook her head wonderingly. *Where the hell did that come from?* She watched as the men and then Therese and Sarah loaded up their plates and headed back out on deck.

Jenny was moving around in the galley, beginning to clear away the breakfast dishes. The young hostess took the last of the bacon and tipped it onto Cadie's plate as she passed.

"Finish that off for me, will you?" she said with a smile. "Otherwise it's just food for fishes."

Cadie grinned back. "Sure thing," she said, scooping a forkful of egg and mushrooms into her mouth and chewing enthusiastically. "Will we stay here all day, Jenny? Or are we just waiting for the new skipper to get here before we move on?"

Jenny turned from the sink and looked at Cadie curiously. "What new skipper?" she asked, puzzled by the out-of-the-blue question from the blonde American. She wiped her hands on a tea towel and leaned on the central counter.

Cadie stopped chewing for a hesitant second and then swallowed with a gulp. *Oops,* she thought. "Ummm...aren't we getting a new skipper? Isn't that where Jo's gone?"

Jenny laughed. "Nope. She just headed over to the resort to get a few supplies and to make a booking for you guys for dinner tonight." She paused, curious. "What made you think she was leaving?"

"Er, I don't know really," Cadie, trying to think around the surge of joy and confusion suddenly welling up inside her. "I think I just misinterpreted something she, um, said last night...maybe..."

Jenny shrugged and got on with the task of cleaning up breakfast and preparing for lunch. If she thought there was anything odd about Cadie's question, she gave no indication.

She's probably had weirder passengers than me, Cadie thought ruefully. *That must've been some trip.* She went back to eating, her thoughts racing as she munched on her bacon.

Oh wow, oh wow, oh wow...she hasn't left. Cadie grinned to herself. *I wonder what happened. I wonder...gosh, how is this going to work?* Reality hit as she realized the next two and a half weeks were going to be fraught with danger. She walked over to the sink in the galley and washed up her dishes, putting them away where Jenny pointed.

Naomi's going to go nuts unless I can figure out a way to stay away from Jo, she mused. *It's a big boat, but it's not that big. I just have to try. I have to give Nay and I a chance to work things out somehow.* She remembered the events of the night before and a dark cloud came over her thoughts. *Part of me wonders why I want to, if she's going to make a habit of swinging at me every time she gets jealous and drunk at the same time.*

Cadie walked aft, into her cabin, and dug out the manuscript of the book she was supposed to be evaluating while she was on this vacation. It was an historical novel written by a new writer who was trying to find a literary agent. No doubt she was one of many agents the manuscript had been sent to, judging by the dog-eared quality of the pages. *Never a good sign.*

But Cadie prided herself on being able to see talent where others had missed it, and she had become one of the Midwest's best literary agents on the strength of that ability. Perhaps this would turn out to be another hidden gem she could proudly add to her stable of authors.

She tucked the manuscript under her arm, grabbed her sunglasses and sunscreen, and headed back out on deck. She made her way forward, approaching Naomi and the other two women. The senator was looking distinctly pink after a couple of hours in the blazing sun. Cadie offered the sunscreen.

"Nay, you should put on some more cream, hon, or you're going to burn badly," she said quietly.

The senator looked at her for a second and then took the sunscreen. "Thanks," she replied grudgingly.

Cadie almost did a double-take. *Don't tell me,* she thought. *Is it possible? Is the great Senator Silverberg looking just a tad sheepish?* She smiled quietly as she waited for Naomi to finish with the cream. She took it back and continued forward, finding a spot in the shadow of the mast. She spread out her towel and sat down, ready for some serious reading.

It wasn't long before Naomi came and joined her, sliding down onto the deck beside Cadie and gazing off into the distance silently.

Cadie slowly put down her manuscript and turned to her partner. "Hi," she said quietly.

"Hi."

The senator looks a little uncomfortable, Cadie reflected. *Can't say I mind that,* she thought with a smile. "What's up?" she asked.

Naomi frowned. "Does anything have to be up for me to sit next to my partner while we're on vacation?" grumped the senator.

Cadie raised her hands. "No, no. It's just you looked a little pensive."

Naomi looked down at her hands self-consciously, and then cleared her throat. "Look, Cadie. I'm sorry about last night. I was out of line." For the first time she looked Cadie in the eye.

"You mean about being jealous of Jo? Or about taking a swing at me?" Cadie asked a little more sarcastically than she'd intended.

Naomi bristled. "I apologized, didn't I? And as a matter of fact I do think you've been acting like an idiot around that woman. You've been making a fool of yourself—and of me—over a woman you barely know." She quieted her tone a little. "But I had no right to raise a hand to you."

Cadie tried not to be insulted by the backhanded apology. She was frankly surprised to get anything out of her famously intransigent partner, let alone an apology, however meager.

"You're right, you didn't. Apology accepted," she said shortly. "But Naomi, know this. However much you don't want to acknowledge it, you and I have some problems we really need to talk through. Because the bottom line is, I'm not happy about the state of our relationship, and I think, deep down, neither are you."

"Jesus, Cadie, what's not to be happy about? We've made it. We're where we always said we wanted to be. I'm a US senator, for God's sake. I bought you a great house, clothes, we get to take long vacations in exotic places." She swept her arm around, taking in Blue Pearl Bay and the *Seawolf.* "I got you started in a career that seems to suit you. What more do you want?"

It was Cadie's turn to bristle. "You got me—" she spluttered. "Excuse me, Naomi, but my career is 100% my own blood, sweat, tears, and trust fund. Don't even try to start taking credit for that,"· she objected.

"Oh come on, Arcadia. You don't think being married to a senator has something to do with the number of high-profile authors wanting you as their agent? Please."

Cadie was almost speechless. "Every single one of those high-profile writers was an unknown until I found them a publisher, Naomi. How can you have the nerve to try and claim credit for that?"

"I know what I know," said the senator smugly.

Aargh. She's not listening to a word I say, thought Cadie in frustration. *Gotta get this back on track.* "Naomi, forget that for a minute. Do you really think I care about the house and the clothes and the money? If you think those are what make me happy, then we've got a serious problem."

Naomi lay back on the deck, with her hands behind her head. "Would you relax? We're on vacation, let's make the most of it. You worry too much."

Cadie sighed. "The whole point was that this would be a good opportunity to do a lot of talking, reacquaint ourselves with each other, Nay."

The senator snorted. "Not much chance of that if you keep flirting with Captain Courageous all day long, is there?"

Cadie winced. "Don't use that as an excuse to avoid working on our relationship, Nay," she said pointedly. "I'm certainly not going to."

Naomi sat up straight again. "What's that supposed to mean?" she barked.

"It means I started this vacation hoping it would give us a chance to salvage something we both used to care a lot about. That's still what I want to do, regardless of whatever paranoia you might have about Jo." *Careful, Cadie,* she chided herself. *Jo was right. She was only reacting to what she saw.*

"Enough," the senator said brusquely. She stood up quickly and towered over Cadie. "There's nothing wrong with our relationship that a little more care and attention from you wouldn't fix, Cadie. As far as I'm concerned, we're just fine."

Cadie was stunned into silence by the senator's arrogance. Naomi took that as a victory and stalked away to rejoin Larissa and Kelli.

Yeah, and don't think I don't know you two weren't listening to every word, Cadie thought with a grimace. *Why the hell am I worrying so much about this relationship? She doesn't give a damn. She's just not taking me seriously. Why the hell am I tear-*

ing myself up over this?

She sighed.

Because I care about her. Because it's 12 years of history I can't just throw away. Because giving up on it without a fight...disrespects it somehow. She ran her hand through her blonde locks. *Life is so complicated sometimes.*

And almost as if to prove her point, she heard Paul firing up the dinghy. She stood and watched him heading towards the beach, where a tall, dark-haired woman stood with a man and a truck.

Cadie's heart leapt at the sight of Jo leaning casually against the vehicle, and she wondered what was going through the skipper's mind.

Jo felt faraway eyes lock onto hers.

How does she do that? she thought. *How do we do that?* She watched Cadie lean against the mast as Paul roared away from the *Seawolf* in the dinghy. *God, she looks wonderful. She looks...golden.* She tried to picture Cadie in the snow and cold of Chicago and failed totally. *She belongs in brilliant sunlight.*

Paul approached the beach and Jo pushed herself off the hood of Tony's truck and walked down to the water's edge to meet him.

She moves like a cat, thought Cadie. *Smooth and graceful, like everything is so easy for her. I bet she can move fast if she has to though.*

The blonde watched as Jo and the other man helped Paul load three boxes of supplies from the truck into the dinghy. The crewman climbed back in and waited while Jo turned back to the other man to say her goodbyes.

"Thanks, Tony." Jo smiled at the dark-haired man. "Are you going to be at your mother's place for dinner tonight?"

"'Fraid not, Jo-Jo. I'm waiting tables at La Scala," he replied. "I'll be able to keep an eye on your loopies for you." He grinned.

Jo gave a couple of seconds' thought to asking her friend to keep an especially close eye on the senator and Cadie, but bit back the idea. *Cadie's a big girl,* she thought. *And I'm already in enough trouble without actively looking for it.* She leaned up and kissed Tony on the cheek. "See ya, big guy," she said.

He reached down and enfolded her in another bear hug. "Don't stay away so long next time, okay, Jo-Jo?" he said softly in her ear. "We miss you."

She smiled and patted his cheek gently. "I promise, Antonio."

"'Bye Jo." He waved as she pushed the dinghy back off the beach and jumped into the front. Paul fired up the motor and pointed them back in the direction of the *Seawolf.*

Hmmm, Cadie thought as she watched the goodbyes on the beach. *I wonder who tall, dark, and handsome is. I know who tall, dark, and beautiful is,* she chuckled. *God, how are we going to survive this vacation?*

Jo looked up as the dinghy drew closer to the *Seawolf.* She found herself raising her right hand and waving at Cadie, who quickly waved back. She grinned. *Oh, we are in so much trouble here.*

Half an hour later the new provisions were loaded and everyone was back on deck luxuriating in the late morning sun. It was just over 100 degrees, but the sanity of all concerned was saved by the sea breeze and the proximity of the water.

Jo took the opportunity to gather all the passengers together to talk about their plans for the next day or so.

"I've taken the liberty of booking you all in to Hayman Island's top restaurant, La Scala, for dinner tonight," she said, folding her arms as she rested her foot on the bottom of the port wheel. "If that doesn't suit all of you, it's not a problem to change the reservation, but I should do that fairly soon as the place is in pretty high demand."

Toby piped up. "What kind of a place is it, Jo?" he asked.

"Top of the range, mate," she replied. "The Michelin Guide gave it three stars, and there are only four restaurants in the whole country with that. There's a pretty strict dress code. Suit and tie compulsory for the guys."

"No problem," he grinned. "We brought our tuxes."

Jo nodded. "If you're all agreeable, we can motor around to the resort late this afternoon. It's only about a half-hour trip, so there'll be plenty of time for you to freshen up." There were general murmurs of agreement to the plan from around the cockpit. "Okay then. Anybody have any thoughts about what you want to do this afternoon?" she asked.

"We're going to do some more snorkeling," Therese said, looking for agreement from her partner. Sarah nodded.

"Jo, is there a walk we can take up to the top of the island?" Jason gestured toward the hill rising up behind the bay.

"Sure is," she replied. "It's not a bad trip. A bit steep at the top, but otherwise not too taxing. About an hour each way."

"I'd like to do that, too," Cadie said quietly, with a smile. "How about you, Naomi?" She turned to her partner.

"Nope. I'm gonna stay here and soak up some more rays," the senator said.

Jo watched the quick flash of hurt and disappointment cross the blonde's expressive face. *Boy, the senator sure doesn't act like someone who wants to spend time with her partner,* she thought.

Jenny emerged from the cabin. "I can fix up a packed lunch for the bushwalkers, if you like. That way you can start out now, and take your time there and back," she said, getting enthusiastic nods from the two men and Cadie. "Ok, done." She disappeared below decks again.

"Now, about tomorrow," Jo spoke again, "if anyone wants to experience the game-fishing thing, we're in about the best place to organize that. Hayman has a terrific charter boat that heads for the outer reef for the day. They pretty much guarantee you'll take some serious trophy fish."

"Yeah, we definitely want to do that!" Toby said excitedly.

Jo grinned. "You two are up for anything, aren't you?"

"You bet," Jason said "This is a once in a lifetime thing. Gotta make the most of it."

Jo nodded. She was starting to like the two men, even if they were in public relations. "For everybody else, the full facilities of the resort are at your disposal tomorrow. Tennis courts, swimming pools, restaurants, and gymnasium. There's even a cinema complex and their cabarets are legendary. They also have an art show going on in the main lobby at the moment."

Everyone seems pretty satisfied with the arrangements so far, she thought. *Even the senator is nodding her head. Yeehah.* She caught Cadie's eye and smiled at the attractive blonde. *All I have to do now is figure out who's going to take them up the mountain,* she mused. *The senator will have a hissy-fit if I go. Jen's gotta do lunch. That leaves...*

"Paulie," she beckoned the crewman over as the passengers dispersed to their various activities, "can you lead the bushwalk?"

"Ah," he said, "not if you want us to have a functional motor in time for tonight, Skip."

"What's wrong with the motor?" she asked.

"Well, it was running a bit rough last night when we came in, so I stripped it down this morning. I was gonna put it back together again after lunch," he said sheepishly.

Jo sighed. It just wasn't going to be her day, she could feel it.

They managed to get ashore without the senator realizing Jo would be leading the bushwalk, largely because the skipper had steered the dinghy to the beach and then swapped places with Paul who dropped them off and roared back to the *Seawolf.* Jenny had prepared little backpacks filled with water, sandwiches, fruit, and chocolate for each of the walkers. They stood together for a few moments on the beach, settling the packs on their backs and getting their bearings.

"Where to, Skipper?" Toby asked.

Jo pointed up the beach to a break in the undergrowth. "That path loops up to the top and back again," she said. The two men quickly made for the track. "Fellas, hang on a second." She grinned at the impatient duo who were obviously keen to set a record for making the summit. "Do me a favor okay? When you get to a fork in the path, go left. At least that way we'll know exactly where each other is." The men nodded. "And let's stop for lunch at the top, yeah?"

Jo turned to Cadie, who had been standing quietly behind her left shoulder. "Ready?" she asked. The blonde just nodded. Jo smiled at her. *She looks a little blue,* thought the skipper. *Probably anticipating the response when we get back on board.* She sighed.

The two men were already powering ahead as Jo and Cadie walked from the beach and under the cool, green canopy of trees.

"How did I know those two would be racing each other to the top?" Cadie asked and then laughed. "They're terminally competitive."

"They sure are," Jo replied. "But at least they're enjoying themselves. Hard to argue with that."

Silence fell as the pair settled into a walking rhythm, Jo moderating her long strides to allow the shorter woman to keep up without discomfort.

Jo knew she owed Cadie an explanation. "Look, um, I'm sorry I'm here," she said hesitatingly. "Well, that is, I'm *not* sorry I'm here...I mean—"

She felt a gentle hand on her forearm, halting her words.

"I know what you mean," Cadie said with a smile. "And I have to be honest; it's not going to be easy." She looked up into troubled blue eyes. "But I am glad you're here." She watched Jo's brow unfurrow. "What happened?"

Jo sighed. "My boss doesn't have anyone else to replace me. We've got one guy out sick and another one out with another group. He couldn't see a way to make it work."

Cadie nodded. "Well, we're just going to have to make the

best of it." She hesitated. "Jo..."

"Yes?" the skipper asked quietly.

"Thank you for trying." She smiled and Jo held her breath as their eyes met again. "I don't want you to try again, okay? Um, this is going to sound kind of out there, but," she hesitated again, "I missed you when you weren't here when I woke up. I mean, I really felt it."

Jo nodded, glad to know she hadn't been alone in feeling an emptiness at the prospect of leaving. "Come on," she said with a smile, "or we're going to get too far behind the Wonderboys."

Cadie grinned and they picked up their pace a little. She gazed around and took in the lush surroundings. "This is gorgeous, Jo. Is this what they call rainforest?"

"Pretty much," the Australian replied. "Though the soil's a bit too sandy to be true rainforest. But it's still a pretty rich environment with a lot of wildlife around."

"Will we see any?" Cadie asked, looking down at her feet quickly.

"It's a pretty well-used path, so the animals probably know to stay away, but you never know your luck," Jo replied.

A wild and startled yell from further up the path caught their attention and Jo broke into a run, taking the steadily increasing incline in long, strong strides. She could hear Cadie running behind her and concentrated on listening for further sounds from in front of her. She rounded a corner and came across the two men, standing stock still in the middle of the path.

"What's wrong?" she asked breathlessly.

Toby pointed further up the track.

"S-snake," Jason said shakily. "I nearly walked on it. Scared me half to death."

Jo stepped between them to get a closer look at the reptile that was curled in an angry, hissing pile in a patch of sunshine in the middle of the track.

"Bugger," she said quietly, recognizing a nasty customer when she saw it. "It's a good thing you didn't step on it, Jason. That's a taipan. See the rectangular head and red eyes?" She pointed at the distinctive characteristics.

"They're poisonous?" Jason asked.

"Oh yeah," she understated.

The two men took another step backwards. Cadie came up beside Jo to get a better view. "Can we go around it?" she asked, looking skeptically at the relatively narrow track.

"I don't think he's going to appreciate us getting that close somehow," Jo muttered, thinking hard.

"I was afraid you were going to say that," Cadie said. "What's the plan?"

"I'm working on it," Jo said, keeping one eye on the alarmed reptile while searching for a likely tool. She spotted a handy looking long stick that had a fork in it and reached for it, trying not to startle the snake with any quick moves.

"Maybe we should just go back?" Toby offered.

"Come on, fellas. Where's that sense of adventure we've come to expect from you?" Jo grinned as she trimmed the branch down to a long pole with a narrow fork at the top. "Okay," she said as she folded her Swiss Army knife back up and put it in her pocket. "Here's what's going to happen. You three are going to stay right where you are, where he can see you. I'm going to try and sneak around and behind him, then pin his head still with this little gizmo." She waggled the stick and smiled. "Ready?"

"I notice you get out of range of his fangs while we get to stay his target," Cadie said with an uncertain smile.

"Well sure. You three are a bigger target than little old me, so he'll stay focused on you guys and won't notice me." She paused. "Hopefully." She grinned again. "Okay, here we go. Oh, and if he comes for you, try and scatter three different ways."

"Jesus Christ," Toby muttered, still focused on the hissing, flattened snake.

Jo edged her way to the right-hand side of the track, stepping off the dirt and into the underbrush, moving slowly around the snake, giving him a wide berth. *So far, so good. Hell of a moment to be trying this for the first time, Madison.* She broke a twig suddenly and the snake rotated sharply around to seek her out.

"Whoa! Here, Mr Snake," Cadie yelled, flapping her arms, trying to attract the snake's attention away from Jo. It worked and he swung back towards the trio, standing up a little on his neck muscles.

"Fuck, Cadie, whaddaya doing?" Toby shouted, stepping back again.

Brave girl, Jo thought, as she was in position beyond the snake and making her way back up onto the track behind him. *I wonder if she would have done that if she knew how mean taipans are. Don't think I'll mention that right now, though.*

She readied her stick and began cautiously lining up the fork with the back of the snake's head. *Christ I hope I get this right first time, or he's going to be incredibly pissed off. Oh well, in for a penny, in for a pound.*

With a long lunge, Jo thrust the stick forward and hit her

mark, pinning the snake by his head to the ground. Quickly he uncoiled himself, thrashing his long body around in a vain attempt to get free from his trap.

"Come on, you lot, get around him," Jo urged, trying to avoid the flailing tail.

Cadie led the way with the two men scurrying past.

"Okay, now back off some up the track, 'cos when I let go of him, he's going to be pretty angry, and I have no clue what he'll do," Jo said. She hoped like hell he'd slink off into the scrub, given her exposed legs were the nearest targets. "Here we go."

She pushed the stick away from her as she let it go, hoping it would force the snake further away. It worked. Once released the angry reptile took one look over its shoulder and with a powerful flick of its tail, was off into the scrub to the side of the track.

Jo turned around to three impressed Americans. "Nice one, Skipper." Toby grinned.

Cadie's sea-green eyes met hers and held her gaze for what seemed like an age. The blonde smiled gently. "Very impressive," she said softly.

Jo cleared her throat and tried to ignore the blush she was sure was climbing up her neck.

"Well. Uh, yes, um, welcome to the Australian bush, folks. Shall we see if we can get to the top without endangering any other innocent creatures?"

Chapter
Five

The foursome made it to the top of Hayman Island without
further encounters with the wildlife. The last 200 feet had been
hard work, as it was much steeper than the rest, but they were well
rewarded for their efforts. The Queensland Parks and Wildlife
Service had built a small platform and benches with a spectacular
view looking south down the length of Whitsunday Passage.

"Wow," Cadie said, reaching for her camera. She took a long
series of pictures panning from east to west before finally swinging her pack off her back and sitting down on one of the benches.
"Do you ever pinch yourself, Jo? Living in such a gorgeous part
of the world, I mean?" She looked at the tall skipper who was
standing with one foot propped on a rock, gazing out at the panorama. *She looks like a goddess.*

"Oh yeah," Jo replied softly, knowing Cadie could have no
clue just how much like a dream this was in comparison to the
world she once inhabited.

Toby and Jason had settled on the other bench and were happily munching the sandwiches Jenny had prepared for them.

"Is this home for you, Jo?" Toby asked. "I mean, were you
born here?"

Jo turned back to face them all, dropping her pack at her feet
and sitting down on the rock. "No. My parents are sheep station
owners, out in the west of New South Wales," she said.

"Station?" Cadie asked. "You don't mean trains?"

Jo laughed. "No. Station, as in, um, ranch? A farm, I
guess." Cadie nodded in understanding. "I pretty soon figured
out that farming was not for me, and as soon as I was old enough
to drive myself, I moved to Sydney." *Ran away like a coward in
the night, more like,* she reminded herself. "Then just over five
years ago I came up here." She took a large bite out of a sand-

wich, using the mouthful as a reason to shut up. She felt Cadie's eyes on her, and for the first time in almost five days, couldn't meet them.

"Did you sail boats in Sydney?" Jason asked.

"No," she replied bluntly, taking another bite and chewing slowly.

A goddess who doesn't like talking about herself, apparently, Cadie thought. *Interesting. She needs some help here before the boys give her the third degree.*

"Toby and Jason are the new whiz kids of the political world back home," she said quickly before either of the men could delve deeper into Jo's past.

"Is that so?" Jo asked, grateful to have the focus off herself. "I know you're the senator's public relations team. But what does that mean, really?"

"They make her look good," Cadie said dryly. Everyone laughed. "It's true."

"Well, kind of, I guess, Cades, but I'd like to think our job is a bit more..." Jason looked to his partner for inspiration.

"Principled," Toby said for him.

"Yes, that's it," Jason agreed. He turned back to Jo. "Naomi can't be everywhere at once. She can't always have the answers at her fingertips. We just make sure her message gets to the right people at the right time."

Jo raised one eyebrow quizzically and looked at Cadie. This time it was the blonde who couldn't meet her eyes. "And what's the message?" she asked.

"Strong, stable government. Equal rights for all," chorused the twosome in unison.

Cadie stirred the dirt with her toe, silently.

Jo watched her sympathetically and then turned back to the men, smiling quietly. "Sounds very...reasonable," she said. She glanced back at the blonde, wondering if she had any right to ask her questions, given her own reluctance to answer queries about herself. The decision was made for her when Cadie's sea-green eyes lifted and met her own.

"I'm a literary agent," Cadie said.

Jo smiled. "Cool," she said. "You find publishers for writers, yeah?"

"Exactly," Cadie said, smiling back. "And occasionally I find writers for publishers—if they have a specialist book they want written for example."

Jo nodded. She cocked her head a little and studied the smaller woman. "It suits you," she said.

"Suits me?"

Jo nodded again. "Mhmm. You're in the right job. It...fits."

Cadie smiled. "I like to think so," she said.

They held each other's gaze for a few beats before Toby cleared his throat pointedly. "Time we got back, don't you think, Skipper?" he asked quietly, exchanging a quick look with Jason.

Jo looked down at her watch, aware that both she and Cadie were blushing. "Yep," she said. "If we go back down now, there'll be time for a swim before we head around to the resort."

"God, that sounds wonderful," Cadie said with a groan. "I'm sweating buckets."

They made it back to the beach in good time after sticking together on the return journey, partly due to Toby and Jason's reluctance to come face-to-face with any more wildlife on their own, and partly a silent, but mutual, agreement between Jo and Cadie that being alone together was probably not a good idea.

Paul drove the dinghy up onto the beach and the two men headed for him, throwing their backpacks into the boat. Cadie took the opportunity for a quick conversation with Jo.

"Is there any reason why I shouldn't swim back, Jo-Jo?" she asked.

Jo smiled at the familiar diminutive, loving how it sounded coming from the blonde. "No, but it's further than you think." She paused. "You're worried about Naomi, aren't you?"

Cadie nodded. "I just think any chance to keep us separated is a good idea at this point."

"Mhmm. I'll go back with Paul. If you get too tired, yell out, though, okay? The distance really is deceptive."

"Okay. I'll be fine." Cadie grinned up at her. "Thanks for a lovely walk."

"My pleasure." She watched the American walk down to the dinghy and drop her backpack and camera into the boat, before stripping off her shirt, shorts, and hiking boots. Jo tried not to stare as her compact, bikini-clad form came into view. *God,* she thought, *what I wouldn't give to be within arm's reach of her right now.* She sighed.

Cadie waded into the water and dove under, kicking out towards the underwater forest of bomboras, and the *Seawolf* in the distance. Jo climbed into the dinghy and settled in with the three men.

"Let's go, Paulie."

As it turned out, their arrival back on the boat was barely noticed by the senator and her entourage, who had spent more of the afternoon exploring the bottom of various bottles of alcohol than the sandy bottom of Blue Pearl Bay. Naomi was asleep on her back, oblivious, and snoring in the afternoon sun.

By the time Cadie climbed back on deck, Jo was hunkered down with Paul in the engine compartment, piecing the motor back together. They were both sporting smears of grease on their faces and were bantering back and forth.

"You do this to me every trip, Paulie," Jo said with mock weariness as she cranked away on a stubborn bolt.

"I'm telling you I heard something," came the muffled reply from the blond crewman who was head down, backside up in the confined access panel under the central mound of the helmsman's cockpit.

"Yeah, yeah, you heard something. The Abominable Snowman is still out there too somewhere. And the Loch Ness monster and the Yowie and—"

"All right; all right; all right," he grumbled, just as exasperated as she was. He sat upright again.

Jo grinned at him fondly. "Face it, Paul. You just love pulling this thing apart and putting it back together again, don't you?"

He chuckled.

Jo looked up as Cadie stepped past them, making her way down to the main cabin. "Good swim?" she asked, trying desperately not to notice the American's toned and dripping body. *There's only one thing sexier than Cadie Jones in a bikini,* she thought. *And that's Cadie Jones in a soaking wet bikini, on the deck of my boat.*

"Great. Thanks," grinned Cadie, her skin tingling as the skipper's eyes swept over her and then flicked away. *Like she's trying not to look,* she chuckled to herself. *God, I wish...* She shook that thought away. "You were right, though, it was further than it looks. I'm beat."

"Well, if Paul the Intrepid Mechanic here has done fart-arsing about with the engine, we can fairly shortly be on our way to the resort," Jo said, slapping the crewman across the shoulder with her work glove.

"I don't mind if you never get it going," Cadie said, disappearing down the companionway.

By 7pm the *Seawolf* was safely tucked into her assigned berth in the Hayman Island marina and locked down for the night. Jo, Paul, and Jenny were sprawled around the main cabin, talking quietly as the guests readied themselves for their evening ashore. Jenny had set up a tray of champagne flutes filled with ice-cold bubbles on the cockpit's central table for the passengers to sample on their way out.

The lack of sleep from the night before was beginning to catch up with Jo and she rested her head on the back of the couch, listening to Jen and Paul speculate about their own evening ahead.

"God, I hope Rosa makes those little dumplings with the red stuff inside. I love those," Paul said.

Jo laughed. "She makes that every time we go to her place for dinner, Paul. It's a fair bet she'll make it again."

"Great. I'm drooling already," he replied.

Jo smiled and closed her eyes, letting the two deckhands' conversation drift over her as her thoughts wandered. *I'm gonna sleep tonight, that's for damn sure.* She listened with half an ear as some of the passengers started to emerge. Jenny whistled at Toby and Jason in their tuxedos, and the two men began a running fashion commentary as the women came out of their cabins.

"Therese and Sarah are resplendent this evening in matching Dolce and Gabbana power suits, one in burgundy and the other in teal," Toby said.

Jenny and Paul applauded as the two attorneys got into the spirit, parading down the length of the cabin. Jo watched sleepily from where she sprawled, laughing at the antics.

"Senator Silverberg of Illinois is all style and class in a classic tailored dinner suit by Armani," Jason announced as Naomi hooked her jacket collar with her forefinger and flicked it over her shoulder. She then followed the attorneys up on deck as Larissa and Kelli flounced out of their berth in full supermodel style.

She could actually be a supermodel, Jo thought as the stick-thin Kelli sauntered by, spinning once before climbing the companionway to the cockpit. Larissa, sporting a red sequined sheath, shimmied after her.

"Come on, Paul, grab a bottle," Jenny said, picking up a freshly opened bottle of champagne. "At the rate these guys drink, they'll be yelling for a second glass any minute now."

Paul followed Jen up onto the deck, leaving Jo to her own thoughts. She stayed as she was, head back, eyes closed, letting the sounds of the boat flow over her. The passengers laughed and clinked their glasses against each other and then started moving above her, making their way ashore and to the restaurant.

I wonder if they even realize Cadie isn't with them, Jo wondered. *How can they not miss her? I miss her whenever I can't see her.* She laughed quietly to herself. *When did that start happening?*

Cadie was flustered. Naomi had taken forever in the tiny bathroom and there just hadn't been enough room to work around each other, so she had sat quietly on the bed, reading her manuscript. Finally the senator was ready, and walked out to meet the others. She barely grunted when Cadie had complimented her on her outfit.

Now Cadie was stuck. She'd hurried into her dress and had managed to get the zip two-thirds of the way up her back, but no matter how she contorted herself, she couldn't reach the rest of the way. Up until a couple of minutes earlier she could hear the others either in the main cabin or up on deck but now everything seemed silent.

They left without me, thought Cadie. *Well, if that doesn't just sum it all up.* She sighed. *God, I'm tempted to just stay here. Screw them. It's not like they're gonna miss me.* She growled quietly to herself and made another attempt at the zipper. *God dammit. I'm gonna have to enlist some help.*

She padded over to the door and cracked it open. She was surprised to see Jo, half-reclined on the galley sofa, her feet on the seat opposite, head tilted back, dark hair flowing over her shoulders.

One brilliant blue eye opened and focused on her. A stunning wide smile followed. "Hello."

"Hi, Jo. Umm, I don't suppose you know if Naomi is around?" Cadie asked, suddenly shy under the tall skipper's intense gaze.

"Er, no. Actually, they already left," Jo said, sitting up straighter and bringing her feet down to the ground. "Is something wrong? Apart from the fact they left you behind?"

"No big surprises there," Cadie muttered. She decided to bite the bullet. "Well, yeah, kind of. I, um, need a little assistance getting into this thing." She opened the door completely to reveal the simple, elegant, black lace dress.

Jo was stunned into silence. She knew her jaw dropped but there was nothing she could do to prevent it. Cadie was utterly gorgeous to behold. The dress was just the right length to show off the athletic blonde's toned legs to best effect. The neckline plunged perfectly.

Cadie's sea-green eyes sparkled at the look on Jo's face, and she felt a warm glow beginning somewhere south of her waistline, spreading up and through her like a shot of brandy on a winter's night.

She cleared her throat softly. "Now look who's staring," she said quietly, remembering the previous night's moonlight encounter.

She's breathtaking, Jo thought. *Just...breathtaking. Come on, Madison, connect your brain to your motor centers. Move.*

"I'm sorry," she said hastily, stumbling to her feet like some kind of clumsy newborn colt. "Um, it's just I wasn't expecting...you look so..." She took a deep breath. "You are beautiful, Arcadia."

I've never liked my name. Until now, thought Cadie, thrilling at the sound of Jo's warm contralto rolling around her full moniker.

"Thank you," she said, feeling the blush rise as Jo walked slowly towards her. Cadie turned her back on the tall skipper. "Could you?"

Oh boy. Jo swallowed and walked closer to the petite American. Awkwardly she wiped suddenly sweaty palms on her shorts then reached for the jammed zipper. She was close enough to smell Cadie's apricot-scented shampoo and... She inhaled deeply. "You smell wonderful," she said softly, her fingers fumbling slightly with the zip. "Is that Obsession?"

Cadie nodded slowly. *If she comes any closer I'm going to faint, I just know it.* Every now and then she could feel Jo's fingertips brushing against her skin and each fleeting touch sent rivulets of warmth through her.

I want to touch her so badly. Jo tried to absorb every tiny sensation of Cadie's skin that she could. *So soft.* The temptation to run her hands over the blonde's back and shoulders was almost too much for her and she hesitated as she finally unsnagged the zip and gently pulled it closed.

"Can I ask you something, Cadie?" she asked, staying close behind her.

Where is she going with this? Cadie thought. *God, Jo, please don't ask me for something I can't give right now. I don't want to say no to you. Don't make me, please.* She found herself holding her breath as she nodded again.

"These people...they're not really your friends, are they?"

Cadie turned to face Jo, surprised by the question. "No they're not. Not at all. They're all Naomi's friends," she replied quietly, looking up into hooded blue eyes. "I didn't even know they were coming with us until they met us at the airport in Chicago." Jo cocked her head to one side, listening. *It's so cute the way she does that,* Cadie thought.

"That really sucks. I'm sorry. Doesn't make for much of a vacation for you."

"To be honest, I've gotten kind of used to it," she said sadly.

"That doesn't make it right," Jo said softly, looking deep into the blonde's eyes.

Her eyes are so hypnotic, Cadie thought. *I could spend hours...days...long, endless days...lost in them.* Instead she reached up and gently cupped Jo's cheek, smiling at her softly.

So warm, thought Jo, leaning into the touch slightly.

"Thank you for the good thoughts, Jo. I really appreciate them. And thanks for the..." She flicked her thumb over her shoulder, indicating the troublesome zip.

"No worries." *Oh no, no worries at all.*

"If I don't get going, they're going to be halfway through their appetizers before I even sit down," Cadie said. She slipped on a pair of black heels and picked her purse up from its resting place on the bed.

Jo backed out of the cabin, letting Cadie past. As the blonde headed for the companionway, the skipper had an idea.

"Cadie, hang on a second," she said. She reached around and unhooked her cell phone from its place on her belt. "Do me a favor, take this with you? Paul and Jen's numbers are programmed into the speed dial." She keyed the relevant menu buttons to show her where. "They're going to be with me all evening. If you need anything, or if you just want picking up at some point, call. Okay?"

Cadie gazed up at the tall skipper gratefully. "Thank you," she said softly.

Two hours later Jo, Paul, and Jenny were up to their armpits in good food, friendly company, and several very drinkable bottles of lambrusco. Jo drained another cold glass of the sweet red wine, only to have it refilled by Roberto, Rosa's gregarious husband.

"Drink, drink, drink," he bellowed, making the rounds of the table, splashing more wine into everyone's glasses, regardless of whether they needed refilling or not.

Jo grinned. It was hard to have a bad time at Rosa's dinner table, and as she looked around she was unsurprised to discover that she wasn't the only one letting her hair down.

Paul and Jenny were enjoying each other's company, ribbing and poking fun under the maternal wings of their hostess at one end of the table. Jo was beginning to have her suspicions about her younger crewmates and she could tell by the twinkle in her eye that Rosa was also making note of the chemistry between the two. Jo smiled at the thought. *They certainly look good. I hope they are getting together. They make a terrific team.*

Down on her end of the table, Jo was sitting opposite the youngest of Rosa's children, 12-year-old Sophie, the baby of the family. The dark-haired, brown-eyed girl had a bad case of hero worship when it came to the tall skipper, something Jo found flattering but uncomfortable at the same time. Sophie had spent most of the evening gazing adoringly at her.

Roberto sat down heavily in the end seat next to Jo and placed a large, rough hand on her shoulder. "You don't eat enough, Jo-Jo," he exhorted. "None of you do. Look at you three, you are skin and bone, all of you. Come, come eat more of Rosa's ravioli or she will make my life a misery. Come, come." He spooned another enormous helping of the creamy concoction onto Jo's plate, then tore off a hunk of garlic bread and popped it into her mouth when she opened it to object. "Do not tell me you do not have room, Jossandra, I know better," he said.

Jo didn't need her arm twisted. Rosa had outdone herself. The spinach ravioli, stuffed with ricotta cheese, was covered in a creamy herb sauce and sat on a bed of fragrant pumpkin mash. She scooped another forkful up and happily munched away. The table was piled high with wonderful food. Paul had his dumplings, but there was also veal parmigiana, and a huge dish of spaghetti bolognaise.

God, I may never eat again, Jo thought, glad she'd opted for a pair of sweatpants rather than tighter-fitting jeans. She'd gained a second wind since feeling so sleepy earlier in the evening. She sighed happily and wondered how Cadie was doing. *I wish she were here,* she thought. *She could use some real fun.*

"Jo-Jo?"

"Yes, Sophie?" Jo leaned forward to grin at the young girl. "What can I do for you?"

"Can I have some of your wine, pleeease?" The cherubic smile and batting eyelids were all innocence, but Jo had long ago learned to recognize a flirt when she saw one.

She's going to be a heartbreaker, that's for sure, she thought with a smile. "Now, Sophie, you know your mother would have my guts for garters if she knew I was giving you this stuff," she admonished. "Besides you've got some right there in your glass." She nodded her head in the direction of the small amount of watered down lambrusco the girl had beside her plate.

"Pleeease, Jo-Jo? I promise I won't bug you anymore." Big brown eyes pleaded.

"Tell you what," Jo said, "instead of lambrusco, how about you come sailing with me next time I have a free day? How does that sound?"

Sophie's squeal of delight and enthusiastic hand-clapping drew the attention of the whole table.

"What promises are you making my daughter, *bella* Jossandra?" Rosa laughed as Sophie sprinted around the table and smothered Jo in an all-embracing hug that nearly knocked her off the chair.

"Oof...just a little sailing, mamabear," Jo replied, happily returning the youngster's hug.

"Can I, mama?" Sophie begged.

"Maybe. If you are good and stop squashing Jo-Jo, I will consider it," Rosa said with a mock fierce look at her baby. "Now sit back down and finish your meal like a civilized human being."

The child happily complied, planting a big wet kiss on Jo's cheek before she climbed down.

"God, Rosa, I swear your cooking just gets better and better," Paul said around yet another mouthful of dumplings. "I have no idea how you make these but they're the best thing I've ever eaten."

Rosa reached out and patted the big crewman's face gently. "Paulo, for you only I make them, so they are made with love," she said cheerily.

"You are so full of shit, mamabear," he grinned back at her. "But thank you anyway. They are delicious."

"It's all delicious, Rosa," Jo interjected, grabbing the passing salad bowl from Jenny. "Thanks for inviting us."

"Aaah, Jo-Jo. You three are my...how do you say it...*i miei bambini quando non ho di bambini*...um, my children when I don't have children, you know? I worry about you when you are not here. And when you are here, I want to feed you and keep you safe and make sure you have love in your life, *lei capisce?*"

"Aaaaw, Rosa, that is so sweet," said Jenny, reaching over to hug the larger woman impulsively.

Jo smiled quietly to herself. Sometimes she had to pinch herself when she found herself surrounded by these friends of hers. Friends who never asked about her former life, trusting what she was now. It wasn't that they didn't care where she had come from, it was more that it bore no relevance to their opinion of her now. And they loved her; she knew that. And more often than not, she marveled at it.

One day I will feel safe enough to tell them who I am, she thought to herself. *Who I was... But right now I need these people too much to risk losing them. I want to believe they will still love me when they know the truth, but...*

For long moments, she found herself looking at her hands as if they didn't belong to her. Hands that were holding a knife and fork, pushing food around the plate. Hands that had, on more than one occasion, wrung the life from another human being.

Jo swallowed hard, fighting back an aching tug in her throat. *And Cadie...sometimes I feel as if she already knows all my secrets,* she thought. *Especially when she looks into my eyes like she does. But she doesn't know them. So it's not true and it never will be true. Because even if I ever get that brave, in a little over two weeks' time she'll be gone...*

"Jossandra?"

"Hey, Jo-Jo!" Paul yelled at her, breaking her reverie.

Jo looked up quickly, seeing five pairs of eyes watching her quizzically. *Jesus, where the hell was I?* she thought. "Sorry," she said shortly. "I was away with the fairies there for a minute. S'been a long day...night...day." She laughed.

"Bloody hell, Skipper, what planet were you on?" Paul teased.

"Planet Sleeping-On-Deck, Paulie. A planet you're going to be visiting tonight, by the way."

"Oooo goodie," the crewman said unenthusiastically.

Rosa caught Jo's eye as other conversations resumed around the table, and the rotund woman smiled knowingly at the tall skipper. She leaned around behind Jenny to speak to Jo. "I was hoping your mystery woman would come with you tonight, little one," she said softly.

A sad smile passed across Jo's lips. "No chance, mamabear. She needs to be doing what she's doing and I need to let her. There's nothing I can do about any of that."

Rosa nodded. "But you remember what I told you this morning, Jo-Jo. *Che sarà, sarà.*"

"It would be so nice to believe that, Rosa," she said quietly. "It really would. But I can't let myself do that, because I'll only be disappointed."

Cadie slowly twirled the scotch glass with her fingertips as it rested on the table in front of her. She leaned her elbows on her right knee, which was crossed over her left, and watched the room full of people in front of her.

Dinner at La Scala had come and gone, and half the group had moved on to Hernando's, one of the resort's nightclubs. Toby and Jason had opted instead for a moonlit walk around the resort, while Therese and Sarah had headed for the theatre where a world-class jazz band was playing.

Hernando's was smoky and dark, save for the swirling, flashing patterns flicking across the dance floor, which was packed with writhing, sweaty bodies pulsating to the deafening blasts of house music.

Cadie was alone at the table, the others somewhere in the maelstrom of dancers. Naomi, it seemed, was taking advantage of the freedom of her anonymity outside the US to acquaint herself with every woman in the room. The only thing louder than the music was the pounding headache making Cadie's temples throb. She knew the Chivas Regal probably wasn't helping in the long term, but for now it made her feel better.

She hadn't missed much by being late to the restaurant. Naomi and the others were still sitting at the bar when she arrived. Conversation had rather ominously stopped as she had approached the group, and all night long Cadie had had the rather paranoid suspicion that there was another whole layer of conversation going on around her that she just wasn't a part of—an undercurrent.

La Scala had been everything Jo had promised. The food was divine, the service was immaculate, and at one point Cadie had recognized one of the waiters as being the man on the beach with Jo this morning. He wasn't assigned to their table though he had nodded and smiled at her a couple of times when she caught his eye.

One thing was concerning Cadie greatly. Several times during the meal, Larissa and Kelli had whispered conversations with one of the other waiters. And now, here he was again, out of uniform and dancing his way towards the couple who were entwined around each other in a corner of the dance floor.

Jesus Christ, could they be any more obvious? Cadie thought disgustedly as she watched the furtive exchange of small packages from hand to hand. *What the hell am I going to do about that?* she wondered as the waiter melted back into the crowd. Larissa and Kelli shimmied their way through the crush, seeking out the senator.

Cadie felt her heart sink as all her worst fears looked close to being proven. She watched as Larissa and Kelli found Naomi and after a few seconds' conversation she saw the senator glance her way. Shortly Naomi was back at the table, sitting down next to

Cadie and leaning in for a shouted conversation. *Oh, I know what this is going to be about,* the blonde thought.

"Why don't you head back to the boat?" the senator yelled over the music.

"Why Naomi? So you and the girls can get high without worrying about whether I'll see anything?" Cadie shouted back.

Naomi's face darkened in anger. "You're imagining things, Cadie," she warned. "All I meant was you're looking tired."

The blonde snorted in derision. "You must think I'm blind as well as stupid, Senator. I'm not going anywhere. You're going to have to do whatever it is you want to do with me sitting right here." She took another mouthful of scotch and swallowed it quickly.

"Suit yourself," Naomi growled, standing quickly and slamming the chair back under the table.

Oh boy, thought Cadie. *I think we just reached what might be called a turning point. God, I wish Jo was here.* She reconsidered. *Actually, I wish I was wherever Jo is.*

Jo was flat on her back on the floor of Rosa's living room, belly bulging slightly from an evening of good food. She was laughing like a loon at the antics of Paul, who was trying to come up with a charade. She had no idea what movie he was miming but he was leaping around like a demented orangutan, much to the amusement of everyone.

"Jurassic Park," Sophie yelled.

He shook his head, then leapt up the stairs to the second floor, hanging off the banister.

"King Kong," Jo said.

"God, fiiinally," Paul said, jumping down. "I thought I was going to have to kidnap a beautiful young maiden and climb up onto the roof before you got it."

Just then Jenny's cell phone rang, barely heard over the laughter. The deckhand flicked it open and stuck one finger in her other ear, trying to hear whoever was calling.

Jo watched as Jenny answered then caught her eye. "Hang on, I'll get her," she said into the phone, and then passed it to the tall skipper. "American. I think it's Cadie."

Jo nodded and took the phone, turning away from the rest of the room to try and block out most of the noise. "Cadie?"

"Yes. I need some help, Skipper," a tired reply came.

She sounds wrung out. "What's up?"

"What isn't? Larissa and Kelli are high as kites and making

no sense at all, and I'm afraid Naomi might be, too. I can't tell though because she's basically unconscious. I can't get anywhere with them. And if it wasn't for the fact that I don't know where the hell I am, I'd leave them all to it."

Jo could hear the ragged sound of tears very close to the surface in the American's normally gentle voice. *Need to calm her down a little, so I can get a clue where they are.* "Okay, hon, we'll come and get you. Do you have any ideas at all about where you are?" she asked, trying to keep her own voice as calm as possible.

As far as Cadie was concerned, it worked. She took a few deep breaths and tried to stay focused on the soothing sound of Jo's voice on the other end of the phone. She looked over to where Naomi was lying flat on her back in the middle of a patch of lawn. Larissa was giggling mindlessly at nothing in particular and Kelli—*oh fabulous.* Kelli was throwing up in a perfectly manicured flowerbed.

"We were in a nightclub," she said shakily. "I'm pretty sure Kelli made a connection through one of the waiters at the restaurant and they got their hands on something—I don't know what—and now Naomi's out cold, Larissa's seeing pink elephants, I think, and Kelli's adding protein to the local flora. Help, Jo."

Jo suddenly found a knot of tension forming deep in her guts. *That's all I need, a boatload of junkies,* she thought. *Christ.* "Okay, Cadie. Was the nightclub called Hernando's?" she asked. By now Paul, Jenny, and Rosa were standing around Jo, trying to figure out what was going on.

"Y-yes, I think so."

"Right. How far away from it do you think you are?"

"Well, I lost track of them while we were still in the nightclub. After about half an hour I decided to go back to the yacht, so when I left I just pointed in the general direction of the water and started walking. That's when I ran into them again. We're in kind of a little garden."

"Is there a pool over to your left?"

"Yes. Do you know where we are, Jo-Jo?"

"I've got a pretty good idea," she replied. "Listen, you just sit tight right where you are. I'll be there with reinforcements in about 10 minutes."

"Thank you," Cadie said quietly.

"It's okay. We'll see you soon." There was a soft click as Jo hung up, and Cadie tucked the cell phone back into her purse. She glanced at her watch. *Close to midnight. I'll be glad when this day is over.* She watched as her partner rolled onto her side and curled up into a fetal position in the grass. *And maybe...just maybe, I'll be glad when this relationship is over.*

It was a grim thought, and for the first time she wondered if it really was worth the effort to resurrect her marriage. *Where did she go, that woman I married?*

Cadie sank down on to the ground, wrapped her arms around her knees, and rocked herself gently, oblivious to the damp grass, or to the silent tears that were coursing down her cheeks.

That's where Jo found her quarter of an hour later.

The three *Seawolf* crewmembers, Rosa, and Tony, who had pulled up to the house just as they were about to leave, were piled into Tony's truck. Jo had seen Larissa first, the tall brunette stumbling around just off one of the resort's more dimly lit paths. They pulled over and while Jenny and Rosa went to reel in her and the retching Kelli, Paul and Tony put their heads together to figure out how to move the comatose senator.

Jo walked slowly around the patch of grass until she spotted Cadie, a small and silent ball of misery sitting on the edge of the path. She crouched down in front of the crying blonde and gently placed a hand on her shoulder. "Hey there," she said softly.

Cadie lifted her head off her hands and looked up into smiling azure eyes. "Hi," she said weakly, sniffling slightly.

"You look like you could use a lift back to a cup of coffee and a good night's sleep," Jo said.

"God, that sounds wonderful," Cadie replied, managing the smallest of smiles.

Jo stood and reached down with a hand. Cadie grabbed it and pulled herself up, keeping a firm grip on the skipper's fingers. She found herself hard-pressed to look the taller woman in the eye.

"I'm sorry, Jo," she said awkwardly.

"Hey." Jo lifted the American's chin with a gentle finger, meeting and holding her gaze. "You have nothing to apologize for, okay? I don't see you out cold or puking in the petunias. And somehow I don't think you're the type to be doing whichever brand of dope they were doing tonight."

Cadie shook her head slowly. "No. The really sad thing is," she nodded her head in the general direction of Naomi, by now slung over Tony's shoulder, "she used to be as against drugs as I am." She felt her resolve slipping again and her chin started to wobble. "I...I don't really know when that changed."

Suddenly Jo had her arms full of sobbing woman as the tension of the last couple of days caught up with Cadie. She threw her arms around Jo's neck and burrowed her face into her shoulder. Gently Jo wrapped her arms around her, the feel of the compact body against hers a revelation. *I want to hold you like this forever, Cadie Jones*, she thought as a wave of protectiveness washed through her. She held the blonde tightly, looking over her shoulder at the sympathetic glances from her crewmates.

Cadie let the tears flow, feeling overwhelmed by all that had happened since they'd arrived in the Whitsundays, but also aware of the comforting presence of the tall woman wrapped around her. *I feel safe*, she realized. *Safe and so familiar. Like she's held me all our lives. And she smells so...*

She smells so good, Jo thought, closing her eyes for a brief moment, savoring the feel of Cadie in her arms one last time. She felt the blonde pull away finally and she reluctantly let her go, smiling down at her. "Ready to go?"

"Oh yeah."

They walked back to the truck where Naomi, Larissa, and Kelli, all three now blissfully unaware, were safely installed in the tray. Tony, Paul, and Jenny climbed in with them to keep them company. Tony tossed the keys to Jo with a smile. She patted him on the arm as she passed him and opened the passenger side door for Cadie to clamber in.

Rosa followed the blonde into the truck as Jo walked around and climbed into the driver's seat.

Well, this isn't quite how I pictured these two meeting, Jo thought to herself. *But it will have to do.* "Cadie, I'd like you to meet Rosa Palmieri. Rosa, this is Cadie Jones." She watched as the two women smiled and shook hands with each other. "Rosa is kind of the *Seawolf's* figurehead. Whenever we're close enough she feeds us and mothers us and tucks us into bed."

"Tch, Jossandra, such lies you are telling. You should be ashamed," Rosa said with a smile. She looked at the small blonde sitting between them and nodded her head slowly. "I am very glad to meet you Miss Cadie. Already I have heard much about you from this...how do you say...*la bevanda lunga di acqua*...long drink of water, here."

Cadie laughed, albeit a little shakily. "My God, that's a scary thought, Rosa, given we've only known each other five days."

"It's been a hell of a five days though, hasn't it?" Jo asked softly, keeping her eyes on the road ahead.

"Oh yeah," Cadie said equally softly. She was very aware of Jo's thigh pressed against hers, the warmth of the skipper's long limb seeping through both their clothes. It was both comforting and deeply sexy. *God, she makes me feel so much, so often, all at once,* thought the blonde.

Jo groaned inwardly. Cadie's mostly bare thigh was leaving a hot brand on her own leg and she never wanted it to end. *Jesus, Madison, the things you get yourself into,* she admonished herself. *A gorgeous woman I find myself so drawn to I can't believe it, her drugged-up partner unconscious in the back of the truck, and Rosa with that match-making glint in her eye. Can this get any more complicated?*

Rosa smiled quietly to herself. It didn't take any special second sight or magic to see the chemistry between the two women beside her. Part of her was very happy, seeing two soulmates finding each other. And another part of her was sad, knowing both women had difficult journeys to take before they could be together. She patted Cadie gently on the knee. "Everything, it is going to be all right, Miss Cadie," Rosa said. "You ask Jo-Jo here, she will tell you, I do not lie. And I am telling you that everything will work out exactly as it should."

Cadie sighed. "Right now, I'd settle for a cup of coffee and a good night's sleep."

Jo chuckled and pointed the truck towards the marina.

They managed to get the groggy trio on board the *Seawolf* and into their respective berths without too much difficulty. Toby, Jason, Sarah, and Therese were already back and in their cabins, thankfully.

Jo and Cadie lowered Naomi onto the bed where the senator rolled over of her own accord into a curled up position in the middle of the bed. Cadie stood looking down at her, slowly rubbing her temple with a weary hand.

Jo gently took her elbow and gestured toward the main cabin. "C'mon, we need to talk," she said softly.

The American nodded and followed slowly, slumping into a corner of the sofa. She looked up as Jo took a seat opposite. Rosa and Jenny moved around the galley quietly, making coffee for everyone.

"Do you have to report them to the police, Jo?" Cadie asked anxiously.

Jo shook her head and smiled reassuringly. "No. Bottom line is, unless Paul and Jenny found any drugs on them," she looked enquiringly over her shoulder at the *Seawolf's* hostess, who shook her head, "then we don't have any proof that they weren't anything but drunk. It would be good if you could give Tony a description of the waiter, though. At least we can get his arse kicked off the island."

"Okay, I can do that. Jo, I'm really sorry."

"Cadie, like I said before, you don't have anything to apologize for." Jo squirmed a little, making herself more comfortable. "But we do have a bit of a problem," she said. Cadie looked at her steadily and Jo felt warmed by her gaze. "Every now and then the Australian Customs Service makes random inspections of tourist boats. For example, we've been checked three times since August." She decided not to mention that she suspected her own supposedly expunged record had something to do with the frequency of the ACS' visits to the *Seawolf.* "If they find any illegal substances on board, it's big trouble for whoever owns the dope, for me, and for Cheswick Marine."

Rosa handed them both a cup of hot, steaming coffee and Cadie gratefully took a sip. "I'm pretty sure they don't have anything on board, Jo," she said. "We had to go through customs in Sydney and we were all searched."

"Okay, good enough." She smiled softly at Cadie, who looked totally worn out. "You think Naomi's involved, don't you?"

Cadie nodded forlornly. "I don't see how she can't be. Kelli and Larissa get a handful of dope, she disappears with them, and an hour later she's unconscious. What else can I think? And," she hesitated, lifting her eyes to meet Jo's again, "I've had my suspicions for a while."

"I'm sorry," Jo said softly.

Cadie nodded. "Me too."

Jo clambered out of the forepeak hatch around 8 o'clock the next morning. She felt rested for the first time in days after taking Paul's berth for the night. Fresh from a cool shower, she bent over, letting her long hair fall down, then she flicked it back, sending a shower of water over the deck. As she pulled it back into a ponytail, she glanced aft, where Paul was talking with Toby and Jason.

"You guys ready to go fishing?" she asked with a smile.

"You bet," Toby said.

"Okay. The Sun Aura leaves at 9am. Paul, can you run them over?"

"Sure thing, Skipper."

"Have fun, guys."

She watched as the three men piled into the golf cart assigned to the *Seawolf's* berth. *Ah well,* she thought. *At least I know those two are going to have a good day.*

Sarah and Therese were also on deck, sitting in the cockpit eating a light breakfast of fruit and cereal. They were dressed for golf so it wasn't brain surgery to figure out where they planned on spending their day. Jo sat down opposite them and smiled. "Did you have a good night, ladies?"

"Oh yeah. You weren't kidding about La Scala, Jo. The food was amazing," Therese said. "Thanks for organizing it for us."

"No problem." Jo smiled. "What time's tee-off?"

"Not till 9.15am," Sarah said.

"Cool. That'll give Paul a chance to get back. He can run you over to the clubhouse."

"No need," Therese said, taking another juicy bite of mango. "We're going to walk over, do a little exploring, a little shopping, on the way." She took Sarah's hand and pulled her up. "Come on, babe. Let's go."

Jo looked up to see Cadie walking across the gangplank from the marina. *I thought she'd still be sleeping,* thought Jo. *She still looks exhausted. Gorgeous,* she pondered, taking in Cadie's figure-hugging mid-thigh shorts and tank top, *but exhausted.*

"Good morning," she drawled.

"Hi," Cadie replied as she sat down next to the skipper.

"How'd you sleep?"

"I ended up on the sofa in the galley," she said. "Naomi was an immovable object." She ached in places she didn't realize she had muscles.

"Did you pull out the sofa bed?" Jo asked.

"There's a sofa bed? Are you telling me I spent the night squashed onto that narrow sofa when I could've been stretched out?" Cadie slapped her gently across the shoulder.

Jo grinned. "Yup."

"Why don't the crew use it, instead of sleeping out on the deck?" the blonde asked.

Jo shrugged. "Because it's a bit of a pain in the arse, frankly," she replied. "You have to take the table apart and then figure out how to unfold the bed and blah, blah, blah." She grinned.

"Show me." Cadie stood and started down the companionway.

Jo grabbed a grape from the platter on the table before she followed, running straight into Cadie's back halfway down the steps.

"What's wrong?" she asked, falling silent at the look on Cadie's face. The blonde had her hand over her mouth, her eyes wide. "Cadie, what is it?"

Cadie backed into Jo, shushing her with a finger against her own lips.

Jo listened and finally heard what had brought the American to a standstill. Naomi, Larissa, and Kelli were in Cadie's cabin and they were talking rather loudly.

"I told you back in December that it was time to do something about her, Nay." Jo was pretty sure that was Larissa. "She's been a fucking liability to you for years."

"Yeah, yeah, I know. To be honest I almost kicked her out after that New Year's Eve debacle," came the deeper tones of the senator. "She just walked out in the middle of a goddamn cocktail party we were supposed to be hosting together."

"You've got to do something about her."

Jo felt Cadie cringing back against her, and for the second time in 12 hours Jo wrapped her arms protectively around the smaller woman. "C'mon," she tried to pull her back up on deck, "you don't need to be hearing this."

Cadie resisted. "Yes. Yes I do, Jo," she whispered.

"Okay, hon." Jo stopped pulling her and just held tight. Cadie pressed back against her, making the most of the feeling of safety as the awful conversation continued inside the cabin.

"So why didn't you kick her out then?" came the whiney tones of Kelli.

"I don't know really," Naomi replied. "It's not like she's good for anything anymore. Not even in bed." She laughed derisively. "Goddamn frigid bitch."

Cadie buried her face in her hands, shrinking back even further into the warm embrace of the skipper pressed against her back. *God, I can't believe this is happening*, her mind said. *This is a nightmare.*

Jo felt an overwhelming rage building inside her. *I don't care if these bitches are paying customers, I'm going to kick their arses any second now.*

"Well, regardless, she's out when we get back home," the senator said. "This vacation is it. Payment for services rendered, and then she's gone."

Jo growled softly and made to move past Cadie. The blonde turned quickly in her arms and restrained the angry woman by holding her face in her hands. "Stop, Jo," she whispered. "You'll only make it worse—for me and for you. Just let it go. Please." She pleaded with her eyes, holding the skipper's rage-darkened blue eyes for long seconds. "Please."

I'd do anything for you, Jo realized with a start. She nodded slowly, trying to relax the tension she felt through every muscle.

"Thank you," whispered Cadie, suddenly very aware of the arms wrapped tightly around her. "Come on. Let's go find somewhere else to be. I've got some decisions to make."

Chapter
Six

The blue and red-striped float bobbed up and down hypnotically with the movement of the water. Jo watched it with half-
closed eyes, trying to ward off the worst of the glare off the glassy
sea. She shifted slightly, making herself more comfortable, even
wedged as she was in the curve of the bowsprit rail, her left foot
pressed against the vertical strut, her right dangling over the
water. From her position she was looking out to sea. If she
turned her head to the left she could see down the length of the
Seawolf back towards the helm.

A heat haze shimmered all around the boat as it floated in the
wide expanse of blue. The atmosphere was still and muggy, the
sun relentless out of the cloudless sky. There was no need to move
to work up a sweat. Perspiration just oozed out of the body, the
humidity sucking the moisture out.

The float bobbed again and Jo reached for the rod, feeling for
the nibble she hoped wasn't too far away. *Nope. Not this time.*
She let her eyes drift down the fishing line again, tilting her head
back and absorbing the sunshine on her skin.

It was three days since they'd left Hayman Island. The *Seawolf* had cruised south to Whitehaven Beach, on the reef side of
Whitsunday Island, the largest of the group. It was a long, curv-
ing stretch of pristine white beach, lapped by clean, calm water. It
truly was paradise. On the beach, the crew had set up a camp that
served as a great base from which to explore the jungle behind the
beach, as well as somewhere different to eat meals and sleep if the
passengers were so inclined.

Cadie felt like she was in heaven. She stretched out on her
back on the deck of the *Seawolf*, her rolled-up shirt and shorts acting as her pillow. The sun was viciously hot, but the blonde

American was covered in sunscreen, her newly browned skin glistening. She felt remarkably sanguine, lulled into a half-dozing state by the heat and the gentle swaying of the boat.

The three days since the disastrous night at Hernando's had been bizarre, not so much for what had happened, but for what hadn't. After the initial shock of the overheard conversation had passed, a sense of calm had settled over Cadie. The dynamics between her and Naomi had definitely changed, almost as if the senator had realized that she was being listened to that morning below decks. She and Cadie had barely exchanged more than half a dozen words, and though the blonde had gone back to sleeping in their assigned cabin, the contact between the two had been minimal. Cadie no longer felt the need to make a particular effort to stay away from Jossandra, and so far, the senator hadn't commented or made an issue of it. Cadie knew it was only a matter of time before there was a confrontation—she knew her own temper well enough to admit that—but for now, she was content to keep her own counsel and make the most of her vacation.

Payment for services rendered, huh? You'll pay, Naomi, that's for damn sure, Cadie thought for the hundredth time since she'd heard the senator dismiss their 12-year marriage in a five-minute conversation. *You've certainly helped me make my decision. I used to think there was a chance you might want to save our marriage. Now I know that's the last thing on your mind. Now I can stop wasting my time and energy on it, too.* Cadie felt a wave of sadness wash through her, followed by a shot of trepidation. *How is this going to pan out?* It was a measure of how far along her thinking was that she now spent most of her time running through an inventory of her belongings back in Chicago.

She shifted slightly, moving with the position of the sun.

The ironic thing is I pretty much have all I need with me right here. My laptop, my diary, and contact books. I was running the business from home anyway, so that's not going to be affected. She thought about the closets full of expensive clothes, and dismissed them. *I don't need any of them. That just leaves my books and CD's, and a few pieces of bric-a-brac.* Cadie shook her head in wonder. *I'm going to leave her. Amazing. And what's really mind-blowing is I have no hesitation about it anymore. I know it's the right thing to do. I'm looking forward to it.* She laughed out loud with relief. *Thank you, Naomi, for that, at least.*

Jo turned in the direction of the soft laugh. She gazed at the American sprawled on the deck and felt a flood of warmth, some of it affection, some of it out and out chemical reaction.

She seems to be so much more relaxed now, Jo thought with a smile. *She was right. She did need to hear that conversation. It's helped her make whatever decisions she was fighting with.* The tall skipper couldn't help but feel somewhat melancholy, however.

It really changes nothing for you, Jo-Jo, she told herself. *Leaving Naomi is one thing. Being with you is another thing altogether. We barely know each other and when she finds out the truth she won't want to know me.* Her eyes drifted slowly along the American's compact, athletic body. *God, she is beautiful.*

Jo allowed her head to rest back against the rail, and she half-closed her eyes, keeping Cadie in her field of view. She imagined herself leaning over the reclining woman. *Applying some sunscreen for her maybe,* she thought, with a tiny smile. *Her skin would be so soft.* Jo's fingers tingled from the memory of the brief touches she had stolen while helping Cadie with her zip a few nights earlier.

Oh yes, so soft. In her mind, her hands drifted down Cadie's body, barely touching her, palms sparking from the light contact. As she watched, the American shifted again, arching her back slightly as she repositioned herself. Jo groaned quietly, imagining how that would have felt if she'd been holding herself just above the smaller woman. *I want to feel her pressed against me,* she realized. Cadie turned her head slightly, away from the skipper. *And I want to kiss her just there,* Jo thought, pinpointing what she was sure was a sensitive area of Cadie's neck, just below her ear.

She continued to watch as Cadie reached for her bottle of sunscreen, mesmerized as she followed the movements of the American's fingers removing the cap and squeezing an amount of the creamy fluid onto the fingertips of her left hand.

Oh God, thought Jo. *What is she going to do with that?*

Her question was soon answered as she watched Cadie's fingers slowly stroke across her own cleavage, reapplying the sunscreen. The blonde's fingers dipped briefly between her breasts and Jo had no problem imagining caressing that very spot.

Only I wouldn't use my fingers, she found herself thinking. *God, this is torture.* Cadie's fingertips continued to trail across her skin, sliding just under the edge of her bikini top. Jo held her breath, her own fingers tingling just at the thought.

Finally the blonde was finished, and Jo exhaled slowly, very aware of the aching desire she felt. She knew she was flushed, and that, combined with the delicate stretching pull of fresh sunburn on her skin, left her feeling as if jolts of electricity were passing through her.

Cadie turned her head back towards Jo and blue eyes met green across the 15 feet between them. They held each other's gaze for long, endless seconds.

What is she thinking? Jo wondered, lost in sea-green depths, her whole body alive with sensation. The color rising in Cadie's cheeks gave her a strong clue, and she found herself beaming at the gorgeous blonde.

Cadie smiled back.

I'm sure she can read my mind, the blonde thought. *She's blushing almost as hard as I know I am.*

Finally Jo broke away from the intense gaze, feeling that if she didn't she would be hard-pressed not to do something about the insistent, tugging ache low in her gut. She tried to focus once more on the bobbing float on the end of her fishing line.

I'd crawl 15 miles over broken glass just to sweat in her shadow, the skipper thought.

Cadie couldn't help but smile at the tall woman's discomfort. *I know how she feels, but I just don't want to stop looking.* She swept her eyes across the dark-haired woman's body, greedily taking in every detail. Jo had her long bangs swept back in a loose ponytail, exposing a statuesque neck that cried out to be kissed, and Cadie was more than happy to picture herself doing just that.

God, especially when she tilts her head to one side like that, she thought, watching the skipper concentrating on her fishing. Jo was wearing a cut-off midriff-hugging tank top that was barely more than a sports bra. The lack of material showed off her toned stomach deliciously. Cadie laughed quietly to herself. *When was the last time you thought of someone's stomach as delicious, Jones?* She groaned at the thought of trailing her lips and tongue over the smooth, brown skin.

She gasped softly as, almost as if by some silent command, Jo's hand moved to her stomach.

Oh yes, Jo, Cadie thought, *touch yourself for me.*

The skipper's long, strong fingers almost caressed across her abdominal muscles. Cadie watched intently as one finger caught a trickle of sweat and slowly wiped it away. The blonde groaned inwardly and her eyes traveled lower.

I wish it were my hands caressing you and not just my eyes, she thought wickedly. The shorter-than-short denim cut-offs Jo was wearing were clearly well-loved and ragged around the hem, their pale bleached color highlighting the golden hue of the skipper's long, long legs.

Cadie gulped as a tantalizing picture formed in her mind.

I want those legs wrapped around me. I want to feel captured, tangled up in her. I want to feel that safety mixed with sensuality again, she thought, remembering being held by Jo as she had eavesdropped on that humiliating conversation. *She felt so good around me, surrounding me.*

Ohhh, Cadie, what are you doing to yourself? she thought. *Where are you going with this? You're at most, a couple of weeks away from leaving the only major relationship of your life. Do you really want to leap straight into another one? A complicated one at that?*

She rolled away from the view Jo afforded, sitting up to rest her forehead on her hand as her elbow balanced on her upraised knee.

But there's something there between us, no question. Would I be walking away from the one person in the world I'm supposed to be with? She couldn't help laughing at herself. *I don't know her.* She glanced back at the skipper, who was giving a good impression of being asleep, if it weren't for the slivers of blue peeking out from beneath slightly cracked eyelids. Cadie smiled softly, knowing those eyes were focused firmly on her. *And yet, I do know her. How that's possible I haven't a clue. She has secrets, but they don't matter. I know her heart.*

She knows I'm watching her, Jo thought. *I wonder if she knows how badly I want to be sitting behind her, cuddling her against me, with my legs wrapped around her, kissing the nape of her neck...*

A tugging on the fishing line almost distracted her, but it wasn't until the tiny bell on the end of her rod started tinkling that Jo finally came to her senses.

"Whoooaaa!" she yelped, sitting bolt upright as she grabbed the rod. "Holy shit, I've got a big one hooked here. Cadie, grab that net, will ya?" Jo stood up quickly, bracing herself against the rail as she applied some drag while the line played out.

Cadie sprang to her feet and grabbed the long pole Jo had indicated, swinging it around so the round net on the end hung out over the water. The skipper was battling to reel in what was clearly a decent-sized fish. She hauled on the wildly bending rod, winding frantically as she dropped it low, then leant back, groaning on the upstroke.

"You're going to snap that line, Jo," Cadie warned, hopping from one foot to the other with excitement.

"No way." Jo grinned, sweat starting to break out on her forehead. "This one's mine. Can you see any color yet?"

Cadie leaned out over the rail, trying to follow the line below the waterline. "No." She paused. "Wait. Yes! Yes, yes. Kind of flashes of pink."

"Woooohoooo!" yelled Jo with delight. "I bet it's a red

emperor. We eat well tonight!"

Cadie laughed. "Like we haven't been eating well anyway," she said.

"Yup, but there's nothing beats eating something you've caught yourself," Jo said smugly. "And wait till you taste this fish, Cadie—smooth, creamy, sweet flesh..."

"Hey, Captain Ahab, ya gotta catch it first," the American chided with a smile.

"Piece of cake," Jo replied. "Get ready with the net, 'cos this sucker is about ready to land." With one last big upstroke, Jo flicked the fish out of the water just as Cadie moved in closer and came in underneath it with the net.

"Yes!" Cadie cried, triumphant. "We did it!" She grinned up at Jo, who answered with a brilliant smile of her own.

"Yep, we sure did." The two women high-fived each other as the large red emperor flopped around on the deck.

Cadie looked down at it uncertainly. "Um...now what?" she asked.

"Well. Now I've got to kill it," Jo replied, reaching around for the small truncheon-like piece of wood she had in her back pocket just for that purpose.

Cadie bit her bottom lip. "I don't think I'm going to like this bit," she said quietly.

"I promise it'll be quick," Jo said noticing the anxious look on the blonde's face. "Don't look if it's going to upset you."

"No, it's okay," Cadie said. "I'd rather know the reality." Their eyes locked again for a few seconds.

Jo grabbed the fish's thrashing tail and swiftly tonked it on the forehead with the cosh. Cadie winced at the strangely hollow sound. The fish immediately dropped lifeless and still. "Done," the skipper said.

Jo picked up the fish and began to turn to walk aft. Cadie gently stopped her with a hand on her elbow, pulling her back around to face the American.

"What's wrong?" the skipper asked.

"When will you tell me, Jo-Jo?" Cadie asked softly, not knowing quite what made her ask the question at this moment.

"Tell you what?" Jo flicked her eyes away, suddenly uncomfortable with the scrutiny.

"Whatever it is that you seem to think would be so terrible for me to know," Cadie replied, ducking her head to recapture Jo's eyes. "There isn't anything you can say that will stop me..." She hesitated, not sure how far she was prepared to go. "Nothing that will stop me caring about you," she went on.

"You don't know what you're asking, Arcadia," Jo said, another wave of melancholy hitting her. "Trust me, you don't want to know." She paused, the warmth from Cadie's fingers on the inside of her elbow giving her chills. "Let it go. Please?"

Cadie squeezed the skipper's arm gently. "Trust me, Jo. Trust me to know my own feelings," she said.

"You have a lot more to think about than my dark, mysterious past," Jo said pointedly. "Don't make your life any more complicated than it already is, Cadie."

Cadie's crooked grin lightened the mood a little. "Oh, so you *do* have one then?" she cajoled, poking Jo gently in the ribs.

"One what?" Jo asked, gritting her teeth against the tickling sensation the poke provoked but unable to keep from grinning.

"Dark and mysterious past. That's the most you've told me so far."

"Mmmm...well, it'll take a lot more than a poke in the ribs to get me to tell you the rest." With a quiet smile Jo turned away again. "Come on. Let's give this to Jenny."

Cadie stood watching for a moment as the tall skipper walked away. *What could possibly be so awful,* she wondered. She shook her head quickly and making a decision that surprised her with its intensity. *It doesn't matter. She's a good person; I can feel that in my heart. And I don't give a damn what happened in that "dark and mysterious past."* She strode after Jo, following her down the companionway into the main cabin where Jenny was in paroxysms of delight over the large catch.

"Put it on ice, Jen," Jo was saying. "Paul can clean it up later." She rubbed her hands together in anticipation. "I'm drooling already." She grinned.

"Aye aye, Captain." Jenny mock saluted.

"Oh shut up," Jo replied good-naturedly.

A distant thrumming noise caught all their attention just at that moment.

"What's that?" Cadie asked, making her way back up on deck. She gazed up into the cloudless azure sky, spinning around.

"Helicopter," Jo said shortly, from just behind her. "And if I didn't know better, I'd say it was..." She turned towards the rise of Whitsunday Island, looking west. She laughed triumphantly as she caught sight of the small aircraft heading over the hill towards them. "Yep, it's Billy." She grinned.

Cadie looked up over her shoulder at the tall skipper. "Who's Billy?"

Jo chuckled. "A fly boy. A rich, spoiled, handsome, totally likable, fly boy." She turned with Cadie, following the path of the chopper as it circled closer and lower. "Around here the Air Sea Rescue Service is funded totally by donations, so it needs all the help it can get. Billy inherited a squillion from his parents—they used to own a bunch of newspaper and television stock. He bought himself a 'copter for fun and kitted it out with all the rescue gear, just so he can help the service out when they need it."

Cadie snorted, watching as the chopper circled the *Seawolf* one last time and started to come down for a landing on the wooden pontoon anchored in the middle of the bay about 200 feet from the *Seawolf.*

"He's a good bloke," said Jo, laughing at the incredulous look on the American's face. "He's just a bit of a lair as well."

"Lair?"

"Yeah...um...a show off."

"Ah. That would explain the entrance," Cadie said with a chuckle.

"Oh yeah."

The helicopter's engine died and the rotors slowed as a man clambered out of the cockpit and waved at them.

"Hey Jo-Jo!!" he yelled. "Are you gonna make me swim?"

"Yep," she shouted back.

"You asked for it," he replied. The sounds of bad singing wafted across the water towards them as Billy made a passable attempt at the Stripper theme. He pulled off clothing as he danced on the pontoon, flinging apparel in all directions.

Cadie laughed at the performance and Jo grinned at her. "Like I said. He's a bit of a lair," she said.

"I see that," Cadie replied.

Finally the big man was down to just his board shorts and he dove into the clear water, stroking easily out towards the yacht.

"Prepare to be boarded," Jo said.

"Aye aye, Captain," Cadie said just under her breath, catching Jo's eye with a smirk as the skipper did a double take.

"I heard that," she muttered.

Cadie giggled as they watched the man plowing his way through the water, finally reaching the transom and pulling himself up onto the boat. Billy was a big man, built like a footballer and with the height to carry it. Cadie thought he would tower over Jo by a good few inches, and he soon proved it by bounding up to the two women and pulling the skipper into his arms.

"Hello, gorgeous," he bellowed, swinging Jo down into a deep dip and planting a long noisy kiss on her lips. She struggled for a couple of seconds and then went with it, catching her breath as he backed off and pulled her upright.

"Yuck, Bill, that was gross," she protested, wiping the back of her hand across her mouth. "Hello to you too, you big bastard." She grinned back at the tousle-haired man.

He started to say something else but caught sight of Cadie, immediately captured by her bikini-clad, blonde good looks. He pushed past Jo, much to her amusement, and headed for the American.

"Well, who do we have here?" he asked smoothly. "Aren't you going to introduce us, Jo-Jo?" He took Cadie's hand and bowed over it, kissing it softly.

Cadie looked back over his shoulder at Jo, raising an eyebrow comically. The skipper laughed out loud. "Cadie Jones, meet Billy Maguire, the Whitsundays' own millionaire playboy," she said.

Cadie did a double take. "Maguire, as in Robert Maguire, media magnate?" she asked incredulously.

"Ah, daddy dearest, how I do miss him," Billy said mockingly, his hand over his heart.

Cadie looked at Jo again. "Boy, you weren't kidding about those squillions were you?"

Jo grinned and shook her head.

"Please don't hold it against me, Miss Jones. I promise I'm only half the scoundrel my old man was." He beamed down at her.

She chuckled. "I believe you, I believe you. Nice to meet you, Mr Maguire."

"No, you must call me Billy. Everybody does, y'know."

"And you call me Cadie. Miss Jones makes me feel like a schoolteacher."

He swept his eyes admiringly down and back up her length. "If I'd had a teacher like you, Cadie, I would have stayed in school way past 14." He grinned at her winningly.

She smiled back, liking him despite his brashness. Or maybe because of it.

"Okay, lover boy," Jo said, sitting down in the main cockpit. "What brings you out here?"

Cadie and Bill also sat down.

"You of course, beautiful." He grinned.

"Yeah, yeah, yeah."

"I was down at Shute, ran into Doris from Cheswick, asked after you and she said as far as she knew you were out here at Whitehaven. I felt like a bit of an outing, so here I am." He spread his arms wide. "I wondered if you and any of your guests would like a trip out to Heart Reef."

Cadie nodded enthusiastically. "I'd love to go. Toby and Jason went fishing out near there the other day and they came back raving about it. So, yes, count me in," she said.

Jo flicked her cell phone on and keyed Paul's number. He was ashore with the two men, Naomi, Larissa and Kelli.

"Hey, Paulie," said the skipper when he answered. "Billy's here, wondering if anyone wants to go out to Heart with him for the day." She paused. "Okay." She looked at Cadie and Bill. "He's asking them. Apparently the senator has a pretty fierce card game in motion."

Cadie rolled her eyes. "She's a terrible poker player. But she can't stand losing, so they'll be at it all day."

Paul obviously replied to Jo and the skipper nodded. "Okay, mate. Have a good day." She paused again. "Yeah I will, I think. Okay, see ya." She hung up. "No takers there. The boys are climbing for coconuts." She rolled her eyes and laughed. "And the card school has settled in for the day, as you predicted. Where are Therese and Sarah?"

Jenny came up from below just as she was asking. "In their cabin, Skip," she said. "With the do not disturb sign up."

"Ah. Okay. You want to come, Jen?"

The brunette had wandered over to Billy and sat down on his knee, the big man happily wrapping her up in a bear hug. "Nah," she said. "That mob'll need lunch." She indicated towards the beach with her head.

"Looks like it's just Cadie and me, Billy."

"Cool," he said, patting Jenny's backside as she stood up.

Ken Harding was sweating like an old, fat horse. Partly that was from the climate, partly it was because he was strapped into a Queensland Police Service helicopter. There were two things in the world Harding hated more than anything. One was drug dealers. And the other was flying. Particularly when that flying was in a tiny glass-sided box with a ceiling fan strapped on top.

Fuck this, he thought, wiping his brow for the 50th time since they'd taken off from Mackay. *Christ, I need a cigarette.* It had been an hour since his last desperate puff between getting off his plane from Sydney and waiting for the police chopper to show up.

He'd flown up on a whim. A nagging, nasty, cold slimy whim that had been burning a hole in the back of his brain for about a week.

It had been over five years since he'd last seen Jo Madison. She'd walked out of his dingy office in Sydney and disappeared into the night, as mysterious and untouchable as she'd ever been. He'd tried to keep tabs on her though. His colleagues would make fun of him on a regular basis whenever he called in a few favors to pin down her whereabouts. It wasn't like he did that for any of the other state witnesses lurking out in the real world. But he couldn't help it. He had always had a thing for Madison. A strange half-paternal, half-lustful thing that made him care.

He didn't understand it himself. He just knew that when Marco di Santo, former henchman of Tony Martin—Madison's ex-boss—had mysteriously disappeared two weeks ago, it was time to do something.

When Jo had turned state's evidence that cold night five years ago, Martin had been the first she'd grassed up. In the barely controlled chaos that followed, di Santo had been one of the few to slip through Ken Harding's fingers. He'd kept his nose clean since then, inhabiting Martin's old haunts but never quite doing enough to warrant police attention.

But that had changed three weeks ago when someone slipped a stiletto between Tony Martin's ribs in the shower block at Pentridge Prison. He'd bled to death on the floor while a roomful of criminals looked on. No doubt most had been more than happy to see his life washing down the bathroom drain.

Soon after that di Santo had gone underground. And Harding had a hunch the two events were not unconnected.

He's eliminating the people he sees as a threat to him taking over Martin's turf, Harding thought in an attempt to keep his mind off the thin layer of perspex between himself and a 1000-foot drop. *He's taken out the boss, and now he's going after the only one left who can threaten him, either by killing him or putting him away. I'm sure of it. Madison's in danger, and she hasn't exactly made it difficult for anyone to find her. Damn her.*

He had never understood Madison's attitude to the witness protection program. Whether it was arrogance or a death wish, her decision not to hide or change her identity had always rankled with him. He knew she was far from stupid, so he had to assume she felt she could handle anything—or anyone—that came her way. And it was hard to argue with that. He had seen her handiwork, more than once.

But he also knew she had been out of the loop for over five years. There was no way she could know what was coming.

Assuming your hunch is right, Harding. This could just be a complete waste of time and di Santo is rotting under a pile of garbage in some Sydney dump somewhere.

The helicopter swung sharply towards the group of islands in the distance and Harding clutched the edge of his seat, his knuckles white with fear.

Oh Christ, I need a cigarette.

Cadie floated across Heart Reef, barely six feet above the coral heads and tropical fish. She was making no effort at all, just drifting in starfish position, absorbing every little detail she could. Jo was behind her in the lagoon made by the reef's unique natural heart-shaped formation. The current took the blonde closer to the outer edge of the reef and she caught her breath as she slid over the precipice. Suddenly the bottom dropped out from under her and the water went from crystal clear to dark indigo beneath her.

Cadie took a deep breath and dove down using her flippers to propel her down the face of the reef wall as far as she could. Fish flashed and dipped around her, filtered sunlight bouncing off their silver scales. A dark shadow passed overhead and Cadie's heart stopped for an instant, till she looked up and recognized the shapely silhouette. There was no mistaking the long legs and fan of dark hair floating across the surface.

The American grinned around the snorkel's mouthpiece and finally listened to the burning in her lungs. She shot back up toward the surface, bursting up a foot or so from the smiling Australian.

"Having fun?" Jo asked, lifting her own mask and snorkel off her face.

"Oh, you bet," Cadie enthused. "I can't believe the colors down there. It's gorgeous! I just wish I could hold my breath for longer, and go down deeper."

"Why don't you take some scuba classes?" Jo asked, as they started to stroke back across the reef and into the lagoon.

"I can't. I'm asthmatic. They wouldn't give me a medical clearance," Cadie replied somberly.

"Ah. Well, we'll have to see what we can do about getting you down a bit deeper somehow," Jo said. "There's a couple of mini-sub companies we could try hooking up with."

Cadie trod water and beamed at the skipper. "That would be wonderful."

"Come on. They're about to serve lunch," Jo urged and they struck out for the pontoon on the other side of the lagoon.

Several tour companies used the pontoon on a daily basis, and there were groups of tourists dotted around the large square, wooden platform. The company that owned the pontoon also provided food and anchorage. Apart from two helicopters, there were also several boats moored around the outside of the reef.

Fifteen minutes later they were dry and happily munching on a shared plateful of sandwiches as they sat next to each other, legs dangling over the edge of the pontoon.

"There's a storm coming," Jo said, nodding at the dark clouds gathering away to the south. "We should probably head back after lunch—give Billy a chance to get home before the weather closes in."

"Okay," Cadie said, gazing at the thunderclouds. "My first tropical storm. Cool." She grinned. "Um, will we be okay anchored at Whitehaven?"

Jo considered. "It's a little exposed. We'll move around the point onto the leeward side of the island." She looked at Cadie. "Another reason to head back after lunch."

Cadie took it all in as she chewed on her sandwich. "Jo, how long have you worked for Cheswick?" she asked the tall skipper.

"About five years," Jo replied warily, her defenses automatically rising, a reaction not lost on the blonde.

"Relax, Jo-Jo," Cadie said, patting the woman's arm. "I'm not going to dig for anything you don't want to tell me. I was just wondering if you've ever thought about running your own business."

Jo nodded thoughtfully. "Mhmm, I have," she said. "I'd love to have my own boat. I'd keep it small and aim for an exclusive market. Fully crewed and catered trips. And I'd focus on 'family' tourism."

"Family as in gay, or family as in kids?" Cadie asked, grinning at Jo.

"Ew no, no kids. Family as in gay." Jo swept her arm around the horizon. "There's so much to see out here that's different for so many people. And there really isn't a specialist tour operator who can create a safe space for gays. Ron's pretty good. If a group comes along—like yours—he's happy to give them what they're after, but he doesn't specifically aim for that part of the market."

"Is that why you're our skipper? Because you're gay, too?"

Jo smiled. "No, not really. It was just the way the roster worked out. But it did make sense. And I probably would have suggested it to him if he'd assigned you lot to another skipper."

Cadie studied Jo's pensive profile. "So what stops you doing it, Jo? Running your own company, I mean. Money?"

Jo glanced at the American, and smiled. "No, actually," she said, thinking of the untouched ill-gotten gains burning a hole in her bank account. She sighed. "I don't really know what I'm waiting for. I like working for Cheswick, and when I see how much stress Ron has, I don't see any reason to take on more responsibility."

"But you've just outlined how your business would be different," Cadie said gently.

Jo grinned, and began pulling on her socks and hiking boots. "I know. Shot myself in the foot there, didn't I?" She chuckled. "Perhaps I'm just too chicken shit to take the plunge, Cadie. And maybe, too, I feel like I owe Ron a lot, and doing the best job I can for him as a skipper could be the most appropriate way of paying him back." She shrugged her shoulders slightly.

Cadie bumped Jo's shoulder with her own. "Somehow I don't think you and 'chicken shit' should be in the same sentence, Jo-Jo," she said. "Pinning down a taipan with a twig kind of blows that image don't you think?" She nudged her again.

Jo snorted. "That was just common sense," she demurred.

"Riiight." Cadie grinned at the slowly blushing skipper until Jo finally gave in and met her gaze with a sheepish smile.

"Okay, okay." She surrendered to the compliment, and then gazed back out across the reef. Something clicked in her head and she decided to share it with Cadie. "It's almost like..." She paused, trying to find the words. "It's almost like I've been resting...recovering, in a way. There was my life before I came up here, and it was," she sighed, "complicated. And stressful. And...awful...in so many ways." She looked down as she felt Cadie's hand creep around her forearm reassuringly, tiny tendrils of warmth jumping across her skin. Jo glanced up and caught warm, sympathetic green eyes gazing at her. "And I know this isn't making any kind of sense, is it?"

"It's okay," Cadie said softly. "Anything you want to tell me is okay by me, Jossandra."

Jo tingled at the way the American's soft accent caressed her name. "Mmmm," she murmured. "Anyway. When I came up here I wanted to get as far away from that life as I could possibly go. And part of that was letting go of any unnecessary stress and decision-making."

Cadie nodded. "I understand," she said. Jo looked at her from under a raised eyebrow. "Well, I kind of understand, given I don't know the details," she qualified. "You know what's really ironic, Jo?"

"What's that?"

"You're a natural-born leader. You can't help taking responsibility and making decisions. It's just what you do. I may not have known you very long, but that much is obvious. I can't imagine you taking a back seat, especially if leadership is what's needed."

Jo had to admit that was true. It had to be or she would never have gone for her master's ticket in the first place. "Mhmm. I guess maybe I feel like I'm coming to the end of that recovery part of my life," she said slowly, only realizing it as the words formed on her tongue.

Cadie smiled softly. "Feel like there's a big change in the wind, huh?"

Jo turned her head and caught the blonde's green eyes with her own azure ones. Another long moment of connection passed between them. "I guess you know that feeling, huh?" she asked gently.

The locked gaze continued.

"Oh yeah," Cadie whispered.

Their reverie was broken by the insistent sound of Jo's cell phone. Cadie giggled as she recognized the musical tone as the theme song from a cult television show.

"Xena, Warrior Princess?" She laughed.

"Hey, I'm a fan, all right?" Jo smirked as she picked up the phone to answer it. Cadie laughed again and stretched out on the pontoon, soaking up the sun. "Yeah, hello?" Jo answered casually into the phone.

"J-Jo? It...it's J-Josh."

Something about the teenager's tone sent icicles of fear lancing through Jo. His breathing was ragged and his voice high and anxious. She sat bolt upright, suddenly alert. Cadie's brow furrowed at the quick change in the skipper's posture.

"Josh? What's wrong, mate? Are you all right?"

"N-no...they've got me, Jo, they—" She heard the phone roughly pulled away and the sickening, but unmistakable sound of a fist hitting flesh and bone, then a body hitting the ground.

What the fuck is going on there? she thought desperately. Her world telescoped around her as a voice from her past curled around her heart and squeezed hard.

"It's been a long time, Madison."

Marco di Santo. Jesus fucking Christ. Jo fought hard to breathe, the sudden tightness in her chest making her head swim for a moment. A long buried part of her scrambled to the surface and a cold, hard mask slammed down over the skipper's normally open face. "Marco." She knew it was her voice but she barely recognized the sound.

Cadie sat up slowly. *Something very weird is happening. Whoever she's talking to is either someone she doesn't like at all, or they've just given her the worst kind of news.* She studied the skipper's face closely. *Maybe both.* The rich blue eyes that were usually so open and expressive were now pale and—Cadie shivered involuntarily—and cold. Tension washed off Jo in waves that the blonde could almost see. She was overwhelmed by the urge to comfort her somehow. Hesitantly she reached out to touch Jo's arm, but the dark-haired woman shrugged her off quickly, her focus totally on the voice at the other end of the phone.

"Did you miss me, Madison?"

Jo swallowed hard. Flashing visions of that dark back-alley nightmare flickered across the back of her eyes as she tried to focus on what the scumbag was saying. *What has he done to Josh? Where did he come from?* She felt a trickle of sweat at the back of her neck. *Think, Jo. Clear your mind and think.*

"Back to your old tricks, Marco?" she asked coldly, feeling her dark persona settling into place like a well-worn favorite overcoat. *Scary how easily that came back.* "Hurting the young and the innocent to get what you want?"

He laughed, an evil sound low in his throat that made the hackles on the back of Jo's neck rise. "You always were a mouthy bitch," he growled. "But this is the end of the line for you, you treacherous slag. Get yourself here, and give yourself to me, Madison, or this young pretty boy you keep will find himself getting uglier piece by piece."

She kept silent, not wanting to give him any satisfaction. Instead she hung up. For a few seconds she sat calmly, gathering her thoughts into an embryonic plan. Jo tasted bile in her mouth and she knew she was afraid. *Enough,* she told herself. *There's a time for fear, and there's a time for action. And now is the time for action.*

Cadie continued to watch quietly as her friend struggled with something. Jo was in another world now, she could tell. *I get the feeling the dark, mysterious past just jumped up and bit her on the ass. She said it was awful. If that look on her face is anything to go by, she was understating it.*

Suddenly Jo came to life, as if she'd just made a decision. Without a word she sprang up and started striding towards the helicopter, which was parked on an adjoining pontoon. Cadie scrambled to catch up.

"Jo!" The skipper kept walking, her steps long and purposeful. "Jo!" Cadie reached forward and grabbed the taller woman's elbow. *It's like she doesn't even know I'm here,* the blonde thought.

Jo blinked at Cadie unseeingly, not recognizing her for a

moment. "What?" she asked roughly.

Cadie stopped uncertainly. "What's going on Jo? What's happened?"

"I have to go," Jo replied curtly. She looked around the pontoon until she found the chopper's pilot, who was chatting up a pretty tourist boat hostess. "Billy!" she yelled. He looked her way. "C'mon on, I've got to go!"

He waved at her and turned back to the girl, continuing his line. Jo strode over to him and grabbed him by the arm.

"I'm not kidding Bill," she muttered menacingly in his ear. "We have to go...now!" She let him go at the startled look on his face. "Seriously. I've got an emergency."

"Okay, okay, Jo. Jesus. I was just saying goodbye."

"You can say goodbye another day. Come on."

The big man looked at her with a puzzled expression on his face, but followed, trusting her enough to know she meant what she said.

Cadie met them at the helicopter. "Where are we going, Jo-Jo?" she asked quietly, as Bill walked around the chopper, doing his pre-flight checks.

"You're not going anywhere," Jo replied gruffly. "I'll get Billy to come back to take you to the *Seawolf*, after he's dropped me off."

Cadie shook her head. "Jo, look at the sky," she gestured back over her shoulder at the increasingly menacing line of thunderheads. "You said yourself there wouldn't be enough time for Billy to get back if we didn't leave for the boat straight after lunch."

Jo knew the blonde was right, but the last thing she wanted was Arcadia Jones anywhere near Marco di Santo and his ilk. And right now, she knew, she herself was one of his ilk.

Bill fired up the engine and the chopper's rotors started to turn. Jo turned and glared at the shorter American, the downdraft whipping her hair around as she held open the door to the craft's main passenger compartment.

"I don't have time to debate it with you, Arcadia," she said, more harshly than she intended. "Get in. After Bill drops me, you two can go wherever you need to go. But you're not coming with me, okay?"

Cadie tried to ignore the stinging hurt, but climbed into the helicopter without further argument. She strapped herself in and watched as Jo did the same in the seat opposite her. Most of the space in the back was taken up by the rescue equipment Billy had installed—a cable winch and reel, lifejackets, harnesses, and a large first aid kit. Jo pulled on a headset, and Cadie did as well, plugging herself into the same audio channel as the skipper and the pilot. They lifted off.

"So. Where to, Skipper?" Billy asked.

"My place, Bill. As fast as you can." Jo looked at Cadie, wishing like hell she had stayed on the pontoon.

The American almost flinched under the cool, distant gaze from those pale chips of ice. *She's gone somewhere I can't even conceive of,* thought the blonde. She felt a stab of fear, wondering what was ahead. *It's certainly never dull wherever she is. Well, wherever that is, I'm going too,* she resolved, setting her jaw.

"There's nowhere to land up there, Jo," Bill said warningly.

"Don't worry about that. Just get me there. Just get me home," Jo replied shortly. She looked across at Cadie, who met her gaze questioningly, a tinge of hurt in those green eyes. *Dammit,* thought Jo. *Don't ask me to be human right now, Cadie.* She sighed. *Like I have a choice. She gets into my heart like nobody I've ever met. Even now.*

She reached forward and touched the blonde's knee with her fingertips. "Trust me."

There was a long moment as their eyes met.

"I do," Cadie said softly, knowing it for an unshakeable fact.

Chapter
Seven

Jo turned her attention back to the immediate problem: how to get herself from the helicopter to her house without alerting Marco.

Wait a minute, she brought herself up short. *He's not alone. Josh said "they've got me". Okay, that makes it just that bit harder. It figures that bastard would bring along reinforcements to take on one woman. The question is, how many?*

She keyed the microphone on her headset. "How long, Bill?"

"Less than five minutes, Jo-Jo," the pilot replied. "I've got a huge tail wind. That storm is coming in fast."

"Okay," she acknowledged. A plan started to form in her mind. "Bill, you know the dirt road up to my place?"

"Sure," he replied. "But Jo, I can't land there. The road's too narrow and the canopy's too thick."

"You're not going to land. You're going to hover just long enough for Cadie to winch me down on the harness."

They both objected at once.

"Jo, I don't know how to operate—"

"That's nuts, Jo, in this wind?"

"I don't have time to argue this with either of you," she barked. "Bill, fly the damn helicopter. Cadie, come here and I'll show you what to do."

Cadie unstrapped quickly and moved to join Jo next to the large barrel of the powered cable winch. She shoved down her apprehension and tried to take in what the dark-haired woman was telling her.

"Here's the indicator that tells you how much cable has been played out," said Jo quickly, pointing to a small gauge on top of the control panel. "This switch powers the winch, see?" She pointed at a large toggle. "Forward plays it out, back to the middle applies the brake and backward reels it back in. You got that?"

Cadie nodded silently, starting to feel swamped by the sudden change of circumstances and bizarre situation they were in. "I can handle it, Jo, but please...what the hell's going on? You're not seriously going to try this are you?"

Jo stood up gingerly as a crosswind buffeted the chopper. She reached for the harness and stepped into it, hooking the wide belt under her arms and double-checking the metal clip that connected the belt to the cable. "Cadie, listen to me," she said as she made some minor adjustments to the fit of the harness around her. "Someone from my former life has come back to haunt me. He's got a friend of mine at my house, and he'll hurt him, or worse, if I don't get in there now and do something about it. It's my fault, my responsibility, and I'm going to do whatever I can to fix this."

Cadie stood as well, bracing herself with her hands against the ceiling of the passenger compartment. "Why not just call the police?" she asked.

"Because he asked for me. If anyone else shows up, he'll kill Josh."

Cadie looked skeptical.

"Cadie," Jo stepped forward and lifted the blonde's chin with her fingers, "these guys don't fool around. They're the real deal. You're from Chicago. You should know about these things." She smiled slightly, hoping Cadie would accept the mood-lightener for what it was.

Cadie tried to smile back, but her eyes were full of apprehension and worry. "What were you?" she whispered.

"Trouble," Jo replied softly. "And now I have to be trouble again. I can't think of anything else other than stopping Marco and getting Josh, and hopefully myself, out of there in one piece. I can't be worrying about anything else, Cadie." She looked deep into the blonde's anxious green eyes, hoping she could convey what she was feeling with just a look. "Do you understand?"

Cadie nodded silently. *She's asking me not to give her cause to be distracted,* thought Cadie. *Okay. I can do that.* "Is there anything I can do to help, Jo?" she asked quietly.

"Yep. Get me down on the ground and then let Bill get you somewhere safe and dry for the duration of the storm. Give me a couple of hours and then call the police, okay?" She unclipped her cell phone and gave it to the blonde. "In fact," she thought carefully for a moment, "remember how you accessed Jenny's number?"

Cadie nodded.

"Do the same thing, but look for a guy called Ken Harding. He's a cop in Sydney. He knows the whole story and he'll be able to organize some back-up. Just give me time to get Josh the hell out of there first, okay?"

Cadie took the phone and looked up at the dark-haired woman. "Okay," she said quietly.

Bill's voice crackled in their headsets. "Coming up on your place, Jo."

"Right. Bill, circle round and approach from behind the hill. With luck they will hear the chopper but won't be able to see where you're hovering."

"Roger," he replied, swinging the helicopter around and away from the front of Jo's house.

Jo moved to the door of the passenger compartment and looked back over her shoulder at Cadie. "Brace yourself. It's going to get a bit windy."

Cadie knelt behind the winch and held on to its bulk. Jo cracked the door and pulled it aside, air rushing in as the chopper leaned into its turn around the hill. She slid down till she was sitting on the floor, her legs hanging out of the compartment. She looked down and double-checked the harness one more time.

Jo found her mind drifting for a few seconds. *I can't believe this,* she pondered glumly. *I thought I was done with this shit. It took me so long to put that life behind me. And now, in the space of an hour, it's all come back. I haven't changed at all. I'm still that animal.* A sudden aching tug in her throat threatened her composure, and the animal inside shook itself fully awake. *Get over yourself, Madison. Get in, get Josh, and get out. Save the sentiment for later.*

Cadie had been still, watching Jo quietly as Bill maneuvered the helicopter into place above the dirt track leading up to the skipper's home. She watched as a world of emotions swept back and forth across Jo's face.

She looks so lost. Cadie felt her heart breaking for the tall woman who seemed to be fighting for control of her emotions. *And there's nothing I can do but follow her instructions and pray. This is so unreal.*

Just then Jo turned her head towards the American. A cold, ice-blue stare sliced through her and Cadie felt herself flinch away from the intensity of the gaze.

Whooooaaaa. I almost feel sorry for the asshole she's going after, Cadie thought as she took one more look at the winch control panel.

"We're there, Jo," came Bill's voice. "We're at 65 feet. That's as low as I can go in these winds." He grunted as a strong gust buffeted the chopper. "Get down as quick as you can, will ya?"

"Okay, Bill. Hold her steady." Jo looked up at Cadie. "Put the brakes on at 60 feet. I can jump the rest." She slid down until she was standing on the helicopter's landing strut, the downdraft whipping around her. She lifted off the headset, throwing it back inside the cabin, and turned towards Cadie.

She raised a thumb and Cadie nodded, flicking the winch switch forwards. The thick steel cable began playing out and Jo allowed herself to go with it, trusting her full weight to the harness wrapped around her. Stepping off the strut was an exercise in faith, but she gritted her teeth and let go. Soon she was swinging under the chopper, the harness pulling under her arms painfully.

Another wind gust pushed the chopper sideways and Jo was jerked around even as she continued to drop. She went into a spin, the ground beneath her circling wildly.

Christ, I hope I get down before I throw up, she thought with grim humor. She felt Bill correct for the wind gust and slowly the world righted itself. *Bill's doing a fine piece of flying,* she thought to herself. He was managing to keep the chopper lined up with the road and she drifted down between the treetops. *Please, God, just don't let me get tangled up in the trees.*

Cadie watched the gauge intently. *20...25...30.* The chopper rocked wildly as the storm pushed the wind ahead of it. Suddenly she was slammed against the wall of the cabin as a strong gust caught the tiny craft. She grunted and pulled herself back upright, refocusing on the gauge. *35...40...45.* She heard Bill cursing mightily in her headsets.

"We okay, Bill?" she asked nervously.

"If the fucking wind would just decide which direction it's coming from we would be," he replied, grunting as he strained to hold the helicopter steady. "Is she down yet?"

50...55...60. Cadie flicked the switch back to the middle position, watching the cable stop unraveling from the reel.

"She's at 60 feet now," she answered. Quickly the blonde scrambled on her stomach to the open door of the chopper, pulling herself forward till she could look down. What she saw made her heart jump into her throat. Through all the noise and buffeting from the wind and rotors she saw Jo, flailing about on the end of the cable. "Jesus, Bill, you've got to hold it steady, she's being thrown around down there."

"Doing my best," he muttered through what she guessed were gritted teeth.

Jo fought the spinning cable frantically, trying to give herself the best shot at landing without hurting herself. Her arms felt like they were close to being ripped from their sockets by the strain on the harness.

She arched her back and looked up through the small gap in the canopy of trees, seeing Cadie's anxious face gazing down at her. She gave the blonde a thumbs-up signal and got one back in return.

Well, I guess this it, she thought to herself. *All I've got to do now is figure out how to get out of this fucking thing.* She fumbled with the harness attachment for a minute but grabbed on hurriedly as the helicopter once again slewed sideways. Jo just had time to duck her head slightly as she was slammed into a tree-trunk with sickening force. All the air was forced out of her lungs as the left side of her back caught the full impact. She didn't have long to think about it however, as she was quickly swung back into the middle of the path as Bill corrected for the wind gust.

Jesus Christ, she thought, trying to catch her breath. *I've gotta get out of this thing.* Again she reached for the metal clasp holding the harness together and fumbled with it as the world spun around her. Finally it released and the belt slipped off her, dropping her to the ground with a painful thud.

Jo tucked and rolled as she fell, moving as quickly as she could away from the cable which was now flailing around in the swirling wind. Again she looked up and saw Cadie, their eyes locking. She waved them off and the American waved back, clearly talking into the headset's microphone. Soon the chopper climbed and banked away as the cable began to retract. Jo stood staring at the retreating craft for a few seconds, imagining that she could still see the worried look in the blonde's soft green eyes.

The helicopter disappeared over the rise of the hill, and suddenly Jo felt very alone.

I want to see her again, she thought to herself. *Even if it is just to hear her say she wants nothing to do with me, I still want to see her again.* She fought back tears. *God dammit. Gotta concentrate. Gotta focus on getting Josh out of there. No matter what it takes.*

"No matter what it takes," she repeated out loud, hardening her resolve. She took a deep breath and allowed the cold deep down inside her to envelop her once again. "No matter what."

She took a moment to look around at her immediate surroundings. She was at the bottom of the hill behind Shute Harbor, on the landward side. Her house was on the ocean side, out of sight. She hoped that, and the height of the trees all around the house, had prevented the occupants from seeing where the helicopter had been hovering. She had an inkling that Marco did not know where she was coming from or how long it would take for her to arrive.

So, she thought, *at least I have some element of surprise working in my favor.*

The dirt track up to the house was too obvious a route so she took to the bush, making her way through the thick undergrowth as quickly and quietly as she could. There was at least a half hour of walking and climbing in front of her, she knew, and there was always the chance Marco had men out here looking for her.

She glanced up at the thick, black clouds rolling in from the southeast. A slightly feral grin split her face, though her eyes remained cold and hard.

That might just work in my favor as well, she thought. *Nothing like a tropical thunderstorm to wreak a little havoc and create a little diversion.*

Even from their height Cadie could see the brilliant blue of Jo's eyes looking up at her. She waved back at the tall Australian when she saw she was all right and then keyed the microphone on the headset.

"Jo's down okay, Bill," she said, reaching for the switch on the winch and starting to retract the steel cable.

"Roger," he replied. "Let's go find somewhere quiet to land, so we can figure out what the hell to do next." He banked the chopper steeply away and headed in a wide arc around the hill, back towards Shute Harbor.

Cadie wasn't arguing. Once the cable and harness were back on board she clambered into her seat and refastened her seatbelt. She reached for Jo's cell phone and switched it on. The power came on just fine, but the indicator showing the strength of connection sat stubbornly on zero.

God dammit. "Bill."

"Yeah?"

"I can't get a line on Jo's cell phone."

"Not surprising. There's too much electronic equipment and interference in here. And the storm won't be helping. Wait till we get on the ground and I can shut this thing down."

Double God dammit. "So where to?" she asked.

"Shute," he answered shortly. "There's a helipad at the end of the pontoon. Keep your fingers crossed that there isn't anything else already there."

Cadie sat back in her seat, trying to will her heartbeat to slow. She didn't mind admitting that she was scared witless. Whatever

Jo was mixed up in, there was no question the tall Australian was in danger. Something inside Cadie told her Jo was more than capable of looking after herself, though.

But still, she thought, *I've never seen her eyes so hard. Like there was someone else looking back at me. I want to see my Jo back again.* She laughed at herself. "My Jo?" *Who am I kidding?* She sobered up quickly. *I want to see her face again. I don't know how it's happened but she's important to me now. Very impor- tant.*

Ken Harding was a frustrated man.

He was standing on the pontoon outside the Cheswick Marine office at Shute Harbor, gazing through the locked glass door at the unoccupied building. He was soaking wet, thanks to the drench- ing tropical downpour that had hit just as his helicopter was land- ing. And there wasn't another human being in sight. Clearly everyone had seen the storm coming, battened down the hatches, and made for dry land.

He wished he'd thought of that before the police chopper had dropped him off before disappearing inland for safer air.

"Son of a bitch," he grumbled aloud. Just then a huge bolt of lightning crackled on the near horizon, grounding somewhere out to sea. "One elephant, two elephant, three..." he muttered. The resounding crack of thunder made the glass door behind him rattle and Harding found himself hunching his shoulders in a protective response. "Fucking goddamn weather."

The rotund detective flipped up the collar of his jacket in a useless gesture against the driving rain which was coming in almost horizontally as the storm built towards its peak. As quickly as he could for a fat man in a suit and street shoes on wet wood, he hurried back along the pontoon, hoping there would be somewhere open on the main pier where he could shelter.

And if the gods were really smiling on him, there would be someone there who knew where the hell he could find Jo Madi- son.

The woman in question was almost unrecognizable. Jo was drenched, mud-covered and crawling on her belly through the undergrowth near the small clearing in which her house was nes- tled. She hadn't seen hide nor hair of Marco or any of his goons, but she knew if they were out here at all, they would be patrolling the edges of the clearing.

Slowly Jo crawled forwards, ignoring the scrapes and scratches she was accumulating on her knees and elbows, until she came up against a large, half-rotten, fallen log. She knew exactly where she was. The log marked the top of the track she usually took on her morning runs and just beyond it, she knew, was the large patch of grass that served as her back lawn and beyond that again, the back entrance to her garage.

Jo opted not to extend herself beyond the cover of the log just yet. For now she just wanted to listen. Not that the storm was making it easy. Cracks of thunder and the pelting rain rattling off the foliage all around her made hearing anything else an exercise in concentration.

Come on, Madison, she thought. *This used to be like breathing for you. Focus, damn it.*

Jo took a deep breath and closed her eyes, allowing the sounds around her to fill her senses. As she had done since she was a hungry teenager on the streets of Sydney, she pictured the noises arranged almost like an orchestra inside her head.

Okay, she thought. *Rain, and thunder, all around in the background. Crickets, tree frogs,* she smiled quietly at the familiar creaking of the small, green creatures, *toads. There's something alive inside this log.* She registered the slow, deeper rustling under her fingertips. *Let's hope it's friendly. And over to my right...*

She held her breath and tried to place the unfamiliar sound. Her eyes opened wide as she finally figured it out. *Someone taking a drag on a cigarette.* She listened again, and caught the slow intake of breath and the faint crackling of burning paper and tobacco.

Carefully Jo crawled to the right-hand end of the log, moving like molasses, slow and steady. She risked a peek, staying low to the ground. In front of her was 30 feet of lawn, and there, in the shelter of the overhanging verandah, stood a man, his cigarette dangling from the corner of his mouth, and a sawed-off shotgun resting casually over his arm. He gazed off into the half-distance blankly, clearly unimpressed by his current assignment.

Jo smiled the feral grin of an assassin who recognized an easy mark.

Marco would have your balls on a plate if he knew you were more interested in staying dry than in keeping an eye out for me, arsehole.

She withdrew back behind the cover of the log and contemplated her next move.

Weapons, her mind answered. *Got to get some weapons.*

She backed slowly down the hill until she was once again well hidden by the trees and undergrowth. Then she turned and headed for a place she had planned on never visiting again after the last time.

Cadie had never been happier to be on solid ground than she was the moment she stepped out of Bill's helicopter onto the pontoon at Shute Harbor. The last few minutes of their flight had been a nightmare as they'd found themselves deep in the teeth of the storm. The blonde had a bump on her eyebrow, a bruise already developing where she had had a close encounter with the chopper's internal bulwark during one particularly wild wind gust. She clambered out on shaky legs as soon as Bill gave her the all clear and waited until the pilot joined her. They ran together through the pouring rain towards the Cheswick Marine pontoon.

"No offence, Bill, but I'm in no hurry to get back in that thing again," she said breathlessly.

"None taken," he replied.

They arrived at the door of Cheswick Marine only to find the office locked and empty.

"Well, I guess that figures," Bill said. "They would have seen the storm coming, secured the boats, and buggered off for the day. They're not going to do much business in this weather."

"Oh great," Cadie grumbled. She tried again to get Jo's cell phone to connect to a network, any network. "And this goddamn thing still won't work. Damn, Bill, I've got to get to a phone." She looked up at the big pilot and noticed his bottom lip was bleeding. She reached up and gently wiped the blood away with her thumb. "What did you hit?"

"Huh?" She showed him the blood. "Oh." He laughed humorlessly. "I guess I bit my lip trying to get us down onto the pontoon." He caught her eye somewhat sheepishly. "One of my hairier landings. Sorry about that."

She patted his arm reassuringly. "Don't worry about it. Given the circumstances I was just happy to be on the ground in one piece." She looked up at him again. "Come on. Help me find a phone. We've got to get Jo some help."

He gestured in the direction of the main pier. "Well, there's a coffee shop just over there that should still be open. Let's give that a whirl."

They both looked bleakly out at the torrential rain as a large crack of thunder rolled around the harbor.

"Last one there's a drowned rat," Cadie said, sprinting off

into the downpour.

Jo came upon the huge paperbark gum tree suddenly. She hadn't been sure she would be able to find it, but here it was, tall and imposing, the only one of its species in this part of the forest. She circled it carefully, looking for the mark she had placed on its trunk five years earlier.

There. A barely visible arrow scratched into the bark.

Jo dropped to her knees and quickly swept away layers of leaves and twigs. The rich, damp smell came on strong as she disturbed years' worth of mulch and debris. Finally she was down to the loose, dark topsoil and she began digging in earnest.

Three torn fingernails later she found what she was looking for—a plastic-wrapped package. She pulled it up out of the ground and sat back against the trunk of the tree, shooing away a large huntsman spider as she did so.

Jo turned the package over in her hands, looking for the way in. She ripped the plastic apart and pulled out the oilcloth-wrapped bundle inside. She balanced it on her knees and gently unfolded the cloth. She gazed at the contents for a few moments.

Never thought I'd see you again, old friends.

She picked up the piano-wire garrote, the small wooden handles smooth in her hands as she pulled the wire taut experimentally. Carefully she curled the weapon into a loop and tucked the handles into her belt. Next, she took up the thin, long-bladed knife, testing the blade carefully with the pad of her thumb.

Razor-sharp, just the way I left you, she thought grimly, as she slid the stiletto into her sock.

Last of all she picked up the gun, its familiar weight alarmingly comforting. The Colt had been custom-built for her, the grip tailored to fit her palm perfectly. As Jo curled her fingers around it, a wave of memories washed through her. Faces from the past, gunshots, and the smell of spent bullets.

You and me again, huh? I hope to Christ I don't have to use you today. She inspected the gun carefully. *And if I do, I hope I remember how to use you well.*

Somehow, though, she doubted that was going to be a problem, as her hands found their way into old routines seamlessly. She tipped the .45 caliber bullets out of their box and into her palm, quickly sliding the magazine out of the gun and clicking the bullets into place, before sliding it home again. She stood, tucking the gun into the waistband of her shorts just behind her right hip.

Time to go.

They made it into the shelter of the kiosk just as the storm seemed to redouble its efforts. Cadie spared a thought for the *Seawolf* and her passengers, trying to imagine what it would be like out on the water in this, even if the anchorage was sheltered. For right now though, her biggest concern was finding some back-up for Jo. A quick look around the shop yielded little cause for optimism.

Half the space was given over to a souvenir and gift shop. There were carousels of postcards and piles of t-shirts and garish tea towels hanging along the walls. The other half was a slightly seedy-looking coffee shop. There were only three customers—a Scandinavian couple hefting two enormous backpacks and over in the corner, a middle-aged man in a cheap, wet suit.

Cadie headed straight for the counter and caught the attention of the waitress who was sitting reading a paperback romance.

"Excuse me?" the blonde asked. "Is there a chance I could use your phone? It's an emergency and I can't get a line on my cell phone."

The woman stood, pulling the shop's phone over with her. "You're welcome to try, darl, but the line always goes down in storms like this. There's a big transformer between here and Airlie Beach that always seems to get hit by lightning every single time."

Cadie's heart sank as she picked up the receiver and jiggled the button hopefully. Nothing. *Fuck. Now what do I do?* She turned and walked back to where Bill was sitting, his wet clothes forming a puddle under his chair. Cadie slumped into the seat opposite him, her mind running at a million miles an hour.

"No luck?" Bill asked. Cadie shook her head forlornly. "Jesus. Cadie, what the hell's going on?"

She raised her eyebrows, surprised by the question. "I was hoping you'd tell me, Bill. You've known Jo a hell of a lot longer than I have."

He shook his head. "She never talks about her life before she came up here. And people in this part of the world don't ask those kinds of questions. This is a place people come to get away from questions and trouble."

Cadie bit her lip anxiously. *Trouble. Jo said she was trouble.* "You heard the conversation over the headsets, Bill. All I know is we have to get her some help. Where's the nearest police station?"

"Airlie Beach. In this weather that's probably going to take almost an hour. Assuming we can find someone to lend us their car."

Cadie rolled her eyes. "Don't tell me, your car is in Airlie Beach?"

He nodded grimly.

Another huge crack of thunder coincided, paradoxically, with a cheerful chirping from the cell phone in Cadie's hand.

"Yes!" she yelled, as the LCD showed four bars of connection to the network. Quickly Cadie keyed through the menu items till she found one marked "Harding, K." "Thank you, God. It's ringing," she said, half to Bill and half to the universe. She was vaguely aware of someone else's cell phone also kicking into life somewhere else in the shop, its ring tone vaguely distracting.

"Harding."

Cadie's jaw dropped as the phone was answered in stereo—in her ear, and simultaneously from across the coffee shop. She turned and met the gaze of the seedy-looking fat guy in the corner. She hung up the phone and walked towards him.

"You're Ken Harding?" she asked.

"Last time I looked at my driver's license, that's what it said," he said gruffly. "Who wants to know?" He stood up to meet her.

"M-my name's Cadie Jones," she replied, tentatively reaching out a hand to shake his. *He's got sweaty palms,* she thought. "I'm a friend of Jo Madison."

"You're kidding," Harding said, his eyes lighting up. "What the fuck are the chances of that?" He sat down heavily and Cadie took the seat opposite him, waving Bill over to join them.

"What are the chances of you being here?" she asked the detective. "Jo said you were in Sydney."

Harding took off his battered fedora and placed it on the table next to his cigarettes and his cell phone. He pulled a handkerchief from his jacket and patted his damp, balding forehead with it. "I came up here on a hunch," he said. "Where is Jo? I really need to warn her about something."

Cadie snorted. "I think she's already taking care of what you were going to warn her about. That's why I was trying to get hold of you."

"She's up at her house, trying to rescue a friend of hers who's being held hostage," Bill interrupted.

Harding turned noticeably paler under his florid complexion. "Christ in a wheelbarrow, I hope you're joking," he said bluntly.

Cadie shook her head. "'Fraid not, detective. We need to get her some help."

Harding stood suddenly, shoving his hat back on his head

roughly and gathering up his things. "Come on. It's time to get the cavalry. You can tell me everything you know on the way," he said, moving towards the door and the still-raging storm.

"I was hoping you'd be telling me," Cadie muttered, following the policeman out into the rain.

Mr Cigarette had gained a friend. The second man was older, short and squat, and the Uzi in his hand was a menacing reminder to Jo that she was playing in the big leagues again. The newcomer was arguing with his younger colleague.

"Get out there, you fuckwit," he growled, nudging the bigger goon with the butt of his gun. "This bitch is coming to us. It would be nice if we could have some warning. That means you've gotta get out there and look for her, numbnuts."

"Aw geez, Des, it's pissing down."

That earned him a clip to the back of the head from the short guy's free hand. "You idiot," he snarled. "Which would you prefer? Getting soaked to the skin, or having your teeth extracted through your arsehole when Marco finds out you let Madison sneak up on us? Now, get out there!" He kicked the taller man in the backside, sending him stumbling out into the downpour.

Mr Cigarette flicked his butt into a puddle, cursing softly under his breath as he hoisted the sawed-off shotgun off his shoulder. With all the subtlety of a rampaging water buffalo, he stomped off into the undergrowth to begin a wide circuit of the house through the bush.

From her vantage point deep in the scrub, Jo smiled quietly. This was going to be almost too easy. For about five minutes she tailed the tall man, staying just out of sight. She traveled silently, sometimes sliding ahead of him, sometimes alongside him. Finally, when they were well out of sight of the house, she slipped quietly up behind him, unsheathing the stiletto from her sock in one swift motion.

Jo crash-tackled the man from behind, causing the shotgun to spill out of his hands and land out of range as he hit the muddy ground hard. Her weight pinned him from knees to shoulders. Quickly she slid the knife up under his chin, pressing against his skin, but not drawing blood, while her other hand grabbed his hair and pushed his face into the puddle beneath them.

"Surprise, surprise," she muttered in his right ear. The man bucked under her, trying to raise his nose and mouth out of the filthy water. He spluttered as she pushed him back down. "Now, now, my friend. Don't compound your mistake by fighting me.

You can't win." She let him up for a quick, heaving breath, and then pressed him into the puddle again.

"You've got about 30 seconds to tell me what I want to know, or you're going to wish you were never born." She flicked the dark, rain-soaked hair out of her face. She watched the man struggle to breathe for a few seconds more, than lifted his face clear again. "Ready to talk?"

He nodded quickly, spitting mud and water. "W-what, what do you want to know?" he asked.

She laughed humorlessly. "Boy, you really aren't the brightest light on the Christmas tree, are ya?" she asked. "What I want to know, Einstein, is how many of you there are, and where Marco and the boy are."

He hesitated briefly and she shoved him back into the mud once more.

"Don't test me, ya buffoon." She pulled him back again. "Talk."

"Three," he spluttered. "There's three of us, including Marco. He and the boy are upstairs, in the living room."

"Okay. Is the boy alive?"

The man nodded. "But Marco's been having some fun with him."

Jo set her jaw grimly. She knew all too well the kind of fun Marco liked to have. Without another word she drew her arm back, unleashing a vicious punch to the henchman's head, knocking him stone cold unconscious. Quickly Jo stood and walked to the nearest big tree, where she found a lantana vine winding its way around the trunk. With a grunt she yanked it free and sliced off a length with her knife.

Within a couple of minutes she had hog-tied the man and rescued the shotgun from where it had fallen.

No. Too much to carry. Quickly she buried the weapon under a pile of leaves and branches. *Now for Mr Uzi.*

She worked her way back to the house. There was a cacophony of sound around Jo as the storm intensified. The sky was prematurely dark and the rain was coming down in sheets. Soon she was back at her vantage point behind the log, watching silently as Mr Uzi paced up and down under the shelter of her verandah. Jo looked down at her watch and was surprised to see it was only a little over an hour since Bill and Cadie had dropped her.

Feels like about a month, she thought grimly. She watched as the man paced towards her, his eyes sweeping the bush surrounding him. *He's wondering where his mate's gone. The question is, do I wait for him to come looking for him, or do I go to him? Of*

*course, I could just take him out with a bullet from here, without
him even knowing what's hit him.*

But something, some civilizing thought deep inside her railed
against that notion.

*I don't want to cross that line again. Not if I can find another
way.* For a fleeting few seconds Cadie's face swam in front of her
eyes. *For her. And for me.* A grim thought floated through her
consciousness. *I just hope that hesitation doesn't cost Josh his
life.*

Mr Uzi turned away from her and started walking away,
towards the other side of the house. Jo took her opportunity and
sprang into life, sprinting out of the scrub and across the small
expanse of lawn, banking on momentum and surprise to give her
the advantage.

She was almost right. Something tipped the thug off and he
swung back towards her, bullets spitting from the gun in his hands
even as he turned.

Jo felt time slow down and the world outside the narrow tun-
nel she inhabited seemed to blur around her. *Like that dip-shit
Keanu Reeves flick,* she found herself thinking in a bizarre piece
of mental timing.

Bullets zinged past her and Jo felt weirdly disconnected from
what was happening, even as her body threw itself sideways, twisting in mid-air to avoid a bullet she was sure she could see spinning
around its own axis as it came towards her. A burning, tearing
sensation seared across her upper right arm, and she knew she had
been hit, but she felt detached from the feelings, the seeping red
penetrating the cloth of her shirt not registering as her own blood.

She hit the ground with a breath-expelling thump and rolled
under her Jeep and out the other side. Mr Uzi had moved forward
as he had pulled the trigger and lost sight of Jo as she disappeared
under the vehicle. Now she was behind him and Jo made the most
of her chance, grabbing a tire iron from the back of the car and
flinging it, end over end, at the back of the man's head.

It found its mark with a sickening squishy thump and he
dropped like a rock. Something wild in her laughed with exulta-
tion but she didn't hang around to see if he stood up again.

*Marco knows I'm here now. He had to have heard the gun-
shots. Now I have to move. And quickly.*

She sprinted to the other side of the house, ignoring the sheet-
ing rain that threatened to reduce her visibility to almost nothing.
The far side of the house was a blank wall, covered from ground to
roof with climbing plants, draped across a sturdy wooden trellis.

Hold my weight, Jo prayed. *Just hold my weight.*

She scrambled up, fighting for every toe and finger-hold as the rain was added to by the water sluicing off the roof and the overflowing gutters. Gritting her teeth, Jo ignored the throbbing pain in her arm and the slightly light-headed feeling she had. She refused to look at her wound, concentrating instead on pulling herself up the trellis, as fast and as quietly as she could.

Not that noise was a problem. The storm reached its height, cascades of thunder rolling across the sky like waves advancing onto a beach. Jo pressed on upwards, pulling herself up and over the edge of the roof finally, and slithered across the tiles.

Her objective was a good 20 feet away—the skylight over the main room on the top floor of the house. Jo sized up her options and began crabbing across the front edge of the roof, her grip precarious on the slippery-smooth slate. She reached the skylight and slowly peered over the edge to the room below. What she saw turned her heart to rock-ice.

Josh was slumped on a chair in the middle of the floor. His head lolled backwards and Jo had no trouble seeing the marks of a heavy beating on the teenager's normally handsome face. He was unconscious or close to it, unmoving, and his hands were tied behind his back.

Marco hasn't changed much. Gained some weight maybe. Five years older and slower. She smiled tightly. *And balder.*

The thug circled Josh slowly, but his focus was outwards, and he was alert.

Waiting for me.

Jo looked down, working out angles and heights. *This skylight is not the way in,* she decided. *Josh is too close underneath it and the glass is going to hurt him.*

She rolled onto her back, sliding her heels down to the guttering at the front edge of the roof. Below her, she knew, were her verandah and the glass doors leading into the living room.

Please, God, let those doors be open.

She reached back and drew her gun, checking the action one more time and removing the safety. She inched forward till she was crouching on the front edge of the roof.

Jo looked skyward and waited. It wasn't long before a long, forked streak of lightning lanced across the sky in the near distance. She counted one and then launched herself, twisting as she dropped so she landed facing into the house. Her legs flexed as she hit the wooden deck, absorbing the shock as the lightning's accompanying crack of thunder coincided with her arrival.

To Josh, barely aware, and di Santo, who was standing behind his captive at the time, the effect was devastatingly dramatic. One second the doorway was clear, the next instant a dark, menacing silhouette filled the space, backlit by more lightning, its features shadowed, black hair whipping around in the wind.

Jo raised her arm, ignoring the pain as she trained her gun on the hit-man.

Di Santo recovered quickly from the shock of her appearance, reaching down and wrapping his arm around Josh's neck, dragging the teenager to his feet and shielding himself with the young man's body. Jo found herself gazing down the barrel of a gun very similar to her own.

"Hello, Marco," she said coldly, taking a step towards him.

"Put the gun down, Madison, or the kid is dead meat." He jammed the muzzle of his gun under Josh's chin for effect, the teen's eyes widening perceptibly.

Jo snorted with derision. "Do that and you'll be dead a millisecond later, Marco, and you know it," she replied, taking another step towards them. "Why don't you let the boy go and then you and I can really get down to business." She kept her voice low and intimidating, her natural alto deepening almost to a throaty growl.

For the first time since he decided to come after Jo Madison, di Santo hesitated.

Jo's flinty blue eyes didn't miss the uncertainty that flashed across his wide, flat face. She laughed coldly. "You dumb fuck, Marco. When you came chasing up here, didn't you think it might be a good idea to have some kind of plan?" She grinned wildly, taking another step towards him, her gun aimed steadily at the point where his two eyebrows met. "You can't kill him, because you know that's your death sentence. And you obviously don't want me dead—there are much less complicated ways of killing me, and you certainly didn't have to come here in person for that." She stepped closer again. "So you must want something from me."

She was close enough now to see the beads of sweat on the big man's upper lip.

"So let the boy go, Marco. He's served his purpose. I'm here. Let him go and let's get serious. Because, frankly, I don't care if you live or die." Another step closer and now the two guns were within inches of each other.

Jo could almost hear di Santo's brain churning through the possibilities. He had to know he was no match for her reflexes and speed. She smiled again at him, never dropping eye contact.

Finally, the hit man shoved Josh away. The teenager fell awkwardly since his arms were still tied behind his back.

"Josh," Jo said quietly, never taking her eyes from di Santo, "can you stand up?"

"Y-yes, I think so," he said shakily, struggling to get to his feet.

"Okay. Come here." Slowly Jo lifted her leg and with her free hand, drew her knife from her sock. When Josh limped to her side she slid the blade between his hands, slicing through the ropes around his wrists. "Now get out of here, Josh. Just walk out the door and keep on going. Don't try anything silly, okay?"

He nodded silently, eyes wide and round with apprehension. "Y-you'll be okay?"

She laughed softly, her eyes still locked with di Santo's. "Yes, mate, I'll be fine. Go on now."

He didn't need telling three times. Josh bolted for the front door and disappeared out into the rain.

Jo and di Santo stood motionless, arms raised, guns cocked for several more silent seconds.

"You fucked up, Marco," Jo said quietly. "You came up here with a crappy plan and incompetent back-up. There are only two outcomes here. We kill each other, or the police come through that door." She paused for thought. "And even then I might just decide to kill you to save on the paperwork."

Slowly she lowered her arm, reached behind her and tucked the gun back into the waistband of her shorts. She flicked the knife in her other hand toward the back wall of the living room, where it lodged point first, the blade thrumming.

She took a bigger chance and turned her back on the hit man who hadn't moved. She wandered into the kitchen, opening the fridge and pulling out a can of Coke. Looking up as she cracked open the can, she noticed he'd followed her every movement with the gun. She had to smile.

"You don't mind if I have a drink from my own fridge, do you Marco?" she asked sarcastically. "I've had quite the day." She tipped back the can and drank deeply, welcoming the sugar hit. She had been starting to feel light-headed—*probably from blood loss*—though she still refused to look at the wound on her arm. Jo finished the drink, threw the empty can in the general direction of the garbage bin, and walked back into the living area.

"So what is it, Marco? Was this visit just a revenge mission?" She circled him slowly, forcing the man to pivot around as he kept her in his sights. "Though, really, you should be thanking me. I got rid of Tony, opened up the field for you. Or are things not going quite as well as you'd hoped?"

That hit a raw nerve. "Shut up, bitch. I'm the one here to do the talking."

Jo flopped down onto the leather couch, throwing her arms across the back casually like it was any summer afternoon. "So talk, Marco. Right now you're just spinning like a fat, sweaty top. What do you want?"

He stalked toward her until he towered over her. Roughly he kicked her legs apart and stepped between them, pushing them outwards with his own. "You."

Oh, he shouldn't have done that. Now he's got me really mad.

She turned steely blue eyes on the hit man and dropped her voice to its most intimidating level as she folded her arms across her chest. "And what could you possibly offer that would make me want to be within a thousand miles of you?" she growled, her legs twitching with the urge to kick him across the room.

This time it was di Santo who smiled. He leaned down, resting his left hand on the back of the couch beside Jo's head and using his right to push the muzzle of the gun up under her chin. His bad breath washed over her, but neither unpleasantness made her flinch. "For a start, I won't send someone out west to kill your parents," he said. "Second, you'll be well-paid. Better than Tony ever gave you. And third," he reached down and grabbed his crotch, squeezing it suggestively, "you'll get all you'll ever need of this."

It never fails to amaze me how a man truly believes his penis is the center of the universe, Jo thought with disgust, even as she leaned forward as if to kiss di Santo. She stopped bare millimeters from his mouth. "And what is it you would like me to do in return for all these...favors?" she purred, pushing down the bile rising in her throat.

"What you've always done, gorgeous," he replied. "Kill. Stop me from being killed. And of course, the added privilege of taking a damn good fucking from me whenever I want it."

Jo smiled seductively even as the white-hot rage grew inside her. She kept his focus firmly on her lips by licking them slowly, but her hand snaked out. She waited a half-beat then bit down on the hit-man's fat lower lip as hard as she could, at the same time as her long, strong fingers wrapped around his genitals and pulled down hard.

She bit until she tasted blood and then let go with her teeth, but by then the big man was doubled over and screaming as she felt things tear beneath her fingers. Still she pulled, twisting and yanking as di Santo fell to his knees in front of her.

The cold darkness had Jo in its total control now, and she

gave it full rein, a red haze dropping down in front of her eyes. She let go of the howling gangster's groin just long enough to get behind him and she leaned in so her face was close to his right ear. By now he was whimpering, and tears of pain streamed down his face.

"You and I go back a long way, Marco," she snarled. "And I have a very good memory. Did you really think I could put all that behind me just because I was so dazzled by the prospect of your dick? Which, by the way, is never going to be the same, and was never that impressive in the first place, as I recall."

"You goddamn fucking bitch!" he screamed.

She pulled his head back by what was left of his sparse hair. "Oh please, Marco, don't hold back. Tell me how you really feel." As she spoke, Jo took the garrote from its place on her belt, flicking it around the hit man's neck in one swift movement. "And now I'm going to make sure you never have the chance to hurt anyone else, ever again, you tiny scumbag."

With each word she tightened the thin, metal wire around his throat. At first di Santo was more concerned about his groin, and he moaned again as he realized he was bleeding. The throbbing pain was excruciating. But the garrote began to bite as Jo slowly closed the deadly noose, and he let go of himself, raising his hands to his throat in a desperate attempt to pull the wire away.

Jo laughed coldly, and with images from her past dancing in front of her eyes and lightning flashing across the sky, she began squeezing the man's life away.

Cadie elbowed her way through the group of uniformed police until she reached Ken Harding, who was standing outside the front door of Jo's house.

"I'm going in with you," she declared firmly, hands on hips.

Harding looked down at the blonde American, who was trying to look defiant despite being soaked to the skin. "No, Miss Jones, you're not. I don't know how they do it in your country, but here in Australia, cops don't let civilians wander into the middle of this kind of operation. This isn't an episode of *NYPD Blue*, ya know."

Cadie stepped forward and got in the man's face, her finger poking him in the belly. "That's my friend in there. And I'm going in with you, no matter what you say. So please don't make this any more difficult that it already is."

Her green eyes sparked and he was hard-pressed to resist. He had spent a part of the last hour while they waited for reinforcements from Airlie Beach telling Cadie the little he knew about Jo Madison. It had made him realize that he actually knew very little about the tall ex-assassin. None of what he'd told her had seemed to faze Cadie a bit, but then he had left out the gory details of her friend's former life, telling her the bare facts.

Jesus Christ, he sighed. *I don't have the time to argue with her. And the bottom line is, she's about to get an eyeful of the ugly truth, no matter how much I try to protect her from it.*

"Get behind me here then," he said, pulling her out of the way of the two cops who were swinging a battering ram between them, ready to break down the door. Harding strained to hear what was going on beyond the door but the storm was making that almost impossible. "Do it," he yelled at the uniforms.

Seconds later they were through the door and Cadie pushed her way forward past the debris and shouting policemen. She stopped short, transfixed by the nightmarish vision in the middle of the room.

Jo stood over the kneeling, sobbing man like some kind of dark, glorious goddess. Lightning turned her silver and Cadie could see the wild, wide grin on the tall woman's face. She could also see Jo's blood-soaked right arm. The man was scrabbling at his throat with his hands and suddenly Cadie saw the cruel wire beginning to cut into his neck. Blood was seeping down, soaking his shirt collar and covering his fingers as he desperately tried to ease the pressure.

Jo was vaguely aware of an explosion of sound over to her right but it barely penetrated the red haze of rage that filled her. She felt Marco's hands fluttering around his throat, and then reaching back to try and break her grip. She saw the blood on his fingers and exulted. Gradually she became aware of men shouting around her but she didn't care. She wanted the man at her feet dead and gone from her life forever.

Cadie couldn't bear to watch any longer. The police had circled Jo and had their weapons trained on her from all sides. They shouted and shouted at her but nothing was having an effect on the tall woman. Cadie ran forward, trying to break through the circle, but Harding grabbed her elbow and yanked her backwards. "Stay out of it, Miss Jones," he barked.

She rounded on him hotly. "She's not the goddamn criminal here, Harding," she shouted back, wrestling out of his grasp. She pushed through the line and came to a halt by Jo's right shoulder. But the dark woman ignored her.

Jo felt someone standing next to her, a woman's voice calling her name, but she didn't care. She jerked Marco again, yanking back on the garrote, and he squealed. *Music to my ears,* she thought.

Cadie winced as she saw the wire biting deeper into the man's neck. But she knew she had the best chance of getting through to Jo. *If she will just let me touch her.*

The American reached out slowly and gently rested her hand on Jo's shoulder, careful to avoid the still-bleeding wound on her upper arm. The response from Jo was immediate.

Dark hair whipped around her head as she turned sharply towards Cadie. A deep, threatening growl came from her throat and the stare from her icy blue eyes lanced through the blonde like a hot knife through butter.

Jesus, Cadie thought. *This has to stop.* "Jo." Cadie weathered the intense gaze and held it with her own. "Jo. Stop please." She could see the man's responses becoming weaker as the piano wire sliced deeper. She kept her hand on Jo's shoulder, hoping the warmth of her touch would somehow penetrate. "Please stop now."

The tall woman's only response was to turn back to the man whose life she was toying with.

Cadie felt a wave of frustration and then decided to take things into her own hands. Literally. She leaned forward and pulled Jo's chin around then cupped the woman's face between her hands. She gazed intently into her eyes. "Jossandra," she said softly. The blue orbs blinked at her blankly. "Jossandra, sweetheart...please let him go now."

Jo felt the soft gentle voice sliding into her consciousness, melting her from the inside. Warm hands stroked her cheeks and the most beautiful sea-green eyes were just inches from her own.

Something clicked inside her.

She took a sharp breath in, gasping like she had just come up for air after a long, dark dive. At the same time she released her grip on the garrote, and Marco fell forward. Police rushed in from all sides, dragging the gangster away. But Cadie and Jo stayed still, absorbed in each other. "C-Cadie?" Jo whispered. Her blood-covered hands reached up to hold the blonde's wrists.

"Yes, sweetheart," Cadie replied gently, gazing up at a face that was suddenly years younger and filled with vulnerability. "It's okay. It's all over."

Jo's legs gave out from under her and she dropped to her knees. She wrapped her arms around Cadie's waist and buried her face into the blonde's shirt, desperate sobs wracking her body, welling up from deep inside.

Cadie felt a huge rush of protectiveness and cradled Jo's head against her, stroking the long, black hair and crooning soft words of comfort.

Most of the police were back outside the front door dealing with di Santo, but Harding had remained behind, watching the two women in the centre of the room. The killer in Jo Madison he understood. The sobbing, near-hysterical woman, he didn't get. *But that cute little American sheila sure seems to. I'll give them a few more minutes, but then I've got to ask Madison some questions.*

He began to turn away, but a movement out on the verandah caught his eye and he swung back just in time to see a staggering figure lunging through the door. In his hand was a...

Fuck.

"Madison!" Harding screamed, beginning to draw his police revolver from the holster under his left arm.

Jo heard the urgency in Harding's voice and turned her head in time to see Mr Uzi stumble through the verandah door, his weapon spitting bullets indiscriminately. Without thinking she drove herself upwards, lifting Cadie off her feet for an instant before throwing them both down on the floor.

As she covered the blonde's body with her own she reached back and drew her Colt. Within half a second she was pumping bullet after bullet into the oncoming man.

Cadie had the breath knocked out of her when Jo threw her down, but she was too startled to protest and with the big gun just inches above her head as it fired, she thought it prudent to keep as still as possible. She tucked her head in under Jo's chin and held on for dear life.

Jo wasn't the only one firing. Harding emptied his .45 before the man finally dropped to the floor. The detective scrambled to reload as he ran to the body, nudging it with his foot as the other cops ran in, alerted by the gunfire.

"Okay, okay...it's okay," Harding said breathlessly, re-holstering his gun. "He's about as dead as he's gonna get. Let's get this lot squared away and get out of here."

Cadie peeked out from under Jo's arm. *Oh yeah. He's definitely dead.* She swallowed hard and turned away from the man, his face a bloody mess.

Instead she looked up at Jo's tear-stained, blood-smeared face. The arm holding the gun was still stretched out toward the intruder, but there was a distinct tremble to it now, and Cadie noticed that fresh blood was dripping from the wound near Jo's shoulder. The dark-haired woman's face was a mask of shock and her eyes, normally so blue, were pale and glazed over.

"Jo," Cadie said gently. "Honey, it's over now. You can put the gun down."

Jo's vision cleared gradually and she looked along her arm at the gun, its barrel still smoking slightly. It was only a small leap for her eyes from the gun to the corpse on the floor. "Noooo," she moaned. "No...no...I didn't want to have to do that. Noooo..."

The gun clattered to the floor and Jo sat up quickly, leaning back against the couch and burying her face in her hands.

Cadie breathed in deeply, a part of her suddenly missing the strangely safe and protected feeling she had when Jo's weight was pressing down on her. Instead of dwelling on that she stood up and reached a hand down to stroke the dark head. "C'mon, Jo-Jo. Come and sit up on the couch here with me. It's more comfortable."

She sat down and began to pull Jo down next to her, but the tall woman resisted, her eyes widening as if she'd just thought of something critical.

"Jo, what is it?" *God, please not more thugs with guns.*

Jo yanked her hand away and she darted towards the bedroom Josh had been using. "Mephy?" she called out frantically. "Mephisto...where are you?" She ran back out again and then headed for her own bedroom. But before she could get there, a black streak hurtled out and leapt into the tall woman's arms, where he was promptly wrapped up in a hug. Jo buried her face in the big cat's soft fur as she carried him to the couch, where Cadie had watched bemused.

She is such a contrast, thought the blonde. *So dark and dangerous one minute, and so soft and vulnerable the next.* She couldn't help smiling as Jo sat down, tears now streaming silently down her cheeks, as the cat purred happily in her arms.

Jo had no words. The last few hours, the energy she had expended holding her focus, the things she'd done hit her like a baseball bat between the eyes.

Cadie watched as a range of emotions flew across Jo's expressive face, ending with a look of total exhaustion. "Jo?"

"Yes?" the woman replied softly.

"Let the cops do their thing. Just rest here awhile, okay?" Cadie wrapped an arm around the taller woman's shoulders and pulled her closer.

Jo didn't need any urging. Without another word, she turned towards Cadie and lay down, resting her head in the blonde's lap. Mephisto curled up in her arms, and Cadie stroked the black cat's fur and watched his mistress close her eyes.

She has the longest eyelashes I've ever seen, Cadie thought, as cat and woman fell asleep almost instantly. *Amazing, considering the place is swarming with cops and the storm...* She looked up and saw that the storm finally had broken. Sunlight streamed in through the skylight above them and a cooling breeze blew in the open verandah doors.

   I hope that's a sign. She looked back down at the sleeping skipper and gently stroked an errant lock of hair from her forehead. *I think she's had enough stormy weather.*

Chapter
Eight

Cadie took in the activity around her as if it were some bizarre movie she was watching in 3D. Police swarmed over the house, taking fingerprints and photographs. A contingent had gone with the man Jo had been fighting when they had arrived. He was being taken by air ambulance to the nearest big town. Another group of police had dealt with the body of the second man, sliding it into a body bag and removing it. And now, acting on Ken Harding's special instructions, they were cleaning up, washing blood away after taking samples, sweeping up broken glass. They had even called a handyman to put in a new makeshift front door in place of the one the police had smashed through with the battering ram. The officers had found another man tied up not far from the house and he too had been carted off to hospital.

Harding had said nothing to Cadie. He just moved around the house supervising the Airlie Beach police and giving out instructions. Eventually things seemed to be as resolved as they were going to be and the big detective wandered over, taking a seat opposite the couch. "We're about done here, Miss Jones," he said quietly. "The bad news is I do need to talk to her before I go." He nodded at the still slumbering Jo.

Cadie looked down at the dark-haired woman. Jo was deeply asleep, her face half-buried in Cadie's shirt, her arms loosely wrapped around the black cat, who gazed up at the blonde with sleepy, golden eyes. She swallowed as another wave of protectiveness washed over her, and she looked back up at the detective.

"I'm sorry," he said, his hands restlessly searching for his cigarettes in his inside jacket pocket. "But it's got to be done. Better we sort this out now with one conversation than have to keep revisiting it." He tapped a cigarette out of the damp, crumpled packet. "Tell you what. I'll go out and smoke this while you wake her up, yeah?"

"Okay," Cadie said quietly. She waited until Harding was out on the verandah before she looked down at Jo again, taking in the dark woman's angular features.

She looks so young. Cadie stroked Jo's hair. *It's a shame to wake her.* Gently she shook Jo's shoulder, careful to avoid the wound on her upper arm, which thankfully seemed to have stopped bleeding. *Need to get her cleaned up.* The blonde continued to coax Jo awake with as little drama as possible.

The tall woman stirred slowly, disturbing the cat that stood, stretched, and leaped off the couch in search of food.

"Jo-Jo," Cadie said softly, shaking her shoulder again. "Come on, hon. Wake up."

Jo's response was to make soft, objecting noises as she burrowed even further into Cadie's shirtfront. Cadie's heart melted. *Even covered in mud and blood. Even after the day she's had. She still gets to me.*

One more shake and Jo's eyes fluttered open, blinking sleepily for a few seconds as she tried to figure out where she was and what smelled so good. And what felt so soft and warm against her face.

"Hello there," a voice said. Jo rolled blue eyes upwards to meet the sea-green ones smiling down at her.

"Um, hi," Jo replied. She sat up carefully, pulling away from Cadie, feeling embarrassed about falling asleep on the blonde. Not to mention... "Uh, sorry about that," she said awkwardly, unable to meet Cadie's eyes as she swung around and dropped her feet to the floor. She winced as every muscle and joint in her body protested.

"There's no need to apologize, Jo," Cadie said gently. "You were in shock, and exhausted. And I offered. It's not like you bushwhacked me."

"Bushwhacked?" Jo couldn't help smiling, though she still didn't turn to look at the blonde. "You've been listening to Paul too much." She groaned as she tried to stand up, eventually falling back onto the couch. "God, I hurt."

Cadie nodded. "And you're probably going to need some stitches in that arm."

Jo looked down and gingerly lifted the bloodied sleeve of her shirt. An angry, deep graze sliced across her upper arm. It was crusted over and she poked it experimentally. "Lucky," she grunted. "Bullet just brushed me. Another half inch and that would've been really nasty. No stitches though. Can you help me clean it up later?" For the first time she glanced up at Cadie. "That is...if you..." She stumbled for words.

Cadie leaned forward and placed a hand on her thigh. "We

have a lot to talk about." She watched as Jo visibly swallowed and nodded silently, avoiding eye contact. "Yes, of course I'll help you clean it up. And anything else you need help with, too." Cadie patted her leg again. "And now Detective Harding wants to talk with you before he leaves." She nodded towards the verandah where the big detective was lounging against the rail, cigarette smoke curling around him as he watched them.

Jo leaned forward, elbows on her knees, hands clasped in front of her. She focused on a spot about three feet ahead rather than face Cadie's open gaze. "I guess he told you everything, huh?" she asked quietly, hating the fact that circumstances had taken away the chance to tell Cadie about herself.

Cadie watched her sympathetically. "He told me the bare bones, Jo," she replied. "That you were involved in some criminal activity for a while. But he also told me that because of you a lot of bad people are in jail today." She reached forward to touch Jo's leg again, but saw the tall woman flinch away from the contact. *She's scared to death,* Cadie realized, a light coming on in her brain. *She thinks I'm going to walk away from her because of this.*

Just as she had two hours earlier, Cadie reached out and gently drew Jo's face around with her fingertips. "Listen to me." Wide blue eyes stared back at her, uncertainly. "I want to hear all about it. From you. I'm not interested in Detective Harding's perspective. I want to know what it was like for you. Please?" Jo nodded slowly, and Cadie slid her hand around to cup the tall woman's cheek. She felt Jo lean into the touch slightly. "And I'm not going anywhere, okay?" she said with a smile. "So just relax."

Tentatively Jo smiled back and she let out a breath she hadn't realized she had been holding. *I can't believe she's seen what she's seen today and hasn't run a mile.* Jo watched Cadie get up and go to the verandah door to speak with Harding. *Either she's in shock and the reality of the day hasn't hit her yet or...* Jo swallowed hard. *Or, you idiot, she just might care enough about you not to care about your past.*

Jo shook her head disbelievingly.

But my past was very much here in the present today. That's got to be scary for her. Doesn't it? She watched as Harding tossed his cigarette butt over the verandah and followed Cadie back inside. *Good thing we've had some rain,* Jo thought absently.

"I'm going to explore your kitchen and rustle up some coffee," the American said, gesturing to the kitchen area at the other end of the living space. "Okay?"

Jo nodded quickly as Harding sat down opposite her. "That

would be great, Cadie. Thanks." They exchanged smiles before
Cadie walked off, and Jo sat back in the couch and fixed her gaze
on the big policeman.

Harding looked out of place on the soft leather chair. His
cheap suit was drying in wrinkles and he patted at his shiny forehead with a graying, tattered handkerchief. He looked hot and
tired, perched on the edge of the chair like a middle-aged Buddha
on a bed of nails.

Uncomfortable, Jo thought with a smile. "So," she said,
breaking the silence.

"So," replied Harding.

"How's Josh?"

Harding nodded slowly. "Yeah, he's not too bad," he
answered. "Cuts and bruises. A bit freaked out. We talked to
him and he's agreed to go with the home invasion angle when it
comes to telling his parents what happened. I don't think it'll do
anyone, least of all you, much good to tell them any more than
that, do you?"

Jo winced. Josh's parents were good people. She hated being
less than honest with them about what had happened to their son.
"Not too many burglars come in gangs of three, carrying semi-
automatic weapons, mate," she said to the policeman.

He nodded again. "I know but what's the alternative? Tell
them their son's been cat-sitting for an ex-assassin with underworld connections?" He shook his head. "Keep it simple, Madison. The kid's agreed so go with it."

Jo sighed. Like she had any choice. "Did he need hospital-
ization?"

"Nope. The paramedics patched him up and we took him
home. Gave him the name and number of a head-shrinker type in
case it jumps up and bites him in the arse later on."

Jo nodded. *Standard procedure.* "I owe him and his parents
an apology at the very least," she said quietly, guilt washing over
her in a sickening wave. "I'll give them a call in a couple of hours,
when things have settled a bit." She rubbed her hands over her
face tiredly. "Do we know yet how they got past the security system?"

Harding snorted quietly. "They knocked," he said. "Told the
kid they were cops and he let 'em in. Next thing he knew he was
tied up and getting familiar with the point of Marco's boot."

"Jesus," Jo exhaled. "I should've known. Been more careful.
Not left the kid on his own like that. God damn it."

Harding looked at the tall woman. *She's changed. Time was
it wouldn't have bothered her a damn. Now she looks like she's*

gonna beat herself to death with it.

"Let it go, Madison," he growled. "It's been five years for Chrissakes. Fair enough to think you were beyond all this shit. You weren't to know Marco was just biding his time."

She looked up sharply at the detective.

"Yeah I should've, Harding. Of all the people in the world, I should have known exactly that. Marco's always been a psychotic prick with a long memory." She slumped back in the seat. "I got complacent. Forgot who I was."

Cadie listened quietly from where she stood in the kitchen, fixing three cups of coffee. It worried her to hear Jo beating up on herself for what had happened. Absentmindedly, she stirred a tea-spoon of sugar into Jo's coffee, then wondered briefly if Harding wanted sugar. She glanced over at the big man and smiled as she tipped three teaspoons of the sweet stuff in and stirred. Carefully she picked up the mugs in both hands and wandered back to the sofa.

"That one's yours," she muttered, offering Jo the nearest cup to her. Then she turned to Harding and waited for him to take his before she straightened up again. "I'm going to go sit on the verandah," she said, starting to move in that direction. She was stopped by Jo's hand sliding into hers.

"Stay?" Jo asked quietly, looking up at her with irresistible blue eyes. "There isn't anything I don't want you to hear, or ask about. Please?"

"Okay," Cadie replied softly, following the tug of Jo's hand and sitting down next to her. She sat back and gently placed her hand against the tall skipper's lower back, rubbing in small, light circles.

God that feels good, thought Jo gratefully. *How does she know just what I need?* She looked back over her shoulder and smiled at the blonde, saying thank you with her eyes before she turned back to the detective, who was watching the exchange bemusedly.

"So," Jo said again. "Just how much trouble am I in?"

Harding shook his head. "None." She raised her eyebrows in surprise. "Seriously," he said, reassuring her. "There's nothing I've seen here today that doesn't scream self-defense, Madison, and that's what the paperwork will reflect."

"You've got to be kidding," she said, incredulous. "I killed a guy, Harding. And I..." She swallowed. "And I would have killed another one if...if Cadie hadn't..." She felt Cadie's hand press against her back comfortingly.

"For a start," Harding replied, "there were almost as many of my bullets in that moron as there were of yours. He came in here spraying bullets. It was a good shoot. Forget about it." He took a sip of his coffee, sighing happily at its sweet richness. "Nice cup of coffee, miss, thanks." Cadie smiled at him and he turned back to Jo. "As for Marco, I frankly don't give a shit what you would have done. He came in here intent on hurting you, at the very least, and you defended yourself. That's what I saw. End of story."

"Actually, he was making me a job offer," Jo replied quietly.

"You're kidding?"

She shook her head. "Nope. Offered me my old job, plus the added incentive of being his whore." She ran a hand through her hair, still very aware of the warmth from Cadie's fingers as they circled gently in the small of her back.

Harding snorted in derision. "What a dumb shit." He laughed and looked around at their luxurious surroundings and the panoramic view across the Whitsunday Passage and the islands. "Like you're gonna give up all this to go back to that life."

"Mmm," she replied noncommittally. "I wouldn't have gone back with him if I were living in a cardboard box off Oxford Street. He just pissed me off and then I lost my temper." She wasn't very proud of that, she realized. And she was scared by it as well. *Frightening to know how little it took to make me go back to that kind of violence.*

Harding broke into her reverie as he noisily drained his by-now lukewarm cup of coffee. "Well, I'm going to head off," he said, putting the mug down on the small table next to his chair. "Got some paperwork to do."

"You right for a lift, Ken?" Jo asked, standing up with him. He did a double-take at her use of his first name.

There's a first, he thought. "Yeah, no worries, thanks," he replied. "Got a car waiting for me outside. Listen, swing by the Airlie Beach cop shop in the morning, eh? We'll take a statement and get this all squared away."

"Will I have to testify?" she asked.

"Probably. But not for a while. He's going to be in prison hospital for a bit yet." He grinned lopsidedly at her. "Plus we've gotta do the whole extradition thing back to Sydney, and all that. So don't hold your breath for it. See you in the morning, eh?" He put his hat back on his head, and started for the door.

Jo followed him. "Harding, how did you get up here so quickly anyway?" she asked.

"I was already here," he answered. "Came up on a hunch."

Jo was speechless, impressed he had remembered her at all, let alone been concerned enough to follow a hunch over five years after their last meeting. "Well...Jesus. Thanks, Harding," she said, offering her hand to the man.

He took it, shaking it slowly. "No thanks needed," he replied gruffly. "Besides it was your little mate over there who found me and got me here. Until I ran into her I was wandering around with my head stuck up my arse trying to figure out where to find you. She's a determined little bugger. Wasn't gonna let me keep her out of the action either."

She grinned at him and turned back to Cadie where she had stayed quietly on the couch, flashing the blonde a brilliant smile. Cadie returned it in kind, feeling the blush slowly creep up her neck. "It was blind luck, honestly," she said. "Lucky timing for us all."

"Well, whatever it was, I'm glad you found me. See you tomorrow, ladies," Harding said, tipping his hat and walking out the door. Jo closed it carefully behind him, checking the lock on the rough new door and resetting the security system. She turned and walked back into the living area, suddenly feeling unsure.

Cadie watched Jo stand uncertainly in the middle of the room, gazing out at the view of the Passage. The ocean and islands were slowly turning shades of orange as the sun began to set. The glow made Jo seem golden as she stood there.

She looks like a goddess, Cadie thought, not for the first time. *A dirty, bloodied, lost, scared goddess.* The blonde stood and walked over to Jo, taking her hands in hers and looking up at her. Jo looked down and half-smiled.

"Why don't you go get cleaned up, put some fresh clothes on?" Cadie suggested. "It'll make you feel better."

"Good idea," Jo replied. "Hey, do you still have the cell phone? I'm amazed we haven't heard from the *Seawolf.*"

Cadie looked up at her sheepishly as she unhooked the cell phone from her belt and handed it back to its owner. "Well actually there's a very good reason for that," she said apologetically. "I switched it off."

They held each other's gaze for a few seconds.

"You're worried about Naomi's reaction to us being away together?"

Cadie nodded. "Oh yeah. And if we're going to be away all night she's going to go ballistic," she replied quietly, dreading her next conversation with her bad-tempered partner.

Jo thought hard. "Well, I can try and get you back to the boat tonight," she said, chewing her bottom lip as she tried to figure out how. "But the water taxis stop running in," she glanced down at her watch, "half an hour ago. And the only other way back is Bill's helicopter." She paused. "Hey. Where is Bill, anyway?"

Cadie started pulling Jo towards the bathroom. "He offered to go with Josh when they took him home," she said. "He said he would come back first thing in the morning to hold the fort here for as long as you need him to."

Jo followed her, stopping only at the linen cupboard to pull out a couple of fresh bath towels. "He's a good man," she said. "So...he can't get you back tonight." She bit her lip again as they entered her spacious main bathroom.

Cadie dropped the lid of the toilet and sat down as she watched the tall woman moving around, getting ready for her shower.

"Cadie, I don't think I can get you back there tonight," Jo said worriedly.

"It's okay," she replied. "We just need to get our story straight." She grinned wryly at Jo. "Somehow I don't think telling her the truth is going to make her any calmer."

Jo raised an eyebrow and grimaced a little at the thought. "Nope, I don't suppose it will. She hates my guts now, so telling her I'm a former assassin isn't going to improve my reputation with her." She stopped still when she realized Cadie probably hadn't heard the truth so baldly expressed before. She looked up and met a steady green gaze.

Cadie smiled gently back at her. "The important word in that sentence was 'former,'" the blonde said quietly. "I'm not afraid of your past, Jo. So stop worrying that I'm going to run from the truth. 'Cos I'm not going to."

Jo shrugged. "Why not?" She sat down on the edge of the bathtub and leaned down, untying her bootlaces and pulling the heavy boots and socks off. "I have killed people," she said bluntly. "I killed someone today, and would have done it again if you hadn't stopped me. Why wouldn't you run a mile from that? From me?" She threw the dirty socks over to the laundry hamper in the corner of the room with just a touch of venom.

"Because I know you," Cadie said calmly. Jo looked at her quizzically and the blonde raised a hand to stop the skipper's protest. "I know, I know. I've known you, what? Nine days?" She stood and moved over to help Jo when she realized the tall woman was having trouble lifting her injured arm above shoulder height. "Hang on a minute, let me help here." She pulled Jo's shirt up. "Bend over a little and hold your arms out for me," she said. Jo complied and Cadie slowly slid the shirt off her, mindful of the nasty graze on her upper arm. She turned and tossed the soiled shirt over to the hamper. "Damn, Jo," she said quietly when she turned back to her. "You're a walking bruise."

Jo had stood and was looking back over her own shoulder at her reflection in the mirror. "You should see my back," she muttered.

Cadie walked around Jo and hissed involuntarily at the sight of the left side of the skipper's back, which was a purpling mass of bruising. "What hit you?" she asked.

"A tree," Jo said shortly. "When you guys were lowering me down and the chopper got caught by a wind gust."

"Damn. We ought to get you to a doctor, Jo. Your ribs have got to be badly bruised at the very least." Gingerly Cadie allowed her fingertips to roam over the discolored area, feeling the heat beneath Jo's skin.

Jo winced slightly at the touch, but was relieved not to feel too much more pain than that. "No, I think it's okay," she said, twisting back and forth experimentally. Her eyes widened suddenly as she felt something other than Cadie's fingertips brush against the skin between her shoulder blades, a warm tingle radiating out from the point of contact. *Did she just kiss me?*

I can't believe I did that. Cadie pulled back from where she had planted a tender kiss on Jo's bruises, just under her black sports bra. *Is it hot in here?*

She cleared her throat and moved back around Jo, avoiding eye contact as she felt a blush rising. "Well," she said awkwardly. "I guess I'll leave you to grab your shower." She began backing out of the bathroom. "Or bath. Or whatever you're going to...um...do."

Jo chuckled and grabbed the blonde's hand before she could retreat completely. "Why don't you do the same?" she asked with a gentle smile. "You can use the en suite in my bedroom. And in the top drawer of my dresser you'll find a pile of clean t-shirts and shorts. There should be something in there that will fit you." She squeezed Cadie's hand reassuringly and handed her the other bath towel. "And Cadie?"

She waited until the blonde was forced to look up and meet her gaze. As their eyes met the electricity immediately sparked between them, and both let several seconds pass as they just swam in the warm feeling.

"Mmm?" Cadie murmured, her eyes dropping slightly to focus on Jo's gently-smiling lips.

"Thank you," Jo said softly. "For everything."

Cadie's eyes flicked back to the brilliant blue ones above her and she let the smile she was feeling deep inside reflect in her face. "I just called in the cavalry. You were the hero today. Don't argue with me," she said quickly as Jo opened her mouth the protest. "You got Josh out of there, Jo, and three more bad guys are off the street."

"But if—"

Cadie stepped closer and reached up, resting two fingers across Jo's lips. They both were distracted momentarily by the contact but it was the American who regained focus first. "No buts, Jo. We'll talk about it all later, okay?" She withdrew her fingers, somewhat reluctantly. "Right now you need to feel human again, and I don't know about you, but I could eat a horse." She grinned.

Jo relaxed and smiled back. "Okay. See you in a few."

Jo leaned her forearms against the wall of the shower, resting her forehead on her hands and letting the cool water flow down her back. She ached from head to foot, but slowly the high-pressure jet began to work the kinks out. The events of the day played over and over in her mind, but two things stood out.

It's just possible I may finally be free of that other life. Marco was the last of them. There's none of that old crowd left who would care to come after me. Tony's dead and Marco's going to be put away for a long time.

And Cadie didn't run a mile. She couldn't help smiling at that thought. *She knows the truth...or at least the basics. And she's still here. Not just here, but touching me...kissing me...and wanting to know more about me.* The smile turned into a grin. *How is that possible?*

She reached for the soap and began washing the grime and crusted blood from her body, desperate to remove the evidence of the day's bizarre activities.

Hard to believe that it was just this morning that I was watching her sunbathing and fantasizing about touching her, Jo thought as she stepped further under the spray, rinsing away the soap. *And now she's as naked as I am, on the other side of this wall.*

Jo reached forward and pressed her hand flat against the back wall of the shower, trying to picture Cadie. *Mmm...*

Niiice, Cadie thought, pressing her hand flat against the shower wall. *Why is it we can be at the end of the crazy day we've had and all I can think about is how soft her lips felt against my fingertips?*

She closed her eyes and called up that sensation again, remembering the soft touch and warmth of Jo's breath gentling her skin.

Oh my.

Cadie reached for the shampoo bottle in the shower recess and squeezed an amount onto her palm.

How do I get through this night without...without what, Jones? She laughed at herself as she spread the shampoo through her hair and began to lather up. *Ravishing her? Confessing undying love?* The unspoken dialogue in her mind began a back and forth debate that she'd had many times with herself since Naomi had revealed just how little their relationship meant to her.

I don't want to think about Naomi, she thought morosely as she rinsed the shampoo out of her hair. *It's over with goddamned Naomi.* She sighed. *One step at a time, Jones. Let's just get through this night.*

When Cadie emerged from Jo's bedroom 10 minutes later she found the tall woman sitting on the couch, trying to wrap a bandage one-handed around her upper right arm.

"Hang on, let me do that," she said, sitting down next to Jo.

"Thanks. I was going cross-eyed." Jo pulled up the sleeve of the long, pale blue silk robe she was wearing, revealing the bullet graze on her arm. Now that it had been cleaned of dirt and crusted blood it was weeping again.

Cadie winced. "Are you sure this doesn't need stitches?" she asked uncertainly.

"Positive," Jo replied. Cadie looked at her with raised eyebrows. "Honestly," Jo reassured her. She pulled over the first-aid kit she'd brought out from the bathroom. "Here ya go. Just put a cotton pad over it and wrap it with the bandage."

"It's going to leave a scar, Jo," Cadie said quietly as she tore open the packet holding the sterile cotton pad.

"That's okay," she shrugged. "It'll be a reminder. Besides, I'm not planning on entering any beauty contests any time soon." She grinned.

Cadie smiled back. "You could you know," she said matter-of-factly, putting Jo's hand over the cotton pad while she re-rolled the bandage the skipper had been trying to apply herself.

"Aw quit it, will ya? You're making me blush."

Cadie looked up and noticed it was true. *Well, that's a first.* She smiled as she began winding the bandage around Jo's arm.

She secured it with the two clips provided and patted it gently when she was done. "How does that feel? Not too tight?"

"Nope, it's good. Thanks," Jo said, letting the sleeve of the robe drop.

"No problem." Cadie tugged lightly at the sleeve. "I like this. The color brings out your eyes." She smiled mischievously up at Jo.

"I came out of the shower and realized I didn't have any fresh clothes in there. So rather than scandalize you, I threw this on." She grinned. "I'll go change in a minute."

"No need on my account," Cadie replied. "If you're comfortable, stay as you are."

Jo nodded, letting her eyes sweep up and down the blonde's outfit, which consisted of one of her white t-shirts, about two sizes too big on the American, and a pair of soft cotton drawstring shorts. "I see you found something you could live with," she said, smiling.

"Mhmm. Thanks."

There was a long pause as they contemplated each other openly, eyes drifting and then meeting again, small smiles exchanged.

Finally, Jo cleared her throat. "Um, did you say something about being hungry enough to eat a horse?" she asked.

"God, yes," Cadie replied. "It feels like about three days since we had those sandwiches on the pontoon out at Heart Reef."

Jo nodded in agreement, then rubbed her face wearily. "It's been such a weird day," she said.

And suddenly Cadie could see that lost, uncertain look shading across the dark-haired woman's face again. "Come on," she said, patting Jo's thigh as she stood up. "Let's rustle up some food, and we can talk it out over dinner." She held out a hand and when Jo took it, pulled her up.

"Sounds like a plan," said the skipper, a smile returning to her eyes. "There's just one more thing we need to do before we can relax."

Cadie nodded. "Call the *Seawolf,* yes." She took a deep breath. "Can't say I'm looking forward to that. Are we going to stick with the burglary story?"

Jo looked down at her as they moved into the kitchen. "Do you think Naomi will go for that?" she asked, opening the fridge and pulling out the makings of a salad.

"At this point, I don't think it makes much difference what our reason is. She's just gonna hate that I'm here regardless of why."

Jo placed a lettuce, cucumber, tomatoes, avocadoes and bean sprouts on the counter, along with a glass salad bowl and a bottle of homemade salad dressing she was glad to see Josh hadn't raided too badly.

"Well," she said, "if she's going to be pissed off no matter what we tell her we might as well get it over with. Then at least she'll have until tomorrow morning to calm down about it."

Cadie snorted. "You don't know her very well. She'll just use that time to work up a head of steam about it, if she hasn't already."

She looked so glum about the prospect that Jo felt a pang of remorse. "I'm sorry I involved you in it all, Cadie," she said quietly, beginning to slice the tomatoes on the wooden chopping board. "I should have just had Bill drop you at the boat before we came here."

Cadie shook her head emphatically. "And then how would you have gotten yourself down to the ground, or found Det Harding?" she replied. "You needed me." She grinned up into azure blue eyes that sparkled back at her. "And there really wasn't time, Jo-Jo. Think about how fast that storm came in. We only barely got back to Shute Harbor as it was."

Jo tossed the tomato quarters into the salad bowl and reached for the cucumber.

"That's true, I guess," she answered. "Tell you what. You finish this salad. There are some eggs in the fridge if you want to hard-boil a couple to add in later. And I will call the *Seawolf.* I'll tell her you're asleep, okay?"

Cadie was tempted. The thought of not having to talk to Naomi tonight was definitely a pleasant one, but she knew the senator wasn't going to take no for an answer. "Call them, Jo. But I will talk to her. It'll only make it worse if I don't." She took the knife from Jo and moved around the counter. "But thanks for offering."

Jo picked up the cell phone and tentatively rested her back against the counter, wincing slightly as the hard surface caught the edge of one of her many bruises. She felt Cadie shift and lean slightly against her as Jo pulled up Paul's number on the speed dial. She looked down at the blonde while she waited for her crewman to answer. Cadie looked subdued as she finished slicing the cucumber and Jo took a moment to slide her left hand around the smaller woman's waist. A little smile crept to the corners of Cadie's mouth at the movement and Jo felt her lean more in response.

She's a bit scared of the senator, Jo thought grimly. For about the millionth time since she'd met the odd couple, she wondered how on earth they had gotten together. *I guess tonight is the time to ask,* she thought, realizing they had an interesting evening ahead of them.

Finally, Paul answered the phone. "Jesus, Skipper, where the bloody hell are you?" he shouted good-naturedly. "We'd just about decided you been washed off the pontoon. Is Cadie with you? The senator's going nuts here."

She chuckled. "One question at a time, mate, okay?" she answered. "Yes, Cadie's with me and we're at my place. I got a call from Josh while we were out at Heart, telling me he'd disturbed a couple of burglars. I needed to get here quickly and that storm was coming in fast, so Bill just brought us straight here. By the time I got done with the cops and all that crap it was too late to try and make it back tonight."

"Bloody hell. Is Josh okay?"

"Yeah. A couple of cuts and scrapes but nothing too serious. Scared silly, I think, but he'll be fine. I've got to do a bit more paperwork with the cops in the morning, but we should be back by lunchtime for sure. How did you guys do with the storm?"

Cadie moved around the kitchen, finding a pan for the eggs and filling it with water, before exploring the stovetop and putting the eggs on to boil.

How does she make that outfit look so sexy? Jo thought as she listened to Paul's response.

"Yeah not too bad, Skip. We moved round the south point into the bay and we were pretty sheltered. Things got a bit choppy though. Couple of cases of seasickness on board, but things have settled now." Jo could almost hear his grin.

"That's good," she replied. "Any damage?"

"Nothing too noticeable," he said. "We got everything pretty well tied down before the wind got too strong. I figured we'd stay here till you get back."

"Mhmm, sounds like a good idea. Let those landlubber stomachs settle a bit more." She grinned at Cadie who had looked up quizzically.

"Skipper, the senator's pretty keen to talk to Cadie," Paul said quietly.

Jo pointed at her and mouthed "Naomi." The blonde rolled her eyes and nodded. "Yeah she's here, mate. Put her on." Jo handed Cadie the phone and watched as she rested back on the counter next to her, leaning against Jo's shoulder. Almost immediately she could hear the senator's argumentative tones blaring through the cell phone's little speaker at Cadie. Jo grimaced.

"Naomi—" Cadie tried to find a break in her partner's onslaught, with little luck. "Naomi—" She held the phone away from her ear when it became obvious there was no stopping the senator until she'd said her piece. Finally there was silence. "Are you done?" Cadie asked quietly. "First of all, as much as I'd like to 'get my ass back there' as you so charmingly put it, it's not possible tonight." She pulled away again at another barrage from Naomi. "No, there's no way out there tonight."

She listened again as the senator let rip once more, and Jo found her arm curling around the smaller woman's shoulders in a protective gesture she just couldn't help.

"Damn it, Naomi, would you just listen for five seconds? There wasn't time to take me back to the boat before the storm. Or perhaps you would rather have had us risk flying twice as far in that weather, just to keep you happy? Not to mention that it was important for Jo to get back here as quickly as possible."

Another barrage.

Cadie closed her eyes and dropped the phone away from her face for a couple of seconds before she made another attempt at reasoning with her partner. She nestled in closer to Jo and felt the taller woman squeeze her protectively. *It's almost worth this bullshit just to feel her arm around me,* Cadie thought wistfully as she waited for Naomi to take a breath.

"Naomi, Jo did the safest thing for all of us. She thought we'd be able to get back tonight and it wasn't her fault that we're stuck here. You're just going to have to live with it. No...no, I'm not going to let you rant at her. No."

Jo guessed the senator was giving her a fair bucketing judging by the frustrated look on Cadie's face. *Time to stop this in its tracks,* she thought, gently taking the phone from the American.

"Senator, it's Jo. I will get Cadie back to the *Seawolf* as quickly as I can. But that's going to be tomorrow morning at the earliest. There just isn't any faster way of doing it," she said quickly before Naomi could object. "What's that? Sorry, you're breaking up. Nope, can't make you out at all. Hanging up now. Bye." She closed the connection, feeling Cadie shake with silent laughter against her side.

"Oh, you're baaad," the blonde said with a giggle, slapping Jo gently on the stomach before she moved away to rescue the eggs.

"Sorry, but there's only so much bullshit a girl can take," Jo grumbled, carefully switching the phone off and putting it back on the counter. "I gather I'm public enemy No.1?"

"Oh yeah," Cadie said, draining off the hot water and pouring cold over the top of the hard-boiled eggs. "Plenty of ranting about what she'd do to either one of us if we laid a hand on each other. Blah, blah, blah." She went quiet as she started to peel the eggs as Jo rummaged around in the pantry. "I'm sorry, Jo. She shouldn't take it out on you."

Jo chuckled. "Well, I'd rather it was me than you, to be honest," she replied, pulling out pasta and olive oil. "How would you like to try my world famous veggie pasta?"

Cadie grinned. "Sounds great. That salad dressing is killer," she said, throwing the diced-up egg into the mix and pouring the dressing over the top of the lot, sucking a dribble off her fingertip. "Naomi's always been a very possessive person. It's one of her least attractive qualities. It's always been paranoia in the past, though."

Jo looked over at Cadie. "And this time?" she asked quietly.

Sea-green eyes met hers and held steady. "And this time she's right on the money," Cadie replied softly, letting more than a little of what she was feeling show on her face.

Wow. We do have a lot to talk about.

Before they'd settled in to eat Cadie had explored Jo's CD collection and been delighted to find they shared a similar taste in music. She had selected a disc while Jo had moved around the living room lighting a series of candles and oil burners before they'd settled in to eat. The conversation through dinner had been light-hearted and flirtatious, and despite the events of the day, they had found plenty to laugh about.

An hour and a half later the two women were relaxed, full of good food, and sprawled next to each other on the couch. Jo had pulled a coffee table over and they had their feet up on its glass surface, their plates piled up next to the half-empty bottle of red wine. Both women were nursing their glasses. They were quiet, just enjoying the peace of the cool sea breeze coming through the open French windows and the waxing moon spilling silver across the verandah onto the polished wooden floor in front of them.

"I can't believe you're into Eva Cassidy," Cadie said quietly, leaning back and closing her eyes as the silky tones of the young folk singer filled the room. She slowly twirled the wineglass resting against her belly.

"Hey, this may be a cultural backwater, but there are some of us who like to occasionally expand our horizons." Jo smiled as she leaned towards Cadie conspiratorially. "Don't tell anyone but I even have some Cris Williamson and Tret Fure somewhere." She let the smile broaden, and Cadie found herself just inches away from one of her companion's trademark stellar grins.

Of their own accord, her fingers wandered up to trace Jo's lips, the mutual shock of the contact keeping them both very still. "Jo?" she whispered.

"Mmm?" came the quiet response.

"I think if you don't kiss me very shortly, I'm going to explode." Cadie couldn't take her eyes off Jo's mouth and she caught the slight upturning at the corners as the taller woman smiled against her fingertips. She let her eyes wander up to the brilliant blue gazing down at her. "And I was wondering what you thought about that."

Jo said nothing. Instead she sat up and carefully took Cadie's wineglass out of her hand, placing it on the coffee table along with her own before she turned back to face the blonde. As Jo leaned towards her, a sexy half-smile on her face, Cadie slid her arms around the tall woman's waist, reveling in the feel of the cool silk of the robe and the warm body beneath it. She pulled gently and Jo came closer until they could feel each other's breath on their lips.

"Arcadia?" Jo breathed.

"Mmm?"

"I think it's a very...very...good idea."

Their mouths came together in a tender explosion of sensation that took Cadie's breath away. Softness mingled with a rush of tugging, aching passion as their mouths melted into each other. Jo slipped her arms around Cadie, pulling her closer as the kiss deepened and intensified. She felt Cadie open to her and marveled at it, following the blonde's lead into a slow, delicious exploration of tongues and lips. Small incoherent, passionate sounds mingled with the music that played softly in the background, and it was with a shock that Jo realized she was making at least half of them. Gently she cradled Cadie in her arms as they kissed. Then, as the sensations built up, she shifted position slightly and slowly lowered them down on to the couch, never breaking contact.

Cadie's mind had come to a complete standstill, overwhelmed by the surging ache that built, then receded, and climbed again as she and Jo moved sensually against each other. She felt Jo take her down till she was flat on the couch, and she surrendered to the sensation, tugging the taller woman down with her, loving the feel of Jo's weight above her. She slid her hands down to the small of Jo's back, pulling her even closer, eliciting a groan from the dark woman that gave Cadie chills as she deepened the kiss once again.

Every gaze, every spark of the past nine days coalesced in the long embrace. Hands moved slowly, tugging at clothing, teasing. Legs tangled together.

Cadie's hands moved slowly up Jo's sides and across her shoulders until she cupped the taller woman's face, her fingers tangled slightly in her long, dark hair. Jo broke the kiss and pulled back as they both gazed deep into each other's eyes, breathlessly. Cadie looked up into startling blue orbs, their color deepened by desire.

"Oh, Jo," she whispered, brushing fingertips across the dark, full lips inches from her own. "This feels so...familiar." She smiled at the slightly raised eyebrow that elicited.

"Familiar, as in boring and unexciting?" Jo asked softly, leaning down to nuzzle the blonde's neck, working slowly towards the soft spot just below Cadie's ear, the tip of her tongue drawing a long, low groan from the American. Jo chuckled softly, a deep rumble close to her ear that made Cadie shiver. "I guess that answers that question," the skipper whispered.

Cadie nodded, smiling as she tried to find the words to explain what she meant. "I am *so* not bored and unexcited, trust me," she whispered and felt Jo laugh again. "I guess I meant that this feels like..." She hesitated and Jo pulled back again to gaze down into the blonde's gorgeous green eyes. "It feels like we have done this before. Like our bodies know just how to..." Her eyes drifted back to Jo's mouth again and Jo closed the distance till they were almost kissing once more. "Respond...to each other..."

Jo's answering "mhmm" mingled into another deep, melting kiss and they both forgot all thought for a few more minutes as the sensuality washed over them. This time was less urgent, but no less pleasurable. When Jo's hand gently cupped Cadie's breast through the soft fabric of the t-shirt, it sparked the blonde into an arching stretch that gave the tall skipper goose bumps. The intensity of it took them both by surprise and once again they found themselves blinking at each other breathlessly.

"Wow," Jo said quietly, shivering.

"Oh yeah," Cadie agreed. Impulsively she pulled Jo close again, wrapping her arms around her and hugging tight, burying her face against the tall woman's shoulder and neck. She suddenly felt tears close, overwhelmed by what she was feeling and what the consequences might be for them both. *For all three of us,* she reminded herself. Jo sensed the tears and held her close, making soft, comforting noises until they subsided, content to let Cadie tell her what was happening in her head when she was ready.

Finally the blonde loosened her hold somewhat and Jo let her lie back on the couch, reaching out and gently wiping away a tear with her fingertip.

"Sorry," sniffled Cadie. "I don't usually do that as a response to being..." She laughed weakly. "So...incredibly...turned on." Jo smiled broadly. "Although, when I think about it, I'm not sure that's true," Cadie corrected.

"What do you mean?" Jo asked, puzzled.

"I mean, Jossandra Madison, that I don't think I have ever in my life felt like this. So I don't really know if this is how I'd usually react." She smiled softly at the confused look on Jo's face.

"It doesn't feel like this with..." Jo jerked her thumb over her shoulder, roughly in the direction of the *Seawolf*, lying at anchor off Whitsunday Island.

Cadie shook her head and had to laugh at the slight widening of Jo's eyes. "Never. Not ever." She reached up and cupped Jo's face with her left hand. "You and I, my love, are in a lot of trouble." She tried to make light of it, but Jo caught the flash of fear and uncertainty that crossed her face.

"You're scared?" Jo asked softly, afraid of the answer. Cadie nodded distractedly and Jo pulled away. "Of me," she said with certainty and a sinking heart. She sat up quickly, swinging her feet down to the floor and resting her head in her hands dejectedly. "I can understand that. I mean, you saw me at my worst today. I'm a killer and it doesn't matter how many years go by, that's what I'll always be."

Damn, Cadie thought as she felt doors slamming closed. *Gotta be more careful. She's so quick to condemn herself.*

Quickly she sat up and slid in behind the tall woman, wrapping her arms around Jo's waist to hold her firmly between Cadie's legs. "No," she said definitely, gently shaking Jo for emphasis. "Understand this, Jo." She waited for the skipper to turn her head slightly towards her. "I have never felt safer than when I'm with you. And that included this afternoon when you had Marco where I know you wanted him." She smiled gently, seeing the slight upturn of Jo's mouth. "It's not you I'm afraid of, Jossandra. And no matter what you've done, or will do in the future, it's not possible for me to be afraid of you."

She leaned back into the couch, pulling Jo with her until they were sprawled together, Jo's feet back up on the coffee table and her head tucked under the blonde's chin, against her right shoulder. Their hands were clasped together across Jo's belly.

This probably doesn't look it, but it's so comfortable, Cadie thought, contentedly, certain she'd soothed Jo's fears, at least for the time being. *I want her to feel as safe with me as I do with her.*

Jo relaxed, loving the warm rush as Cadie enfolded her. "So

what is it that you're afraid of?" she asked softly.

There was a pause as Cadie reached for the right words. "Change," she finally answered. "To borrow a line from an old movie, you and I changed our direction tonight, and it's going to have a ripple effect."

"You mean you and Naomi."

"Yes, but not just that."

"But after that conversation we overheard, you weren't planning on staying with Naomi regardless of what might happen with us. Were you?" Jo asked uncertainly, a cold trickle of fear working its way through her guts.

"No. But Jo—and this is something else you're going to have to understand about me—I am going to leave her, but I have to do it the right way." She looked down at Jo, who suddenly felt restless in her arms. "I want to be with you, Jo. But it will be better for both of us if I make sure I come to you with all loose ends tied."

"Okay," Jo said, nodding slowly. "So, what's the right way?"

Cadie sighed, resting her cheek on the top of Jo's head. "Right now Naomi thinks she's just going to dump me at her convenience." She pushed down the rising anger she felt just remembering that damn conversation, and Jo's thumb brushed reassuringly across the back of her hand. "Well, I'm not going to let that happen, because I'm going to leave her the moment we get back to Chicago. But I need her to understand why I'm leaving her. That it's about her and me, and not about meeting you. If you'd turned out to be a hairy man with a wooden leg and bad breath, I'd still be leaving Naomi."

Jo chuckled. "Damn. You've discovered my real dark and mysterious past," she said quietly.

Cadie laughed out loud, hugging Jo close as they both shook from the belly laughs.

"I understand what you're saying," Jo said when they'd both recovered. "You don't want to give her any excuse to duck responsibility for what's happened to your relationship."

"Exactly."

"You don't think maybe it's a little late for that? I mean, she's been thinking the worst of me from the moment she met me. You're going to have a hard time convincing her that this isn't all about you and me."

"I know," Cadie sighed. "But I have to try." She hesitated a little before going on, not sure how Jo would react to what she had to say next. "Honey, there is something else that concerns me." Jo looked up at her questioningly. Cadie took a deep breath.

"I've never lived alone." She felt the tall woman go very still in her arms. "I went straight from my parents' home to college and then I was with Naomi. I think..." She hesitated again. "I think I might need some time to myself."

Jo's heart sank, but she had known that being with Cadie was never a *fait accompli.* There were just so many complications. She swallowed. "Cadie. I never expected us to have even this," she gestured generally. "Anything you can give me..." She swallowed, suddenly choked up. "I'll take any time I can get with you, and call myself lucky to have known you."

Cadie squeezed Jo tight, fighting tears of her own. "I want to be with you Jo," she said fiercely. "I do. I just have so much I need to get cleared up first. Some time to get my ducks in a row, if you like."

Jo nodded. "I understand," she said softly. She disengaged herself slowly and stood up, picking up the dinner plates and wineglasses as she did so. She wandered over to the kitchen and placed the dirty dishes in the sink before walking back to the stereo system and selecting another CD.

Cadie watched all this silently, wondering what was going on behind the cool, blue eyes. *I've hurt her, and that was the last thing I wanted,* she thought sadly.

Jo's mind was going in 15 different directions, but the one thing she was sure of was that she wanted to make the most of this evening. She keyed the stereo and the funky, mellow rhythms wafted out. She walked back to Cadie who was looking up at her with uncertain eyes. She smiled and held out a hand.

"Dance with me?" she asked softly. Cadie beamed back at her and took her hand. Jo pulled her gently into her arms, and she snuggled in, fitting herself to the tall skipper's contours as they swayed together to the music. Several minutes passed in companionable silence as they let the music flow through them, directing their movements. Jo rested her cheek against Cadie's head and she could feel the blonde's warm breath on her neck.

"Which old movie?" Jo asked suddenly.

Cadie looked up at her quizzically.

"You said you borrowed a line from an old movie," Jo reminded her.

"Oh." Cadie laughed quietly and burrowed back into Jo's embrace. *"An Affair to Remember."*

"Hmmm. Don't think I've ever seen it."

"Mmm. Deborah Kerr. Cary Grant. They fall in love on a cruise. It's very romantic." Cadie felt Jo squeezing her gently, as they fell back into comfortable silence. "Jo?"

"Mmm?"

"Are you angry with me? For starting something I can't finish yet?"

"No," she answered simply. "For a start, you beat me to it by about two seconds." She felt Cadie laughing. "And for another, I think it's been inevitable for about a week, don't you?"

"How do you explain it?" Cadie wondered. "I've never felt this before. Not even in the earliest days of my relationship with Naomi."

Jo considered her response for a few moments. "Do you believe in soulmates?" she finally asked.

Cadie looked up at her. "You mean, two souls going through time, meeting each other again and again? That kind of thing?"

"Mhmm."

"I never really thought about it before," she said honestly. "You think that's what's going on with us?"

Jo shrugged slightly as they danced. "Well, think about it. When was the first time you felt like you knew me?" She looked down into curious green eyes.

"That's easy," Cadie replied quickly. "I saw you from my hotel balcony when you pulled the *Seawolf* into the Hamilton Island marina. I can remember thinking how I felt like I'd seen you before somewhere." She grinned up at Jo, whose eyes had widened perceptibly.

"That was you, wasn't it?" she asked wonderingly. "Wow."

Cadie nodded. "So maybe your theory is right," she muttered, snuggling back into Jo's arms, squeezing her softly. "This certainly feels right."

"Yes it does," Jo murmured, kissing the top of Cadie's head. She started to quietly sing, following along with the music they were dancing to.

"Mmm," purred Cadie. "You are so good at that."

Jo smiled. "I only do it when I'm inspired," she said, lifting Cadie's chin and ducking her head to meet soft, willing lips. She felt the blonde's hand slide to the back of her neck and into her hair, pulling her closer. Jo moaned softly into the kiss and Cadie met the sound with one of her own, their bodies surging together as the passion intensified once more.

"Oh God, Jo, I want you so much," Cadie gasped when they broke off again. Jo's hands slid down to her backside and lifted her up. Quickly she wrapped her legs around the tall woman's waist and found herself, for once, at eye level. It was an intriguing perspective.

"And I want to make love with you all night." Jo growled and kissed the blonde again, deep and soft and open. Cadie melted against her. "Instead, I'll make do with the next five minutes," she muttered as she started to walk them both into the second bedroom. Cadie groaned, recognizing Jo's willpower was the only thing stopping her from breaking her own promise to herself.

They kissed hungrily as Jo backed up against the bed and sat down slowly, giving Cadie a chance to unwind her legs before she leaned back onto the mattress. The blonde straddled Jo's hips, her hands on either side of her head. She gazed down.

"You are so beautiful," Cadie murmured, tracing Jo's collarbone with her lips. The tall woman's hands on the blonde's hips pulled her closer and both women groaned at the contact. "You are so beautiful and from the moment I saw this robe, I've been wanting to peel it off you." Her fingers trailed down the edge of the robe, teasing the skin below.

"Almost as much as I want to pull that t-shirt off you," Jo replied, even as she used her greater strength and body weight to flip them over, pinning Cadie. They grinned at each other breathlessly. "And you too, are beautiful, Arcadia," she said softly, leaning down and kissing the hollow at the base of the blonde's neck. She lingered, brushing her lips against the soft skin. "And I cannot wait for the day...or night...when I can undress, and tease, and excite you." She interspersed each phrase with a kiss up Cadie's neck, until finally she reached her mouth, parting her lips tenderly with her own, beginning a long, deep exploration.

Cadie moaned softly, arching under Jo, aching to be touched.

"Two out of three isn't bad, Skipper," she muttered when the kiss finally ended, and she felt Jo's smile against her neck. "I'm sorry, Jo," she said quietly.

The skipper pushed up on her elbows and looked down at Cadie.

"Don't apologize for any of this, sweetheart," she said gently. "There are two of us here and, if you hadn't noticed, I seem to be a more than willing participant." She kissed the blonde once more and then reluctantly disentangled herself. "But right now, I'm going to leave you here, before we *both* explode."

They spent a few more seconds gazing at each other with open desire, and then sighed in unison. Jo growled in frustration as she stood up, provoking a giggle from her supine companion.

"Sleep well, gorgeous," Jo said as she walked out of the room.

"Aye aye, Captain," Cadie replied cheekily, saluting the retreating woman.

"Oh, shut up," came the response.

Cadie laughed quietly and lay back on the bed, hands behind

her head. Her body was still tingling with desire and she just absorbed the feelings for a few minutes, listening to Jo moving around in the living area before going into her own bedroom.

What a day, she thought as she slid the shorts down over her hips and off, tossing them on to the chair in the corner. *She's a complicated woman and I...* She gasped, suddenly realizing what she was thinking. Cadie crawled under the top sheet and curled up on her side.

Jo slid out of the robe, dropping it on the foot of the bed. She stretched wearily, feeling every ache in her muscles and joints, as well as the more pleasant ache of lust. She smiled softly and walked to the dresser, pulling out another old t-shirt and slipping it over her head. Seconds later she was curled up in bed, gazing out at the moonlit ocean and wondering at the strangeness of the day.

I should be exhausted, she pondered. *But I feel like something new has begun. And Cadie...God, she makes me feel so good.* She grinned at the moonlight. *I don't care how long I have to wait for her. She's worth it.* Jo closed her eyes, letting the pleasant tingling echoes of Cadie's touch ripple across her skin.

"Jo?" Cadie called out.

"Yes?"

"Goodnight." *I love you, Jo.*

Jo smiled again. *I love you, Cadie.* "'Night."

Cadie wasn't sure what woke her but she suspected the big, black cat sitting next to her might have had something to do with it. The wind had picked up again, and occasional flashes of lightning through her bedroom window suggested another storm had rolled in. She reached out and scratched under the feline's chin.

"Hello, Mephisto," she whispered. "Did the thunder scare you, boy?"

A soft meow answered her and the cat jumped down from the bed and headed for the door. He stopped once to look over his shoulder and meowed at her again.

Intrigued, Cadie disentangled herself from the sheet and padded after him. "If this is all so you can show me a half-chewed dead mouse, I'm not going to be happy, cat," she muttered.

Finding a black cat in a dark room wasn't the easiest task, but finally an opportune sequence of lightning showed her the way. He sat, washing his face, in front of Jo's open bedroom door.

"Okay, so what's up?" she whispered.

Fortunately she didn't have to wait for him to answer. She

could hear low sounds of distress coming from Jo's room and tentatively she stepped through the door.

She's crying. As her eyes grew accustomed to the dim light she could make out Jo's long shape moving restlessly under the sheet, her face framed by the fan of dark hair splayed out on the pillow. Her head turned from side to side as she moaned through whatever nightmare visions she was experiencing. Cadie could see tears streaking Jo's cheeks.

"Nooo, no please," Jo moaned. Her hands came up in a defensive gesture and she squirmed.

To Cadie's eyes it looked like she was trying to back away from something menacing. The blonde's heart melted all over again at the sight and she moved forward slowly and sat down on the edge of the bed. She reached out and gently took Jo's shoulder, shaking her slightly.

"Jo." The dreaming woman thrashed away from her touch but Cadie persisted, leaning over Jo and taking both her shoulders in her hands. "Honey, please wake up," she said firmly.

Suddenly Jo surged forward. Sitting bolt upright with eyes wide and frightened, she initially pushed Cadie away. As the dream dropped away and she came fully awake, Jo pulled her back, clinging desperately to the smaller woman. The blonde wrapped her arms around her, stroking Jo's hair as the skipper took in deep, gulping breaths.

"It's okay, baby, it was just a dream," Cadie soothed, rocking them both back and forward slowly.

"S-sorry," Jo muttered.

"There's nothing to apologize for, Jo-Jo." She felt her shivering. "Do you want to tell me about it?"

Jo shook her head. "N-no. D-don't want to go back there now. Maybe in the morning?"

Cadie nodded. "That's okay, sweetheart. Do you want to try and go back to sleep?" Jo's only answer was to hug her even closer. "How about if I stay with you?"

She felt Jo relax perceptibly against her, and Cadie suspected she was already drifting back towards sleep. But she was still shivering.

"Come on, Jo-Jo. I'm not leaving you on your own like this, so let's get snuggled in." Gently she pushed Jo back into the bed and watched the half-asleep woman curl up on her side, facing the ocean. Cadie slid under the sheet and cuddled up against Jo's back, wrapping arms around her and tucking her head against Jo's shoulder blade. She felt Jo take her hands and pull her closer and she smiled, placing a kiss against the soft cotton of Jo's shirt.

"Thank you," Jo mumbled sleepily.

"Ssshhh. Go back to sleep, gorgeous."

"'k."

As Cadie drifted off, Mephisto jumped up onto the bed, circled a couple of times, and then settled into a furry ball behind her knees. She smiled softly. *Guess that's the feline stamp of approval,* was her last cogent thought.

Chapter
Nine

Sometime in the night, once the second storm had passed, Mephisto found it too warm, nestled as he was against Cadie's skin. He stood and arched his back before he stretched out and flexed his claws. He then padded nonchalantly across the two sleeping women. When he reached the corner of the bed he coiled himself up and leapt high, landing on top of the tall bookcase with practiced ease. One circle to make his nest and the big black cat settled down, front paws tucked under his chest like a sphinx. He gazed down at the two humans with sleepy, half-lidded golden eyes, waiting for the day to begin.

The first suggestion of sunrise touched the two sleeping figures in the bed and seemed to stir them, though neither woke. The cat watched as Jo stretched and rolled over, turning in Cadie's embrace until they faced each other. The blonde responded by pressing closer, murmuring incoherently as she continued to slumber. Mephisto uncurled and rolled over onto his back, matching the lazy comfort of the women.

Jo felt herself swimming up through a deep, sound sleep towards the pale light of dawn. She protested quietly and tightened her arms around the warm body cuddled up against her left side. Content, she buried her nose in the sweet-smelling hair against her face and settled back down into a drowsy half-awake state.

That's when it hit her.

Eyelids flew open, revealing startled blue eyes. She stiffened slightly when she realized it was Cadie she was hugging. Jo glanced down and confirmed what her tingling skin told her.

"Hoo boy," she muttered, her brain scrambling to remember how exactly they'd ended up in this position when she was sure they'd gone to bed in separate rooms. Flashes of her nightmare came back to her and a light went on in her head.

I woke Cadie up with my dream, she thought. She looked down again at the blonde woman tucked under her chin, blissfully unaware. *Dangerous. She's so beautiful and I want to keep holding her.* Wistfully she planted a tender kiss on the top of Cadie's head before she gently tried to extract herself from the blonde's determined grip.

"Noooo," mumbled Cadie, tightening her hold around Jo's waist and casually flinging her left leg over Jo's, effectively pinning her in place.

The taller woman couldn't help but smile and it only took about half a second to give in to the impulse to stay just as she was. "Okay, sweetheart," she muttered. "I'm not going anywhere." She kissed Cadie's forehead once more and let herself slide back down into the drowsy warmth. *I guess it can't hurt. We're only sleeping.*

Cadie burrowed deeper into the nest of sensual safety. Part of her brain knew it was Jo's arms that held her close, but mostly she was an unthinking ball of sleepiness, content to feel the warmth of another human at her fingertips and against her face.

Happily she snuggled closer, burying her face against the soft smoothness of Jo's neck. Unconsciously she kissed the warm skin, murmuring incoherently as her lips made their gentle way up the line of the taller woman's neck until the blonde was nibbling at the soft spot below her ear.

Lips and tongues merged and tangled as Jo and Cadie's bodies did what their minds hesitated to permit in wakefulness. Inhibitions forgotten, their movements slowly became more and more passionate as desire overtook tenderness, even in sleep. Legs wound around each other, Cadie's left hooking over Jo's right hip as the skipper's long fingers stroked down the outside of her thigh. Sunlight crept across the bed, bathing the two languorously moving figures in light and warmth.

Finally, consciousness, like the sunshine, snuck up on the pair and the deep kiss they shared was enough to pull them both awake. Breathlessly they gazed at each other, blinking groggily despite the waves of tingles coursing through them both.

"Wow," breathed Jo, mesmerized by the brilliant green orbs just inches from her own. She suddenly became very aware of her hands, one possessively cupping Cadie's buttock, the other wrapped around the smaller woman's waist.

"Very wow," the blonde agreed quietly, wondering just how her leg came to be wound around the dark woman's hips. "That's one hell of a way to wake a woman up, Skipper."

"Mhmm..." Jo murmured, savoring the feel of the compact American's body against hers. "I don't know about you, Miss Jones," she whispered as she leaned in to claim Cadie's lips again, "but I could stand to wake up this way every morning." They kissed again, slowly, both riding a gradually rising tide of desire. Only the thump of an impatient feline landing on the foot of the bed interrupted them.

Cadie giggled as she watched Mephisto stalk up the foothills of the lumpy mountain the two women made under the sheet.

"Ow, ow, ow...claws. Mephisto, mind your claws," Jo protested as the big cat made his way up her long thigh. She winced as the feline bumped a few bruises, reminding Jo of the hard day her body had endured. She and Cadie parted enough to allow him a place to sit between them and he promptly curled into a contented ball with a sound that was half meow and half purr.

"I'm guessing that's his 'stop kissing and feed me' noise." Cadie grinned at the cat's owner who was gazing affectionately at the black feline.

Jo laughed quietly. "Something like that." She turned back to look at Cadie with frank eyes. "And it's probably a good thing he interrupted us if we want to stick to that decision we made last night," she said, somewhat wistfully, fighting the urge to nudge the cat out of the way and throw caution to the wind.

Cadie sighed, desire for the tall skipper warring with the complications of her life that were bouncing insistently off the inside of her skull. "Probably," she agreed sadly. "But I don't have to pretend I like it, do I?" She pouted slightly, a look that drew a charmed smile from Jo, who ran a gentle finger down the line of Cadie's jaw.

"No, sweetheart, you don't have to like it," she replied softly. "Here's an idea. It's early and we've got some time. Why don't I get up and feed the monster here?" She ruffled the fur on top of the cat's head playfully. "I'll put together some breakfast for us as well and then we can spend the next few hours in bed getting to know each other."

"In the Biblical sense?" Cadie quipped hopefully, grinning at the belly laugh that erupted from the tall skipper.

Jo leaned forward and kissed her soundly before sliding out of bed. She groaned as she stretched stiff and sore limbs. "Don't go away. I'll be right back," she said, padding gingerly around the bed.

Cadie couldn't keep her eyes off the lanky Australian whose t-shirt barely covered the tops of her long legs.

"Mmm," she murmured. "Don't worry, I'm not going anywhere."

Jo lifted one elegant eyebrow in response to the lascivious look on the blonde's face and chuckled as she headed out the door to the living room. "C'mon Mephy, tucker time," she called out.

The feline sprang up, used Cadie's stomach as a stepping-stone, and bounded out after his mistress.

"Oooofff...claws!" yelped the blonde, giggling quietly to herself when she heard Jo laughing at her distress.

Jo was still laughing as she crossed the living room into the kitchen, retrieving the cat's bowl from the corner where it had been kicked in all the commotion of the day before. Remembering just what a bizarre day it had been brought her up short for a moment and she glanced over to the front door where the crudely-fashioned makeshift replacement paid testament to the day's events.

Was that really me? Do I still have that violent animal inside me? She poured a handful of kibble into the bowl and placed it on the floor for Mephisto, crouching next to him and absentmindedly running her fingers through his fur as he tucked into the food. *So much has happened in the last 24 hours. So much that was awful.* She glanced toward the bedroom where she could hear Cadie pottering about, humming tunelessly to herself. *But she made it wonderful,* Jo thought with a smile. *All that horror, and she wiped it away with one touch and one word.*

She shook her head in disbelief and opened the fridge in search of the contents for a suitable breakfast-in-bed.

I can't get over the connection I feel with her, she thought as she pulled out mangoes, strawberries, and a couple of bananas. *It feels...old...and deep.*

A wave of melancholy washed through her as she began slicing the various fruits into bite-sized pieces and placing them on a platter.

Bottom line is it doesn't matter how connected we feel, she thought grimly. *In a few hours we'll be back to reality. Naomi will be breathing down Cadie's neck, and in less than two weeks that gorgeous blonde in my bedroom will disappear from my life like she was never here.* She tossed the knife into the sink with a satisfying clatter. *That kiss may have been a huge mistake, Jo-Jo. You're about to get your heart broken.*

Cadie emerged from the bathroom and took the opportunity to explore Jo's bedroom while the tall skipper was otherwise occupied in the kitchen.

She wandered around the large room, taking in the cool blue and green tones of the largely unadorned walls, and the few knick-knacks sitting on the crowded bookshelves. There was one picture of an older couple she assumed were Jo's parents, arm-in-arm outside a comfortable-looking white bungalow-style house. Apart from that there was nothing to indicate Jo had had a childhood of any sort. Cadie carefully picked up a foot-long clear bottle which held an exquisite model ship, the rigging and sails a mass of delicately executed ropes and spars.

This took hours and hours to make. Cadie gingerly replaced the bottle on its stand. *It's gorgeous.* She ran a finger across a row of books, taking in the titles and learning what she could about her tall companion. *Hmmm, science-fiction mainly. Biographies, Buddhism.* That raised her eyebrows a little. *And what's this?* Smiling broadly, Cadie pulled out a lesbian romance novel whose author was one of her own stable of talent. *Well, whaddaya know? Tall, dark, and dangerous is a sucker for romance.* She grinned as she slid the book back into its place.

The room was neat and well organized and reminded Cadie of the inside of the *Seawolf.*

Not surprising, I guess. Everything's tucked away and in its place. She smiled as she crawled back into the bed, sliding between the sheets and curling up in a patch of sunlight. *I know so little about her, but I feel like I've known her forever.* Her body shivered slightly at the memory of Jo's touch. *Yesterday was so...bizarre...that darkness that's in her—can I live with that?*

She snorted to herself, rolling back up into a sitting position and hugging her knees to her chest.

God, listen to me. Live with what? she chastised herself. *I'm thinking like I don't have another life. Damn...what am I going to do? Jo's become the most precious thing in the world to me, but it's all so complicated. And I'm not sure I want more complications in my life.*

A small tear escaped and rolled down Cadie's cheek as she rested her chin on her forearms. She sniffed mournfully and gazed out at the spectacular view of Whitsunday Passage.

She felt, rather than heard the quiet presence behind her and turned to see Jo holding a huge platter of fruit as she leaned against the doorjamb. The tall skipper looked worried.

"Hi," the blonde said quietly, brushing away the tears with a quick swipe of her hand.

"Hey," Jo replied. "You look like you could use a hug."

Cadie nodded, disconcerted to find her chin wobbling at the concern in Jo's eyes. The skipper sat down on the edge of the bed and reached over Cadie's legs to slide the platter onto the flat part of the mattress, out of the way. "C'mere, sweetie," the dark-haired woman said, wrapping the blonde up in long, willing arms. She ignored the ache from her injured arm as she rested her cheek on the top of Cadie's head and rocked her gently for a while. "What's up?"

Cadie laughed tearfully into Jo's neck. "Oh, nothing much. Just a few small little things. Like I'm not married to the person I'm in love with. And I am married to someone I don't think I even like much anymore." There was a pause as she gathered herself. "And...and...and in 10 days I have to go back to the States." The words rushed out.

Jo closed her eyes and grimaced, recognizing the pain behind Cadie's words and its mirror image in her own heart. But at the same time a soft, happy little chime sounded in her head. She pulled away from Cadie and ducked her head to catch the smaller woman's eye. "You're in love with me?" she asked, a lop-sided grin giving her a rakish air.

Moist green eyes managed a smile back at her. "Well, um, yes, I think I might be...yes," replied Cadie, feeling the blush rise across her face and neck. "I...um...sorry, that's probably the last thing you wanted to hear right now, what with everything else that I said last night..."

Jo lifted her chin with a gentle fingertip and deliberately locked gazes with the blonde.

"Do I look like I'm complaining?" she asked softly. "I'm glad you said it. I was hoping I wasn't the only one feeling that way." She smiled gently as Cadie looked up at her wonderingly.

"Wow," Cadie whispered. "That's nice to know."

"Mhmm," answered Jo as she leaned down to capture the American's lips in a soul-deep, intense kiss.

"God that feels good." Cadie took a few seconds to savor the feeling but soon Jo could again see the fear in those beautiful eyes.

"Honey—" she started, but Cadie's hands flew up to cover her face as panic overtook the blonde.

"Jesus, Jo-Jo, what are we going to do? This is a nightmare."

Jo sighed and pulled Cadie back into an all-enveloping hug.

"I'll tell you what we're going to do," she said fiercely. "For a start, we're going to live in the minute as much as we can. We

have the next few hours to ourselves. Let's take the opportunity to
ask and answer the million and one questions I know we have."
She felt Cadie nodding against her shoulder and acknowledged the
perceptible relaxation of the American's body. "Then we're going
to go back to the *Seawolf* and deal with reality as best we can."

Cadie whimpered softly and Jo chuckled.

"I know, baby. But then we're going to do exactly what you
said you needed to do last night."

"What's that?" came the muffled question.

"We're going to take it one step at a time, Arcadia. You're
going to work through all the loose ends with Naomi till you get
to a conclusion you can live with." Cadie nodded again. "And
then you're going to spend whatever time you need deciding what
you want to do next." Jo softly kissed the top of the blonde's
disheveled head. "And the bottom line is, darling, I'm not going
anywhere. You'll always know where to find me, if and when
you're ready to."

Jo knew she sounded brave and strong, but she felt a large
part of her heart crumbling under the reality of her own words.
There's a chance I may never see her again once she goes home.

"I love you," Cadie said quietly.

Jo smiled into the golden hair against her face. "I love you,
too," she replied.

Cadie patted the bed on her right-hand side where she could
still feel remnants of Jo's body heat. "Come back to bed?"

A few minutes later they were side by side again with the
platter of fruit between them. They each propped themselves up
on an elbow to eat their breakfast and occasionally they fed each
other a tasty morsel.

"You must have a lot of questions for me," Jo said after a
while, keeping her eyes studiously on the fruit. "Yesterday wasn't
exactly run of the mill."

"No it wasn't," Cadie agreed. *She's not comfortable with
this. She's ashamed of what she was. Let's see if I can make it
any easier.* "Tell me about the nightmare?"

Jo lifted faintly surprised eyes to Cadie's.

"I wasn't expecting you to start there," she admitted with a
small smile. "But it's as good a place as any. It harks back to the
day I started in the business and the day I decided to get out for
good."

"Okay," Cadie said, reaching for a piece of pineapple that was
calling her name.

"I used to work for a man called Tony Martin. He was the biggest drug dealer in Sydney at the time. I was what they used to call his 'minder.' In exchange for rather large amounts of money I would...eliminate...his competition, or people who had done the wrong thing by him."

"You would kill them?" Cadie asked quietly.

"Sometimes, yes," Jo replied, her face flushed and her eyes downcast. "Sometimes it was enough just to hurt them a bit, or scare them badly. But yes, sometimes I had to kill them.

"As time went on he had me take people out for less and less reason." Jo dropped onto her back and threw her right arm across her eyes. Cadie kept still and just let the dark-haired woman talk. "That last one..." She swallowed hard. "She was just a kid who made the mistake of giving him some cheek and re-selling some of the dope he'd given her for nothing." Cadie watched a tear slip from the corner of Jo's eye as she lay there. "She was like I had been 10 years earlier—scared and young and hungry."

Jo dropped her arm down by her side and stared at the ceiling. She sighed deeply.

"I chased her into an alley and held a gun to her head." She glanced over at Cadie who watched her somberly. "She had green eyes, too." Jo rolled onto her side and gazed up into the blonde's eyes. "Something clicked in my head—finally." She shook her head in wonder. "And I couldn't do it. But before I could let her go, our friend Marco came along and took care of us both."

Cadie swallowed the rising lump in her throat. "So she died anyway?"

Jo nodded mutely, playing with the piece of mango in her fingers. "He king-hit me then took her out with my own gun. When I came to, I lost it completely and called Harding. That was the beginning of the end."

Cadie leaned forward and gently took the mango sliver from Jo's fingers, reaching up and placing it against her bottom lip. "Eat, darling," she urged with a smile. Jo accepted the fruit, taking the opportunity to place a few delicate kisses on the blonde's fingertips as she did so. Cadie tried to ignore the run of tingles the action sent up her arm and all positions south. "You said the dream also connected to your first day in the business. Tell me more about that?"

Jo took a deep breath and let it out slowly. *Where do I start that story?*

Cadie chuckled at the perplexed look on her friend's face. "Honey, just start at the beginning." She smiled. "How did you end up in Sydney in the first place? I remember you said your parents own a sheep farm out in the country."

"Mhmm," Jo confirmed, relieved to have a specific question to answer. "It's pretty isolated out there. Our nearest neighbors were about an hour's drive away, and the nearest town was a couple more hours beyond that."

"Really?" Cadie blinked hard, trying to imagine those kinds of distances. "So the farm must be pretty big I guess?"

Jo smiled and nodded. "About 60,000 acres," she said and laughed at Cadie's wide-eyed reaction. "Anyway, there was just me, Mum, and Dad and a few jackaroos most of the year. A jackaroo is like a cowboy," she explained in answer to the quizzical look on the blonde's face. "And the shearers for a couple of months in early summer. So it was pretty quiet." She paused. "Really, really quiet."

"Where did you go to school?" the blonde asked.

"School of the Air," Jo replied. "That's where you do all your work by correspondence and then once a week you catch up with the teacher by radio."

"Wow, that's amazing. You didn't ever get to go to parties or dances, or stuff like that?"

"Oh, Mum and Dad did their best to get me to and from places when they could," Jo replied. "But they were working so hard just to keep the station afloat, you know? There was the occasional B and S but that was about it."

"B and S?"

Jo chuckled at the puzzled look on the American's face. "Bachelor and Spinster's Ball. All the single men and women from around the district drive for miles to have a dance in an old shed. Lots of bush dancing, lots of drinking, and a lot of sore heads in the morning," she explained. "Happens a couple of times a year. But I was a little young for those, according to Mum and Dad."

Cadie nodded.

"I was driving by the time I was 12, so that helped a bit, but then the more I mixed with kids my own age, the more I realized I was different from them," Jo said. She picked up a humungous strawberry and grinned wickedly at the American. "Remind you of anything?" she asked, twirling the fruit by its stalk and quirking an eyebrow at Cadie.

The blonde grinned back. "Why don't you tell me?" she teased.

"Lean forward and close your eyes," Jo said in her lowest, sexiest register.

"Ooo, God you should patent that voice, woman," muttered

Cadie, doing as she was told.

Jo pressed the narrow end of the strawberry against the blonde's lips.

"Open a little and kiss this," Jo whispered, mesmerized by the tantalizing way Cadie's lips surrounded the tip of the fruit. "Mmm, that's it. Now touch your tongue to it and stroke it slowly." She watched Cadie obey and then laughed as the blonde's eyes flew open. "I told you it would remind you of something," she teased.

Cadie responded by grabbing Jo's hand and slowly, sensually devouring the strawberry like it was a part of the taller woman's anatomy that she had coveted for a very long time. Jo felt her temperature rising as she watched the blonde make love to the fruit with her mouth. She swallowed, wondering if the desire she was feeling was as obvious to Cadie as it felt to her.

Clearly it was.

"That'll teach you to tease me," Cadie said smugly around the last remnants of the fruit. Jo leaned forward and kissed off the dribble of juice that slid down the American's chin.

"That'll teach you to tease *me*," Jo replied, smiling softly as she resumed her reclining position and licked her lips.

Cadie cleared her throat. "Where were we?" she asked huskily.

"Damned if I know." Jo laughed.

They both took a moment just to be together before Cadie refocused the conversation.

"You can drive at age 12 here?"

Jo laughed. "No, not legally," she said. "But out in the bush kids learn early so they can help out on the farm. Tractors, trucks, utes, you name it, I was driving it."

"Was that part of feeling different?" Cadie asked.

"Nah, all my friends did the same," Jo replied. "No, it was like...I felt much more self-aware than everyone else seemed to be. What free time I had away from my chores and my schoolwork, I spent reading. My folks were pretty good at making sure I got as wide an education as they could give me. So I wasn't a naïve kid at all. And from what contact I did have with other kids my age, it didn't take me very long to figure out that it was the girls who intrigued me and not the guys."

She and the blonde exchanged grins as they each remembered their own moments of revelation.

"Oh, I can relate to that," Cadie said. "I was at my junior prom in Madison, and I was dancing with a boy called Jimmy Hofsteder. He was shorter than me..."

"Hard to believe," Jo teased and ducked as Cadie flicked a wet slice of mango in her direction. "Hey, no fruit in the bed sheets."

"Brat." The blonde smiled. "Anyway, Jimmy was shorter than me, covered in zits and hair oil, and I found myself looking over his shoulder at Sally Doogan all night. That's when a clue ran in and bit me on the fanny."

Jo spluttered, almost choking on the mango slice. "Fanny?" she managed at last, coughing as she tried to catch her breath.

Cadie was perplexed. "Yeah. Fanny. As in, bit me on the butt," she said, wondering why her companion looked like she'd swallowed a whole chili pepper. She was even more confused seconds later when Jo started giggling hysterically.

"Whaaat?" she asked, poking the skipper in belly.

Jo recovered her composure enough to speak coherent English. "So," she said, wiping the tears away, "fanny means butt in America, huh?"

"Well, yeah," Cadie replied, a light beginning to dawn in her brain. "Why, what does it mean here?"

"Not that, that's for damn sure," Jo said, grinning like a Cheshire cat.

"Tell meee," the blonde pleaded. "Or I'm going to be forced to tickle you."

Jo snorted. "You'd have to catch me first," she replied, eyes widening as Cadie threatened to leap over the fruit platter and make good on her promise. "Okay, okay." Jo laughed. She beckoned with a finger and Cadie leaned across so Jo could whisper in her ear.

"You're kidding?" she asked when she pulled back. Jo shook her head, her smile wide. Cadie soon had a matching grin. "Well, what the hell do you call a fanny pack, then?" she asked, delighted when Jo dissolved into gales of laughter.

"A...a...bum bag," Jo gasped between convulsions.

That prompted a mini-explosion from the blonde and they both spent the next couple of minutes giggling helplessly.

"So," Jo asked as they recovered, side-by-side, leaning back against the headboard, "was she cute?"

"Who?"

"Sally Doogan."

Cadie laughed. "Not particularly, but she smelled way better than Jimmy Hofsteder, that's for darn sure."

Jo chuckled and leaned in to kiss the blonde again. "I, for one, am glad you figured it out," she said softly when they pulled back from each other. "Anyway, to cut a long story very short, I muddled my way through puberty, bored out of my mind. Sydney was like this great emerald city by the sea, you know?" Cadie nodded. "All roads seemed to lead there, most of my friends were trying to get there one way or another. It was like the pot of gold at the end of a very dry and dusty rainbow. We all had this romantic idea that if we could just get to Sydney then our lives would suddenly become glamorous and exciting."

She glanced at Cadie who was engrossed in the story. "But I was the only child of a third-generation farming family," Jo continued. "Mum and Dad wanted me to stay close to learn the business and for a while there I just didn't know how to tell them it wasn't for me."

"Something must have happened to change that," Cadie said softly. "What was it?"

Jo took another deep breath. "My best mate killed himself," she said simply, hearing the American's sharp intake of breath. "Phil...we were both 17 and he'd figured out he was gay too, so that kind of pulled us together, y'know?" Cadie nodded mutely. "He lived about 75 miles south of us so we didn't see each other too often, but we talked pretty much every day on the radio. Did our homework together, that sort of thing." She accepted another strawberry from the blonde and chewed on it thoughtfully.

"He was a tough kid, light of his Dad's life. But that summer his father caught him with one of the shearers and it was all over. Up until then Phil was heading for university—he wanted to be a doctor—but after that his parents told him he wasn't going anywhere. His dad said he'd rather have him on the property where he could keep an eye on him than risk him living a life of deviation." She saw Cadie's jaw drop. "Those were his exact words.

"Phil lasted about a week after that. I talked myself blue trying to buck him up. But one night he just went out to the big shed, took down his father's shotgun and..." The words stuck in Jo's throat and she fell silent, swallowing down sudden tears that surprised her so long after the event. She felt a soft hand on hers and looked up to meet kind sea-green eyes gazing back at her with sympathy.

"That's when I decided I had to get out. Phil and I had a lot in common and I guess I saw my future in what he did if I didn't do something pretty drastic to change things. So one night while Mum and Dad were sleeping I snuck out, threw my things in the back of the old ute and just...disappeared." She dropped her eyes, ashamed all over again of what she had done to her parents.

"It was as easy as that?" Cadie asked quietly.

"Sure," Jo shrugged. "I drove straight through the night,

dumped the ute the next morning once I hit a decent-sized town and hitched the rest of the way to Sydney. From there it was just a matter of blending in. There are thousands of street kids in that city, always have been. I was just one more face in the crowd."

"You lived on the streets?"

"Mhmm, for a while."

"Did you tell your parents where you were?"

"Not straight away," Jo murmured. "It was about a year before I felt established and that's when I called them." She paused. "I really regret waiting so long."

Cadie looked at her quizzically.

"Dad had a heart attack after I left because of the stress of not knowing what had happened to me," Jo continued. "They nearly lost the farm because they had to pay for extra hands to do what he couldn't anymore. By then I was earning money so I offered to send some back to help them out. But they wouldn't accept anything from me. I'll never make up for the pain I caused them."

Cadie squeezed Jo's hand and then kissed the palm softly. "So how did you get off the streets and into a job?" she asked.

"Tony found me."

"This is the bit that relates to the nightmare, right?"

Jo laughed wryly. "I have taken a while to get back to that, haven't I?" She paused for a moment to gather her memories together. "When you live on the streets of Sydney, you're never too far away from the drug scene. I managed to avoid using the stuff—that kind of thing had never appealed to me much. But guys like Tony made good use of street kids. He paid good money to me to make deliveries and run errands. If there's one thing a street kid needs more than food and shelter it's a few extra dollars in the pocket. So I played the game.

"Trouble is Marco had other things in mind for me. One night he cornered me—just like I cornered that girl five years ago—only he wasn't out to kill me."

Cadie gasped. "Oh God, Jo, he didn't..."

Jo smiled wanly. "He certainly tried," she answered quietly. "Tony intervened, luckily for me, and gave Marco a beating for his trouble."

"No wonder he came after you," Cadie said.

"I'm surprised he waited as long as he did, frankly," Jo replied, wincing as she shifted, catching the bandage around her arm on the bed sheet.

Cadie noticed. "Where's the first aid kit, Jo?" she asked. "I'm going to change the dressing on your arm."

"It's okay," Jo demurred.

"Don't argue with me, okay? Where is it?"

Jo smiled, relenting. *A little pampering wouldn't do me any harm. It's been a long time since anybody wanted to.* "I put it back in the main bathroom," she replied.

"Stay right where you are," Cadie ordered, swinging her legs out of the bed and bounding out of the room.

Jo lay back on the bed, gazing up at the ceiling. Dredging up all the old memories was giving her the strangest sensations. *I haven't thought of Phil in the longest time,* she realized. *I wonder how his folks are doing.* She struggled to pull their faces out of her memory banks.

Shortly, Cadie was back, clambering up onto the bed again, first aid kit in hand. "Come on, turn over, so I can get at it," she said. Jo sat up and turned around, lifting the right arm of her t-shirt so the blonde could remove the old bandage. Carefully Cadie started peeling the fabric free, wincing a little in sympathy as the dried blood caught and pulled. "Ouch, sorry," she muttered.

"No worries," Jo replied, gritting her teeth.

"So what happened after Tony rescued you from Marco?" Cadie asked.

Jo sighed, another flood of memories sweeping over her. "He took me off the streets and handed me over to the kung fu school," she said.

"Kung fu school?"

"Yeah. Tony ran a martial arts academy in the middle of King's Cross. By day, the instructors took classes, and by night they patrolled the streets in pairs."

"Why'd they do that?"

"Well, ostensibly they were doing the community a service. You know, keeping the streets safe and all that." Cadie nodded. "But in reality it was a protection racket. Restaurant and store owners paid Tony a fee and in exchange he didn't torch their buildings, or let anyone else torch them. Damn, that smarts."

Cadie stopped cleaning the wound for a second. "Sorry, there's a bit of infection in here, Jo-Jo. Are you sure we shouldn't have a doctor look at this?" She carefully prodded again at the angry-looking graze with a cotton bud.

Jo pulled a face as she tried to get a good view of the wound. "No," she said. "It'll just mean a needle for me and a ton of paperwork for the doctor."

"Don't tell me a big, strong girl like you is a wimp about needles," Cadie teased, resuming her careful exploration of the swollen edges of the cut.

Jo raised an eyebrow and shrugged her shoulders slightly. "Actually, yeah. Can't help it. Lays me out flat every time." She watched as the American started to rewrap the wound. "Anyway...Tony installed me at the kung fu school, gave me a roof over my head, and kept me well away from Marco. I showed a bit of talent for martial arts and he began grooming me to be his personal bodyguard. He was getting to the age where he didn't think he could protect himself enough. And he didn't quite trust Marco."

Cadie finished wrapping a fresh bandage around Jo's arm. "I take it by 'a bit of talent' that you were actually kicking everyone else's butt?" she asked.

"Yeah, I guess so," Jo muttered. "If I'd known where it would lead...I don't know, maybe it would have been different..." For a few moments she seemed lost in a haze of memories.

Cadie fixed the end of the bandage with a clip and gently patted the Australian's arm. "All done." She watched as Jo glumly swung back around and lay down on her back again. Cadie picked up the now-empty platter and carefully placed it on the bedside table before resuming her spot next to the dark-haired woman. She propped herself on an elbow and looked down at Jo.

"Thanks," Jo said looking up into Cadie's smiling face. "Why isn't any of this bothering you?"

Cadie thought carefully about her answer for a few seconds. "Because I don't think that's who you are anymore," she answered. "Because I'm not sure it's who you really were then either. Because something...God, I'm not even sure what...tells me that you're a good person, no matter what you've done in the past." She paused again as a small piece of truth floated up through her consciousness. "And because I just feel safe with you." She shrugged her shoulders and grinned down at her companion. "Don't ask me to explain it all beyond that, darling, because I don't think I can."

Jo suddenly found herself fighting tears. "You're an amazing woman, Arcadia Jones," she whispered.

"I'm in love with an amazing woman, Jo-Jo," came the soft reply. Cadie leaned down and claimed the taller woman's lips for a deep kiss.

Jo melted at the touch, retaining just enough sense to wrap her arms around the blonde and pull her down on top of her. She felt Cadie relax against her and together they deepened the contact into something that lasted minutes rather than seconds. She groaned softly, reveling in the feeling of giving herself over to another person. Cadie's hands roamed her body, sliding slowly up under her t-shirt and Jo arched against her as sensuality radiated out from the blonde's teasing touch.

Cadie could hardly believe the silky softness of Jo's skin, hard muscles rippling just under the surface, speaking of power and control that she found intriguingly sexy. She felt Jo press her thigh between her own and they both moaned as bare skin came up against warm wetness.

The blonde teetered on the brink of just throwing away all rational thought, every care she had for the sake of the passion that threatened to overtake them both. For a moment she hesitated, and then she went limp, whimpering in the dark, warm nest formed by Jo's neck and her hair.

Cadie felt the vibration of a deep, rumbling chuckle from the woman beneath her and she smiled at the skipper's good-natured response. Long arms wrapped her up in a tight hug and Jo kissed her temple softly.

"I'm driving you nuts, aren't I?" the blonde asked wistfully, willing her body's reactions to settle.

"Yes." Jo laughed. "But I understand." She squeezed the smaller woman gently. "God help us the day we get to take this through to its natural conclusion." She grinned.

Cadie looked up at her quizzically. "What do you mean?"

Jo laughed again. "I may just spontaneously combust," she joked.

That brought a belly laugh from the woman in her arms and soon they were giggling hysterically again.

"Oh dear," Cadie gulped, wiping tears from her eyes. "Oh, that felt good. That's one of the things I love about being with you, Jo." She smiled fondly at the dark-haired woman. "You have this knack for making me laugh."

Jo said nothing but took the opportunity to roll them both over, till she was sprawled half on the bed and half over the blonde. She rested her cheek on Cadie's breast, her arm wrapped firmly around the smaller woman. She felt Cadie enfold her in a hug, one hand stroking slowly through her hair. Jo felt a surge of well being that connected her to the American in a way she hadn't experienced with anyone else before.

"I've never felt this good," she half-whispered, making Cadie wonder if she'd heard correctly. "Whatever happens, I'll be forever grateful for the time we've had."

Cadie bit her lip, trying not to succumb to the tears she could hear just under the surface of Jo's words. "I will be back," she whispered back. "I don't know when, but I will be back. I promise."

"Shhh," Jo said, turning and placing a gentle finger on Cadie's lips. "Don't, darling. Don't make promises. Too much has to happen. Let's just take each day as it comes."

"Scary thought," Cadie muttered. "I don't do real well without a plan." She caught Jo's eye as the tall woman raised an amused eyebrow. "I know, I know, loosen up Arcadia."

Jo shook her head. "No, that wasn't what I was going to say. I was thinking just how well you *are* doing given the complete chaos of the last 24 hours," she said.

"Well," Cadie said changing the subject, "you must have a bazillion questions for me. Though I have to warn you, my life is nowhere near as eventful as yours has been."

Jo rolled off the smaller woman and propped herself up on an elbow. "From what I've seen, I like your life just fine," she said, gazing down at the American.

"Ask away." Cadie smiled back up at her.

"I guess the immediate question that springs to mind is how did you and Naomi manage to get together in the first place?" Jo asked. "You're so different from each other, it's hard for me to picture what drew you together."

Cadie sighed and let her eyes drift to the ceiling, even as she felt Jo's soothing hand drawing gentle circles on her stomach.

"We've both changed," she said simply. "Naomi probably more than me, but I've grown up a lot as well." She settled into the story and regained Jo's eyes, finding them interested and sympathetic. "Have I told you lately that you have the most beautiful eyes I have ever seen, Ms Madison?" She was charmed by the fetching blush that colored Jo's face highlighting her high-planed cheekbones and angular jaw.

"Back at you, Miss Jones," Jo replied huskily. "Now get on with the story." She grinned.

"I can't help it if I'm distracted by your gorgeousness, can I?" Cadie giggled at the renewed color in Jo's cheeks, but soon squealed as the Australian's gentle touch turned into tickling. She wondered at the barely-suppressed strength in the way Jo contained her squirming body, inflicting delicious torture. "Okay, okay, uncle!" Cadie yelped.

Jo relented, a wickedly cheeky grin splitting her face from ear to ear. Cadie caught her breath and relaxed back against the pillows.

"Okay," she said, regaining her composure. "Absolutely nothing interesting happened to me at high school. Jimmy Hofsteder didn't last long." She grinned at Jo who chuckled in reply. "But I didn't do anything about my feelings about girls until I was

at college." She paused, wondering just how much Jo knew about
the college system in the US. "I moved out of Madison for that,"
she explained. "I got into Northwestern University in Chicago."

"What were you studying?"

"English literature and art history," Cadie replied. "Which
guaranteed I graduated with the world's most useless degree."

"What were you planning to do with it?"

"All I really knew was that I didn't want to teach. Through
high school my English teachers kept telling me that I should
write, but I could never come up with anything original to write
about."

She was distracted by Jo's finger lazily tracing her lips, triggering a delicious wave of sensation. Cadie took the opportunity
to softly suck the fingertip into her mouth, watching as Jo's eyes
widened, riveted on the blonde's mouth.

"You are so wicked," Jo rumbled. "Maybe you should write
lesbian erotica. You certainly seem to have a knack for it." Gently she withdrew her finger, with a sigh. "God...I'm sorry...I
didn't mean to interrupt you."

Cadie cleared her throat. "I don't mind, trust me," she
replied huskily. "Anyway, I met Naomi in my freshman year at
NWU. That's the first year," she explained at Jo's quizzical look.
"She was a senior."

"That's the fourth year, yeah?"

"Mhmm. She was doing a government and economics
degree."

"Makes sense," Jo said.

"She was a lot different from the person you see now," Cadie
said wistfully. "Any cause that was going, Naomi was up for it.
Student politics, homeless kids, gay rights, national and foreign
policy...you name it, Naomi was campaigning for it. It was kind
of mesmerizing to watch her in action. Inspiring, in many ways."

Jo nodded.

"She's the one who got me interested in politics. There used
to be weekly debates and forums around the campus and Naomi
was always one of the best speakers. I got involved as a volunteer
and one Friday afternoon she noticed me." Cadie shrugged her
shoulders. "That's more or less where it started."

"When did you decide to become a literary agent?" Jo asked.

"Oh, not for quite a while. We both come from pretty privi-
leged backgrounds, so money wasn't really an issue for us, even
early on. By the time I graduated, Naomi was done with law
school and was practicing with one of the big firms in Chicago. It
wasn't too long after that when she decided to make a career out

of politics."

Jo noted the look of quiet sadness on the blonde's face. "Is that something you regret?" she wondered.

Cadie thought for a while before answering. "She was a good politician in those days," she said. "She went into it for the right reasons—I mean she really wanted to change things for people, you know?" Jo nodded her understanding. "And I was very happy to do my bit."

"So you worked for her?"

"Mhmm. For the first few years I worked full-time for whatever campaign she was running. I was the secretary, publicist, speech writer, and gopher all wrapped into one. It was fun." She smiled at the memories of rallies and victory speeches.

"So, when did it stop being fun?"

"Good question," Cadie replied. She rolled onto her stomach and flung an arm over Jo's chest, snuggling into the crook of the taller woman's arm. Mephisto appeared out of nowhere and curled up in a ball on Jo's belly. Both women reached out to stroke him, their fingers tangling together as they met.

"I guess I started to grow up," Cadie reflected. "I started wanting something for myself. By then Naomi was running for Governor." She sighed deeply. "She always blamed me for losing that one, even though she was by far the youngest candidate to try."

Jo looked down at the blonde sharply. "Why on earth would she blame you?" she asked.

"Because that was the first campaign I didn't work on full-time. I'd set up the agency by then and was working pretty hard to establish myself. Naomi felt like I wasn't doing what I promised to do back when we first got together."

Jo snorted. "Shit happens," she muttered. "Life happens. People change and grow."

"I know," Cadie said. "But losing that campaign was the start of the big changes I started to see in Naomi. It suddenly became much more serious. Early on, when she was winning—and winning easily—politics was about helping people. She could afford to have fun with it. But later it became about making Naomi feel good. Her self-esteem became invested in winning, I suppose. I guess I kind of still feel guilty about that."

Jo squeezed the blonde gently. "Don't do that, Cadie," she urged. "You're not responsible for her happiness, I don't care how married you are." She felt the smaller woman go very still in her arms.

"My head knows that," Cadie whispered. "But part of me

feels like if I'd just stayed involved full-time then maybe the whole drugs thing wouldn't have happened."

Jo couldn't bear hearing the self-blame in the American's voice any longer and she pulled her up so they could look in each other's eyes. "Cadie, answer me a question?" She waited for the blonde's tentative nod. "Why did you feel the need to start your own business?"

Cadie blinked a few times as she searched for an answer, her eyes glassy as she cast her mind back, trying to recapture her feelings at the time. "It was like I was disappearing," she said softly. "I was the quiet, behind-the-scenes half of this thing called Naomi-and-Cadie. Everyone saw the politician, but nobody ever saw me. I can remember waking up one morning and knowing that if I didn't find something I wanted to do, I would just fade away to nothing."

Jo smiled at her. "So don't beat yourself up for doing something that was essential to your survival as a happy individual," she said, leaning forward to emphasize her point with a soft kiss on Cadie's willing lips. "And one thing's for certain, Naomi sure as hell thinks of your happiness a lot less than you worry about hers."

Cadie nodded silently.

"Tell me about the drugs?" Jo asked.

"I don't really know if it's been going on for a long time and I just haven't noticed, or if it's a relatively new thing in her life," Cadie said sadly. "About halfway through her first term in the Senate—about two and a half years ago, I guess—she started coming home much later, taking more trips, having meetings at weird times of night...that kind of thing." She caught Jo's eye. "Don't get me wrong, US senators lead busy lives, at least while the Senate is in session, so I never really expected to see much of her. But this was a bit different. When she was home she was foul-tempered and on a hair trigger most of the time."

"Does she use at home?"

Cadie shook her head. "Not that I've ever been able to find," she replied. "To be honest, for a long time I thought she was having an affair. And then New Year's Eve happened and I realized that if she wasn't using drugs, she was at least condoning her friends' use of them, if not supplying them."

Jo's eyes widened. "What happened on New Year's Eve?"

"We were hosting a cocktail party. Kelli was as high as a kite and told me that Naomi had made a never-ending supply of cocaine available to anyone who wanted it."

"Holy shit," Jo muttered.

"Yeah, that's pretty much what I said," Cadie answered. "She denied it, of course, and somehow managed to make it my bad for even suspecting it. And things have been pretty awful between us ever since."

"I'm surprised she didn't offer to cut you in," Jo muttered, increasingly irritated with the senator.

"I'm not," Cadie said. "She may have long since stopped knowing me, Jo, but on this subject she knew damn well I would be immovable. Ever since—"

She stopped, silenced by the familiar lump in her throat whenever she thought of that time.

"Ever since what, sweetheart?" Jo asked softly, seeing that Cadie was lost in some distant and none too happy memory.

The blonde swallowed and lifted her eyes to the gentle blue ones of her companion.

"I had a brother," she almost whispered. The skipper caught the break in her voice and gathered the smaller woman up into the softest, safest hug she could muster. "His name was Sebastian and he was 10 years older than me," Cadie continued. "He was my best buddy." She smiled into Jo's neck and the dark-haired woman felt it and smiled with her.

"When I was eight and he was 18 he went away to college, but that last summer we spent almost every day together." Cadie sat up and faced Jo, beaming with the happy memories. "He was the sweetest guy, Jo. He would take me camping, and sailing on the lake. And he bought me an ice-cream every single afternoon on his way home from his summer job."

Jo grinned, captivated by the blonde's descriptions and the childlike glow as she recalled her sibling. "He sounds like a sweetheart."

Cadie nodded. "The last day before he went away to college, he gave me his high school letterman jacket, and told me that I would always be his best girl, no matter what. He wrote me a letter every week." She fell silent, drifting away again on the memories.

"What happened?"

Cadie sighed. "We don't really know for sure. He was at a fraternity party. One minute he was playing pool with some friends and the next...well, they said he sat down for a minute, and when they turned around to tell him it was his turn to play, he was dead where he sat."

Jo reached for Cadie again, pulling her close and wrapping her up tightly. "I'm sorry," she whispered.

Cadie nodded.

"The coroner said there were high levels of LSD and other drugs in his bloodstream, though his friends always denied there were any drugs at the party. But apparently, that combined with the alcohol...he choked to death on his own vomit." Her voice caught again and she buried her face in Jo's t-shirt. "And...and...nobody knew what was happening to him. He never made a sound."

The tears came freely now, and Jo stayed quiet, rocking the smaller woman until the sobs subsided.

"Oh boy," Cadie sighed. "I haven't done that in a long time. I'm sorry."

"Shhh, don't be," Jo replied. "Thank you for telling me about him."

"He's a big part of me. And I want you to know everything there is to know," Cadie said, sniffling and dabbing at the damp patch she left on Jo's t-shirt.

Jo reached up and cupped Cadie's cheek with a gentle palm, picking up a tear on the tip of her thumb. "And I want to know everything," she murmured.

Cadie smiled wanly and leaned forward into Jo's touch until their lips were almost in contact. "I love you, Jo," she breathed.

To the Australian it felt like she was inhaling pure love, an intoxicating sensation. The kiss laid them both bare like never before. Jo felt herself opening emotionally as the contact between them deepened and intensified in a way that left her breathless and teary. When they broke off she hugged the blonde fiercely.

"Ohhh, Cadie, I love you, too," she said. "Ten days ago..." They pulled apart and looked at each other, both sporting disbelieving grins. "I didn't even know you. Now I'm struggling to know how it's going to be once you've gone again."

"Let's not go there," Cadie said quickly, silencing Jo with a finger across her lips. "We've got another week and a half. I don't want to think beyond that. At least not yet. Please?"

Jo nodded and Cadie moved to straddle the tall woman's hips, easing forward to be cradled in Jo's arms against her chest.

"I don't even want to get out of this bed," the blonde mumbled. "It's like our own little bubble of safety." Jo smiled at the analogy, and squeezed Cadie closer. "It's chaos out there and I don't want to move."

"Mmm, neither do I," Jo replied, scratching under Mephisto's chin with her big toe.

For a few more minutes the couple just lay in each other's arms, watching the sun climb higher in the sky over the islands. *This is bliss,* thought Jo, closing her eyes against the heat. *I want time to slow down so each second lasts a minute. I don't ever want to forget any of this.* She lightly scratched Cadie's back in slow circles, feeling the blonde almost purring under her touch.

"That feels so good it ought to be illegal," Cadie murmured, kissing the hollow at the base of Jo's neck softly. *Please God, don't let this be the last time I feel her arms around me.* She felt Jo sigh deeply. "We have to get moving, don't we?"

"'Fraid so," Jo replied. "My bet is that Bill will show up any minute, and then there's Josh and Harding to visit before we head back to the *Seawolf.*"

"Damn..."

A few hours later they were skidding across the waters of the Whitsunday Passage in a water taxi, part of a fleet which ran people and cargo to and from the islands several times a day. Jo had chartered one especially to get her and Cadie back to the *Seawolf,* which was still anchored off the southern tip of Whitsunday Island. The couple sat in the spartan cabin, looking out salt-smeared windows at the pristine day.

The morning had been in steady decline since they'd left the house up on Shute Harbor hill. *The hour we spent with Josh and his parents was awkward, but we all survived,* Cadie reflected. *It was the meeting with Harding that put Jo's mood into a spiral.*

"So, he said you wouldn't have to testify for a while?" Cadie asked, turning to Jo, who had been very quiet behind her sunglasses.

"Yeah, at least six weeks or so, he thinks," the tall skipper replied shortly. "Apparently Marco was still in surgery well after midnight and it's going to be quite a while before he's fit to sit up, let alone go through a trial." Her tone was grim and she kept looking out to sea, unwilling to look at Cadie.

"Stop it, Jo," the blonde said quietly.

"Stop what?" she replied absently, steadfastly watching a yacht away to their starboard side.

"Whatever it is that you're doing to yourself inside your head," Cadie said, reaching for Jo's arm and pulling her around to face her. "Stop it. You did what you had to do."

Jo snorted. "Right. And that included neutering the guy just for the sheer hell of it? I don't think so." Jo jerked away from Cadie, stalking out of the cabin to the stern of the boat and leaning on the rail.

The blonde sighed and walked after her. She came up along-side the taller woman and leaned back against the rail, focusing her eyes on the boat's only crewman who was up in the cockpit above the cabin. "Jo, you told me this morning that Marco once tried to rape you. You couldn't have been much more than...what? Seventeen or 18?" She turned to see Jo nodding. "Do you really think you're the only young girl he's ever tried that with? Or that every other one he tried it with was as lucky as you were that day?"

Jo looked down into the water being churned by the boat's propellers, her thoughts swirling along with the wash. "So you're saying that he deserved what I did to him?" she asked quietly. "That's kind of Old Testament don't you think?"

Cadie turned, looping her arm around Jo's and sliding her fingers into the dark-haired woman's hand. "Maybe so. But think about this. Even if he wants to ever try that again he's not going to be able to do much about it."

Jo looked down at Cadie. *There's so much about that world she'll never understand. And I'm glad for that. I don't want her to know any more than she has to.* "Rape isn't about sex, Cadie," she said out loud. "It's about power. What he can't do with his penis, he'll do with his fists, or his gun, or...or whatever he wants to use to beat up the next young girl he wants to break."

Cadie shook her head. "Not for the foreseeable future, Jo-Jo. You're about to put him in jail for a very long time." She leaned in and kissed the skipper softly. "Let it go, honey. It's over with, at least until you have to testify. Marco's an asshole. And yes, I think he got what he deserved." She planted another resounding kiss on Jo's lips. "So there."

Jo couldn't help but smile at the blonde's efforts to cheer her up.

"That was nice of Bill to offer to stay at the house," Cadie continued, determined to get Jo's mind away from self-recriminations.

Jo accepted the change of subject graciously, pulling Cadie down on to the bench across the stern next to her and draping an arm across the blonde's shoulders.

"Mhmm. Can't really blame Josh's parents for not wanting him to go back there," she replied. "At least they seem to have accepted the burglary thing."

Cadie nodded. "Well it helped that Josh didn't go into too many details about just who rescued him."

"I think Harding might have had something to do with that. I'll have a good long talk with Josh when this trip is over," said Jo. That thought sobered them both and they fell silent. The only sounds were the rushing wind, the muffled roar of the engine and the slapping of the boat's hull against the chop.

Jo looked around to get her bearings, realizing they were only a few minutes from rendezvousing with the *Seawolf.* "We don't have much time left, sweetheart," she said, turning to face Cadie and taking the blonde's hands in hers. "You ready?"

"No," Cadie said honestly. She sighed. "But I guess I will be if you kiss me one more time before reality hits."

Jo smiled and leaned closer. "I think I can manage that," she whispered, capturing the blonde's lips with her own and surrendering all her concentration to the kiss.

Cadie melted into the contact, trying to forget that it could be the last she shared with this remarkable woman. Instead she focused on the intense sensations.

They began tenderly, almost tentatively exploring each other, but soon they were lost in passion, using their lips and tongues instead of words to convey the depth of their emotions. To Cadie it felt as if the world contracted around them, nothing else existing but the woman who held her close. Jo's lips were soft but insistent, her tongue gentle but sexy, and her arms safe and strong.

Several minutes passed as the kiss waxed and waned, moist and warm and filled with aching tenderness. When they finally broke off they both had tears in their eyes.

Cadie looked up into eyes so blue they rivaled the cloudless sky above them. She caught her breath raggedly. "I don't know how I'm going to survive the next 10 days, Jossandra," she said softly, trying to control the wobble she felt in her chin. "I don't know how—"

"Sshhh..." Jo took the blonde's face in her hands, green eyes blinking at her wetly. "We can do this, darling. We can." She felt a tear sliding down her own cheek, but didn't want to let go of Cadie to wipe it away. Instead the blonde reached up and brushed at it with a gentle fingertip. "Stay strong, my love. Things will work out."

Cadie couldn't speak, so she just nodded, holding Jo's gaze for as long as she could.

"Jo-Jo, we're coming up on the *Seawolf,*" the water taxi's skipper yelled over his shoulder.

The look continued between the two women despite the interruption, but slowly they moved apart on the bench until their fingers were barely touching, invisible to anyone on the fast-approaching yacht.

"I love you, Cadie, never forget that," Jo said as the water taxi maneuvered to come alongside the *Seawolf.*

Finally their eyes unlocked and their fingertips brushed each other one last time as they turned to face the passengers waving at them from the deck of the yacht.

"I'll never forget it, Jo," Cadie murmured under her breath to the skipper, even as she waved back and smiled at the others.

Chapter
Ten

Of all the welcomes Cadie had imagined, being swept up into an all-encompassing senatorial bear hug was the most unexpected. She felt herself lifted off her feet as Naomi squeezed her.

"Welcome back, darling," effused the senator, putting Cadie down and planting a resounding kiss on her shorter partner's lips. "It's good to have you back. I missed you."

Cadie cringed, painfully aware of Jo turning away from the scene and making a show of greeting Jenny and Paul.

"Hello, Naomi," Cadie replied, fighting the urge to struggle out of the senator's grip. *What is with this? Yesterday she was screaming at me on the telephone and today she's all over me. What gives?*

"I was worried about you," Naomi continued, guiding Cadie to a seat in the cockpit. "When Paul told us how Jo had disturbed a burglar at her house, I was concerned. Are you all right?" She looked the blonde up and down, her expression all concern and care as she sat down next to Cadie.

"Yes, Naomi, I'm fine," she replied. "And it wasn't Jo who disturbed the burglar, it was Josh, the young man who was looking after Jo's house for her." She decided to stick with the same story they'd come up with for Josh's parents. "We got there at the same time as the police and they handled it."

"Well, that's grand," Naomi said, patting Cadie's thigh and casually leaving her hand there. "Look, I'm very sorry about my attitude on the phone last night. But, as you can understand, I was scared out of my wits for you." She smiled winningly and looked Cadie in the eye. The blonde felt herself squirming inside.

"It's okay," she mumbled. "Forget about it."

"In fact," the senator continued, "while I'm in the mood to apologize, I'm going to go and tell Jo the same thing, while you settle back in." Before Cadie could object, Naomi bustled off in search of the skipper.

"Look out, Jo," Cadie muttered to herself. "Here comes Hurricane Silverberg." She watched anxiously as Naomi accosted the

tall skipper. She could see Jo's face over the senator's shoulder
and at one point caught her eye, trying to smile in reassurance.
Jo's expression clouded over as the senator shook her hand.

Jo watched the senator hurrying towards her with a large
degree of trepidation. Like Cadie, she had been surprised by the
friendliness of Naomi's welcome, and had stuffed the unexpected
pang of jealousy deep down. But now there was no avoiding the
senator's approach.

Welcome back to real life, Jo-Jo, she thought as Naomi closed
in.

"Skipper, I want to thank you personally for looking after my
partner so well," gushed the senator, placing one hand on Jo's
shoulder and pulling her away from Paul and Jenny. "I know you
were in a difficult situation but she tells me you did everything
possible to keep her safe and happy."

I certainly did. But I'll bet you don't want to hear that. "It
was no trouble, honestly," she said aloud. "I'm the one who
should be thanking her for tagging along when my personal life
was intruding on her vacation."

"Not at all, not at all," Naomi said, grinning from ear to ear.
"It was good of you to keep doing your job in the face of such
problems. And just to show my gratitude..." She reached forward
and shook Jo's hand, pressing a $100 bill into the taller woman's
palm.

Jo caught Cadie's eye over the senator's shoulder and tried to
keep her expression light. But then Naomi leaned forward.

"You really went above and beyond the call of duty, Miss
Madison," she said quietly, and this time Jo saw the glint of something entirely different in the senator's brown eyes.

*And if I do it again I'll be at the bottom of the ocean wearing
cement boots, is what she's really telling me,* thought Jo, keeping a
tight rein on her temper. "Really," she said, trying to keep her
voice calm. "There's no need. And we don't accept cash gratu-
ities." She tried to hand the money back.

Again the senator leaned in, this time her manner infinitely
more menacing. "Consider it payment for services rendered," she
growled, her fingers now biting into Jo's shoulder painfully. Suddenly she released her grip and smiled broadly again, before turning on her heel and heading back towards Cadie.

Jo grimly fought down the urge to throw something large and
solid at the back of the senator's retreating head. Instead she
looked down at the bill in her hand. *Well, that's put me firmly*

back in my place, hasn't it? Angrily she stuffed the money into her shorts pocket and turned back to Paul and Jenny who had watched the conversation.

"What the hell was that all about, Skipper?" the tall man asked bemusedly. "She's been as mad as a cut snake from the minute she found out Cadie was with you. Now suddenly everything's sunshine and happiness."

Jo tried to brush it off. "Beats the hell out of me, Paulie," she replied with a wan smile.

"She hung on to my cell phone after she had a go at you last night," Paul admitted. "Said it was some kind of personal emergency. I didn't see it again for an hour." He saw the grim look on Jo's face and hastily apologized. "Sorry, Skip, but I figured the customer is always right, y'know?"

Jo patted the tall man's shoulder. "Forget it. You didn't have any choice." A slimy thought snaked its way around Jo's brain. "You got it with you now?"

He reached around and pulled the phone off his hip, handing it to her.

"Thanks." Jo flipped through the phone's menu items, searching for the option that stored the calls made. "God damn it," she muttered. "Whatever calls she made, she's wiped the memory." She handed the phone back to Paul, who had a puzzled look on his face.

Jo smiled at him, shaking her head. "Nothing, Paulie. I'm just getting paranoid in my old age." She looked around the deck and tried to clear her head of any negative thoughts. "Let's get her ready, eh? I want to motor back around to the beach."

"Okay, Jo-Jo."

Jo looked around, spotting Cadie still sitting in the cockpit, the senator sticking to her like glue. The skipper caught herself grinding her teeth. *So, the good senator is going to play the saint. No doubt she'll use that winning smile any way she can.* The beginnings of a vicious headache thumped at her temples. *Fuck this. Just gotta get on with it and take it all as it comes.* With a sigh she walked back to the cockpit, where most of the passengers were gathering for lunch.

"Okay people, let's make a move," Jo said as she jumped into the pit and reached for the engine cover. "I'm suggesting we motor back around to the beach. That should take about half an hour and then we can set up lunch on the sand. What do you think?"

She glanced around at the nodding heads, trying not to notice the senator's hand gripping Cadie's knee possessively. "Sounds like a wonderful idea, Jo," the senator said with a wide smile.

"Right then," Jo said and took a deep breath. "Let's go."

The cabin door clicked behind her and Cadie had the bad feeling she was trapped like a fly in a spider's web. She turned around to face her partner, who was looking decidedly green around the gills.

"Are you okay?" Cadie asked quietly, sitting down in the corner chair.

"No," Naomi grumbled, staggering a little against the rolling of the boat as she made her way to the bed. "This goddamn boat is a freaking bucket." She sat quickly and held her head in her hands.

"It's just because we're wallowing while we find an anchorage, Nay," Cadie muttered. "It'll be steady soon."

"It had better," the senator growled. "This vacation has been a fucking torture test. Never again, I swear."

Cadie said nothing, preferring to see where this conversation was going. Naomi could have come below decks alone when she started feeling ill, but instead had insisted on Cadie's company. That meant only one thing.

The rattling of the anchor chain sliding overboard could be heard forward. "So," Naomi said, sitting up as the boat finally ceased its rolling. "Did you enjoy your little adventure?" All semblance of good humor had deserted the senator's face. What was left was not pleasant.

"Nay, why don't you just say whatever is on your mind?" Cadie asked wearily. "Because I'm not really in the mood for playing these games."

The senator moved faster than Cadie could have believed possible. Within a blink of an eye, Naomi was almost on top of her, grabbing the blonde's chin in a cruel grip. Cadie gasped and pressed back in the chair, trying to get away from her partner's intense stare.

"Games, Cadie?" the senator spat, almost nose to nose with the smaller woman. Suddenly her gaze softened, as did her hand, the vice-like grip on Cadie's chin turning into a slow caress. She leaned closer, her lips just brushing the blonde's cheek. "I don't think I'm the one playing games, my love," Naomi whispered.

Cadie stayed silent, the hairs on the back of her neck rising as Naomi's fingers stroked along her jaw and into her hair.

"Did she get this close, Arcadia?"

The senator's hot breath brushed Cadie's earlobe. She swallowed hard and tried not to let her panic show.

"Your silence is telling me a lot, darling," Naomi continued as she dropped light kisses down the blonde's neck. "My guess is you've had yourself quite a night."

Cadie stiffened as she felt Naomi's hands roaming over her body, the stocky senator's leg forcing itself between her thighs. "Don't, Naomi," Cadie muttered.

"Oh come on now," the senator purred. "I know how much you love to be touched here." She kissed Cadie's neck again. "Nobody knows you like me, sweetheart."

This time a hand slid up the inside of Cadie's thigh and the smaller woman tried to pull away from the contact.

"Ah ah ah, Arcadia," Naomi growled, slipping her hand higher and wrapping fingers around the top of Cadie's leg. "Don't fight me darling. All I want to do is make sure you know the kind of person you spent the night with."

"You know nothing about her, Naomi," Cadie said through gritted teeth, turning her head away from the senator's baleful, close scrutiny.

"Oh but you see, I do," Naomi replied.

Cadie steeled herself and turned back to stare Naomi in the eye. "What happened to you?" she whispered, tears stinging her eyes. "I don't know who you are anymore. What happened to the woman I fell in love with?" She felt the tear slide down her cheek, and for a moment she thought she saw something lost and fearful flicker across Naomi's face as her eyes tracked the salty trail.

But then it was gone and the hard, cold stranger was back. A mean little smile touched Naomi's thin lips and she leaned even closer, catching Cadie's tear with the tip of her tongue, licking upwards until the blonde could stand it no longer and jerked her face away.

"I grew up, Arcadia," the senator murmured. "I learned that to get what you want you have to bite and scratch and claw. Good guys really do come last. And life is too short not to have some fun along the way."

"That is the saddest thing I've ever heard," Cadie said tearfully. "You used to care so much about people, Nay. Where did that go? Or have the drugs got that big a hold on you?"

She winced as Naomi's grip on her leg tightened sharply and Cadie bit down on her bottom lip to stop herself crying out.

"If you have any sense at all," the senator growled. "You will *never* mention that word in connection with *my* name again." Cadie blinked wordlessly at her.

Naomi chuckled low in her throat and suddenly backed away,

wandering back to the bed where she sat with her back against the cabin wall. "You have no idea what you're flirting with, Arcadia. You weren't the only one who was busy last night. I was making phone calls and pulling the strings of the people who run this backward little country." The sneer on the senator's face sent a cold dagger of fear through the blonde.

"I know all I need to know about, Jo," Cadie said, grateful to be out of reach once again.

Again Naomi laughed. "You always did have a very naïve view of the world, my love," she said. "Did you know, for example, that the good skipper has the blood of at least 15 people on her hands?"

Cadie felt the color drain from her face. *She really does know...this isn't one of her usual bluffs.*

"What's wrong, darling?" Naomi asked sarcastically. "Don't tell me that in the course of her seduction she failed to mention that she was a professional assassin? Or did she only tell you about the drug dealer she worked for?" The senator raised her knee and rested her chin on her hand, watching Cadie with a tiny smile on her face.

"And how did you find out all this?" Cadie whispered, wondering just what was coming next.

"Like I said, darling. A US senator can talk to whomever she feels like when she has the right telephone numbers at hand. And I have the right numbers. The Australian Attorney General knows all about Miss Jossandra Madison."

"Then he should have also told you that she turned state's evidence in return for having her record expunged," Cadie said quickly.

"That means nothing if she reoffends." The senator smiled.

Alarm bells began ringing in Cadie's mind.

"You wouldn't—" she began.

"Yes, Arcadia, I would. But only if you don't do as I ask from now on." Again Naomi bared her teeth in the kind of smile most often seen on circling sharks.

Cadie felt a rising tide of nausea bubbling in the pit of her stomach. *I don't believe this. No matter what I do here, I'm screwed. Or Jo is.* She looked across at Naomi, who sat patiently, knowing she had the upper hand. *This is so unfair on Jo. She didn't ask for me to waltz in here and turn her world upside down.* She swallowed the lump in her throat. "What do you want from me?" she whispered.

"Stay away from Madison for a start," the senator growled. "And then I want you to do what you agreed to do a long time ago. Be my wife. In every sense of the word. Obey me, support me," she paused, raking Cadie with a long, lingering look, "make love to me. Oh, and one more thing...work for me."

"Give up my business?" Cadie gasped.

"Oh yes," Naomi replied. "Don't you see that everything started going wrong for us as soon as you went off on your own? You need to be with me all the time, Cadie. *We* need you to be with me all the time."

Cadie felt a pounding at her temples which, combined with the nausea, made her feel like she'd been dragged backwards through a bush. "And if I don't agree to do what you ask?"

The senator stood and walked back over to Cadie, leaned down and rested her hands on the arms of the chair, her face close to her shorter partner's. "Then I make a few phone calls, the authorities search this boat and they'll find the drugs I'm sure your tall friend has onboard," Naomi replied.

Cadie looked up into hard, cold eyes. "I'll warn her," she whispered.

The senator snorted with laughter. "No Cadie, you won't," she said. "When I say stay away from her, I mean it. Besides no matter what you tell her, I can move faster. After all," she leaned closer and whispered in Cadie's ear, "I know exactly where the drugs are." She drew up to her full height and looked back down at the blonde. "You don't look well, Cadie. Perhaps you need to take a few minutes to recover." She paused, waiting for the blonde to meet her eyes and nod. "I, on the other hand, feel just grand. See you up on deck when you're better."

And with that the senator turned on her heel and left the cabin, closing the door behind her.

Cadie slumped forward, head in hands. Shock and fear did their work on her emotions and the tears flowed freely. For several minutes she let them, preferring not to think. Eventually the tears dried up but her body wasn't done reacting. A wave of nausea tugged at her throat and she dove for the head, just lifting the lid in time as her stomach rebelled.

What a waste of a great breakfast, she thought incongruously, leaning against the wall as the spasms eased. She let her legs give way and slowly slid down the wall till she was wedged in the corner of the tiny bathroom, resting her forehead on the arm draped across her knees.

For now I've got no choice but to do as she says. At least until we get back to the States and Naomi begins to forget about Jo and moves on to other things. Then I'll think of something. Absentmindedly she chewed on a fingernail. *Until then I've got to stay away from Jo.* That thought provoked a deep pang of grief and the tears stung her eyes anew. *Damn it. I can't just let Naomi win this way. It's so...sleazy.* She squeezed her eyes shut, fighting a wave of panic.

You're well and truly trapped, Cadie Jones. She banged the back of her head against the wall in frustration. *And I can't warn Jo. She'll go in with all guns blazing and that's just what Naomi is waiting for.* She shook her head to clear it some. *I'll have to keep thinking about that one.*

Jo finned silently under the *Seawolf*'s hull, sensing the sudden drop in temperature as she swam out of the sun-warmed water into the boat's shadow. It was mid-afternoon, several hours after they had motored back around the southern-most tip of Whitsunday Island and anchored off Whitehaven Beach once more.

The passengers were dispersed in all directions. Therese and Sarah lounged topless on the small swimming pontoon anchored several hundred feet away. The senator, Cadie, and the two boys were on the beach with Jenny where they had set up a large shade cloth. Lunch had been eaten under its shelter. Larissa and Kelli were on deck, sunbathing.

Jo moved slowly down the length of the yacht's hull, running her bare hands over the smooth surface, searching for any little flaws or barnacles. She'd talked Paul into the maintenance inspection on the pretext that the previous day's storm had been the wildest for quite some time.

"But we didn't hit anything, Skipper," he'd protested half-heartedly, recognizing the determined look in the tall woman's eye.

"Don't care," she'd muttered shortly. "Better safe than sorry, Paul, you know that."

So here she was, dressed in cutoff shorts, bikini top, weight belt, fins and mask. Jo inched her way along the hull, trying not to get tangled in the long breathing tube running from the air pump up on deck. The gentle, cool currents lifted the short hairs on her arms and swirled her long, black mane around her as she moved. Predictably, she wasn't finding too much wrong with the *Seawolf*'s hull, but then she hadn't expected to. She was more interested in finding some peace and quiet.

Just want to hear myself think for a bit. She stopped to pick off a stubborn barnacle with her knife tip. She reckoned on about 20 minutes peace before Paul tired of manning the air pump and hauled her back aboard.

The *Seawolf* floated in water deep enough to give about 10 feet of clearance under her keel. Jo stopped amidships and let the weight belt do its thing, drifting down to the sandy bottom where she let herself hang.

Visibility's incredible today, she thought, turning full circle and gazing for hundreds of yards in each direction through the pristine water. The seabed sloped down from her left to right. The water color varied from the clear transparency of the shallows to the darker azures and indigos of the deeper water where the bay's bottom dropped away to open ocean. Schools of tiny fish ducked and darted around Jo's body as she hung motionless. She let her mind drift with them.

It's been the strangest day so far. God, I hope the rest of the trip isn't like this.

Cadie had emerged from her cabin half an hour after the senator. It hadn't taken a genius to work out the conversation between the two women hadn't been pleasant. Cadie was red-eyed and silent, not meeting Jo's sympathetic gaze for even a second.

Jo was surprised how much that had hurt. Of course she had expected they would have to be incredibly circumspect once they returned to the *Seawolf.* She kicked back up to the hull of the boat and renewed her inspection.

But not even a look, Jo thought, as she scraped some weed from the boat's keel. *Something's badly wrong.* Grim possibilities bounced around the inside of her skull. *If that bitch touches her I'll...* She blew bubbles for a few quiet seconds, settling her temper, but not her resolve. *If she crosses that line, then paying customer or not, I'll take Cadie out of here, I swear, and to hell with the consequences.*

Inspection completed, she drifted aimlessly for a while. She disturbed a sleepy stingray with a wave of her fin, sand billowing up as the disgruntled creature undulated away. Jo watched as he found a new patch of sea bottom, shaking himself until a layer of sand settled over him, providing a perfect disguise.

I wish I could do that. No, I wish we could do that. Just disappear.

There was a tug on the breathing tube and she glanced down at her watch.

Fifteen and a half minutes. Paul's getting impatient in his old age. With a sigh she tucked her knife back in its sheath on her hip. Jo kicked back up to the hull, patted the keel one last time, and pushed up to the surface.

She emerged into the baking sun to find Paul sitting on the deck, legs dangling over the side, breathing tube in one hand and a stubby of beer in the other. The contents were obviously ice-cold, judging by the droplets of condensation running down the side, and Jo found herself craving a taste.

Paul read her mind and grinned. "I figured you'd be panting for a coldie, Skipper," he said, waving another, unopened, bottle at her. "Come and get it."

"You twisted my arm," she agreed and she struck out for the ladder, tossing her mask and fins up on deck before pulling herself up the metal steps.

Unclipping the weight belt, Jo plopped herself down next to the bare-chested crewman and accepted the cold bottle gratefully. She sucked down a long drag of the liquid amber, releasing an unladylike but deeply satisfied groan. She leaned back against the deck cowling and closed her eyes against the sun.

"You all right, Skip?" asked Paul, looking at the lines of tension on his usually sanguine boss' face. "You look like you've gone 10 rounds with Kostya Tszyu."

Jo snorted an ironic laugh, tipping her stubby up again for another lengthy swallow. "Gee, thanks, Paulie. It's just been a long couple of days," she said, clinking her bottle against his in a toast. They both looked back over their shoulders at the sound of the tinny returning from the beach. "Hey Jen," Jo called as the brunette tied off to the stern and clambered aboard.

"G'day," Jenny replied cheerily. "Oh God yes, give me a beer, Paul. I'm parched." The crewman yanked another bottle out of the icebox by his side as Jenny sat down cross-legged on the deck next to them. "Thanks, darl."

Jo was content to listen to the two crewmembers' conversation for a while, closing her eyes again, and trying to block out thoughts of Cadie on the beach with the senator. *She's got to do what she's got to do. And I've just got to find a way to survive it.*

An expectant silence punctuated by Paul clearing his throat forced Jo to open her eyes to find both crewmembers looking at her.

"What?"

Jenny and Paul exchanged a glance, the brunette eventually reaching out with a foot to nudge the big man with her toe. "Go on, Paulie, it was your idea."

"I smell a conspiracy," Jo said, taking another swig. "Come on, guys, spill it."

Paul put his beer down on the deck and leaned back on his hands. "Well, Skip, we've been thinking..." he began tentatively.

"Oooo, scary thought," Jo teased. "I'm beginning to think you want something and that this cold beer wasn't just from the goodness of your heart."

Paul clutched a hand to his chest in mock hurt. "Me, Skipper?" he objected. "Would I be that manipulative?"

Jo grinned. "Bloody oath. Now stop stuffing about and tell me what's on your mind."

"Hamilton Island Race Week," he replied bluntly.

"Ah, I should have known," Jo said, pointing her beer at him accusingly. "Here I was thinking you were sewing that patch on the spinnaker just to give yourself something to do the other day."

Paul had the good grace to blush, but he launched into his argument nonetheless. "Come on, Skip, it's a great idea," he said. "Toby, Jason, and Cadie are pretty handy around the sheets and winches. The others at least know enough to stay out of the way. And we've got a great chance this year."

Jo said nothing but leaned back against the cowling once more. Privately she agreed with Paul, but there was some fun to be had in giving the big man a hard time. Hamilton Island Race Week was one of the biggest yachting regattas in the country, a once a year festival of day-long racing and night-long parties. Yachts of all shapes and sizes could compete in various race categories, and the *Seawolf* had been a narrow loser to arch rivals from another company the year before.

"We only ever compete when we don't have a boatload of loopies, Paul," Jo pointed out. "It's an insurance nightmare if we rub up against someone."

Paul rolled his eyes. "You're kidding aren't you, Skip?" he protested. "When was the last time we hit anybody? You know it's only us and *Bombardier* from ABC Charters who are any good in our class. The rest stay out of our way."

It's certainly a tempting idea, Jo thought. It would keep the passengers interested and was low maintenance for the crew, other than the actual racing, which would be full on. *Don't kid yourself, Jo-Jo. It'll keep you distracted as well. And too busy to be wondering every second where Cadie is and what the senator is up to.* A happier thought occurred to her as she remembered the last time the Americans had been anywhere near a nightclub. *And if Naomi is half the party animal I think she is, she might even leave Cadie alone for a few hours.*

"Is *Bombardier* definitely competing?" she asked, looking at Paul, whose answering grin threatened to split his face in half.

"Too right. They've been talking themselves up, too. They reckon we're too chicken to take them on."

"Oh really?" Jo drawled, her competitive spirit stirring at the thought of a week of match racing. She crossed her legs at the ankle and drained the last of her beer. "Okay," she said finally. "Let's do it." She held a finger up as Paul started to celebrate. "On one condition, Paulie. We still have to run it by the paying passengers. If they say no, then it's no. And even then we have to get the entry forms in somehow."

Paul looked sheepish and Jenny laughed. "He's already lodged them, Jo-Jo," she said, giggling. "Weeks ago."

Jo arched an elegant brow at Paul. "Pretty sure of yourself aren't you, mate?"

He shook his head vigorously. "No, Skip. Pretty sure of you though." He grinned and slid out of her way when she tried to swat his shoulder. "Come off it, Jo-Jo, you know you can't resist a little healthy competition."

Blue eyes twinkled back at him. "I can't resist any competition, Paulie, healthy or un."

"Wooohooo," he yelped, springing to his feet and doing a little jig. "I've been wanting to nail those bastards since last year. You beauty!"

The two women laughed at his antics until the big man finally slowed down, pulling another three beers out of the icebox. Jo accepted her second gratefully, twisting the cap off and tossing it back into the ice.

"So," she asked, "when's the first race?"

Paul flopped back down on the deck. "Friday at noon," he replied. "Then each day at noon till Tuesday, providing the wind holds."

Jo started planning the next few days in her head. "Okay, so assuming the Americans say yes, that gives us tomorrow to get ourselves around to Hamilton and tomorrow night and Friday morning to get race trimmed," she mused.

Paul shook his head. "That won't take us that long, Skipper," he said. "We've been running her pretty tight anyway."

Jo nodded. "Well, I can vouch for the keel and the hull," Jo muttered, taking another swig of beer. "Okay, let's put it to the troops at dinner and see what they think."

"We're gonna kick some serious arse, Skipper, just you wait and see," enthused Paul.

"Suits me, mate," Jo said quietly, settling back against the cowling. *It's not the arse I want to kick, but it'll do for now.*

Even silent, we're still talking to each other, Cadie thought as she leaned forward and poked at the fire with a long stick. She took in the circle of people gathered around the friendly blaze and smiled quietly. Jo had managed to position herself directly opposite her as she leaned back between Naomi's legs. The senator sat on a low chair, her right arm resting proprietarily on Cadie's shoulder. *But Naomi can't see my eyes. And thanks to that cap, she can't see Jo's either.*

The fire's glow turned the tall skipper's pale blue eyes molten gold and Cadie willingly fell into them. Under the peak of her cap, Jo's gaze was open and warm, though she kept her expression impassive.

God, I love her, Cadie thought with amazement, smiling back at the dark-haired woman. A fleeting grin flickered across Jo's mouth in reply, followed by a raised eyebrow and a questioning tilt of her head. *She wants to know what's going on,* Cadie reasoned. *I wish I could tell her. Hell, I wish we could just sail away together.*

Jo watched Cadie flinch slightly as the senator's hand shifted from her shoulder and started playing idly with the blonde's hair.

God damn her. Jo suppressed the growl that welled up in her throat, and ducked her head momentarily to better hide her scowl. *What's going on, my love? I expected us to have to be careful when we got back, but having Naomi all over you all the time isn't usual.*

I can't tell you, angel, Cadie tried to say with her eyes. *Please understand. I'm trying to protect you until I can get her away from here. I'm sorry it hurts.*

Jo couldn't tear her eyes from the blonde's. Other conversations swirled around her and she tried to keep half an ear tuned to them, but for the most part all she saw were the darker than normal, gold-flecked eyes across the fire. *Part of me wants the next 10 days over and done with. At least then things will happen. They may not be good things, but anything's got to be better than watching them together.*

"Tell us about the racing, Jo," Toby said, from over to her left. She disengaged from Cadie's eyes reluctantly and smiled at the man's enthusiasm. The passengers had willingly agreed to them entering the regatta, the men particularly excited by the prospect.

"Well, it's a different triangular course every day," Jo replied, feeling Cadie's gaze continue to track her. "If the wind blows like it normally does around here, then each race should take about three hours, from noon each day."

"Is there any prize money?" Therese asked. She was sitting to Cadie's left.

"Mhmm. A thousand dollars for the winner of each race, and

Cate Swannell

$10,000 for the overall class winner at the end of the week," Jo
answered. "So the racing can get a little serious." She grinned.

"And who gets the money?" That came from the senator,
whose fingers continued to trail across Cadie's shoulder possessively.

It figures she would ask that, Cadie and Jo thought simultaneously.

"Well," drawled Jo, "it's Ron's boat, so technically the money
goes to Cheswick Marine." She grinned again at the slightly disappointed looks around the fire. "Except that Ron made a policy
years ago that whoever's on board shares the money." Smiles
brightened. "So whatever we win, we split between all of us,
okay?"

"Alllriiight," Toby whooped, high-fiving his partner.

Jo laughed. "We haven't won anything yet, mate."

"We will," Jason said confidently.

Jo nodded. "If we sail well we will," she agreed, leaning back
on her elbows and running a handful of sand through her fingers.
"We're gonna need about three of you to help us out at any one
time. You up for it?"

"You bet, Jo-Jo," Toby said. Jason nodded vigorously beside
him.

"I'm up for it," Cadie said quietly. Jo smiled at her and tilted
her head in acknowledgment.

"Me too," the senator said quickly, despite having not once
lifted a finger to help the crew since coming aboard.

Jo watched Cadie's eyes roll and fought hard not to laugh out
loud. Instead she opted to be gracious. "Thank you, Senator,"
she murmured.

Just then Paul entered the circle from one side and Jenny
from the other a few seconds later.

Subtle, thought Jo, an affectionate smile creasing her face.
She caught Cadie's eye again and saw the same thought crossing
the blonde's mind. *Nice to know one shipboard romance is working out okay.*

She looks years younger when she smiles, Cadie thought,
allowing herself a few seconds to just appreciate the angular, dark
beauty of the woman sitting opposite her. She tingled at the memory of Jo's touch. *Hard to believe that was only this morning. It
feels like it was a week ago.* Again their eyes met and Cadie felt
the blush rising, realizing her thoughts and the skipper's were
traveling along similar lines. Dark blue eyes looked up at her
from under the peak of the cap and what she saw there set Cadie's
pulse racing. *Again.*

Jo groaned inwardly, wishing the world would disappear.

"Tacking!" Jo yelled as she spun the wheel as hard to starboard as she could. The three men scuttled around the deck, ducking the boom and clearing the sheets and sails as Jenny and Cadie worked the winches hard. "Go, go, go," she urged as the boom and rigging slammed across the boat, swinging them round in a tight arc. "Go hard. Go hard!"

Jo looked up and held her breath, exhaling as the mainsail filled and they regained momentum. *Didn't lose too much with that one,* she thought, pleased with the efforts of her makeshift crew. *And it's just as well.* She glanced across to *Bombardier,* which was on the opposite tack and pretty much neck-and-neck with *Seawolf* as both yachts plowed down the third and final reach to the finish line. *This is going to be a close-run thing.*

She looked back down the length of the *Seawolf.* Cadie and Jenny were flat on their backs, breathing hard next to their respective winches. They'd lost the first race of the series yesterday, mainly because everyone was scrambling to learn the race routine, but things were much improved today. Jo grinned. "Good work, guys," she shouted. "Maybe two more tacks and we should be there."

Cadie lifted her head up and looked back at the skipper. "Are we in front?" she panted.

Jo watched as *Bombardier* headed towards them on the opposite tack.

"Not sure. It's close," she replied. "Right now it looks like they're going to cross in front of us, but it won't be by much."

Cadie nodded and dropped her head back down, folding arms across her eyes and breathing deeply. *Damn, that grinding is a good workout.* Her shoulders ached and her lungs burned as she tried to recover before the next tack. Something cold touched her knee and she glanced down to see Therese holding a stubby of beer out to her. "Thanks," she murmured as she took the bottle and sat up to drink.

It was a glorious day. The cloudless sky arched above them but the stiff sea breeze took the sting out of the sun's burn. Cadie looked around and took in the view. Hamilton Island was behind them and ahead was an open expanse of ocean, with the yacht club's launch away in the distance, marking the race finish.

Naomi and the other women passengers were lounging around the cockpit, chatting and drinking and generally doing their best to stay out of the way of the crew.

"Here we go," Jo yelled as *Bombardier* loomed up on their starboard side. "Prepare to tack if we need to bear away, people." They were close enough now to hear the crew yelling on the other boat. Cadie jumped up and grabbed the handle on her grinder, ready if they had to retrim the sails. Paul ran to the bow.

"Jesus, it's going to be close," Jo muttered to herself. *Hold your nerve, Jo-Jo. Hold your nerve. You only have to miss by an inch.* The other 50-footer ploughed towards them and Jo opened her mouth to call the bear-away order, but Paul beat her to it.

"You're right, Skipper," he yelled. "She's going to cross in front."

A few seconds later he was proven right as *Bombardier* slid past their bowsprit, close enough to see grinning faces.

"We've got you again, Paulie," the *Seawolf* crewman's opposite number shouted as the yachts pulled away from each other again.

"Long way to go, you mouthy bastard," replied Paul under his breath, as he made his way back to the helm. "Close, Skipper," he said as he grinned at Jo, whose black hair was whipping around her head.

She beamed back at him, feeling the adrenaline rush. *I've missed this.* She caught Cadie's eye as the blonde sat down on the edge of the cockpit cover, dangling her legs over the edge. Their eyes locked for the briefest of moments before Cadie tore hers away, a smile playing across her lips. *I miss you,* Jo mentally projected. *I miss talking with you. I miss touching you.*

"Hey, Skip, where are you?" Jenny blurted. "They're tacking again!"

"Shiiit," Jo exclaimed. "Come on, guys, prepare to tack."

Everyone scattered to their stations again and soon they were repeating the routine, swinging back onto the port tack.

"We're losing ground, Skipper," Paul said shortly after as he watched *Bombardier* cross easily in front of them. "No danger of a collision this time."

"All we can do is trim it tighter, Paulie," Jo replied, looking up into the rigging. "What do you think?"

The big man shrugged. "Bit dodgy, Skip," he said, looking back at her. "We've only got one spare mainsail."

"Don't want to waste our prize money on a new sail," Jo agreed.

"Don't want to go two races down either," Cadie piped up from where she was sitting.

"Easy for you to say, Cadie," Jo retorted, laughing. "You don't have to face my boss." *She's a competitor. I like that.* She pondered the problem as *Bombardier* threatened to take an unassailable lead. "What the hell, Paulie, let's go for it."

"Yes!" Cadie yelled, jumping to her feet, evoking chuckles from around the cockpit.

"And you call me competitive," Jo muttered to Paul, provoking another guffaw from the big man as she took back the helm.

"And her butt is cuter than yours, too," he answered conspiratorially, as he passed her on his way forward.

Can't argue with that, Jo thought appreciatively, taking in the sight of Cadie crouching over her assigned winch. *Can't argue with that at all.*

But then, like a cloud crossing the sun, the senator from Illinois was in Jo's face. The skipper didn't flinch, instead fixing Naomi with the steeliest ice-chip glare she could muster. She took a degree of satisfaction when the stocky American took a backward step.

"Enjoying the view, Miss Madison?" the senator asked coldly. Jo didn't reply, just continued to look Naomi in the eye. "I would appreciate it if you could manage to keep your interactions with my partner purely professional from now on."

"Right now, that includes talking about the race, Senator," Jo replied quietly, aware that Cadie was watching the conversation with wide, scared eyes. *There's something here I'm not getting.* "And as Cadie is acting as part of my crew, I can't really avoid speaking to her."

A deceptively friendly smile played across the senator's lips but never quite reached her eyes. "Then try to do it without leering," she said. "I'm sure you wouldn't want to do something you might regret." With that she turned away, not affording Jo the chance to respond.

Oh, she is begging to be bitch-slapped, Jo found her inner demon saying. *And I am just the bitch to do it. I hope I get half a reason to, that's all I'll need. Paying customer be damned.*

Cadie's eyes were still on her, and Jo took the chance while Naomi's back was turned to flash the blonde a reassuring smile. She got a wobbly response and felt her heart ache.

This so sucks. She willed herself to concentrate as the *Seawolf* neared the mark she'd designated as the place to tack. "All right, let's go," she yelled, pushing everything but the race out of her mind.

Cadie arched her back and rolled her neck around to ease the ache from sitting for the past hour hunched over her laptop. Ear-

lier in the evening she had made the short walk up the hill from
Hamilton Marina to the hotel. There she'd hooked up to the
Internet and downloaded what appeared to be half the planet's e-
mail. Since then she had been sifting through the posts, sorting
the ones that needed a reply from the ones that could wait until
she was back in the States.

Funny how I can't seem to call it home anymore, she pondered, kneading the back of her neck with her thumb.

So far Naomi hadn't pushed the issue of her closing down her
business, but Cadie suspected that was only because it hadn't
occurred to the senator that she needed to push it yet. She was
sure things would be different back in Chicago.

Cadie reached for the computer again, wincing slightly at the
tugging ache across her shoulders and the backs of her arms, a leg-
acy of four days of manning the winches and grinders up on deck.

Four days, four races and all square at two wins each, Cadie
mused. *Tomorrow's going to be a big day. Seawolf* had indeed
gone two races down after the first two days of the regatta but
with each day Toby, Jason, and Cadie had become better and better at making the big yacht race smoothly. Yesterday they had
edged *Bombardier* by the barest of margins but today *Seawolf* had
claimed the money by almost two boat lengths. *And tomorrow
there's $11,000 up for grabs,* she thought excitedly.

She grinned to herself as she remembered Jo's delighted reaction when they had leveled the series that afternoon.

Like a kid in a candy store. And that smile. She closed her
eyes and brought to mind the 1000-watt grin that had split Jo's
face when the gun went off as they crossed the finish line. *Wow.
I'd give a lot to see that again.*

"What's so interesting?" Naomi growled from where she sat
on the bed behind Cadie. "You've been reading that same post for
the last 10 minutes."

Back to reality, Cadie.

"It's from Mom," she said out loud. "She says hello, by the
way." Naomi grunted. "She wants to know if we're going to have
time to go up and visit before we have to get back to DC." Cadie
heard the words coming out of her mouth, but it felt like she was
talking about somebody else's life. *Boy, I wish I could talk to you
right now, Mom. Without an audience.*

"Probably not," Naomi replied. "The Senate reconvenes the
Monday after we get back. And driving up to Madison with jet lag
just to turn round and come back again doesn't really appeal."

"I guess not," Cadie murmured. She found it incredibly hard
to imagine being back in a Midwest winter. *No,* she corrected her-

self. *I'm finding it hard to imagine going back to my old life.* The realization was both liberating and depressing. *But I'm going to have to. At least for now.* She looked around the small, tasteful cabin. *I wonder when I will be able to come back.*

"I'm going to take a shower," Naomi said, standing and picking up a towel from the bottom of the bed.

"Okay," Cadie acknowledged, closing out programs and shutting down the laptop. She sighed. *I wonder which nightclub she's going to drag me to this evening.* "Where's the party tonight?"

"Club up at the hotel," the senator replied gruffly. "Wear something short." And with that she closed the bathroom door behind her.

"Well actually, Senator, I wasn't really looking for any fashion advice," Cadie muttered to the empty room. *It's been a party every night since Friday and there'll be another tomorrow night, especially if we win.* She sighed again. *I need a cup of coffee.*

She opened the door to the cabin and walked out into the *Seawolf*'s main lounge. And right into an open blue gaze that bathed her in a bone-deep wash of warmth.

"H-hello," she murmured, unable, not to mention totally unwilling, to tear her eyes away from Jo's. She moved closer, joining the taller woman behind the counter in the galley.

"Hi there," Jo replied, feeling a quiet joy welling up inside her at the sight of the blonde's wrinkle-nosed smile. "Where's your watchdog?"

Cadie bit her lip. "In the shower," she said, flicking a quick glance towards the cabin door, her stomach lurching at the thought of being caught.

A strong arm snaked around her waist and pulled her close. Cadie turned back and looked up into Jo's warm regard, suddenly feeling a shield of protection envelop her.

"I miss you, Jo-Jo," she whispered.

"And I you, love," Jo replied, leaning down and capturing Cadie's lips in the softest of kisses imaginable. The blonde reached up, sliding her arms around the tall woman's neck and pulling her down, deepening the contact into a sweet exploration. Finally Jo broke away, resting her forehead against Cadie's. She closed her eyes and felt her heart nestling into a very safe place. "What's going on, sweetheart?" she asked quietly.

Cadie touched a fingertip to the soft lips just inches from her own. "Don't ask, please?" Blue eyes flickered open and caught her own, the gaze intense. "Please, Jo?"

Jo stood up tall now, tipping Cadie's chin up with gentle touch. She felt the blonde snuggle closer. "Is she threatening you?" Jo asked, fighting to keep a rein on her growing anger.

Cadie remained silent, dropping her eyes to escape Jo's scrutiny.

A light came on in the skipper's head. *Ah. Now I get it.* "She's threatening me, isn't she?" she asked, reading the acknowledgement in the blinking green eyes that quickly tracked back to hers. "Cadie, she can't do anything to hurt me."

"Yes, Jo, she can." Cadie pulled away from Jo and began putting together two cups of coffee. "You don't understand how powerful she is. She can hurt us both." She clattered cups on the counter, frustration making her hands clumsy.

"Arcadia," Jo said calmly, stepping forward and taking the shorter woman's hands in her own. She waited until the blonde turned back and met her gaze, tears welling in her eyes. "Listen to me. I can handle anything she can throw at me. I've come up against a lot worse than her, I promise."

They both startled at a noise from the direction of Cadie's cabin.

"Jo, please just trust me with this," she said hurriedly, pleading with her eyes. "She can do a whole lot of damage to you, the company, all of it. Just let me get her back to the States and she'll soon forget all about you."

Jo couldn't argue. She leaned forward and again rested her forehead against Cadie's. "I do trust you," she whispered, feeling tears close to the surface. "But this hurts. It hurts seeing the way she's treating you, and not being able to do anything about it. And," she swallowed, "and it hurts that you're leaving with her. I know that was always going to be the case, but the way she's being...just makes it worse."

Cadie cupped her hands around Jo's face. "Nothing's changed in my heart, Jossandra," she said fiercely. "I will come back. I need to come back. But for now I need to keep you safe. And if that means staying away from you and putting up with her touching me..." She shuddered involuntarily and Jo tightened her arms around her waist.

"I hate her touching you," she muttered, squeezing Cadie gently.

"I know. And I hate the way she touches me. But if it means doing what she tells me to do for a while...then I'll do it. Gladly."

A tear overflowed and tracked down Jo's cheek. Cadie caught it with the pad her thumb and brushed it away. "Have you noticed we never seem to cry at the same time?" she asked with a weak smile, leaning in and kissing the tip of Jo's nose. "One of us is always being the strong one."

"Just as well," Jo sniffled. "Otherwise we'd never get anything done." They both laughed softly and then got lost once more in their connection. "Has anyone ever told you, you have the most beautiful eyes, Miss Jones?" Jo murmured.

"Nobody whose opinion ever mattered to me like yours does," Cadie replied, pulling the skipper's head down again for another long, lingering kiss. Louder noises from the direction of Cadie's cabin broke them apart, breathless and hungry for more.

"You'd better get back in there," Jo whispered into the blonde's ear, feeling Cadie's arms tighten around her in response. "I'll be here waiting for you, darling. Always."

"I love you." Cadie disengaged quickly, grabbing the two coffee cups and heading back to the cabin door. She looked back over her shoulder and met an encouraging smile with one of her own, before she pushed open the door and disappeared inside.

Damn. Jo rubbed her eyes with one tired hand. *This isn't getting any easier.*

Twenty minutes later Jo was sitting up on the cockpit cowling with Paul, the spare mainsail gathered around them in large, cream-colored ruffles. They were going over the kevlar with a fine-tooth comb.

"I guess this means we're going all-out tomorrow, eh boss?" Paul asked with a grin as they painstakingly stitched a patch to a needy bit of sail.

Jo cocked an eyebrow at him. "Well, I called Ron, and the prospect of $11,000 on top of the $2000 we've already won has him drooling," she said. "So he said go for it. It'll be a boost for the company if we can win that trophy."

Paul snorted. "It won't do us any harm either," he replied.

"I thought of that," Jo said, beaming.

Just then she caught sight of Naomi and Cadie dressed up for a night out emerging from the main cabin. The blonde was in a shimmering green mini-dress that managed to accentuate both her eye color and her shapely legs. Jo had a hard time tearing her eyes away.

"Pick your jaw up off the deck, Skipper," Paul said softly in her ear, surprising Jo into driving the large sewing needle into her thumb.

"Shit," she muttered, sucking the digit hard to take away the ache. She glanced up again to see Cadie, who obviously knew exactly what Jo had been gawking at and was struggling to keep her laughter silent.

"Not going out tonight, you two?" the senator asked, taking Cadie's hand and pulling her towards the gangplank.

"Got some repairs to do before tomorrow," Jo said shortly, wrapping her bleeding thumb in a cleaning rag she had stuffed in her pocket. "Have a good time." But Naomi hadn't waited for a response, and had already taken them ashore. Cadie gave a small wave behind the senator's back and Jo returned it with a tiny smile.

"Y'know what, Skip?"

"What's that, Paulie?" Jo murmured, watching the Americans walk up the hill towards the hotel.

"The more politicians I meet, the more I wonder what kind of scumbag you have to be to become one."

Jo turned and looked at her crewman, eyebrows raised in surprise at the usually affable man's criticism of a passenger.

"What?" he retorted. "Come on, Skipper, don't tell me you don't agree with me. That one's got a nasty streak as wide as her backside. She treats Cadie like crap."

Jo nodded. "No argument from me, mate," she said softly.

There was a pause as Jo resumed sewing, head bent over her work.

"You're really gone on her, aren't you, boss?" Paul asked quietly, realizing he'd hit the mark when Jo's hands stopped moving and a blush crept up her neck. She glanced up at him, nodding slowly.

"Yeah," she replied. "Yeah, I am."

He whistled softly. "Picked yourself a tough challenge there."

Jo snorted with laughter. "I think the challenge picked me, Paulie," she said, smiling at him as they resumed work on the sail patch. "It just seemed to be there from the moment we met."

He nudged her with his shoulder. "Ya big softie."

"Yeah, yeah...give me a break, will you?" She quirked an eyebrow at him. "Besides, what about you? You've been spotted being more than a little starry-eyed lately yourself."

Jenny came up from below, carrying a tray of sandwiches and cups of coffee, which she slid onto the cowling in front of Jo and Paul. She leaned her elbows on the deck and placed a hand on the crewman's knee. "There's actually a pretty good reason for that, Skipper," said the perky brunette with a grin.

"Thought we were going to wait a while to tell people," Paul said as he put his hand over Jenny's.

"This isn't people, hon, it's Jo. That's different," Jen replied.

"Well somebody tell me something," interjected Jo. "Or am I going to have to torture it out of you?"

"What with? A sewing needle?" Paul laughed.

Both women slapped him on a shoulder at the same time.

"Okay, okay, okay." He threw his hands up in surrender. "Tell her, Jen."

The brunette positively beamed at Jo. "We're going to get married, Skip," she said.

Jo whooped in delight, scrambling forward and leaning down to give Jenny a congratulatory hug.

"That's fantastic! I knew it!" She sat back up and poked Paul in the stomach. "You didn't need to go sneaking around, y'know." She clapped her hands together and bounced up and down on the spot with excitement. "When?"

The couple looked at each other and shrugged.

"As soon as this trip is done," Jenny replied. "It's not going to be a big deal, Jo-Jo. Just you and a few other friends, my parents, and Paul's dad. Just an excuse for a great big party."

"Sounds wonderful to me," Jo said, smiling. They all relaxed into a comfortable silence for a bit. "Aw guys, I think it's great. It's really good to see you both happy."

Jenny climbed up onto the cowling and sat down next to her fiancé, wrapping her arms around him as Paul went back to sewing the sail patch. "Thanks, boss," she said. She and Paul exchanged a look. "So...what about you and the cute blonde?"

Jo groaned.

"Two minutes!" Jo yelled. She watched as her five crewmembers scrambled for their stations as the *Seawolf* jockeyed for position along the start line. "Therese!" The attorney turned at the sound of her name and Jo gestured to her. "Give me a hand for a minute?"

Therese clambered out of the cockpit and made her way aft to the portside helm station where Jo was juggling the wheel with one hand and trying to keep her unruly hair out of her face with the other.

"Take the wheel for me for a bit?" she asked the attorney. "My hair's driving me nuts."

"Um, Jo. I don't know anything about this," Therese said hesitantly as she stepped in front of the skipper and tentatively put her hands on the wheel.

"Piece of cake," Jo reassured her. She leaned forward and pointed over Therese's right shoulder. "See that flag on the bow of that big motor launch ahead of us." Therese nodded. "Okay, just keep her pointed that way. Turn the wheel a bit to get a feel

of how she responds." She waited patiently as the attorney exper-
imented, pulling the *Seawolf* off course slightly. "Great. Now get
her back on the right course. Perfect. Now hold her there."

Therese nodded and Jo stepped aside, ducking down into the
companionway where she had stowed a small bag of supplies
under the map table. She dug out a cap and a hair band, impatiently pulling her dark locks back into a rough ponytail before
securing it with the band.

"Jo!"

That sounded a bit panicky, Jo thought as she threw on the
baseball cap, quickly threading the ponytail through the gap at the
back.

"Jo!"

She sprinted back up the steps.

"Okay, okay, I'm coming," she said as she passed Naomi,
Sarah, Kelli, and Larissa in the cockpit. "Thanks, Therese."

"Sorry, but it looked like they were all coming at us at once,"
said the somewhat flustered attorney.

Jo laughed. "No problem," she said. "I know it looks a little
daunting right now." She looked down at her watch. "One
minute, people." *Time to get your brain in the game, Jossandra.*
She looked around at the teeming waters around the *Seawolf.*

There were 10 50-foot yachts, all jostling for a good run at the
starting line. Any boat that crossed the mark early had to bear
away and do another circuit before being allowed to start racing,
so timing was crucial in the run up to the gun. *Gotta get this
right.* Jo had opted to aim for the northern end of the line, as had
three other yachts, but *Bombardier* and the other five had headed
for the southern end.

Immediately to starboard and ahead of *Seawolf* one of their
competitors was in the process of getting it horribly wrong. The
line loomed as the clock ticked down and the skipper could be
heard yelling at the crew to bear away.

They're gonna miss the start, Jo thought with satisfaction.
One down, eight more to beat.

"Thirty seconds," she shouted. Cadie crouched by her winch
on the port side, immediately in front of Jo, amidships. Jenny was
on the starboard side. Paul and Toby were further forward, trimming the foresail and organizing sail changes. Jason was down in
the sail hold, ready to pull out or stow sails as needed.

"Here we go!" Jo warned the crew, noting their heightened
tension. Gently she eased the *Seawolf* away slightly so they were
running almost parallel to the start line. "Five, four, three, two,
one..." The gun fired and Jo ducked the yacht's nose over the line

instantly, judging the timing perfectly.

"Nice one, Skipper," Paul shouted from the bow.

Jo grinned and set the yacht on the first of many tacks up the reach to the mark. *S'gonna be a long day,* she thought happily.

"Wind's picking up, Skipper," Paul said. He had taken over the helm after they'd turned the first mark. The second reach was another tacking leg, but the third and final reach would be downwind, and Jo planned on a spinnaker run.

She looked up into the rigging, scanning for any visible signs that anything was close to breaking. *So far, so good. But we're not going as fast as we could.* She looked back to find *Bombardier.*

"We've got about a half mile on her, Paul," she said. "But I don't think that's going to be enough once we hit the final reach."

The crewman nodded in agreement.

"They've got eight experienced crew on board," he said. "These guys are learning fast, and they're pretty good." He gestured towards the *Seawolf's* three recruits. "But learning how to get a spinnaker up is going to take some time."

"Mhmm." Jo made a quick decision. "Five minutes till we tack again, yeah?" she asked.

"That ought to do it, Skip," he replied.

"Okay." She stepped up onto the rim of the cockpit. "Toby! Get Jason out of his hole and come on back here." She waited for the two men to come aft and take a seat on the cowling, then she looked around at her crew and passengers. "We're doing pretty well," she said, grinning at the smiles that generated. "We're going to need to increase our lead a bit though, because once we turn the second mark there are a couple of tricky little maneuvers we've got to do that may cost us some time. Hoisting a spinnaker for the first time is always a bit of wild ride." She spread her feet a little wider as the *Seawolf* bucked over a bigger than usual wave, unconsciously adjusting her centre of gravity to maintain her balance.

Look at her, Cadie thought with a grin, more than happy she was sitting above Naomi, who couldn't see her without an effort. *She's like a pirate king...born to be on a boat. Beautiful.*

"So," Jo continued, "we need to ratchet it up a couple of notches. That carries a bit of a risk though because something on the boat may break. So I need you all to be extra careful about safety. Crew, make sure you have your gloves on and everyone, please keep hands and feet away from winches, sheets, rigging

cables, whatever, unless you absolutely have to. Things fly around
pretty quickly when they break. Okay?"

She waited for answering nods from everyone, feeling the
warmth from Cadie's smile wash over her.

Mmm. Race? What race? She laughed at herself and
snapped her mind back into gear. "We're coming up on our next
tack. Let's get that done and then we'll crank it up."

The crew scattered to their positions again. Jo looked down
at the remaining passengers.

"Are you ladies willing to sit on the high side if we need you
to, to give us a little more stability?" All but the senator nodded,
even Kelli and Larissa, who normally were indifferent to the
workings of the yacht.

*Nothing like the smell of impending filthy lucre to get a
junkie motivated,* Jo thought grimly.

Halfway down the second reach disaster struck.

Things had been going well after they rounded the mark. The
crew had wound the *Seawolf* up so tight the rigging was singing,
vibrating with tension as the wind ripped through it. They'd
stretched their lead over *Bombardier* to almost a mile by Jo's reck-
oning and she had been quietly optimistic as they headed for the
bottom mark. She had the crew lay out the spare mainsail along
the deck under the boom just in case.

She looked up at the full, straining sails, knowing they were
at the limit of what they could ask of the big boat. *This is the
point where One Australia snapped in half,* she thought, remembering the moment that particular Americas Cup campaign had
come to a grinding, then sinking halt, scattering the 12m yacht's
crew into the water.

Seawolf tilted over at almost 45 degrees to port, the wind
bearing in hard from the starboard side. The crew and passengers—except for the senator, who sat huddled in a corner of the
cockpit—were lined up along the high side, legs dangling over the
edge. All were wearing lifejackets as a precaution.

Jo looked to her right, blinking rapidly as she recognized the
telltale ruffles on the surface of the water that indicated an
approaching gust of stronger than normal wind. "Paul!" she
yelled. "Bullet!!"

Paul and Jenny leapt up and dove for the winches, bleeding
some tension out of the sails, but it was too little, too late and the
wind gust slammed into the mainsail. The boat tilted to an even
steeper angle momentarily but then the sail exploded with a sound

like a gunshot, a huge rent ripping down its length. The sudden loss of momentum jerked the yacht upright with a rush, the hull slapping down on the water violently. Cadie, who had half climbed to her feet when she heard Jo's yell, was caught off-balance, toppling backwards over the edge and into the sea.

"Paulie, get 'em down," Jo shouted, as she wrestled the wheel, pulling the still moving yacht around until it was pointing directly into the wind, the remaining sails flapping uselessly. Paul, Jenny, and the two men scrambled to pull down the ripped remnants of the mainsail, as well as the foresail, trying to stop the yacht in its tracks as soon as possible. Meanwhile Jo grabbed the nearest life-ring and threw it to Cadie who was, thankfully, fully conscious and seemingly unhurt.

Jesus, the senator is gonna have a cow, Jo thought as she watched Cadie strike out for the floating ring, even as the yacht slipped further past the blonde. *Thank Christ she didn't hit her head on the way in.*

True to form, Naomi was on her feet, screaming at the skipper. "Stop this fucking boat!" she yelled. Jo turned to try and placate the senator, but she was having none of it, brushing past the taller woman and rushing to the stern. "Don't just stand there, woman. Get in there and bring her back!"

"Senator, we're not just standing around. Everything that can be done to stop us is being done. And as you can see," she pointed in Cadie's direction, where the blonde had reached the life-ring and was floating inside its confines, calmly waiting to be picked up. "Cadie is okay. She's not going anywhere and we're doing our best to pick her up as quickly as possible."

"That's not good enough," Naomi shouted. "Get in there and pull her out!"

For God's sake, thought Cadie, brushing dripping hair out of her face and treading water. "Naomi," she yelled, "would you calm down? I'm fine." *I swear she thinks I'm totally helpless. I'm glad I'm getting back onboard any minute. This water is dark and deep.*

She decided not to let her mind wander too far down that track, instead focusing on Jo, who had pushed past the senator and was hauling in the line attached to the life-ring. She felt the tug and let herself be reeled in. *Like a great big sunburned fish,* she thought, giggling to herself incongruously. As she came in closer to the yacht, she grinned wetly up at Jo, who caught her eye and smiled back.

Finally she was in reach of the transom and she levered herself back up onto the platform.

"Nice catch, Captain Ahab," she said softly to Jo who suppressed a laugh.

"You sure you're okay?" she asked.

"Just a bit wet, but otherwise fine," the blonde replied, shaking seawater from her hair.

"Get out of my way, Madison," the senator growled, elbowing past Jo and grabbing Cadie's arm, dragging her back into the cockpit. "I'll sue this goddamn company for all it's worth," she said, threatening Jo with a wagging finger.

"Sue for what, Naomi?" her partner protested as she picked up a towel and began drying herself off. "Wet clothes? Forget about it."

"Skipper!"

Jo looked up and saw Paul standing by the boom, pointing to their port side. She turned in the direction he was looking and saw *Bombardier* bearing down on them at full speed.

Jo glanced around the deck of the *Seawolf,* taking in the expectant faces of crew and passengers.

"Everyone else okay?" she asked. Nods all round. "Right. Let's go. Paul, Toby, Jason—get that new mainsail rigged. Jenny, you and Cadie haul the foresail back up. Let's get this show back on the road."

Everyone exploded into movement, leaving Jo and Naomi holding each other's gaze for a few cold seconds.

Come on you harpy, Jo thought. *Give me half an excuse.*

The senator blinked first. Hissing in disgust and flouncing back to her corner of the cockpit, she grabbed another bottle of beer from the icebox on the way.

She's all bluff, Jo realized suddenly. *I wonder if Cadie has figured that out yet.*

She moved back to the helm and watched as Jenny and Cadie hauled the smaller foresail up, then set about trimming it with the forward winches. It would take a while yet for the men to have the spare mainsail ready, but in the meantime they could make at least some headway.

"Trimmed, Skip," came the shout from Jenny.

Jo waved her response and began the tug of war with the inertia-heavy wheel, forcing the rudder around until the wind began to catch the foresail again. *Bombardier* was now well ahead of them and she knew it was going to take some kind of miracle for them to win the prize.

But I'll be damned if we're going to wimp out on the fight, she thought, feeling the competitive rush flow through her.

We came through hoisting the spinnaker amazingly well, Jo reflected as she took in the crewmembers lying around in various poses of physical exhaustion over the deck. She couldn't see Paul or Cadie and guessed they were forward of the mast still.

Jo looked up and watched the huge, balloon-like multi-colored spinnaker fill and billow, pulling the *Seawolf* along at top speed. Ahead of them, by about half a mile, was *Bombardier.* They hadn't gained any on their main rivals, but they hadn't lost any more water to them either, so for now, Jo was satisfied. The other eight yachts in their class were well behind them.

Jenny recovered enough to pull herself up and wander back to Jo, handing the skipper a beer. "I'll take it for a bit, boss," she said.

"Thanks, Jen. Good job by the way." She grinned at her smaller crewmate and got a tired smile back.

"We're not going to win though, are we, Skip?" Jenny asked, her disappointment showing on her face.

Jo shrugged and drained the stubbie of beer, tossing the empty bottle back into the cooler in the corner of the cockpit. "Not unless they run into some dead air, or break something," she conceded. "But you know this is a fluky game, Jen. Anything can happen." She stepped aside and let Jenny take the wheel. "Keep *Bombardier* at about 10 o'clock, hon. I'll be back."

"Aye aye, Captain."

"Oh shut up."

Laughing, Jo picked her way forward, stepping over bodies and greeting each of the crew and passengers as she came to them. Toby and Jason looked like they'd died and gone to heaven.

"Having fun, fellas?" she asked, fairly certain of the answer.

"Oh you bet, Jo!" enthused Jason. He was sporting a lump on his forehead from a close encounter with the boom, but otherwise seemed happy. "M'just sorry we blew that mainsail out. Doesn't look like we can win it from here."

"Yeah, sorry about that Skipper," Toby agreed.

"Not your fault, guys," Jo said. "Purely mine. I pushed it too hard at the wrong moment. But you two are naturals. You should do more sailing when you get home."

Both men grinned from ear to ear.

"I think we probably will," Toby said. "We're having a ball, Jo. Thanks."

"My pleasure," she said. *Well, at least that's two satisfied customers.*

She continued forward, finding both Paul and Cadie flat on

their backs. Paul appeared to be asleep, but Cadie was shading her eyes with a gloved hand and gazing up into the colors of the spinnaker.

Jo crouched down next to the blonde and gently touched her knee. "Hello, sailor."

That provoked laughter from both supine figures.

"Oh, I'm out of here if that's the quality of humor we've sunk to," Paul groaned and jumped to his feet.

Cadie sat up and met a twinkling set of blue eyes. Just then the *Seawolf* slid down the face of the wave she was surfing and dug her nose into the trough. A spray of seawater engulfed the trio leaving them to shake off like a pack of wet dogs.

Cadie giggled. It was the first time she'd seen Jo look less than impressed by the ocean. But the scowl that touched the tall skipper's face didn't last long, good humor returning as she met the shining green eyes in front of her. "Come on," Jo said. "You shouldn't stay forward of the mast in these kind of conditions."

"I'm okay, Jo-Jo," Cadie replied. "I'm having fun."

Paul chimed in. "She's right, Cadie," he said. "If the mast snaps, you're in the worst possible place up here."

Cadie sighed. "Okay, okay," she grumbled. Paul disappeared aft. "It's also about the only place on the boat Naomi won't follow me."

Jo nodded, suddenly seeing the lines of strain on the blonde's face. *If I think it's bad watching them be together how much worse would it be to be joined at the hip with the senator.* "I'm sorry," she said.

Cadie brightened, shaking her head with a smile. "Don't be," she replied. "I'm actually having a great time. Entering this regatta was an inspired idea."

"Well, we can thank Paul for that," Jo said. She opened her mouth to say something else, but another wave splattered across the bow, soaking them both again. She opened her eyes to find a dripping blonde, giggling at her.

"Sorry, but you look so pissed when that happens," Cadie chortled. "Like somehow you don't expect it."

Jo laughed and sat down next to the blonde. "One of the good things about being the skipper and not the crew, is you get to stay nice and dry in the stern most of the time," she said. She wiped the saltwater off her face. "That's the theory anyway."

"S'not working, Skipper."

"No, it's not," Jo replied, squeezing the water out of the bottom of her shirt. She turned to face Cadie and the sudden sense of connection between them was almost palpable.

"You took my breath away before, you know," Cadie said softly, watching a drip slide down Jo's aquiline nose.

Suddenly bashful, Jo ducked her head, looking up at the blonde through long, damp eyelashes. "When was that?" she asked huskily.

"You were standing on the rim of the cockpit, and you had your arms crossed and you looked like the world was yours for the taking." Jo chuckled, feeling the blush rising despite the cold water. Cadie leaned in towards her. "It was about the sexiest thing I've ever seen."

Jo cleared her throat, fighting the urge to kiss the blonde right here and now, senator be damned. "I think we both need a cold shower," she said, smiling. A movement in the ocean caught her eye. "And I think we're about to get one." *Seawolf's* nose dug deep into the trough of the wave in front of it and again the pair was doused. "Come on, or we're both going to end up over the side."

This time the blonde didn't argue and let Jo pull her upright.

"I think it might be a good idea if I went down into the sail hold and made my way back below decks," the skipper said. "That way Naomi's not gonna know which way's up, with any luck."

Cadie nodded, suddenly glum again. "I'm sorry, Jo. This is an awful lot of shit to go through just for a paying customer."

"Hey," Jo waited until Cadie's eyes lifted to meet her own, "you're not just a paying customer, and I don't think you have been from the moment we laid eyes on each other."

Cadie smiled gently. "What am I then?" she asked.

Jo paused, tilting her head as she thought about it. "I think you're who I'm supposed to be with," she said.

Cadie's heart lurched in her chest and long seconds went by as they gazed wordlessly at each other, just enjoying the connection, oblivious to the bucking of the deck under their feet.

"Oh, we are in so much trouble," Cadie muttered, laughing at the rakish grin that lit up Jo's face.

"Understatement," the skipper replied. "Now get going, crewman."

"Aye aye, Captain," Cadie responded, snapping a smart salute.

"Oh shut up," Jo laughed, watching the very wet blonde turn and make her way aft.

"We're running out of water, Skip," Paul said.

"Yup, I know mate," Jo replied. She was sitting on the rail of the stern, holding the wheel in place with her right foot, propping her chin on her hand, elbow on her other knee. The spinnaker reach had been a straight speed run, with no tactics involved beyond picking the right sail and the fastest line to the finish. "Not much we can do about it. It's..." She stared hard at the stern of the *Bombardier.* "...in the lap..." She reached for her binoculars. "...of the gods." She gazed through them for several seconds.

"What is it, boss?"

"Whooohooo. The gods are smiling, Paulie!" she yelled, standing up and clapping her hands together. "They blew out their spinnaker!"

Paul grabbed the binoculars from around Jo's neck, almost lynching her in the process. "Get the fuck outta here," he exclaimed, climbing up onto the rail. Jo jumped down and picked up Jason's gloves, which sat on the rim of the cockpit. She tossed them at the American.

"We're back in the hunt, folks. Let's kick it up a notch, eh?"

Whoops and hollers greeted the news, and people scattered in all directions. Cadie manned her winch, releasing the slack in the sheet and taking the tension on the grinder, waiting for the order to wind. She glanced back and watched Jo at the helm. The tall woman was wound almost as tight as the rigging, and Cadie grinned at the obvious glint in the steely blue eyes. *A pirate queen. My pirate queen.*

Jo grabbed the trophy with both hands, tipping the silver cup up and drinking long and deep from the contents. The champagne threatened to spill over and she let it, not caring how much she wasted down the front of her shirt. There was plenty more where that came from. Tucked into her back pocket was $1180 cash— her share of the $13000 the *Seawolf* had won over the past five days.

The best part was hoisting the trophy over the heads of the assembled crowd with Paul holding the other side of it. She grinned, took another swig of the ice-cold champagne, and passed the trophy on to Jenny, who happily buried her head in the silverware.

And the worst part...Jo looked around the deck of the *Seawolf,* which was packed to the gunwales with the crews from the other boats in their class.

The worst part is Cadie isn't here to share in it, she thought, sobering. Typically, Naomi had pocketed her share of the winnings and, along with Kelli and Larissa, had disappeared into the night, dragging Cadie behind her. *She looked like she was about to burst into tears,* Jo remembered. *Damn, I wish she was here. She worked just as hard for this as the rest of us.*

She gazed around at the marina, which was fully booked for the biggest night of the regatta. Over 200 yachts and motor launches snuggled up to each other. There were several other parties on different boats across the marina, as the winners of each class hosted their own victory celebrations. Lights twinkled against the dark backdrop of the island rising behind them in one direction, and the open waters of Whitsunday Passage in the other.

Jo sighed. *There are a couple of green stars I'd like to see twinkling right about now,* she thought wistfully. But she didn't have long to get introspective as a loud war-whoop announced the arrival of Paul by her side.

"We did it, Skip!" he yelled, picking her up bodily and spinning her around. "We kicked their bums!"

Jo giggled. "Put me down, ya big goon." He complied and she reached up to ruffle the big man's blond curls. "We got lucky, Paulie. That's all."

"That's bullshit, Jo-Jo," he protested, waving his stubby of beer wildly. "We could've given it away when we blew the mainsail. But we didn't. You put us in the right place at the right time so we could have a go when we got a chance." He kissed her soundly. "And now Jen and I have enough for a honeymoon as well as a big party."

She grinned at him cheesily. "My pleasure, big fella," she said, patting him on the belly.

Someone below decks cranked the music up and soon the boat was rocking as 70-odd happy sailors settled in for a big night of partying. The skipper of the *Bombardier*—a bearded man with a pot belly—sauntered up to Jo and bowed deeply.

"Congrats, Jo-Jo," he said graciously. "You got us a good one. Jen's just told me half your crew was a bunch of rookie Seppo tourists. You must've been training the buggers for weeks."

Jo beamed from ear to ear, proud of the makeshift crew. "Actually, Jacko, we only decided on Wednesday to give it a go." She laughed as his jaw dropped.

"Well, bugger me," he said. "All power to you, Skipper, you deserve it." He shook her hand and pumped it vigorously. "We'll get you next year though," he added, wagging a finger at her as he headed back into the crowd.

Don't count on it, Jacko, she thought happily.

It was almost midnight as Cadie wandered back down the hill towards the marina. Parties were still in full swing all over the harbor, and she grinned at the thought of finally joining the *Seawolf* crew in its celebration.

She and Naomi had become separated in the crush of the dance party on the other side of the resort and she'd opted to make her way back to the boat, rather than try and find the increasingly intoxicated senator.

That's my story and I'm sticking to it, she thought with a smile as she caught sight of the *Seawolf. Is that...* She laughed out loud as she recognized the figure halfway up the mast as Paul, hanging happily in a harness, singing his head off. *Looks like it's already been quite the night.* Her eyes swept around the deck. *No sign of Jo though.*

She walked up the gangplank and waved at Jason and Toby who yelled their greetings as they cha-cha-ed past.

I've gotta get out of these heels, Cadie thought, as she stepped into the cockpit and down the companionway. She emerged into the cabin to find Jo sitting with her back to her, head propped on the back of the sofa. Nobody else seemed to be around, so Cadie tiptoed forward and slid her arm over Jo's right shoulder, pulling the skipper close as she ducked down to whisper in her left ear.

"Hello, sailor," she burred, kissing the rim of Jo's ear softly.

"Mmm, hello gorgeous," Jo responded, tipping her head back even further to look up into green eyes. "You managed to sneak away, huh?"

"Mhmm, something like that." Cadie smiled down at the dark-haired woman, letting her fingers tangle in the long locks. *Oh, I can't resist.* She bent again and took Jo's mouth passionately, her tongue probing as bolts of desire rushed through her as Jo responded in kind. Strong hands reached up and cupped her head, pulling her closer.

Jo groaned into the contact, aroused beyond belief by the blonde's initiative. *Damn this sofa,* she thought blearily, wishing she could just pull Cadie over the back of the sofa and into her arms.

Cadie could taste champagne on the skipper's tongue and she smiled as she gently pulled away. They rubbed noses and she kissed Jo lightly. "You all done partying?" she asked.

Jo leaned forward and picked up a cup of coffee. "No fear," she answered. "Just getting my second wind." She leaned back and watched Cadie ease her high heels off her feet with a happy groan. "How about you?"

"Well, I'm done wearing these torture devices," she said. "I'm going to change into something more comfortable." She laughed at Jo's raised eyebrow. "Not that comfortable, darling," she said, patting the skipper's shoulder. "I want to get some fun in before Naomi figures out where I am."

Jo nodded. "Okay. I'll see you back on deck." Jo drained her cup and stood up. "Unless...um..." She grinned wickedly. "Unless you need some help in there." Casually she wandered over to where Cadie was laughing, one hand on the cabin door.

"Oh, Jo-Jo, my love. Don't tempt me." Cadie stood on her tiptoes and kissed Jo softly again. "But the way my luck is running, Naomi would swim by and crawl up through the head just to see what I was up to." She smiled regretfully as Jo nodded her agreement.

"Come up and celebrate with us, Arcadia," the tall woman said softly. "We missed you." She paused and cupped the blonde's cheek again with a gentle palm. "I missed you."

Cadie pulled on her jeans. As she had been doing for close to a week, her mind turned over the problem of what to do about Naomi's threats and demands. And as had happened every time, she ran into a brick wall. She smoothed down her shirt distractedly and looked around the cabin.

The drugs are the key. She's threatening to plant drugs on the boat and blackmail Jo with them. So... She spun in a slow circle. *She wouldn't keep the drugs on her because...well, just because that's too big a pain in the ass for Naomi. And she's barely set foot in other parts of the boat. I doubt she even knows where the crew goes at night. That leaves the main cabin, where anyone could stumble over it, or...in here.*

She glanced down at her watch.

Just after 1am. My guess is she's going to be at least a couple more hours. Plenty of time to search this room from top to bottom.

Chapter
Eleven

The cell phone rang with obscene volume so close to Jo's ear that it brought her upright with explosive speed. She cracked her head on the ceiling of the cramped crew quarters, driving her back down onto the bunk, hands pressed to her temples.

"Oowww. Fuck."

She scrambled to silence the offending gadget. Sleepy hands fumbled as muffled curses floated up from below where Paul and Jenny were curled up in a sodden ball together.

"Hello?" Jo mumbled into the speaker, hoping she'd pressed the right button.

She had.

"Is that Jo Madison?" came an unfamiliar male voice.

"It's her pitiful outer shell speaking," Jo replied, wondering just how a hangover could possibly feel any worse.

"I'll take that as a yes, then. Look, it's Constable McDonald here, from the Hamilton Island police." Jo's hangover got worse instantly. "We've got three of your passengers here. One of them claims to be a US senator."

Jo groaned, rubbing her eyes with the back of her hand.

"Are they lost or something?" she asked, wishing fervently the man would just go away. "Want me to come and collect them?"

"Oh no, Miss Madison, you misunderstand. They're not lost. They're arrested."

At the same time Jo was slamming her head into the ceiling of the crew quarters, Cadie jolted back to consciousness, face down, head buried under a pillow. *You couldn't really call that waking up,* she thought fuzzily.

"Oh God," she groaned, not knowing quite what had woken her. Blearily she lifted her head, shoving the pillow off the bed with a flailing arm and revealing disheveled blonde locks. A sharp pain knifed through her brain. "Oh Jesus, take me now." Someone mean and vicious was pounding jungle drums between

Cadie's ears and it took half a minute for her to realize someone actually was knocking on the cabin door. "Come on in," she mumbled into the mattress.

Jo pushed open the door and gingerly stepped into the cabin. Her own skull was still feeling hollow. She walked carefully around the small piles of discarded clothing Cadie had obviously left on her way to bed. The tall skipper was stopped in her tracks by the sight of the petite blonde. Cadie wore a very brief set of pajamas, sporting tiny Winnie the Poohs.

Or is that Winnies the Pooh? Jo thought disjointedly as she took in the sprawled figure on the bed. The sheet was twisted around one of Cadie's legs and the other was exposed all the way to the bottom of the blonde's shorts. *Now there is an instant hangover cure.* Jo brightened considerably.

A bloodshot green eye peeked out from behind shaggy blonde locks. "Are you the vindictive bitch who spiked my tequila with more tequila?" Cadie asked hoarsely.

"That depends," Jo said, managing a half-smile at her friend's obvious discomfort, "was that before or after you started that game of Fuzzy Duck?"

Cadie moaned piteously and Jo decided to be merciful. She stepped forward to help the blonde swing her legs over the side of the bed and sit up. Cadie had obviously been in no fit state when she put on her pajamas as the buttons were misaligned, giving her a slightly off-centre look. *My God, could she be any more adorable?* She crouched down in front of Cadie and placed her hands on the smaller woman's knees, relishing the warmth and softness under her fingertips.

Being upright seemed to make Cadie feel better and she reached up and swept her errant hair back off her face with one hand. The other she placed on top of Jo's. For a few seconds the two women just enjoyed each other's presence, reveling in their connection.

"Hi," Cadie said softly, smiling down into twinkling, if somewhat tired, blue eyes.

"Hi yourself," Jo replied. "Quite a night, wasn't it?" She found herself in no particular hurry to break the news about the senator. *Can't think why.*

"Mhmm. And I sure made up for getting to the party late, didn't I?" Cadie winced as a memory of a particularly vigorous round of limbo resurfaced. "I guess my image as a perfect young lady is shattered for good, huh?"

Jo replied by leaning forward, placing herself squarely between Cadie's legs. *Funny how it doesn't bother me when she does it,* Cadie thought as a gentle wash of desire chased the worst of the hangover away. Jo's hands slid up the blonde's thighs and came to rest on her waist. Dark hair spilled against her chest as Jo planted the gentlest of kisses on Cadie's breastbone, nuzzling a path between the folds of her pajama top.

She smells so good, Jo's mind whispered as she brushed her lips across soft skin.

Cadie wrapped her arms around Jo's shoulders, resting her cheek on the top of Jo's head in a gentle hug. "Mmm you feel so good," the blonde murmured. She felt Jo smile.

"I was just thinking the same thing," Jo replied, letting herself float in a golden haze.

Suddenly Cadie's brain caught up with the rest of her and green eyes blinked wide. "Ummm, Jo?"

"Mmm?"

"Where's Naomi?"

Damn. Jo sighed and reluctantly pulled away from the blonde. She sat back down on the floor, resting her weight on her hands. "Well, that's actually why I came to see you," Jo said carefully, unsure just how Cadie was going to react to the news.

"Oh, I have a bad feeling about this," muttered the blonde.

"Naomi, Larissa, and Kelli have been arrested for being drunk and disorderly and are currently sleeping it off in the Hamilton Island lock-up."

Cadie's hands flew up to cover her eyes. "Aargh. Shit, Jo, this isn't good." She dropped her hands and glared at the sprawled woman who was obviously having a hard time keeping the smile off her face. "It's not funny."

Despite her best efforts, Jo's grin widened and Cadie felt a giggle welling up from deep inside. "Stop it, Jo, don't you dare laugh."

Wicked blue eyes twinkled back up at her through long dark lashes and Cadie felt the corners of her mouth twitching up into a matching grin.

"Stop iiit."

In a rush, laughter exploded from both women. Cadie doubled over while Jo collapsed back onto the floor, both helpless for a solid half-minute of merriment.

"Oh God," Cadie moaned, wiping tears from her face with the backs of her hands. "It's not funny, really, darling. She's going to be so pissed."

That brought another hoot of laughter from the prostrate skipper. Running footsteps sounded above them as someone came aboard and then scrambled down the companionway.

"Skipper!"

"In here, Jen," Jo called back, sitting up. The *Seawolf* hostess trotted into the cabin, taking in Cadie's disheveled appearance and Jo's casual posture on the floor with barely a fleeting grin.

But then she was all seriousness.

"We've got trouble, ladies," she said, holding out a copy of *The Weekend Australian*, the country's biggest, most prestigious newspaper. Splashed across the front page in glorious color was a six-column photograph of the Republican Senator from Illinois, hair askew, and eyes glazed. She held a martini in one hand, and a redhead—Kelli, looking like something the cat dragged in—was tucked under her other arm. Above the unflattering photo the headline screamed "Underworked, overpaid and over here!"

Even Jo winced. She handed the paper to Cadie who blanched and went very still. "That really isn't funny," the blonde murmured. "This is the national paper, yeah?" Jo nodded quietly. "So the television networks will get to the story. And if the networks get it, word will get home before lunchtime."

"I went up to the resort to pick up some supplies," Jenny said. "There's already a pack of journalists waiting outside the cop shop."

Jo looked up into pleading green eyes. *Awww, shit, how am I supposed to resist that?*

Jenny was reading the accompanying story. "The good news is, there's no mention of Cadie, so there's a fair chance they think Kelli is the girlfriend."

Cadie groaned. "Not back home they won't. So not only will they think Naomi's a lush, they'll think she's cheating on me, too. Great, just great." She flopped back on the bed, arms crossed loosely over her eyes.

"Jen, go roust Jason and Toby," Jo said. "I have a feeling we're going to need some spin control on this." She paused for thought. "Cadie, are Therese and Sarah criminal attorneys?"

"No," came the muffled response, "but they'll do. She's going to need a lawyer."

Jo turned back to Jenny. "Get them up, too, mate."

"Aye aye, Skip," the crewmember said on her way out.

Jo ran her hands distractedly through her mussed hair as she tried to figure out what to do next. She looked up at Cadie who had pulled a pillow over her face and was trying desperately to shut out the world. Jo pulled herself up, then sat down on the bed and stretched out next to the blonde, propping herself up on an elbow. "Sweetheart."

"Tell them all to go away, Jo-Jo, pleeease?"

Jo smiled, reaching out a hand and sliding it under Cadie's pajama top, searching for the soft skin of the blonde's firm belly. Once there she started slow, soothing circles with her fingertips.

Cadie groaned subvocally. "Boy, you've really got my number, haven't you?" she muttered sleepily, still holding the pillow over her face. Jo reached up and pulled it away, tossing it behind Cadie and smiling down at the blonde. "They're not going to go away, are they?"

"'Fraid not, gorgeous," Jo said softly. Her hand drifted back under Cadie's shirt and she leaned down until their lips were just brushing. Tender butterfly kisses nibbled at the corners of the smaller woman's mouth and she let herself float in the tingling glow of Jo's attentions. "I would give anything for some uninterrupted time with you, darling," the skipper whispered as their breath mingled. "But somehow..." Doors slammed out in the cabin and Jason and Toby could be heard yelling at each other. "...I don't think today is the day."

"Cadie!" Jason called, and Jo rolled away from Cadie, standing up and walking out into the main cabin before the blonde could reply. "She's getting dressed, mate," Jo said quietly, watching the American hurriedly pulling on a shirt with one hand while he tried to read the newspaper with the other. *At least he hasn't noticed I was in her cabin. All I need is a report on that to the senator.*

"Christ, this is a nightmare," he said worriedly. "What do we know, Jo?"

Jo shrugged. "Not much more than the story says. The cop told me they were at the dance party on the other side of the resort. There were a couple of thousand people. There was a bit of a scuffle late in the night and the cops moved in and grabbed who they could. Apparently there was some Ecstasy doing the rounds but he didn't find any on our three girls. But as you can see," she nodded at the newspaper, "they weren't exactly clean and sober."

Jason cursed under his breath and handed the paper to his partner who had just emerged from their cabin. Toby whistled softly, adjusting his glasses and running a hand through his sleep-mussed hair. "Have they been formally charged, Jo?" he asked looking up at the skipper.

Jo nodded a greeting to Therese and Sarah who arrived at that moment. "I'm not sure, mate. He said they'd been 'arrested.' Whether that means formally charged, I don't know."

"We'd better get over there," Therese said. She looked over Jo's shoulder as Cadie emerged, tucking her shirt into her jeans, a pair of sunglasses held in her mouth by the arm piece. She still looked a little disheveled. "I know we're all probably feeling a little rough around the edges," the attorney said. "But it would help a lot if we tried not to look like we feel, okay?" She paused while everyone started smoothing down hair and straightening clothes. "Great party, by the way, Skipper."

Jo grinned. "We live to serve."

The group made its way up on deck, where Jen handed out last-minute cups of coffee. Paul sat miserably on the edge of the cockpit cowling, his sore head in his hands. Jo patted his knee sympathetically, smiling quietly at the memories of the big man swinging from the mast.

"I hate to do this to you, Paulie, but I think we're going to have to get ready to get out of here in a bit of a hurry. If we can get the senator out of the joint, she's going to want to get as far away from dry land as possible."

Paul groaned. "Shoot me now," he muttered, provoking a laugh from the dark-haired woman.

"Just say 'aye aye, Skipper'," she said.

"Oh shut up," he moaned.

Nothing the American attorneys said had any impact on the laconic custody sergeant in charge of the Hamilton Island lock-up. Despite the urgency of their pleas to see their clients, he was moving with all the speed of—*well,* Jo reasoned, *all the speed of a cop who's been up all night dealing with the vagaries of Race Week.* She couldn't help but smile at the frustration evident in the tourists. Even the usually unflappable Toby was beginning to get frayed around the edges.

They had managed to run the gauntlet of the press phalanx outside, mainly because nobody had recognized them. That wasn't going to be the case going out, Jo knew, and she was already planning their exit strategy. *Assuming we can get the Terrible Trio sprung at all,* Jo thought. *And judging by our lack of progress so far, that's not a given.*

She looked over to her left where Cadie was sitting quietly, head resting back against the wall of the police station. The petite blonde looked slightly stunned. Jo reached over and gently placed a hand on the woman's knee.

"You okay?" she asked quietly.

Green eyes met hers gratefully. Cadie nodded. "I'm just trying to figure out what I'm supposed to be feeling," she replied, an ironic smile touching her lips. "Naomi hasn't exactly given me

too many reasons to think fondly of her lately." Jo arched an eyebrow at her. "Yeah, I know. Understatement." She leaned closer
to the tall skipper, till their shoulders touched. "But this could
mean big trouble for her. Career-wise, I mean."

Jo smiled sympathetically down at her. "And that's been the
focus of both your lives for so long, you don't want to see it dam-
aged," she extrapolated, nodding. "I understand, love." She
smiled again as Cadie squeezed her hand quickly. Jo looked back
at the group of Americans trying to make headway with the custody sergeant. Then she glanced at Cadie again. "Why don't I
give Harding a ring?" she asked.

A flicker of hope crossed the blonde's face. "You think he
might be able to help?"

Jo shrugged. "It can't hurt. He's pretty high up down in Sydney and at the very least he'll know a few people to call."

An adorable wrinkle-nosed grin was her reward.

"I guess that means yes," Jo said, patting Cadie's knee and
starting to reach for the cell phone on her own hip. She was
stopped by a hand on her arm and she looked back to see the
blonde biting her lip anxiously. "What's up?"

"There's something I need to tell you first," Cadie said.

"Okay," Jo replied slowly.

"Remember the conversation we had a few days ago? About
Naomi threatening you?" Jo nodded. "Well, she implied that she
would plant drugs on board the *Seawolf* if I don't do what she
wants from now on." She held Jo's hand tightly as she felt the
thrumming vibration of rising anger in the tall skipper. "Jo, last
night before I joined the party, I searched our cabin from top to
bottom."

That explains why it took her so long to get changed, Jo realized. "And what did you find?" she asked softly, pushing her
anger into a manageable bundle at the back of her brain.

"Not a damn thing," Cadie replied. "Which means she's
either put them somewhere else on the boat or..."

Their eyes met.

"Or she's bluffing," Jo finished.

Cadie nodded.

Jo leaned forward, resting her forearms on her knees, hands
clasped in front of her as she tried to think the situation through
calmly and rationally. She turned her head to look up at the
blonde. "You think maybe this little fiasco might make her forget
about hassling me?" she asked.

Cadie considered the question. On the one hand, she had
never seen Naomi as jealous and possessive and...downright

nasty...as she had been about the *Seawolf*'s skipper. *But then you've never been in love with anyone else, either, Arcadia,* she reminded herself. *On the other hand...*

"My guess would be yes," she replied. "If she follows her usual pattern, then her No. 1 concern is, and will always be, her career. She's going to be too busy trying to save her political hide to be messing with you." She paused and caught blue eyes dark with concern. "I hope." She smiled wanly.

Jo snorted. "Well, I don't think we can take any chances," she said, flipping open her cell phone and dialing Paul's number.

"Hey Paulie, it's me. No, we're going to be a while, I think. Listen, I need you to do something for me. There's a rumor going around that we may have some drugs stashed somewhere on board." She eased the phone away from her ear as Paul protested loudly. "I know, mate. But the way things are right now, it's in our best interests to turn the boat over, just in case. If you find anything, ditch it any way you can. No, don't worry about Cadie's cabin; she's already been through it." Jo glanced up at the group of Americans still trying to negotiate with the custody sergeant. "No, Paulie, I don't give a rip about their privacy right now. If we ever get out of here, we're going to have a pack of press and God knows who else on our tail, and I don't want any nasty consequences for the company."

Cadie watched as the dark-haired woman calmly went about organizing things with Paul. She reached out and placed a hand on the small of the skipper's back, rubbing gently with her fingertips.

I'm so glad she's here, Cadie thought, noting the fatigue evident on Jo's face as she scrubbed at her eyes with her free hand. The blonde remembered the Jo who had rescued Josh and blown away the man with the machine gun. *That woman is a part of her all the time,* she considered, recognizing the realities and history there. *You can see it in the way she handles every crisis. Calculating. Smart. Cool.*

"Thanks, Paul." Jo turned off the phone and closed her eyes for a moment, savoring the feel of Cadie's fingers slowly working the tense muscles in her lower back. *She's turned my world upside down,* she thought. *But I've never felt luckier.*

They were both brought out of their reveries by a particularly frustrated outburst from Therese.

"Okay," Jo said, pushing herself up. "Time to get this bullshit done with." She walked forward, tapping the attorney on the shoulder. Therese looked at her inquiringly. "I think I can help," Jo said quietly. "Let me make some phone calls."

"Great, Skipper, go for it. We're having no luck getting through to this idiot."

The sergeant bristled and Jo raised her hands in placation.

"Let's just all settle, shall we?" she asked, directing the Americans to the seats along the wall where Cadie was resting. She turned back to the by now far less friendly policeman and rewarded him with one of her most winning smiles.

Cadie smirked at the charmed look that immediately softened the man's craggy features. *Putty in her hands,* the blonde chuckled silently.

"Sarge," Jo started, pressing her hands down on the countertop and leaning conspiratorially towards him, "I know you've had a long night, and the last thing you want, really, is a pack of Americans on one side and the press just outside the door. Am I right?"

"It has been a long night, that's true, miss," he said, reaching up and loosening his dark blue tie, unleashing the top button of his uniform shirt. "But I can't go letting those ladies go just because they're tourists, now can I?"

"No, no you can't," Jo agreed solemnly. She rested her forearms on the desktop and considered her options. "The thing is though, you'd be doing me an enormous favor if you let me make a few phone calls and try and get this sorted out. See, these guys are my responsibility. And if my boss gets wind of this, he's going to kick my backside from one end of the Passage to the other."

The policeman knew enough to know he was being played, but he was enjoying the beautiful woman's attentions too much to make Jo stop. "I can certainly understand why you'd want to clear this up as quickly as possible, miss," he said agreeably, leaning down next to her.

"So how about letting me make those calls?" she asked, smiling up at him.

He reached under the counter and pulled up a phone, plunking it down on the desktop with a nonchalant smile. "I'll even let you use my blower, miss," he said.

That's my girl, Cadie thought with a smile as she watched Jo grin at the officer.

Meaty, nicotine-stained fingers fumbled for the jangling phone that was out to torture Detective Ken Harding. A jaundiced eye peeled itself open enough to take in the clock radio's red glare.

Who the fuck is calling me at 8am on my day off? His first attempt at answering failed miserably when all he produced was a hoarse gargle. "What?" he barked, second time lucky.

"Hello, Ken," purred a dark, rich female voice that could only be one woman on the planet.

Harding felt things shifting in his boxers that hadn't moved of their own accord in months. *Hell, years,* he admitted to himself. *But, damn, that voice could move mountains.* He rolled himself upright, swinging his legs off the bed. "That you, Madison?" he growled redundantly, his gonads telling him exactly who it was.

"Mhmmm," she drawled. "Hope I haven't gotten you up too early?"

Jesus. Now's she's psychic. "It's 8am. And it's my first day off in two weeks. What do you think?" he muttered, scraping fingernails through itchy chin stubble.

She laughed a rolling sexy chuckle that made him think of satin sheets. He morosely flicked a dead toenail clipping off the thinning polyester number he was sitting on and tried to concentrate on what the woman was saying.

"Sorry, mate," she said. "But I need your help. Again."

Harding immediately sat up straighter. "What's happened? Those bastards been after you again?"

"No, no, Ken, it's nothing like that. I just need a favor. A big one," Jo said. "I'm not even sure you've got the pull to get it done for me."

"Try me," he said, reaching for his cigarettes. He lit up his first for the day as he listened while Jo told him about Naomi's arrest. "Jesus, she sounds like a pain in the arse," he muttered at one point and he could almost hear Jo grinning.

"Oh, she is that," the skipper answered quietly. "What do you think, mate? Can you help us get them out of here without any charges being brought?"

Harding considered his options, taking a deep drag on the cigarette. "You're positive there's no hint of drugs on these three?" he asked.

"Positive," she answered quickly. "Just drunk and disorderly. Though I will admit they've all got a history with the stuff. Thankfully this time they just got tanked on gin and vodka."

"Okay," he said. "Look, I think I can get it done. Ya gotta give me an hour or so, though. The Commissioner gets cranky this hour of the morning. Leave it with me, okay?"

"Great, Ken, thanks." He could hear the relief in her voice. "You've got my cell phone number, yeah?"

Tattooed on the insides of my eyelids, baby. "Yeah, I've got it," he replied. "I'll call you as soon as I've got something organized. But you know it's going to be hard to keep this outta the newspapers. I can't do much about that."

"It already is. But at least her spin doctors can make some mileage if we can get them out of here unscathed."

Harding stubbed his butt out in the overflowing ashtray next to his bed. He was a little puzzled. "I don't get it," he said. "I mean, apart from the fact they're clients, why do you give a shit?" There was a pause on the other end of the phone and Harding pictured those gorgeous baby blues blinking as she came up with an answer. *Sensational.* He heard her sigh.

"It's for Cadie," she finally replied.

Aaah, the cute blonde. I should've known. What a waste of a couple of great looking sheilas. "Fair enough," he said gruffly. "I'll do what I can."

"Thanks, mate. Talk to you soon." She hung up.

Harding stood as he dropped the receiver back on the hook. With a grunt he pushed his hands behind his hips and arched, stretching out the kinks in his overladen backbone. He lumbered towards the bathroom, scratching himself as he walked.

Jesus, I look like something the cat puked up, he thought, staring at his reflection. *Ah well.* He picked his toothbrush up and scrubbed away for a couple of minutes. *At least I look better than I feel.* He walked back into the main room of his tiny, disorganized bed-sit. *Okay, let's see who I can piss off at this time of the morning,* he thought as he reached once again for the phone. *Anything for long, dark, and dangerous.*

Jo looked around the room. The Americans had settled into a resigned silence and were scattered around the periphery. There wasn't a one of them who wasn't feeling the effects of a huge night of partying and it was starting to show on their faces.

Including mine, I'm sure, Jo thought wearily as the dull pounding at her temples forced its way to the forefront of her awareness. With gritted teeth she pushed it back again. *God I hope Jen is making us all a big fried breakfast. We are so going to need it.* She glanced over to where Cadie was sitting, her head resting back against the wall. *Is she asleep?* Her question was answered when green eyes blinked open and locked onto hers instantly. *I guess not.* Jo smiled, receiving an answering grin. *How do we do that, I wonder?*

Any further thought was interrupted by her cell phone. Jo looked down at her watch as she flipped the phone open. *Forty minutes. Not bad.*

"Madison," she said.

"It's done," she heard Harding say. "Your little mate behind the desk there should start getting phone calls any minute now." Sure enough the phone on the counter loudly announced itself and the custody sergeant reached for it.

"From your mouth to God's ear, Harding," Jo muttered. "I owe you one, mate. Another one."

"Forget it," he replied. "Just get yourself down here in a couple of months when that slimeball Marco is fit enough to put on trial."

"Count on it," she promised. "How is he, by the way?"

"He's talking again," Harding said. "Of course he's talking in a falsetto since you ripped his nuts off." Jo winced as she listened to the cop's rough laughter, and she caught Cadie's eye. "But he won't be walking around for a while yet. I'll call you when the court dates are set."

"Okay, Ken," she said. "Thanks again, mate." She tucked the phone back into its holster and wandered over to the empty seat next to Cadie.

"Bad news?" Cadie asked quietly. "I saw you wincing before," she explained at Jo's quizzical look.

"Oh. No, not at all, actually." She nodded over at the custody sergeant who was still on the phone, his forehead creased into a frown. "In fact, I think our friend over there is just getting the word now." She looked down at Cadie and smiled. "It's going to be okay, love," she whispered.

"Oh, I adore you," Cadie replied, just as quietly. She wrapped a hand around Jo's bicep and squeezed gratefully. "So what was the wince for, Miss Miracle Worker?"

Jo chuckled. "Just an update on Marco's medical condition." That earned her another empathetic squeeze. "And I'm not the miracle worker. Harding got it done."

"Remind me to send him a bunch of flowers," Cadie murmured, watching as the desk sergeant hung up the phone and disappeared out the door to another part of the police station.

"He'd appreciate a carton of cigarettes and a bottle of scotch more," replied Jo. She leaned sideways, intending to drop a kiss into the soft, gold locks that were so close. But a sudden realization that Sarah was watching them with a curious expression on her face brought her up short. *Whoa, Jo-Jo,* she thought. *Remember where you are. She's not yours to kiss.*

"I want to thank him, not contribute to his early death, Jo-Jo," the blonde replied with a smile, for once oblivious to the thoughts crossing the skipper's mind. She glanced up, surprised to find a very guarded expression clouding Jo's usually open face. "What is it?" she asked.

"Hon, you might want to let go of my arm," the taller woman whispered. "The children are watching."

"Ugh," grunted Cadie, sliding her hand away from the warmth of the inside of Jo's arm. "Sorry."

"Don't worry about it," Jo said. "I think that's going to be the least of our worries for the next few hours or so."

"Oh gee, thanks, that's reassuring." The blonde laughed.

They were saved from further anxious moments by the return of the charge sergeant who walked through into their part of the room. "Ladies and gentlemen," he said. "I've been informed by my superior officer that there will be no charges brought against the three ladies and they are free to leave." Sighs of relief and subdued cheers rang around the room. "I reckon you don't want to be taking them out through the front door, so if you'd like to follow me, I can let you all out the back way."

Toby leapt to his feet. "Okay, here's what we're going to do," he said. "Jason and I are going out to give the press a statement. That will give you all a chance to get back to the boat without having the hacks on your heels. Leave us a buggy and we'll catch up with you as soon as we can."

Jo nodded and stood. "Sounds like a plan," she said. She turned and followed Therese and Sarah through to the part of the police station that housed the overnight holding cells. She felt Cadie at her back. *The sooner we get out of here, the better,* Jo thought, the smells and sounds of the jail bringing back some distant memories she would rather forget.

A reassuring hand on her back let her know Cadie was making a good guess about her thought processes and she couldn't help but smile.

They rounded a corner and there sat Naomi, Larissa, and Kelli. Cadie and Jo moved rapidly away from each other.

The blonde warily approached her partner, who sat in a corner of the room, her expression as dark and threatening as any she'd ever seen. Naomi was unkempt and clearly feeling very much the worse for wear. *Handle with care,* Cadie thought to herself. *Apart from anything else, a humiliated Naomi is a dangerous Naomi.* "Hi, Nay," she finally said.

Slowly the senator pushed herself up out of her seat. She glowered at Cadie with an intense fury that forced the blonde backwards a step. Jo felt the hairs at the back of her neck rise and she made a move towards the pair, stopped only by a quick look from Cadie.

"Where the fuck were you?" Naomi growled, low and soft. "You were supposed to be with me, and then you were gone. None of this would have happened if you'd just stayed where you were supposed to stay. Where..." She moved closer to Cadie. "...the fuck..."

Jo felt herself rock onto the balls of her feet.

"...were you?"

Cadie tried to stay as still and calm as she could. Inches in front of her face, Naomi oozed venom. Behind and to the side of her, she could feel Jo radiating a kind of protective anger that felt warm...but dangerous.

"It was crowded, Naomi," she said quietly, acknowledging to herself that her own long fuse was sparking. "I got separated from you in the crush. I could just as easily ask where you were. I looked for you for an hour and then decided the best thing was to go back to the boat. Perhaps if you'd thought about it a little more, that answer would have occurred to you."

Two things then happened in quick succession; so fast, in fact, that Cadie barely had time to blink and it was over. Naomi raised a hand to slap the blonde and a dark blur swooped over Cadie's left shoulder, pinning the senator's hand in an immovable grip.

"Don't even think about it," Jo murmured, nose to nose with the infuriated senator. "You'll regret it for a very long time."

Ooo, my hero, Cadie thought, wondering at the casual strength humming through the tall woman. *But it's not a good idea to let this go on much longer.* She looked at Naomi and for the first time, saw fear on the older woman's face. "Jo," Cadie said quietly. "I think you can let her go now."

Without taking her eyes from the senator's, Jo released her hand and stepped back. Naomi lowered her arm, breathing heavily.

"Ladies," Therese said sharply from behind them. "We really don't have time for this bullshit. Let's go."

Jo nodded, and then gestured to the door, waiting for Naomi to make a move. With a low growl the American did so, walking out the door and into the brilliant sunshine.

"Thank you," Cadie said as she and the skipper followed Therese and Sarah out. "Though I don't think she would really have hit me."

Jo raised an eyebrow. *The hell she wouldn't. She was going to...she was all set to.* "I wasn't going to take that chance," she said aloud. "Not now, not ever. I don't care what plans she has to blackmail us." Jo looked down at the blonde. "I know it's going to make her angrier, but I can't—won't—let her hurt you." She shrugged. "Sorry. That's just the way I am."

Cadie watched as Therese, Sarah, and Naomi climbed into one golf buggy, while Larissa and Kelli clambered into the back of the other. "I wouldn't have you any other way," Cadie murmured without looking back up at the blue eyes she knew were fixed on her. "I think I'd better go with them." She gestured at Naomi's cart.

"Mhmm," Jo replied. "See you back at the boat. If you see a journalist, run over it."

Cadie snorted a quiet laugh.

Toby and Jason faced the media like the seasoned professionals they were. Toby, ever the front man, took control.

"Ladies and gentleman, if you would gather round please, we have a statement from Senator Silverberg." He waited as reporters, photographers and news crews bustled around him, hurriedly setting up microphone stands and tape recorders. "My name is Toby McIntyre. This," he indicated his partner, "is Jason Samuels. We are the senator's press liaison team.

"Last night, while celebrating Hamilton Island Race Week with other members of her party and crew from the boat she has been staying on for the past two weeks, the senator was accidentally detained by the Hamilton Island police. Contrary to this morning's newspaper reports at no stage was the senator under arrest, nor was there ever any question of that being the case. She and her companions have been released unconditionally. Thank you."

A hubbub of questions rose from the assembled pack but Toby backed away from the microphones.

"There will be no further comment or questions answered at this time," Jason said, before he too turned away and walked back into the police station.

"What do you think?" he asked *sotto voce* to his partner as they retreated.

"I think we'd better get out to sea pretty damn quickly," Toby replied.

The *Seawolf* sliced through the water heading due east from Hamilton Island, towards the outer banks of the Great Barrier Reef. Jo had a destination in mind that wasn't marked on any of the tourist maps and didn't even have a name on the nautical charts. It was a tiny horseshoe-shaped reef and lagoon she knew nobody else would find in a hurry, least of all a pack of journalists with no local knowledge.

They were cruising at about nine knots, the yacht listing with the wind and making good time. Jo didn't have to do much to keep the big boat on track and she relaxed against the bulwark of the port crew cockpit, her right foot resting on a spoke of the wheel, keeping them on a steady course.

It had been a very subdued group of passengers who had made it back to the boat without further incident. Toby and Jason had helped the crew get the *Seawolf* out to sea but since then the Americans had done little else but sit around the cockpit talking in low voices. The senator had disappeared below decks for a while but had since returned, showered and refreshed, to her usual spot in the corner. *She's said barely a word,* Jo noted. Even Cadie was keeping a low profile by helping Jen in the galley.

Jo took another bite on the big bacon sandwich in her left hand, grateful for the hangover-curing miracle the tasty treat was working. Jen and Cadie had made enough to keep passengers and crew going until they could prepare a late lunch once they found anchorage. The skipper hadn't had much chance to talk with Paul and Jenny since their return to the *Seawolf,* other than to issue sailing orders, but she watched as the big man skillfully made his way towards her across the moving deck.

"Hey, Jo-Jo," he greeted her, stealing half a sandwich from the plate tucked into a niche in the side of the cockpit.

"Hiya, Paulie," she returned.

"Pretty quiet group," he said between mouthfuls.

"Mmm. I suspect they're just realizing the good senator is in a fair amount of poo, mate," she replied. She looked over at the big man. "So how did the search go?"

He shrugged as he wolfed down the last of his bacon.

"Came up dry, Skip," he said.

"You searched everywhere?"

"Hell, yeah," he reiterated. "I shone a torch in any space a human hand can get into. From the bowsprit to the bilge pumps. Nothing. If there are drugs on this boat, I'll bare my bum and do a dance down Main Street."

"Okay, okay, I believe you." She chuckled at the mental image. *So it was a bluff.* A tiny flicker of hope sputtered into life in her heart. *Maybe, for once, the senator isn't going to have things all her own way. Perhaps Cadie will actually get to do what's good for her. It could be a start, at least.* It was an unexpectedly bright thought in an otherwise grim morning.

Jo's gamble had paid off. The small coral cay had proven to be uninhabited and the *Seawolf* was safely anchored in the lagoon. The weather was idyllic; warm, and a cloudless sky but with an ocean breeze blowing from the east, where the breakers crashed against the leading edge of the reef. Their anchorage was sheltered and calm, a perfect spot for swimming or walking the coral.

The dark-haired skipper sighed as she balanced on the bowsprit, binoculars in hand. It should have been the ideal place to bring a boatload of tourists, but instead the Americans had settled into a morose kind of stupor. Only Larissa and Kelli, who were apparently oblivious to anything other than their own enjoyment, were making the most of the location, snorkeling not far off the boat's port beam.

Jo lifted the binoculars to her eyes and scanned the sea between them and the mainland.

So far, so good, she thought. *Which is more than I can say for the mood.* Therese, Sarah, and Naomi had had a shouting match of epic proportions not long after they'd anchored. The attorneys were apparently none too pleased about being caught up in Naomi's escapades. At one point Therese had pointed out that the senator was on the brink of blowing 10 years' hard work for one idiot night of partying. *Hard to believe it could get that ugly.*

She glanced up as Cadie picked her way over the deck fittings towards her. Despite it all, the blonde still managed to conjure up her trademark smile, the top of her nose wrinkling as green eyes met blue.

"Hello, Skipper," Cadie said softly, resisting the urge to invade the tall woman's personal space just so she could feel those long arms wrapped around her. Instead she nervously held her hands behind her back.

"Hi," Jo replied. "How are you doing with all this?"

Cadie shrugged and Jo noted the barely reined in tension in the blonde's compact body. "I'm okay, I guess," Cadie said, not meeting Jo's gaze.

"Uh-huh," replied the skipper skeptically. "Try again, kiddo."

Cadie chuckled. "Hey, I'm only a couple of years younger than you, grandma, so who are you calling kiddo?" She grinned as she said it, and Jo was relieved to see a sparkle return to those gorgeous eyes. Cadie looked around at the other passengers dotted around the deck. "I guess we're all just waiting, and it makes me nervous."

"Waiting for what?" Jo asked. "I mean, if we can get through till tomorrow morning without the scumbag media finding us, it'll all blow over."

Cadie shook her head slowly. "I wish that were true, hon," she said. "It may well blow over with the Australian media. But it's the middle of the night in the US. Hopefully we didn't make the evening news, but for sure it's going to hit the airwaves first thing in the morning. And then..." She shrugged again. "Who knows what will happen?"

Jo had never had much reason to think about the internal machinations of US politics. "So what are we talking about here? A rap over the knuckles?"

Cadie leaned back on the bowsprit rail, taking the opportunity to brush the back of her hand against the warmth of Jo's thigh. The two women took a couple of seconds just to enjoy the tingles that set off in both of them until, with an effort, Cadie pulled her eyes away and focused on answering the question.

"Well, Jason thinks she'll be recalled straight away," she replied.

"By the Senate?" Jo guessed.

Cadie shook her head. "No. By the senior party members. The leaders of the Republican Party, in other words," she clarified, seeing the crease appear on Jo's forehead.

"And what will they do?"

"Good question. I don't really know to be honest. She's never managed to get herself into trouble like this before."

Jo shifted around a little so she could place a hand against the blonde's shoulder blade, where she began a gentle rubbing. "Is it really such a big deal?" she asked, smiling as she felt Cadie lean back into her touch. "She's surely not the first politician to get caught with a glass of alcohol in her hand. Hell, here a pollie's looked at suspiciously if they *don't* take a drink."

Cadie chuckled, shaking her head. "I'd believe that." She smiled. "Unfortunately, the Republican Party is a very conservative institution. Having an openly gay senator in the party was something of a novelty to say the least. There are still large factions of the party that have been waiting for an opportunity to tear Naomi to shreds."

"And she's just given them that opportunity," Jo murmured.

"Yes," Cadie quietly agreed. "It could get very ugly."

"Ugly as a hatful of arseholes." Jo grinned at the belly laugh that erupted from the blonde. Cadie quickly tried to stifle it as heads popped up in the cockpit. "Sorry, love," Jo said. "Didn't mean to do that to you."

Cadie wiped away a tear as she finished giggling. "God, I adore the way you talk," she said, beaming back at the tall Australian, who arched an elegant eyebrow in reply.

"Perhaps you'd better back off a little, darling," Jo said softly. "Last thing we need right now is Naomi going off on another rant."

Cadie sighed and turned around again to lean back on the rail. "Well, the good news is she's got way too much on her mind right now to worry about what I'm doing," she muttered.

Jo sensed the change in mood and saw the look of quiet resignation in the blonde's eyes. "And the bad news?"

Cadie's head dropped and she fiddled nervously with the gold band around her ring finger. "The bad news is I still have to go back with her, Jo-Jo."

Jo smiled quietly, unsurprised by that. "I know, honey." She resumed gently circling her fingers between Cadie's shoulder blades, feeling the tension rippling under the surface of the soft skin. "Just to set your mind at ease a little, Paul and Jenny didn't find any drugs anywhere aboard."

Cadie straightened up and Jo saw her jaw muscles working as she ground her teeth together. "So she was just trying to bluff me," the blonde growled. "And I let her."

"Ssshhh. Don't be so hard on yourself. She can be bloody intimidating." That drew a smile from the American. *Was wondering if I'd see that again.*

"This from the Queen of Dangerous." Cadie was pleased when she felt the rumbling laugh from the tall woman behind her. *And I'm going to give her an hour to stop that rubbing.*

"Like I said before, I've seen a lot worse than Naomi Silverberg," Jo said quietly. Cadie nodded silently and Jo felt a wave of sympathy for the younger woman. "You have a lot of history with her, Arcadia. I understand that you feel a need to support her through whatever happens next."

"It's not just that, Jo," the blonde replied. "There are so many loose ends."

"I know. I'll be here when you're ready, sweetheart."

Cadie turned to face her, sliding a hand over Jo's nearest knee and squeezing softly. "Have I told you lately how much I love you?" she asked softly, feeling a thrill as their eyes met, a solid jolt of desire warming her belly. Blue eyes blazed into hers and she knew Jo felt it too. A long thumb slid gently back and forth across the skin of the back of her hand.

"No," Jo replied, teasing, "but feel free to tell me as often as you like from now on."

"Okay." Another long smiling moment passed between them. *Crisis? What crisis?* "I love you more than air," she said tenderly, lifting Jo's hand to her mouth and brushing her lips across the palm gently.

A shiver unbalanced Jo momentarily and she quickly grabbed on to the bowsprit with her free hand, the strength of her physical reaction to Cadie's touch surprising her. She exhaled on a long, ragged breath.

"Wow," Jo muttered. They blinked at each other for a few seconds. "Did you feel that, too?"

"Oh yes."

"More than air, huh?" Jo asked. Cadie nodded solemnly. "Oh, we are in so much trouble."

They'd decided on a late supper, and by 10pm everyone was starting to mellow out just a little. Soft music drifted up from below decks and though the moon was only about half full, phosphorescence shimmered in the water around the boat. The air was still and the sounds of the open ocean half a mile away could be clearly heard in the background. There had been no sign of any media either by sea or air.

Cadie sprawled across the cockpit cowling, her belly full of fresh seafood, including lobster caught by Paul and Jo just that afternoon. She looked up into the blanket of softly twinkling stars. *There must be more stars in this southern sky than back in Chicago,* she thought wistfully. Here, away from the masking lights of any big cities, the inky sky seemed crowded with twinkling pinpoints. *Beautiful.*

She shivered as the slight suggestion of a breeze brushed coolly over her bare arms and shoulders, making the ever-present sunburn tingle in response. Cadie heard a movement to her left and started as a cream-colored sweatshirt landed in her lap.

"It gets cool quickly out here," a familiar, warm voice said softly from below her. Cadie glanced down and saw two night-darkened eyes blinking back at her.

"Thanks," the blonde replied quietly, flicking a glance at Naomi who hadn't moved from the same spot in the corner of the cockpit all day. The senator didn't even give them a second glance. Cadie let her eyes drift back to Jo, a smile flirting between them.

"My pleasure," the skipper murmured before she moved away again.

Cadie pulled the sweatshirt over her head. Her senses tingled when she recognized the cinnamon-tinged scent as a combination of the soap Jo used and the tall woman's own distinctive aroma. *And something else,* she pondered, breathing the comforting essence in deeply. *Sunscreen,* she realized, smiling. *God, I hope she doesn't plan on getting this back any time soon...if ever.* She giggled softly at herself.

From where she sat in the crew cockpit, playing random notes on Paul's guitar, Jo watched the blonde affectionately. *That thing's way too big for her,* she thought as Cadie pulled the sweatshirt on and wriggled around in it till it was sitting comfortably. *She could wear it as a dress.* She found herself grinning as she caught Cadie pulling the front of the garment up to her nose and apparently sniffing it. *What is she...* She tilted her head inquiringly but all she got back in reply was a silly grin. *I'm guessing that's the last I'll see of that shirt,* she thought affectionately.

The music piped up from below ended and Jo began humming softly as she plucked the guitar's strings, letting her voice and the instrument find their own path together. She felt rather than saw Cadie's eyes fix on her and she tried to make the music just for one person, weaving a slow, melodic counterpoint around the guitar's notes.

That's magic. Cadie stretched out on her side, head propped on her hand as she listened intently. *When I get back I want to hear a lot more of her singing. Need to get her out here on the water and relaxed. Just the two of us. Because any minute now...*

"What time is it in DC?" Naomi interrupted. Jo, who didn't know, ignored the question and continued playing.

Toby came up from below and sat down opposite the senator. "It's 7am, Nay," he said quietly.

"Jesus Christ," Naomi exclaimed, standing suddenly and beginning a restless pacing up and down the length of the cockpit. "I can see it now. They're all choking on their muesli as they watch *Good Morning America.*"

"I can't see Trent Lott eating muesli," Toby muttered incongruously. "He's more of an eggs benedict kind of guy."

Jo laughed quietly between codas, ignoring the evil glare she got from the senator as she resumed singing softly. Suddenly a cell phone rang somewhere below decks.

Naomi swung on Toby. "I thought we didn't bring any phones," she snapped. He put his hands up in a gesture of innocence.

"It's mine," Paul shouted from below. The ringing stopped as he obviously answered the call.

"But the GOP does know where you are, right, Naomi?" Toby

asked as the senator resumed her seat.

She snorted. "It was all I could do to stop them from turning this into a diplomatic mission instead of a vacation," she answered grumpily. "They were all for me giving some stupid, pointless speeches every other day. As if we give a damn what anybody in this backwater thinks of us." Cadie winced and flashed Jo an apologetic look. "We compromised. I gave them all the details of where we'd be, including the company's phone number, and I agreed to answer them when they called."

"Which is exactly what they want you to do," Paul said from where he stood at the top of the companionway. He reached out to Naomi with both his cell phone and a piece of paper. "That was Ron," he explained. "There's an urgent message for you, Senator."

Nice to see her intimidated for a change, Jo couldn't help thinking as she watched Naomi tentatively take the phone and message from her crewman.

"Fuck," the politician growled as she read the note. "It's from Lott," she told Toby and Jason. "Wants me to call him immediately."

The two men sat silently, neither willing to give any advice. Jo watched as she continued to play, humming softly now. Cadie sat up, swinging her legs over the edge of the cowling.

Feels like everyone is just holding their breath, Jo thought, catching Cadie's slightly shadowed eyes. Water slapped against the hull softly as everyone on board waited for Naomi to make a move. She sat still for several seconds, turning the cell phone over and over in one hand as she tugged at her bottom lip with the fingers of the other.

"So..." she finally said. "I guess I'd better call him." She stood and climbed up out of the cockpit, picking her way forward to find a little more privacy.

Cadie wondered briefly if she should follow, but thought better of it. *She'll be letting us all know exactly how it went, if I know her.*

Sure enough, it wasn't many minutes before Naomi's fate became obvious to all. Subdued talking was followed by a protracted pause. Jo, the only one with an unobstructed view of the front of the boat, watched the senator's silhouette. After being almost rock-still for several minutes, Naomi suddenly exploded into motion, letting loose a long ragged howl of frustration and tossing the cell phone high and far.

The ensuing silence was punctuated by the distant splash of the electronic projectile.

"Tell me that wasn't my phone," Paul muttered.

"Okay, that wasn't your phone," Jo lied grimly.

Further conversation was prevented by the return of the senator who stomped back down into the cockpit and slumped in her usual corner.

"What's the news?" Toby asked quietly.

Naomi sighed. "They want us back there as soon as possible."

It's always "us" when she's in trouble, Cadie thought ruefully.

Toby grunted and turned to Jo. "Don't suppose you know the airline schedules off the top of your head, Jo?" he asked.

Jo nodded. "I know enough to know the first plane to Sydney's at 9.30am tomorrow," she replied. "That will get you there in time to connect with the outgoing lunchtime flights to LA or San Francisco."

"And you can get us back to the airport in time for that?"

Jo did some rough calculations in her head. "Not unless we sail at night, which isn't the best plan. But there's no problem. We can organize a water taxi to get out here by, say, 5.30am. Early enough to get you to Hamilton Island in plenty of time."

Toby nodded. "Then I suggest we all start packing," he said quietly.

Larissa piped up from where she leaned against the starboard rail. "Why do we all have to go back now? There are still a few days to go," she whined.

Naomi stopped her progress towards the companionway and Cadie watched as she closed her eyes and took a deep breath. *Ohhh, Larissa, that was not a good move,* the blonde thought with a guilty feeling of relief that the oncoming blast wasn't going to be directed at her.

The senator turned, walked over to the lanky brunette, and leaned down so she was inches away from Larissa's slightly startled face. "I'll tell you why, Larissa," she hissed. "Because I paid for the whole damn thing. Because it's my reputation that got you out of jail in the first place." Jo and Cadie exchanged glances, the blonde smiling slightly at the skipper's eloquently arched eyebrow. "And because I goddamn well said so. Is that all right with you?" Larissa nodded mutely, shrinking away from the senator's intimidating presence. "Right. Let's get on with it then, shall we?"

The senator stomped down the companionway and disappeared below. For a few seconds the other passengers just sat in silence, absorbing their changed circumstances. Then, one by one, they stood and trailed down after her. Cadie was the last to go, jumping down off the cowling and casting a sad smile in Jo's direction.

Unexpectedly Jo found it hard to swallow for the tugging ache in her throat. She tried to smile back at the blonde before Cadie turned and headed below decks, but she knew her response had been wobbly at best. *Damn. I thought there would be more time before I started feeling like this.* She was aware of Jenny watching her quietly from the top of the companionway and she turned away from the crewman's scrutiny. *I refuse to cry. If I cry now, how the hell am I going to cope when she leaves in the morning?*

"She threw my goddamned phone into the ocean," Paul lamented from where he stood near the boom. "Can you believe that?"

Perfect end to a perfect day. She reached around and unclipped her own cell phone, keying in the Cheswick Marine office manager's home phone number. "Hi, Doris, it's Jo," she said when the woman answered. Jo glanced down at her watch, grimacing at the lateness of the hour. "Yeah, I'm really sorry about disturbing you at home this late. But we've got a bit of a problem and I need you to make some quick arrangements for me..."

Cadie moved quietly around the cabin, collecting odds and ends that still needed to be packed, and sliding them into nooks and crannies in either her or Naomi's bags. Normally she wouldn't have worried about who ended up with what, but a little voice in her head told her to keep her stuff close by.

I've already started separating our lives, she realized with a rush. She thought about all the logistics leaving Naomi was going to entail and the complexity of it felt overwhelming. She fought down a slightly panicky feeling. *Make like Scarlett O'Hara, Arcadia. Think about today, today and worry about tomorrow, tomorrow.* She glanced over to the bed where Naomi was sprawled untidily. The senator had fallen asleep not long after they had started packing, preferring, as usual, to let Cadie do the work.

Cadie watched the familiar outline of her partner's face for a while. She was again struck by how much the woman had changed from the young college activist she had connected with 12 years earlier.

I should feel sadder about the prospect of leaving you, Naomi. She lovingly tucked a certain cream-colored sweatshirt into the corner of her suitcase. *But I don't. I'm scared, and I don't know when it's going to happen, but I don't have any doubts about it any more. Being with you hasn't been what I've wanted for myself for a long time. And it only took a couple of weeks around Jo to make me see that.* She snorted quietly at herself. *Hell, truth be told, it took about two hours.*

She shivered slightly, rubbing her arms to chase away the pre-dawn chill. She knew the water taxi would be coming for them soon.

I don't want to leave. I don't want to leave Jo. She leaned over the suitcase, hands pressed onto the top of her clothes, eyes closed as a wave of melancholy threatened to unbalance her. *Oh God, Jo-Jo. I don't want to go, because I don't know when I can come back again. And the truth is I don't want to spend another minute without you. I've gone from being someone else's partner, to being totally and utterly yours. Lock, stock, and barrel.* A picture of the tall skipper's sexy, lopsided grin floated behind her eyelids and Cadie felt herself smile. *Not that you would put it that way, my love. But that's how it feels to me.*

A light knocking on the door tore at her attention.

"Come on in."

She looked over as Jenny stuck her head around the door. "Water taxi will be here in about half an hour, Cadie," the hostess said softly.

"Thanks," the blonde replied. She glanced over at her slumbering bedmate. "We'll be ready, despite all appearances to the contrary."

Jenny smiled back before disappearing again and Cadie sighed. She walked over to the bed and reached down, shaking the senator's shoulder gently. "Come on, Naomi, time to face the music."

Jo hugged her knees up to her chest and stretched her sweatshirt over them to fight off the pre-dawn chill. She gazed out to the east where pale pinks and yellows were starting to tint the sky. A long, thin line of cloud banded the horizon, its underside glowing orange as the sun threatened to peek above the waterline.

The dark-haired skipper rested the back of her head against the mast, content to let the growing activity below decks carry on without her. Jo hadn't slept at all but she felt strangely alert, her senses were buzzing.

I don't want to forget any of this. I don't want to forget a single detail of the last time I see Cadie. If she manages to get back here someday I want to have something I can compare that happiness to. The perverse logic of that tickled her sense of humor. *If she manages to get back here.*

She could feel and hear the passengers start to move around below. Jenny had done the rounds, warning everyone the water taxi was closing in, and already Paul was helping to move luggage up on deck.

Jo glanced down at her watch. *Barely 5.30am. They should get back to the island in time to pick up their spare gear and get to the airport,* she mused.

Doris had made some hasty phone calls late the night before and managed to book the Americans onto flights all the way back to Chicago.

Almost 9000 miles away. Nine thousand miles and one enormous goddamn ocean away. Jesus, I don't even have her phone number. As the sun breasted the horizon, bathing the tall woman's angular face in pale warmth, Jo fought the panicky knot of tension in her stomach.

"Jo-Jo!"

The skipper looked back over her left shoulder to see Jenny waving from the stern. The hostess pointed towards the mainland and Jo squinted. There in the distance was a large yellow motor launch churning through the waves towards them.

"Water taxi, Skipper!"

Jo waved back in acknowledgement and picked herself up off the deck. As she brushed off her shorts she noticed the Americans making their way up on deck. Everyone stood silently watching the approaching vessel. Therese and Sarah had their arms around each other. Toby, taller than his partner, had one arm draped over Jason's shoulder, his chin resting on top of the shorter man's head. Larissa and Kelli, as usual, slouched indifferently away from the rest of the group. Naomi was pacing again, up and back in a tight arc that wore Jo out just looking at her.

Damn she's wired tighter than the rigging, Jo thought.

Last one up on deck was Cadie. Unlike the others, the blonde was not looking out towards the water taxi. Instead she turned to find Jo. Their eyes locked and like so many times in the past two and a half weeks, the pair felt the world contract around them. Jo slowly began walking towards the stern, while Cadie stood silently in the cockpit. The skipper crouched down on the cockpit cowling, clasping her hands in front of her as she leaned her forearms on her thighs.

"Good morning," she said softly.

Cadie shook her head slowly back and forth, and Jo could see the early light catching tears that were close to brimming over blonde lashes. "Not really, no," Cadie replied shakily.

"I know," Jo said. She swallowed back a large chunk of ache and cleared her throat. "You should get to the airport in plenty of time. The folks from the hotel are going to meet the water taxi with your extra luggage and then drive you to the terminal." She knew she was just filling air, and she knew Cadie knew it too, as the blonde nodded her silent response.

Cadie gazed up at the woman she loved, taking in Jo's mussed hair and the dark circles under hooded blue eyes. *She hasn't slept a wink either. I can only imagine what this feels like for her.* She took a step closer to Jo, wanting desperately to say so much more than just goodbye.

"I'm sorry, Jossandra," she said. "I know how much this hurts."

"Ssshhh," Jo said, putting her finger against her own lips. "Don't. Please. Just don't forget me."

A sob threatened to escape Cadie's lips and she put her own hand to her mouth in an effort to contain her emotion. Jo saw anguish close the beautiful eyes she adored and her own heart ached.

"Never," Cadie whispered. "I will be back, Jo-Jo."

Jo shook her head slowly. "No promises, Arcadia," she said quietly. "Just do what you need to do for you. I'll be here."

Cadie nodded, but further communication was pre-empted by the arrival of the water taxi. Jo pushed herself up, but stayed put, knowing Jenny and Paul could handle things. The two crew tossed lines to the bobbing launch, pulling it closer till it was alongside the *Seawolf*'s transom. They then started passing luggage to the two men onboard the taxi.

"Skipper!" It was Jason, and Jo smiled as the blond man bounded across the deck and threw himself at her in a huge bear hug. She chuckled as she returned the embrace.

"I wanted to thank you," Jason said, stepping back and clasping Jo's hand. "Regardless of all the bullshit with Naomi, Toby and I have had a fantastic time. We want to come back again on our own schedule and spend some more time with you guys." He grinned.

"It's been a pleasure having you both aboard, mate," Jo replied graciously. "And you're both welcome, any time. Good sailors will always find a berth on the *Seawolf*." She grinned back at him.

"I'm sorry she's been so difficult," Jason said quietly, nodding his head to where the senator continued to pace.

"Forget it," Jo shook it off. "Not your fault for a start, and I've had more difficult than her to contend with." She smiled again at the shorter man. "Good luck on the way home, though."

Jason rolled his eyes. "God, I think we're going to need it," he laughed. "Anyway..." He let go of Jo's hand and started backing away towards the stern. "Thanks again, Jo, and take care."

"You too, Jason."

She looked over and waved to Toby who gave her a thumbs-up as he clambered into the water taxi. Therese and Sarah, too, turned and waved to the skipper, calling out their thanks as they followed the two men. Larissa and Kelli barely looked back. *Big surprise,* thought Jo, grateful to see the back ends of the two women. The senator followed, casting one last malevolent look at the tall skipper who just raised an eyebrow in response.

Cadie was the last one to leave. She turned away from Jo to say goodbye to Paul and Jenny. She gave the hostess a quick hug and got a warm smile in return. "I hope the wedding is everything you want it to be, Jen," she said, trying her best to smile back.

"I'll show you the pictures next time you're here," Jenny said with a knowing smile, catching the blonde by surprise.

"Um...yes, yes please do that. I'd love to see them." A genuine grin touched Cadie's eyes at the crewmember's confidence. "Thanks, Jen. For everything."

Then she turned to Paul. The big crewman scooped her up in a hug, and Cadie giggled as she felt her feet leave the deck. "You take care of yourself, sailor, you hear me?" he said gruffly as he put her down.

"I will, Paulie," she replied. She looked intently up into the tall blond's brown eyes. "Do me a favor?" she asked.

"If I can, you know I will," he responded, half-knowing what she was wanting.

Cadie glanced briefly towards Jo, who was standing in place, looking down at her feet miserably. "Look after her for me? She's hurting." The big man nodded silently and Cadie kissed his cheek. "Thank you." She turned to disembark, but was halted by a hand on her shoulder, spinning her back around. She looked up into wide blue eyes that sparkled with unshed tears.

I didn't even hear her coming, Cadie thought as she felt long arms sliding around her. *How does she do that?* All further thought was driven from her mind as Jo dipped her head and claimed Cadie's mouth in a long and searing kiss that drew the blonde up and closer. She slid her hands up to cup Jo's face and poured her whole heart into her response.

Jo's knees buckled and she felt one of Cadie's arms quickly drop and wrap around her waist to support her. They were vaguely aware of a disturbance on the water taxi behind them, but nothing broke the sanctity of the kiss, until finally, breathless, they pulled gently, slowly apart.

"I'm sorry," Jo murmured. "I couldn't let you go without..."

Cadie's fingers silenced her and Jo lost herself in the warm safety of the fair-haired woman's gaze. "I know. I'm glad you did," Cadie replied softly, gently unraveling herself from Jo's embrace, sliding her hands into the skipper's and taking a reluctant step back. "I love you, Jo-Jo."

"And I you." Just their fingers were touching as Cadie backed towards the transom and the waiting water taxi. Over Cadie's shoulder Jo could see the infuriated senator being held back by Jason and Toby. *I just made things a lot harder for her,* the skipper knew, acknowledging at the same time that nothing could have stopped her kissing the blonde.

Finally their fingertips brushed, then slid apart, and Cadie silently gave Jo a small wave, which the skipper returned with a crooked smile. Then the blonde took Paul's offered hand and stepped up into the motor launch. Once aboard she dodged around Naomi and quickly made her way to the stern as the engines fired up and the boat turned away from the *Seawolf.*

Jo watched the blonde take up her position. She gently raised her fingers to her lips again and blew Cadie a kiss, stretching out her arm towards the departing launch. Cadie replied in kind and Jo caught the kiss, pulled it to her heart, and held it there.

Cadie looked back at the skipper silhouetted against the rising sun, her hand over her heart. Tears slid down the blonde's cheeks as she held her own arm outstretched. *Look at her. My goddess.*

There goes half my heart, Jo thought, watching the love of her life slipping away to the horizon. Finally the ache in her throat took over and tears welled up and overflowed. For a few long minutes all she could do was stand there, one hand over her heart, eyes fixed on the rapidly shrinking motor launch, until finally it disappeared. She closed her eyes and let the tears flow unchecked. Vaguely aware of Paul and Jen moving quietly around the boat, giving her plenty of space, she slumped down onto the deck, head in hands. *This hurts so much. I didn't know it would hurt this much.*

Suddenly her phone rang, startling her as it pierced the early morning silence.

"Jesus," she exhaled, reaching for the device. "Who the hell is calling this early?" she muttered, fumbling for the right key. "The day can't get any worse from here, can it?" Finally she pushed the right button. "Madison."

"Jo, it's Doris." It was just as well the Cheswick office manager identified herself because her voice was almost unrecognizable, hoarse and ragged with what sounded like panic.

"Doris? What's wrong?" Jo asked immediately.

"It's Ron, Jo. He's had a heart attack. Come back in as soon as you can. Please. It's bad."

Jo closed her eyes again, squeezing back the thumping headache, which had sprung into life at Doris' words. *Wrong again, Madison. Wrong again.*

"We're on our way," she muttered, scrambling to her feet.

Chapter
Twelve

Even after the *Seawolf* disappeared over the horizon, Cadie remained at the stern of the water taxi, gazing out to the east, blinking against the glare of the rising sun. If she closed her eyes she could still see the vision of her love—dark hair whipping around her head, golden circle of the sun blazing behind her, a hand clasped over her heart. It was a lovely picture, but Cadie felt only pain as she committed the details to memory.

A million thoughts and emotions churned through Cadie's mind. Sorrow, love, indecision, anger, and frustration all warred for their place in her consciousness. Chief among them was an overwhelming sense that she was doing the wrong thing by leaving.

But how can that be? No matter how screwed up Naomi and I may be right now, we had something good once. Didn't we? Cadie covered her face with her hands, momentarily swamped by indecision. *That's why I'm here, isn't it? Because of our history. Because of all the loose ends. Because she needs me to help her get through this. Doesn't she?*

Behind Cadie, Jason and Toby had managed to wrestle the infuriated senator into the cabin of the water taxi. She sat between the two men, anger and jealousy radiating off her in malevolent waves. Naomi muttered and squirmed in her seat, shaking off Jason and Toby's hands which had circled her upper arms.

"Goddamn it, Naomi, you have got to get a grip on yourself," said Toby earnestly, barely resisting the urge to shake some sense into the woman. "Don't you realize that she's crucial to how things work out for you in the next few days?" He gestured towards the blonde leaning against the stern rail.

That caught Naomi's attention and she tore furious eyes away from Cadie and fixed the PR man with a grim stare. "Explain," she growled.

"Well, Jesus, it's not brain surgery," a frustrated Jason said from her other side. "You're about to walk into a firestorm. The press think you were not only wasted on God knows what illegal substances, but that you were with a woman other than your part-

ner at the time. The Australian media may not understand the sig-
nificance of that, but once we hit US soil, Naomi, there's gonna be
hell to pay. You're the first openly lesbian Republican senator, for
Christ's sake. Part of why you were elected at all was the stability
of your relationship with Cadie. You know that."

His partner took up the argument.

"Naomi, if you can walk off that plane in Chicago with Cadie
at least looking calm and happy by your side, it will go a long way
to helping this whole nightmare blow over. Turn up alone or looking like you both do right now, and things will get degrees worse,
very quickly," Toby said.

Naomi glared from one to the other. "That slut," she hissed,
"is the reason this 'whole nightmare' happened in the first place.
If she'd just stayed away from that bitch and..." She was silenced
when Toby roughly grabbed her arm and covered her mouth with
his hand.

"Shut up, Naomi," he said fiercely. "For once, just shut up,
and listen to the advice we're giving you. That is what you pay us
for, after all." He waited until the senator finally nodded and he
lowered his hand. "I'll be honest with you, Nay, I don't give a
good goddamn who's to blame for what anymore. I don't even
care what you and Cadie do in the long term. But I'm telling you
that if you want to salvage this situation with any degree of dig-
nity and more importantly, credibility intact, you'll march off that
plane with her on your arm. And look like you want her there."

The stocky woman slumped back in her chair, all the fight
seemingly drained out of her.

"Think about it," Jason said quietly. "The last 10 years of
your career—and the next 10, for that matter—rest on what happens to you in the next few days. Don't waste my time, Toby's
time, or any of your other supporters' time. At least mend enough
fences to convince Cadie to play along until we can get you both
out of the media spotlight for a few days."

Both men stood and turned away from the senator. They
walked back out into the sunlight and sat down next to Therese
and Sarah, starting a quiet conversation with the two attorneys.
No one went near Cadie.

She needs me, right? Cadie thought to herself. *I mean that's
why I'm doing this, isn't it? Twelve years of history and I care
about her, right?* She looked back out to sea and her heart fled
back over the horizon towards a tall, dark-haired skipper with
shining blue eyes. Finally, she turned to face the other people on
the boat. Immediately her attention was caught by the ferociously
angry glare coming from the shadows inside the taxi's cabin.

Cadie firmed her jaw and stared back.

And I want her to understand that when I leave, it's because she and I don't work together any more, not because I met someone else. She has to know this is about her, not Jo.

Memories of that overheard conversation came back to haunt Cadie and again doubts welled up in her. *She's gonna kick me out anyway,* she thought in frustration. *God, why am I bothering?*

A little voice piped up, persistent as ever. *Because it's the right thing to do, Arcadia. It might be hard to define and it might feel like crap, but it's the right thing to do.* She sighed, knowing that going against her gut instincts was a short path to an ulcer, if not insanity.

God, Jo, I miss you already. I'd give anything to feel your arms around me right now. Cadie hugged herself instinctively, and looked around at the scenery as the taxi flew across the water. *Colors are so bright here,* she reflected, taking in the brilliant aquas and greens of the sea and islands. She took a deep breath and turned her face to the sun, closing her eyes and savoring the warmth and rushing salt-wind. *I hope the universe brings me back here. Soon.*

Cadie stayed that way for the rest of the journey back to Hamilton Island, moving only when she felt the boat decelerate as it entered the shelter of the marina. She looked over and saw two dark-windowed limousines waiting at the dock. Toby was talking to the water taxi's skipper, and it wasn't long before the PR man came back to talk to the group.

"The hotel's already loaded the rest of our luggage into the limos," he said. "So we can go straight to the airport. The press still doesn't know what we're up to, but it's a fair bet they'll have someone waiting at the airport. It's time for the game face, people. Let's try and look like we're all one big, happy family, okay?" He looked up at the dock, where two chauffeurs and a number of hotel staff were waiting to assist them. "Because the children are already watching," he emphasized. "It's only a matter of time before the press tracks us down."

Naomi emerged from the cabin looking like a new woman. There was no hint of anger or unhappiness on her face and she had made an effort to smarten up her appearance.

Every inch the politician, Cadie thought wryly, standing up straight as Naomi approached her. *Just as always, when it counts.* The blonde had a brief flash of the goodbye kiss she and Jo had shared and was suddenly filled with apprehension about the senator's possible reaction. But for now, at least, she had nothing to worry about.

"All right, people, let's go," the senator said, brushing past Cadie with barely a glance. Quietly the others followed the politician off the launch and up the stone steps of the dock to the two cars. Toby gently nudged Cadie in the same direction as Naomi, but he needn't have bothered.

I know how to play this game, the blonde thought resignedly as she climbed into the spacious limousine and slid across the leather seats until she was next to Naomi. The senator turned away and stared out of the tinted window. *And that suits me just fine.* Cadie breathed a sigh of relief as it appeared she was to be left alone.

Jo was frustrated beyond belief. It seemed to her that almost from the moment Cadie had disappeared over the horizon, everything had started to go horribly wrong. In their haste to get back to Cheswick's base at Shute Harbor, Jo and the two crewmembers had rigged the boat as tightly as they could and picked the most direct route. But Mother Nature wasn't playing fair. The wind had died to almost nothing and the *Seawolf* was crawling along on a glassy sea.

"God *damn it*!" Jo thumped the wheel with the heel of her hand in frustration. "Where the fuck did the wind go, Paulie?" She raised her binoculars to her eyes again, casting about for any signs on the water's surface of an approaching wind gust.

"Beats me Skipper," the crewman said quietly. He was trying to keep a lid on his own emotions. He was just as anxious to get back to Ron as Jo was, but he was becoming concerned about the levels of stress radiating off the tall woman. Jo was restless and angry and Paul knew it had just as much to do with Cadie's departure as with Ron's illness. "Time to fire up the engine, Jo-Jo?"

The skipper growled with exasperation. "Fuck it. Yes. Crank it up, mate."

Paul jumped down into the cockpit and scrabbled around, lifting the engine cover. Within a couple of minutes the boat was under power and Jo watched as Jen and Paul pulled down the useless sails and stowed them away.

Jesus, she thought. *Today of all days. Perfect weather for the whole trip and the one day I really want to get somewhere fast— nothing.* She threw her cap into the companionway in sheer frustration and slumped onto one of the benches. *I wish Doris would call back and tell us what's happening.*

She knew Ron had a history of heart problems. *Running the business doesn't help with the stress levels either, damn it.*

She ran her hand through her hair anxiously. Her feelings about the big Cheswick boss were pretty black and white. He'd given her a job when she'd needed one badly. He'd accepted her without asking too many questions, and he'd taught her everything he knew about sailing and looking after tourists. Ron Cheswick had left no stone unturned in helping Jo get her life back on the straight and narrow. He had been a father figure when she had needed one most. The thought of him being in pain—in trouble—somewhere wasn't something the tall skipper could stomach very easily. *Especially when there's not a goddamn thing I can do to get back there any faster.*

Her thoughts wandered back to Cadie and she looked down at her watch. *They'll be on their way to Sydney by now.* Unconsciously she looked up into the cloudless sky, looking for a plane that would be hundreds of miles away by now. *Safe travels, my love.* She dropped her head again and caught Paul watching her from his position at the helm. A wry smile forced its way to her lips. "Relax, Paulie. I'm okay," she said dryly.

"I'm under orders," he reminded her. A raised eyebrow told him exactly what she thought of that. "You wouldn't want me to let Cadie down now, would you?"

Jo snorted. "I see she's got you wrapped around her little finger," she replied.

"Riiight. Like you're not," Paul responded, mustering up a grin from somewhere.

He's got you there, Jo-Jo. There's not a damn thing you wouldn't do for her, given half a chance. She brushed some dried salt from her knee absentmindedly. *I wonder if I'll ever get that chance.*

Cadie selected a tiny banana muffin from the buffet table and slid it onto her plate next to the grapes and sliced pineapple she had already collected. Lack of sleep and all the emotions of the past 24 hours were beginning to catch up with the blonde. She was distinctly frayed around the edges. It had made the breakfast buffet in the first-class private lounge at Sydney International irresistible. She put down her fruit plate to pour herself a large cup of strong black coffee, then made her way back to the cluster of comfortable armchairs the rest of her group had claimed for themselves.

Naomi had been blissfully silent since they'd left the Whitsundays. Cadie glanced at her partner. The senator was gazing out the window at the line of jumbo jets parked along the terminal. She had a half-smile on her face and Cadie found the hairs on the back of her neck prickling at the sight.

She's planning something. Cadie carefully broke the muffin in half and popped a morsel into her mouth, chewing thoughtfully. *That can't be good.* Uneasily she looked around the spacious lounge, which was largely unoccupied. Thankfully there was no access to anyone but first-class passengers here, so it was a good bet they were safe from the press, at least for the time being. So far they had managed to elude any media complications at both Hamilton Island airport and the Sydney domestic terminal.

But it had been a different story once they reached the international terminal. Word had spread and soon a pack of journalists and camera crews had been on their trail. The lounge was a safe haven, at least until it was time to board their flight. Then, Cadie knew, they would have to run the gauntlet until they were safely aboard.

Another look at the senator and Cadie was convinced the older woman had something up her sleeve for that last run to the departure gate. *The timing makes sense. Give a good impression to the Australian press here, then have 27 hours flying time to let that impression filter back to the US, and perhaps by the time we arrive in Chicago a lot of the sting will be taken out of the story.* Cadie munched slowly on the remains of her muffin. *The question is what part is she going to have me play in all this.* A growing knot of tension made itself known in the pit of Cadie's stomach and she suddenly regretted eating anything. *Oh, I have a bad feeling about this.*

Jo jogged down the ward corridor of the Mackay Base Hospital, head turning from side to side as she tried to figure out where they were keeping Ron. She reached the nurses' station and slapped her hand impatiently on the countertop when she realized there was no one there to answer her questions. *Damn it's just been one of those mornings,* she thought in frustration.

The *Seawolf* had finally made it back to Shute Harbor, but too late. The office staff informed Jo that Ron had been airlifted to Mackay, and that Doris had gone along with him. He had been arguing on the phone with an insurance rep when the heart attack had struck. *How many times have I told him to spread the load around a little?* Jo fretted. She had grabbed the keys to the company car and headed south, trying to make the hour and a half's drive considerably shorter by keeping her foot to the floor. An hour and one speeding ticket later, she was pounding the bell on the top of the nurses' station desk.

A formidable woman in a pale blue uniform advanced on her from the far end of the corridor. "Can I help you?" she asked.

Jo nodded. "I'm looking for Ron Cheswick," she replied. "He was airlifted from Shute Harbor. Heart attack."

The nursing sister searched her records briefly, a stubby finger running down the page of the book on the desktop. "Ah yes. Mr Cheswick is in ICU, at the end of the hallway. But I can only allow family members in there." The woman's expression brooked no argument, but Jo wasn't about to be deflected at this late stage.

"Ron doesn't have any blood family," she said bluntly. "At least, none that cares enough to be here. Me and Doris are as close as it gets. So, how about it, huh?"

"Doris, I take it, is the lady who arrived with him?" the sister asked. Jo nodded again. "And can I ask your name?"

"Jo Madison." The tall skipper shifted anxiously from one foot to the other. "Please, I really need to see him."

Again the older woman consulted her list and Jo was just on the brink of throwing caution to the wind with or without her permission when she looked up and smiled fleetingly.

"You can go through, Miss Madison," she said. "I should warn you, though, not to expect too much in the way of conversation from Mr Cheswick. He's very ill."

A cold chill shivered through Jo. "Okay," she said grimly. "Thanks for the warning."

She was painfully aware of her sneakers squeaking on the polished linoleum floor as she walked down the corridor. Scary smells and sounds assaulted her senses, reminding Jo that hospitals were about her least favorite places to be. *Right next to jails, courthouses, and dark alleys. God, Cadie, I wish you were here to hold my hand.*

At the end of the hallway was a darkened ICU unit, and Jo tentatively looked in, one hand on the doorjamb. She peered through the dimness and could make out four beds, each occupied by lumps of humanity connected to every machine imaginable. Away in the far corner from Jo, she could see Doris, her face illuminated by the eerie glow of several monitors. The older woman was slumped in a chair, and she was rubbing her eyes wearily. Ron was obscured from Jo's sight by the curtain half-pulled around his bed. The skipper swallowed around the lump in her throat and hesitantly stepped forward.

She crouched in front of Doris, taking in the tear streaks on her cheeks. Gently she shook the office manager's shoulder, trying not to startle her out of sleep.

"Oh, Jo!" Doris exclaimed, pulling the skipper close in a desperate hug. "I'm so glad you were able to get here. It's just been awful, and I'm so scared."

Jo returned the hug and then disentangled herself. They both stood and turned to look at Ron. The big man's face was almost totally obscured by breathing tubes and other contraptions that gave Jo chills just looking at them. A heart monitor reassuringly blipped when it should have, but there was no movement at all from the Cheswick Marine boss. His face was slack and a tiny sliver of drool trailed from the corner of his mouth to the pillow. Somehow, that made everything so much worse. Jo reached for a tissue from the box on the bedside cabinet and gently cleaned her boss' face. She brushed an errant lock of hair off his forehead.

"Hey, Ronny," she whispered. "It's Jo-Jo. Paul and Jenny send their love. They're minding the store for us." Ron's eyelids fluttered and she watched him struggle to open his eyes. "Take it easy, mate," she said, placing a calming hand on his chest, which seemed to relax him.

Doris approached the head of the bed from the other side and Jo glanced up at her. "Did you contact his ex-wife?" Jo asked quietly. Doris nodded.

"But she didn't seem too interested in coming up," Doris said bitterly. Ron's 23-year marriage had ended in acrimony three years earlier, foundering on the rocks of the death of their only child, Raymond, in a car accident. Since the divorce the former Mrs Cheswick hadn't been sighted north of the Sydney social scene.

"No big surprise there," Jo murmured. She took Ron's right hand in hers and smiled when she felt him squeeze hers weakly. "Hey, digger. You hang in there. We've got your back." She patted his hand and placed it gently on his stomach before she and Doris moved out into the fluorescent glare of the ward corridor. "What did the doctors say?"

The older woman rubbed her face with her hands for a few seconds as she gathered her thoughts. When she dropped them again, her expression was one of exhausted misery. "He's in trouble, Jo-Jo," she said. "They said the attack did massive damage to the heart and that he's going to need bypass surgery. But they can't do it yet because he's too weak and unstable. They're worried that he might have another attack before they can get him strong enough to survive the surgery."

Jo nodded. *Not good, in other words.* She tried to form an encouraging smile for Doris' benefit. "So," she said, "we wait. And we keep our fingers crossed."

"And we pray," Doris murmured.

Certainly can't hurt. God, Cadie, I hope your day is going better than mine, and a lot better than Ron's.

"This is the first boarding call for all passengers traveling aboard United Airlines flight 815 to Los Angeles. Please present your boarding pass at departure gate 68."

Cadie's stomach sank into a by now familiar cold, tight knot as she stood in front of the restroom mirror.

Moment of truth time, she thought as she splashed cool water on her face. *I feel sick to my stomach. If this is doing the right thing, then give me the wrong thing every time.*

"God damn it," she muttered as she headed for the door. She walked out into the lounge just behind where Toby and Jason sat flanking Naomi. All three had their backs to Cadie and they were engaged in a heated conversation.

"Naomi, you had better start doing some very fast ass-kissing," Toby said pointedly, jabbing the senator's shoulder with his finger. "If you and Cadie go out there now looking the way you both do right now, that pack of piranhas is going to rip you apart. For Chrissakes, talk to her."

Cadie decided to see where this conversation led, and she leaned quietly against the wall.

"And tell her what, Toby?" the senator retorted sarcastically.

"Anything!" he exclaimed. "Promise her anything, Nay, for crying out loud. All you have to do is get past the departure gate and on to the plane without looking like you hate each other. Apologize to her, for a start."

The senator swung on him. "For *what?*" she snarled. "For letting her hang all over that goddamn overstretched bitch for the past three weeks? For making a complete idiot of me?"

"Jesus." The exasperated PR man collapsed back in his chair. "You try, Jason. She's not listening to me."

Jason paused for a few seconds to gather his thoughts.

At least he has the decency to look uncomfortable about this whole thing, Cadie thought ruefully as she continued to listen.

Jason leaned forward. "Naomi, none of that matters now," he said quietly. He held up a hand as she opened her mouth to protest again. "Honestly, it doesn't. I'm sorry if your feelings are hurt or your pride is wounded, or whatever, but none of that matters a damn right now."

Cadie suddenly realized that the usually soft-spoken man was furious with the senator.

"The facts are these, Senator," he said with a quiet intensity. "There are people back in the States who cannot wait to get their hands on you. They've been waiting a very long time. They're the ones who never wanted you in the GOP in the first place, let alone elected to the Senate. They're the ones who fought tooth and nail to stop your nomination. All they've been waiting for is a tiny little chance to prove you to be the promiscuous, substance-abusing homosexual that they believe all gays and lesbians are."

Toby nodded his agreement.

"And you know what, Naomi?" Jason continued, leaning even closer until he was almost nose to nose with the glowering politician. "You've given those bastards that chance. Because, the bottom line is, you've been playing pretty fast and loose with your career." Naomi moved as if to get up out of the chair, but both men pulled her back with a hand on each arm. "No, you're going to listen to this, Nay," Jason insisted. He waited until she reluctantly sat back in her chair.

"You've forgotten how hard it was to get you elected," Jason said, allowing some of his anger to show. "You've allowed yourself to think that now you're here you can do what you like. Maybe that's been partly our fault," he admitted. "We've closed our eyes to some of the things we know you've been doing—the drinking, the affairs..."

Cadie swallowed hard, a missing piece of the puzzle of her last few years with the senator finally sliding into place.

"...and yes, the drugs." He paused, exchanging a sad glance with his partner. "We should have called a halt then." He looked down at his hands and re-gathered his thoughts. "You're a US senator, Naomi," he stated flatly. "Do you want to still be one next week?"

She looked at him sharply. "It won't come to that," she said quietly.

"Won't it?" That was Toby. "We're not so sure."

Jason pressed the point home. "Cadie's your only chance of creating a good impression between now and arriving back in Washington on Monday morning. You have to make the most of it."

"All right, all right," Naomi growled. "I'll talk to her."

"Do more than that, Senator. Be nice, promise her the world. Just get her back on your side," Toby said just before he stood and walked away to gather the rest of the troops.

Jason stood to do the same, and as he did so he caught sight of Cadie leaning against the wall. He flashed her an embarrassed and apologetic look before he turned and walked away.

Cadie wandered slowly over to her carry-on luggage. Her mind was spinning in seventeen directions, but none of them were leading her to any kind of solution she could live with. *I'm just a marketing ploy,* she thought with disgust. *That's all I've been to her for a very long time. Maybe that's all I ever was to her. I don't know anymore.* She glanced over at Naomi and caught the older woman staring at her intently. Cadie walked back to the senator's group of chairs and sat down next to her. *Might as well see which way she wants to play this,* she thought resignedly.

Naomi turned to look at her with a weary half-smile. "I know you have no reason to want to do me any favors," the senator said quietly, leaning close to keep their conversation as private as possible.

Cadie decided discretion was the better part of valor, at least for the time being. She held her tongue, keeping herself very still.

"We've been through a lot together, Cadie," Naomi continued, keeping her voice low. "All I'm asking is that you help me through the next few minutes until we're on the plane and away from the press."

"Why should I, Naomi?" Cadie replied sadly. "You've made it very clear over the past few weeks that not only have I been a liability all these years but that this holiday was—how did you put it?—oh yes...payment for services rendered." She paused to let that sink in, vaguely satisfied to see the senator flush. "You're going to kick me out once we get home anyway. That was the plan, wasn't it?"

She watched while Naomi ground her teeth, the muscles in her jaw bunching and unbunching in quick succession.

"Look, I'm sorry you had to hear that," she muttered hoarsely, clearly hating every second. "That was for Larissa and Kelli's benefit. Just to shut them up and get them off my back, y'know?" Cadie remained silent. "You know I would never kick you out, don't you?" She was almost pleading now.

"I don't know anything about you anymore, Naomi. All I know is I can't trust you. Not with us. Not with anything."

The stocky senator leaned closer still, desperation written all over her face now.

"Please, Cadie," she whispered fiercely, "just play along until we're on the plane and then we can talk. Maybe we can try and figure out how to get things back on track for us."

Cadie shook her head in disbelief, still amazed by the way the politician's mind worked, despite everything she had seen. "I've been trying to get you to do that for months, Naomi," she replied quietly. "You're not interested in us. All you care about is power and having a good time."

"Stop it, Cadie, please," Naomi begged. "All I'm asking is that you pretend for the next 10 minutes until we get on the plane. That's all. Then whatever you want, you can have."

How can I believe anything she says? Cadie bit her tongue, watching Naomi squirm under her scrutiny.

"Please?"

"I can promise that I won't embarrass you, Senator," Cadie agreed finally.

"Okay, folks," Toby said from across the room as he gathered up his hand luggage. "Time for one last joust with the press before we get home." He waited as the others clustered around him. He nodded at Naomi, who, along with Cadie, stood and walked over to the group. "Are you ready, Senator? Because this has to be good...the next five minutes are going to be replayed on the US networks for the next day and a half."

"Don't teach your grandmother to suck eggs, Tobias," the senator said lightly, straightening her clothes and smoothing her hair. She turned to Cadie and put on one of her most charming smiles. "Ready, darling?"

Cadie silently wondered just which direction the ambush was going to come from. *At least I know one's coming,* she thought ruefully.

Naomi held out a hand, inviting her partner to take it. Warily Cadie did so and the senator beamed at her with her best baby-kissing, campaign smile. They stepped through the door into a barrage of camera flashes and a forest of microphones. Questions lobbed at them from every side, but for now at least the senator ignored them all, following Toby and Jason's lead in the direction of the departure gate. The two men plus Therese and Sarah formed a protective phalanx around Naomi and Cadie as the group pushed a path through the crowd of journalists. For a few moments Cadie was unnerved by the jostling, but soon they were into a clear space just before the gate.

Once there, Naomi turned to face the press, pulling Cadie around with her. She waited a heartbeat to give the journalists a chance to gather around. "I'll take a few questions before we leave," she said with a confident smile, tightening her grip on Cadie's hand.

The blonde could almost feel the senator's intensity increase. *She feeds on this kind of thing,* she thought not for the first time in their 12 years together. *You can almost feel her grow more confident the longer she's out here in the glare of the lights. God, I hope she doesn't get overconfident.*

Questions again came from everywhere and the senator waited with practiced ease until one became discernable in the confusion. Cadie felt all eyes, and cameras, turned on her.

Oh, Jo, I wish you were here, she thought. She had a brief flash of her dark-haired friend riding in on a white charger, complete with shining armor and flashing sword. *Only in fairytales, Arcadia,* she thought ruefully as Naomi held her hand up to dampen the chatter from the press corps.

"Senator, were you using illegal substances the night you were arrested?"

Naomi laughed casually. "First of all, let me correct the misapprehension y'all seem to have that I was arrested. I was not arrested. My friends and I were simply caught up in the confusion of what was a very large dance party on Hamilton Island. Like a lot of other people that night, we were questioned and then released in the morning. And no, at no stage then, or ever for that matter, was I, or anyone I was with, using illegal substances."

"But you were drinking, Senator?"

"I had a couple of martinis, yes."

"Who was the woman you were photographed with, Senator?"

Naomi pointed in the direction of Kelli, who stood to the side, arm wrapped around Larissa, both women wearing broad smiles and innocent looks. "My friend, Kelli Mathieson," she said simply.

"Is there any truth to the rumor that your relationship with your girlfriend is in trouble, Senator?" That question had an American accent and Cadie wondered which US network had spent the money to get a journalist here just in time to turn around and fly back again.

She felt Naomi look down at her and glanced up, tentatively returning the senator's smile. Another barrage of flashes blinded her momentarily.

"This is my partner, Arcadia Jones," she heard the senator say. "And as you can see, we are very much together and happy. Isn't that right, darling?"

Cadie felt fingers tightening around her hand. She didn't trust her voice, so instead she just smiled and nodded. She felt Jason move in to stand close on her left, Toby mirroring his movement on Naomi's right. *Getting ready to move us on to the plane,* she thought with relief. *I've had just about enough of this.*

But Naomi wasn't finished yet. Cadie had a sinking feeling as she sensed the senator's confidence growing. And a gnawing suspicion that she had had something else in mind from the very start. *Uh-oh.*

"In fact, we have a couple of announcements to make," Naomi said, beaming from ear to ear. "You'll be the first to know."

Cadie felt a cold dread crawling through her intestines. *Oh Jesus, where is she going with this?*

"As soon as we get home to Chicago, Cadie will be giving up her business as a literary agent because we have decided to start a family. We've wanted this for a long while and now the timing is perfect for us. We hope that Cadie will become pregnant some time in the next few months, God willing."

There was an empty silence for several seconds and Cadie took in the stunned expression on Toby's face as well as the unmistakably vicious glint in Naomi's eye as the senator looked triumphantly at her for a reaction.

Unbelievable, Cadie thought, momentarily dumbstruck by her partner's audacity. *Now I've seen everything. She's actually willing to use a baby to keep her career on track.* At long last the blonde's temper reached its breaking point. *I'm not going to give you the satisfaction.* She saw an escape route. *In fact, I might just see your bet, and double it.*

"And that's why," she picked up Naomi's thread, smiling broadly at the wall of cameras and microphones, "that's why I'm going to stay a little longer in this wonderful country while Naomi and our friends go home. I'm going to spend a couple more weeks resting up for what's going to be a very big year for us both." She turned to the senator whose jaw was now in danger of hitting the floor. "Isn't that right, sweetheart?" She raised an eyebrow at Naomi, challenging her to create a scene in front of the phalanx of eagerly waiting journalists.

Cadie watched Naomi's eyes widen as she realized the predicament she was now in. A red flush crawled slowly up the stocky woman's neck and though her practiced smile remained plastered in place, the blonde easily read the fury and dismay in the brown eyes staring at her.

Seeing the senator floundering for an appropriate response, Jason stepped in and called a halt to the impromptu press conference. "No more questions, ladies and gentlemen," he said quickly. "As you can see they are holding the plane for us and I think we've delayed these good people for long enough."

Cadie stepped closer to Naomi and kissed her on the cheek. "Safe travels darling," she said brightly. Naomi began to protest but Cadie pressed closer and whispered in her ear. "Ah, ah, ah, Senator. The eyes of the world are watching. Goodbye."

"You and that bitch will pay for this," Naomi growled softly. "Count on it."

No doubt, Cadie thought as she watched Toby edge the politician through the departure gate. *But in the meantime, I know I'm doing the right thing. For the first time in weeks, I'm doing the right thing.* Naomi turned for one last photo opportunity, and Cadie obliged, waving and smiling before the senator disappeared down the ramp-way to the plane.

"Jason, give me my bag, please," Cadie murmured, taking the slouch-bag that he had been holding for her. Calmly she slung it over her shoulder and without a backward glance turned away and began walking towards the main terminal building.

Jason hooked her elbow and pulled her back. "Cadie, wait." She looked at him and half-smiled. "Are you ever coming back?" he asked quietly.

"I'm sorry, Jason," she replied. "Not this time. I can't do this anymore. I can't keep letting her do this to me."

"Look, I know what she just did is unforgivable," he conceded. "But why not let things cool down then come home and have it out with her?"

A light came on in Cadie's head. *Finally. Finally, I get it.* A realization slid home in her heart and she shook her head. "I *am* home, Jason," she said. "Nothing she can do or say can change that. And she's done too much damage in here." She tapped her chest lightly. "I know it's going to create huge problems for you, and for her, but I have to look after me...and Jo...now."

Jason stared at her for a few seconds and she held his gaze, more sure than she'd ever been that she was finally making the right choice for her. And then it was like he saw it too and the blond man smiled back at her. He pushed his glasses up his nose. "Good luck to you, Cadie," he said softly. "You deserve better. I hope you find it." He looked around at the press corps, most of whom were hanging around, still curious about the turn of events. "You'd better get out of here," Jason muttered.

He spotted an idle people-mover not far away, its driver leaning lazily on the wheel, waiting for someone to need a lift somewhere.

"Here, come on." He grabbed Cadie's elbow and steered her to a seat in the vehicle, then dug in his trouser pocket for some banknotes. "Buddy, you take this lady as far from that pack of journalists as you can get her." He pressed the money into the man's hand and then quickly kissed Cadie on the cheek. "Go, sweetie."

"Thanks, Jason. For everything," she said with a smile. Journalists were beginning to move towards them and Cadie touched the driver's shoulder. "Take me to the nearest cab, please," she said urgently.

She sat with her back to the driver and waved at Jason as they began to move away from the departure lounge. A detached part of herself kept waiting for the soundtrack to start. *Marianne Faithful should start singing "The Ballad of Lucy Jordan" right about now,* she thought dispassionately.

A small pack of hardy photographers sprinted after her, motorized shutters whirring and clicking even as they ran. She looked over her shoulder at the driver.

"I don't suppose this thing can go any faster," she asked.

"Not much, miss, but I can give it a go," he replied. "Hang on tight, now."

Cadie turned back to see the photographers dropping off the chase. She was relieved that for the time being at least she would be left alone.

Now what? She closed her eyes and mentally projected loving thoughts at Jo. *I'll be home soon, my love. I just need to get some sleep and figure out which way is up. And then I'll come to you.* She wearily watched the hectic world of the airport slipping past her. *I just turned my world upside down. For good. I hope you're ready for that, Jo.*

Hell, I hope I'm ready for that.

Jo leaned wearily back against the wall and took a sip from the hot cup of coffee in her hand. The coolness of the hard corridor wall pressed against her back and she took the opportunity to stretch and loosen her shoulders. She had just swapped places with Doris after spending a few hours sitting by Ron's bed and she welcomed the chance to straighten a few cramped muscles.

A glance at the clock told Jo it was mid-afternoon. Ron had been holding his own for the most part, though the big man hadn't fully regained consciousness at any stage. Jo swirled her coffee and gazed at the brown liquid pensively. *There's no knowing how long this will go on. But I guess every hour he doesn't have another attack is a good thing.*

Reluctantly her mind turned to more practical matters.

Frank's got another three days to run on his trip. At least the Seawolf has an extra week up her sleeve before she takes on another load of tourists. We're gonna have to come up with some contingency plans. She spared a look back up the corridor towards the ICU where Doris was sitting with Ron. *Especially if*

Doris is going to stay down here with him.

She worried away at that for a few minutes, gnawing at her bottom lip while the business of the ward went on, a stream of people flowing incessantly around her.

Cadie will be somewhere over the Pacific by now. She felt her emotions teetering on the brink of a very dark abyss at the concept of the increasing distance between herself and the lovely American. *Boy, this week went to hell. Hard to believe that two days ago we were winning that damn trophy. Ron hasn't even gotten to see it yet.*

Jo suddenly became aware of a shift in the atmosphere of the ward. Staff members were hurrying towards the ICU and two nurses were pushing an ominous-looking blue cart at top speed.

Oh shit. Jo took off at a sprint, leaving her half-empty cup suspended in mid-air before it splattered on the floor. She reached the door of the ICU where Doris was standing, her hands to her mouth. Inside doctors and nurses crowded around Ron's bed, calling instructions to each other with a controlled brand of chaos Jo found chilling.

"What happened?" she asked breathlessly.

"I don't know," Doris sobbed. "H-he started twitching and the heart monitor went crazy. Then there were doctors everywhere and they told me to get out of the way."

Jo clenched and unclenched her fists as she watched the people around Ron. She felt sick to her stomach—partly from helplessness but also the growing feeling that her mentor was in deep, dark trouble. She felt Doris' hands circle her upper arm and she winced slightly as the older woman's fingers put pressure on the still tender bullet scrape there. Doris rested her chin on Jo's shoulder, watching the activities in the darkened ICU.

Dread washed over Jo as she perceived that the urgency had suddenly drained out of the room. Low murmurs didn't quite carry to the waiting women, but soon a doctor was walking slowly towards them. He wearily brushed his hand through his short-cropped hair, fatigue obvious in his every movement.

"Are you Mr Cheswick's family?" he asked quietly, his message already obvious on his face. Doris ducked her head, resting her forehead against Jo's shoulder, stifling the sob that escaped her. Jo just nodded mutely. The doctor took her hand and patted it in a way that part of the skipper's brain found oddly out of place. "I'm sorry," he said. "Mr Cheswick just suffered a massive myocardial infarct and we were unable to revive him despite our best endeavors."

This just cannot be happening. Doris' arms slipped around

her waist and she could feel the older woman crying freely now against her back. Jo swallowed hard. "Th-thank you doctor," she stammered. "C-can we see him?"

"Yes, of course," he replied. "Just give the nurses a few minutes to remove all the machines and then you can take your time." With one last pat of Jo's hand, he was gone, leaving the two women to their grief. Jo squeezed her eyes shut, fighting the urge to just sit on the floor and bawl.

"Come on, Doris," she finally muttered, pulling the office manager around and sliding an arm around her shoulders. Several nurses with sympathetic expressions passed them, pushing various monitors and trolleys full of machines. Jo and Doris moved back to Ron's bed where one nurse remained. She handed Jo a small plastic bag containing Ron's personal effects. "Damn, look at that," Jo murmured. "They cut his wedding ring off."

Doris flopped helplessly into a chair, overcome with tears. Jo moved forward and leaned down, placing a gentle kiss on the big man's cool forehead.

"Goodbye, Ronny," she whispered. "Safe travels."

Cadie pressed her forehead against the cool glass of the hotel room window. She gazed out at a panorama that normally would have thrilled her. Darling Harbor, one of the biggest and most picturesque of Sydney Harbor's coves, stretched out before her. Its huge shopping mall, sweeping monorail and ferry terminus bustled with promise, and in any other circumstances, Cadie would have been the first one down there exploring.

But being a tourist was the last thing on her mind. Cadie had come straight from the airport to this hotel on the recommendation of the cab driver. Staying at the airport, even if it had meant a flight straight back to the Whitsundays, just wasn't an option with the press pack prowling around. She hadn't even waited around for her luggage to be pulled off the international flight. Fortunately a quick call to the airline once she had reached the hotel had solved that problem.

The practical implications of what she had done were beginning to sink in. She had handed over her credit card to the hotel receptionist—a joint card she shared with Naomi—with the realization that once the senator reached Chicago, she could expect to have that financial resource cut off.

And of course it's the credit card with no cash advance capability, she realized wearily. *Great.*

Cadie turned away from the window with a sigh. She knew

she should have been feeling free, excited even, to be going back to Jo so soon, but instead she just felt exhausted. She had no luggage and soon, no money. And that nagging worry was still there in the back of her brain.

What will Naomi do for revenge? Everything she's threatened so far has been nothing but bluff and bluster. But still... Maybe I should take the opportunity to go and find Detective Harding.

Cadie sat on the end of the bed and kicked off her shoes.

God knows, she can't do anything else to me. I have my laptop with me and the business' finances are separate so she can't touch those.

She let herself fall backwards onto the bed, staring at the spackled ceiling that seemed to be standard in hotel rooms around the world. There was a knock on the door and Cadie startled out of a light doze. She rolled off the bed and went to stand by the door. Looking through the peephole she could see a distorted image of one of the hotel's bellhops.

He knocked again. "It's room service, ma'am," he called out. "I have your luggage."

With a sigh of relief, Cadie pulled open the door. "Thanks," she said. "You can just put it on the bed." She scrabbled in her slouch-bag for some change to give the man as a tip. Instead her hand came up against an odd-feeling wad at the bottom of the bag. Puzzled, she pulled it out and found herself staring at a roll of banknotes. A silly grin plastered itself on her face and she giggled hysterically.

Eleven hundred and eighty dollars, she reminded herself. *My share of the Seawolf's winnings. That's perfect.* She laughed again. *Thank you, Jo-Jo.*

The bellhop was looking at her like she was an alien from a distant planet.

"Sorry," Cadie giggled, pulling off a smaller-sized note from the roll of cash and giving it to him. "It's just been a very, very long day."

"No worries, miss," he replied, tipping his cap and moving back to the door. "I've seen a lot nuttier than you." He grinned cheekily and closed the door behind him.

I bet you have. She chuckled and tossed the wad of money from hand to hand for a few seconds, relishing her luck.

I could have so easily put this in the other bag with Naomi's stuff. Score one for me! She flipped the money back into her bag and crawled onto the bed, pushing her luggage away to the other side. A wave of exhaustion rolled over her, and she was asleep almost before her head hit the pillow.

Jo pointed the Cheswick Marine SUV north and let her mind drift as she and Doris began the trek back to Shute Harbor and Airlie Beach. The office manager was stretched out along the back seat, dead to the world. Jo wished fervently she could do the same, but she had the sinking feeling there wasn't going to be much sleep for her over the next few days.

She had hastily arranged for Ron's body to be transported up to Shute in the morning. Then, realizing there was nothing else she and Doris could do in Mackay, she opted to drive them home that evening. Now, with the highway stretching out endlessly in front of her, she was beginning to regret the decision.

If Cadie were here I'd be pointing things out to her. Things that are everyday to me would be so interesting to her. She smiled quietly into the fading light, wondering if the American was thinking of her right now. *I hope so. And I hope that bitch sitting next to her is giving her some peace and quiet, too. She deserves it.*

As the sun began to sink below the level of the low hills to her left, Jo tried to keep her weary mind alert. Traffic coming towards her already had lights on, and absentmindedly she flicked on her own. Something away in the distance on her side of the road caught her attention and she frowned, trying to make out the details.

The big red kangaroo stood on the soft edge looking for all the world like an old man trying to decide whether to cross or not. At six feet tall and a couple of hundred pounds, the 'roo wasn't anything Jo wanted to tangle with, whether in a car or not. She slowed the SUV right down as she approached the marsupial.

"Come on, you bugger, make up your mind," she muttered. Tentatively he took a couple of small hops, holding his front paws together in front of him. "Come on then, cross."

Just to be contrary the 'roo stopped and Jo decided to take a chance. She accelerated to give him a wide berth. As she reached cruising speed the animal changed its mind again and bounded out onto the highway.

"Bastard!" Jo exclaimed, slamming on the brakes. She heard Doris give a yelp as the sudden deceleration rolled her off the back seat, but Jo was more concerned with the 'roo. He swerved almost in mid-air, kicked hard with his enormous back legs against the bull-bar on the front of the SUV and then sprang off into the bush on the other side of the highway. "God damn it," Jo muttered, heart pounding in her throat. "You okay, Doris?" she called over her shoulder.

"What the hell was that?" grumbled the older woman as she scrambled up from the floor.

"Dumb 'roo," Jo replied. "I think he's bent the bull-bar." She scrubbed at her eyes wearily. "Should've known better than to try and do this drive at sunset. They're always on the move then."

"Do you want some company up there, Jo?" Doris asked, worriedly noting the tired slump of the skipper's shoulders.

Jo shook her head. "M'okay, D," she murmured. "I just want to get home." *Except home's about 30,000 feet up and several thousand miles away by now.*

Cadie replaced the receiver on the hook. She had had a frustrating morning. Despite several attempts the blonde had been unable to get through on Jo's cell phone number. That was unusual for the skipper and it worried her.

She had worked out her finances, disconcerted to find that the airfare back to Hamilton Island was going to take a bigger chunk out of her prize money than she was willing to risk. *Looks like it's a bus ride for me. Damn, is nothing going to be simple?* She quickly double-checked her calculations. *Enough for one more night in the hotel, a few meals, a bus ticket and, with any luck, one call home to Mom.* She knew she could just charge everything to the credit card now, while it was still functioning, but something made her reluctant to do that. *That life is done with. I want to do this on my own.* And there was something deeply satisfying about using the money she'd earned on the *Seawolf. A new life.*

There was a tap on the door and she got up to answer the knock, expecting to find a housekeeper wanting to change the towels. Instead a camera flash went off in her face as soon as she opened the door.

"Hey!" she yelped, shielding her face from any further flashes. The man behind the camera stepped forward and she recognized him as one of the pack of journalists who had been at the airport the day before.

"Hello, Miss Jones," he said with a grin. "I'm Tom Saunders from the Sydney Gazette."

"It might have been polite to ask before you took that photo, Mr Saunders," Cadie retorted.

"Ah, but you would have said no, Miss Jones, and then I would have copped an arse-kicking from my editor. I'll do anything to avoid that," he said.

"What can I do for you?" *Like I don't know.*

"I just have a couple of questions," he said, pulling a notebook from his back pocket and sliding a pen from where it was stowed behind his ear.

"That was the point of yesterday's press conference, Mr Saunders. To answer any possible questions."

"I know, miss, I know, but I'm a particularly stupid sort of bloke and I wasn't quite quick enough taking notes. So I was hoping you would answer them again for me." Cadie stayed silent, waiting for the reporter to get on with it. "I'll take that as a yes, then," he continued. "May I come in?"

"No you may not," Cadie said shortly.

"Fair enough. Okay, then. Well, yesterday you said that you would be staying on for a while. Any idea how long exactly?"

Cadie thought carefully before answering. "A couple of weeks," she said finally.

"But you won't be staying here, will you?" Saunders asked, smiling. "Because you're only booked in here on a night by night basis."

So much for guest confidentiality, Cadie thought ruefully. "No," she said aloud. "I'll be returning to the Whitsundays tomorrow, to stay with friends."

"So you had planned all along to stay beyond the senator's departure then?" he asked.

"Yes."

"Then why did the flight have to be delayed further yesterday while they unloaded your luggage?"

Cadie had been a politician's wife far too long to let anything other than calm reserve show on her face, even though the question was a bolt out of the blue. "Mr Saunders," she smiled at him. "I'm afraid I'm going to disappoint your editor because I don't have anything further to say beyond what was stated yesterday. I'm sorry you've come all this way for so little." She retreated back behind the door of her room and leaned against it as she slid the lock into place. A glance through the peephole told her when the journalist had left.

"Jesus," she muttered. *I was hoping the story would hold together a little longer than that.* She glanced down at her watch. *Early evening in Wisconsin.* She picked up the phone again and dialed a long number. When it was answered, she smiled at the familiar voice. "Hi, Mom," she said quietly.

Chapter
Thirteen

Jo sat quietly in her chair up on the slightly raised stage of the Shute Harbor chapel. She looked out over the steadily-filling pews, nodding occasionally in greeting to the people walking in. Ron had been a popular character around the twin towns of Shute and Airlie Beach and both were pretty much shut down for the day. The skipper's eyes scanned the room. Paul and Jenny were already here sitting quietly on either side of Doris in the front row. Every other Cheswick Marine employee was present too, including Frank and his crew from the Beowulf, whose passengers had kindly offered to cut short their trip by a day.

Again Jo swept the room, her eyes faltering only when they fell on the beech wood casket placed just in front of the stage. Ron's weather-beaten sailing cap was placed on top, resting on the white Australian naval ensign he was entitled to as an ex-Navy man.

Jo sighed. The last three days had been a blur. Funeral arrangements had been largely left to her, and Doris had needed all the help she could get to keep the Cheswick Marine office up and running. Ron had left specific instructions for his farewell, something for which Jo had been incredibly grateful.

Planning this from scratch would have been just too tough. The service in the chapel would be followed by a private cremation and then the *Seawolf,* and any other boats that cared to, would sail out to the far side of Whitsunday Island and scatter Ron's ashes over the stretch of water he adored most.

Why can't I cry? So much that has happened over this past week has hurt. And I miss Cadie like... She swallowed. *That hurts like nothing I've ever known.* She closed her eyes and conjured up the blonde's sweet face in her mind. *Where are you now, my love? I would give anything to have you close.* She tried to imagine Cadie back in the snowy winter landscape of Chicago. *I hope you're okay, angel.*

Jo was brought back to reality by the gentle coughing of the presiding priest. The chapel was now full. In fact there was standing room only at the back and Jo felt a quiet sense of pride in the number of people who had come to pay their respects. She refocused, trying to concentrate on the priest's words as he began the service.

You may not have had much in the way of blood family, Ron, but take a look around, mate. You were loved.

Cadie was jolted awake by the sudden cessation of the bus' swaying motion. She came close to rolling off the three seats she was sprawled across, but just managed to brace herself with an out-flung elbow into the back of the seat in front of her.

"Damn it," she muttered to herself. It was only about the trillionth time that had happened during the 29 interminable hours she had been on this bus since it left Sydney. *Oh yeah. This was a good idea.*

The blonde sat up to ascertain where exactly they were. The few remaining passengers were gathering together their belongings and making their way off the bus. Cadie stood and caught the eye of the driver.

"Airlie Beach, miss," he said in answer to her unasked question. "End of the road."

"Thank God," she muttered. Two days ago the bus had seemed like the best option, given the relatively restricted nature of her finances. As predicted, her credit card had ceased to function within hours of Naomi's estimated time of arrival in Chicago and Cadie had been trying not to spend money ever since. Twenty-nine hours and a rumbling stomach later, she was beginning to question her own wisdom.

"I wouldn't expect to find too much open in town, though, miss," the bus driver volunteered helpfully.

"Why's that?" Cadie asked, wondering how long it would take her to track down Jo. She gathered her bags together and shuffled towards the door. *God, I hope they have cabs in this town,* she thought, only half-listening to the man.

"Everyone's gone to Big Ron's funeral," the driver replied. "I'm heading there myself now."

"He must have been a popular guy," Cadie murmured wearily. She dropped her bag out the door and turned back to pick up the other.

"Oh, that he was," he said. "Nobody better than Big Ron Cheswick."

"Well, thanks for getting me here," she said, biting back the sentiment that she was amazed she was sane and in one piece.

"No worries, miss," he said cheerily as he prepared to pull the door shut behind her. He restarted the big coach just as Cadie stepped onto the tarmac of Main Street, Airlie Beach. Moments later, the bus chugged off south towards Shute Harbor and she was enveloped in a cloud of choking exhaust fumes.

"Perfect," she muttered, coughing the garbage out of her lungs. When the air cleared she looked around at her surroundings. Main Street was essentially one long street lined by souvenir shops, restaurants, trendy boutiques, and coconut palms. The bus had dropped her outside JC's, a bar and steakhouse. She vaguely remembered Jo telling a funny story about a night she and her boss had tied one on here.

Cadie wandered a little closer to the restaurant, happy to see that it was open. Her stomach growled again.

If Jo and her boss think this is a decent place to eat, then who am I to argue, the blonde thought. Something was nagging away at the back of her brain. *Jo and her boss...Jo and...ohhh shiiit.*

Cadie sprinted back out onto the road, looking in the direction the bus had headed, but it was already long gone around the corner of the bay. Her heart was hammering in her chest and a wave of longing for Jo welled up inside her.

Damn it, I've got to get there, she thought desperately. *Of course, it would help if I knew where "there" was.* She stepped back onto the footpath in time to see someone coming out of JC's. *As good a place to start as any.*

"Excuse me?" she asked as the man turned back to lock the door of the restaurant.

"Yes, miss?" he replied, smiling as he tucked his keys into his pocket and walked out towards her.

"I'm trying to get to Ron Cheswick's funeral, but I don't have a clue where it's being held, or how to get there from here. I was wondering if you could help me out?"

The man smiled, revealing a sparkling gold tooth. "As a matter of fact, that's where I'm headed myself," he said. "Would you like a lift?"

Relief washed over the American like a cold shower. "You know, that's the best offer I've had in days," she said, smiling back at him tentatively. "Thank you, yes."

The swarthy man bent down and picked up her biggest bag. "Come on then. I'm parked over there." He gestured to the other side of the road. "You look like you've had a long trip. Are you a friend of Ron's?"

Cadie swung her slouch-bag over her shoulder and trotted after him. "Not exactly," she replied. "Actually I've never met him." He looked at her quizzically. "But I am a friend of Jo Madison. My name's Cadie by the way." She offered a hand.

He took it. "They call me Slick," he said, smiling at her curious look. "Don't ask," he laughed, opening the trunk of his car, and tossing her bag inside. "It all goes back to a very long night in the 70's." Cadie nodded in understanding. "A friend of Jo-Jo's, eh? She's a diamond in the rough that one."

The blonde smiled at the description. "Do you know if she's okay?" she asked once they were in the car and under way. "I've been trying to call her cell phone for three days but she's had it switched off."

"Not very surprising," he said, negotiating around a slow-moving caravan going up the hill above Shute Harbor. "She's had to organize the funeral and it's been a bit hectic, I think. She came in for a drink a couple of nights ago, and she looked like hell, to be honest."

Cadie's stomach was tied in knots. *Ohhh baby, I'm sorry I haven't been here. Damn it, I should never have left. Why do I always come to the right conclusion just that day or two too late?*

"Are you all right?" Slick asked, watching the blonde's fists ball up as they rested on her thighs.

She nodded, making a conscious effort to loosen up. "Yeah," she breathed. "I just really need to get there."

"You got it," Slick replied, flooring the pedal.

It was Jo's turn to speak, and she suddenly wished she'd had some more time to think about what she was going to say. The preacher finished his introduction and there was an anticipatory silence as Jo felt eyes all round the chapel settle on her. With a slightly shaking hand she brushed a piece of lint from the knee of her pantsuit and cleared her throat. She pushed herself up and walked slowly to the podium.

A couple of hundred faces turned her way and her mouth went dry. Public speaking was not Jo's cup of tea. Oh, a boatload of tourists was one thing but putting together coherent thoughts— paying respects to someone they all cared about—that was something else altogether. She reached for the glass of water balanced on the podium and quickly took a couple of mouthfuls.

Cadie, I need you, she thought miserably. *I'm tired and I'm sad and I don't want to deal with this on my own anymore.* She could hear people coughing and shuffling their feet. *Not that I have much choice about that.* She took a deep breath and began.

"When I first met Ron Cheswick he was interviewing me for a job as a deckhand. He had no reason at all to employ me. I'd never sailed before, I was new in town, and I'm sure I had that 'lean and hungry look' that made me appear a little desperate." A low ripple of laughter rumbled around the room as others recognized themselves in the description. Encouraged, Jo pressed on. "He saw something in me that I still, to this day, don't understand. That was one of the gifts Ron had..."

Cadie hesitated outside the door to the chapel.
I am so not dressed for a funeral, she thought self-consciously, glancing down at her jeans and rumpled, slept-in shirt. *Bit late to be worrying about that now, Cadie.*
She reached for the doorknob but was transfixed by a familiar and very welcome sound—Jo's rich alto being projected through the chapel's speaker system. She closed her eyes as a thrill of anticipation ran through her, provoking a tugging ache low in her guts that surprised her with its intensity.
Ohhh, Jossandra, what you do to me. She shook her head and opened her eyes again, almost laughing at her visceral reaction to the woman she loved. *I'm at a funeral for crying out loud,* she chastised herself. *Melting into a big, horny puddle is not an option right now.*
She pulled open the door and stepped in to the cool of the air-conditioned chapel. Her first glance told her the place was packed. There was nowhere to sit that she could easily see, and the standing room was crowded enough to leave her out in the aisle. Her second glance was to the tall woman occupying the stage.
Jo was dressed in an elegant black pantsuit over a pale blue silk shirt that brought out the color of her eyes. Cadie's breath caught in her throat at the sight of her. The skipper was as easy on the eye as always but it was the dark circles under those blue eyes and the lines of tension that most caught her attention.
God, I wish I could just go up there and hold her. She looks like she could use all the support she can get. Instead she held her ground in the middle of the aisle, mentally projecting as much love as she could in her friend's direction.
Jo was working the room as best she could, trying to pull everyone into the story of Ron's life. Somewhere in her mind she was vaguely aware of some latecomers entering the chapel, but as her eyes scanned the chapel the last person in the world she expected to see was...
Cadie? Whatever she was saying stalled in her throat and Jo was left speechless. *Oh my God...Cadie.* The blonde's sparkling

green eyes beamed love and joy towards her and the skipper felt her heart stall in her chest, then rush to catch up to its rhythm. *Damn, Jo-Jo, don't faint now.* She was hard-pressed to keep the grin from her face, before she remembered why she was there and continued her eulogy.

That's more like it, my love, thought Cadie triumphantly, relieved to see the beginnings of a grin flicker across the tall woman's face. *Hang in there.*

A few minutes later Jo finished her tribute to the big Cheswick Marine boss and the formalities of the ceremony were completed. Paul joined her and four others of Ron's closest friends as pall-bearers, carrying the casket to the hearse. As they passed her, Cadie felt a warm, long-fingered hand slide into hers and squeeze briefly before moving on. Then she was caught up in the large crowd that filtered out into the brilliant sunshine.

Cadie leaned against the outside wall of the church, watching quietly as Ron's casket was loaded into the hearse and people dispersed to their cars for the next phase of the funeral. She had no trouble keeping Jo in her sights, the dark-haired skipper's height making her easy to follow above the heads of most of the congregation.

Finally Jo was done with the arrangements and was free to come looking for her favorite American. The two women approached each other slowly, grins adorning both their faces. Cadie couldn't wait any longer and broke into a run, jumping into the taller woman's arms.

"Oomph." Jo rocked back on her heels as Cadie's compact body thumped into her but she quickly regained her balance, throwing her arms around the American and steadying them both. Cadie squeezed her hard, legs wrapped round the skipper's hips.

"Oh my God, I am so glad to see you," Jo said breathlessly, close by Cadie's left ear.

"I'm so sorry about Ron, sweetheart," the blonde replied.

Jo closed her eyes and just savored the feel of Cadie in her arms. *Wasn't expecting to feel her again for a long time. If ever,* she admitted to herself. Gently she lowered the blonde to the ground and stepped back a little, reveling in the warm wash of love between them. Soft green eyes gazed up at her. "What on earth are you doing here?" she asked, her voice cracking with emotion. She reached out with a hand and gently stroked the blonde's cheek. "You're supposed to be in Chicago by now."

Cadie took a second to lean into Jo's touch, hungry for continued contact with the tall woman. Then she shrugged and looked up into deep blue eyes that brimmed with unshed tears.

"Things got pretty ugly at the airport in Sydney," she said simply. "I suddenly realized that I have the right to happiness as much as Naomi does. She was trying to dictate my life and it hit me that I didn't have to put up with that." She smiled up at Jo, feeling calm and right about her decision for the first time since she'd driven away from Naomi.

Jo smiled softly at her. The relief she felt wasn't just for herself. Knowing Cadie had the strength to see what was right for her, and had the courage to go after it, was gratifying. "We have a lot to talk about," she said quietly.

Cadie nodded, still smiling. "Yes we do," she agreed. "But at least now we have some time. I have another two months left on my visa."

Jo beamed at her. "I don't think I've ever been so happy to see someone in my life," she said, shaking her head in wonder. "It's been a tough week." Cadie heard the tears close to the surface in the taller woman's voice and she stepped forward again, wrapping the skipper in the warmest hug she could muster.

"I know, baby," she whispered. Jo buried her face against the shorter woman's shoulder and neck, letting the tears come for the first time in days. "It's okay, sweetheart," Cadie soothed. "Let's just get through today and then we can relax a little, yes?"

Jo sniffled and nodded before standing up straight again, her equilibrium restored. A tantalizing thought occurred to her as Cadie wiped away her tears with the soft pad of her thumb. Jo ducked her head again, this time kissing the blonde lightly. "And I think there's a big, safe bed waiting for us somewhere," she whispered when their mouths parted.

"Ohhh," Cadie gasped, surprised by the intensity of the bolt of desire which shot through her at the taller woman's words. "God, Jo. That's not going to make the day go any faster." She smiled shyly.

"I know," the skipper said with a lopsided grin. "But I couldn't resist teasing you." She sighed. "Still got a lot to do here, though," she said, looking around at the still-dispersing congregation, some of whom were looking curiously at them. "You want to tag along for the rest?" she asked hesitantly, unsure of just how much Cadie was up for.

"Of course," the blonde answered immediately. "Jo, I'm not letting go of you again. You're stuck with me."

Jo looked at her wide-eyed, recognizing the commitment and fierce determination on Cadie's face. The blonde hesitated at Jo's expression, suddenly unsure.

"Is...I mean...that is okay, isn't it?" she asked nervously, rattled by the surprised look on the skipper's face.

In answer, Jo scooped her up in another enthusiastic hug. "Oh God, yes," she whispered fiercely in Cadie's ear. "I'm sorry, I didn't mean to throw you. You just caught me by surprise." They pulled apart again. "Come on," Jo said, offering Cadie her hand. "Let's go get this done." Grinning, Cadie slid her hand into Jo's larger one, happily falling into step beside the tall woman.

"Bye, Doris. See you in a few days." Jo took the office manager's hand and steadied her as she made her way back across the *Seawolf's* gangway and onto the Cheswick Marine pontoon. Doris was the last of the passengers to leave. All the Cheswick employees had decided that as the next load of tourists wouldn't arrive till early the following week, a few days off were in order. Doris had agreed to switch the office phone over to her home number and they were all looking forward to some time away from the water.

And time with each other, Jo thought with a smile as she watched Cadie chatting amiably with Paul and Jenny. The couple had decided they would get married on the weekend and the three-some were happily discussing plans while Jo pottered about stowing away pieces of equipment and battening down.

The two crewmembers had welcomed the blonde back enthusiastically, and in true Whitsunday tradition, hadn't asked questions about why, but had just accepted the American's presence happily. *Got a few questions about that myself,* Jo thought. *But it can wait. For right now I just want to hold her.*

The afternoon had been a fitting farewell for Ron. Jo had sailed the *Seawolf* out beyond Whitsunday Island with a boatload of his closest friends, and there they had scattered his ashes. The journey back to port was a truly Irish wake, with much food, drink, laughter and singing. For the first time in days, Jo felt herself start to relax.

Cadie looked over at the lanky skipper and smiled. *Time to take her home,* she decided. *She looks like she could use a distraction or two.* "Jo-Jo?" she called out.

"Mmm?" Jo answered, looking up from where she was winding a sheet into a neat coil.

"Take me home?" Cadie asked quietly, feeling a surge of anticipation at the look her question provoked.

The skipper felt a slow, burning ache deep in her guts just looking at the easy smile on her friend's face. *Soon to be more than a friend, I'm guessing. I want her so badly, I could...*

"I think I can do that," she said aloud instead.

"I'll lock her down, Skipper," Paul said obligingly.

"He means the boat, Cadie," Jenny reassured, noting the suddenly startled look on the blonde's face.

They all laughed.

"Thanks, Jen, I was beginning to worry," Cadie giggled.

"Hey, Jo-Jo. Who's the suit?" Paul asked, gesturing with his head to the man standing on the pontoon looking at them.

Aw geez, now what? Jo wondered, recognizing him. "It's Ron's lawyer," she said. "Come aboard, John," she called out.

He waved back and stepped out along the gangway as Jo jumped down into the cockpit to join the others. She reached out to shake his hand. "John Jacobs, meet Paul Burton, Jenny Gulliver, and Cadie Jones," she said quickly, hoping the man would get through his business in good time. "What can we do for you?"

The lawyer remained standing, holding his briefcase nervously in front of him. "Well, I was rather hoping I could have a private chat with you, Miss Madison," he said diffidently.

Jo looked at him in puzzlement. "No need," she replied shortly. "We're all friends here."

"Very well, then," the thin little man said. "May I, uh..." He indicated the cockpit bench.

"Yes, yes, please," she invited him quickly. "Have a seat."

He did so, placing his briefcase beside him and flipping it open. He took out a sheaf of papers. "Basically I need to talk to you about certain aspects of Mr Cheswick's will, of which I am the executor," he said quickly. "As you know, he died without any children and he specifically did not wish his ex-wife to receive anything."

Paul snorted.

"No surprise there," Jo murmured. She looked over at Cadie who was listening quietly. "It wasn't a friendly divorce," she explained. The blonde nodded in understanding, wondering just how ugly her own break-up was going to become.

"Yes, well," the lawyer continued. "Mr Cheswick specified that all his assets, other than those attached to Cheswick Marine—the house, his car, furniture etc—be sold and the proceeds poured into the business' coffers."

Makes sense, thought Jo. *Then whoever buys the business will have a fair shot at a new start.* She looked at Jacobs expectantly. "So when will the business get sold off?" she asked, hoping whoever took it on would keep things running for a while at least.

The lawyer looked at her strangely. "Well, that rather depends on the new owner," he said, handing her the sheaf of papers.

"Obviously," she said impatiently. "What are these?"

"The deeds to the business," he replied matter of factly. "Including the registration and ownership papers to the *Seawolf* and the *Beowulf.*" He leaned forward at her baffled expression. "In other words, you are the new owner of Cheswick Marine, Miss Madison."

A stunned silence settled over them. Jo's eyes widened as the words started to sink in.

"You have got to be kidding me," she finally blurted out. She looked over at Cadie to find the blonde's hands covering her mouth and her eyes twinkling with delight. "He's kidding me, right?" Jo asked desperately.

"Er, no, Miss Madison. I am most certainly not, er, kidding you," the lawyer reassured, tucking some errant papers back into his briefcase and closing it again. He stood and looked down at the woman who held the documents close to her chest in astonishment. "Please take a couple of days to look through those," he said. "And give me a call if you have any questions. Then we can talk about a business plan." With that he headed back across the gangway and along the pontoon.

"He's kidding me, right?" Jo asked eventually, triggering an explosion of merriment from the other three.

Paul whooped and Jen squealed, while Cadie just applauded, her eyes brimming with tears as she watched sudden understanding, and then slow delight creep into Jo's wide blue eyes.

"Congratulations, darling," Cadie said, beaming as the two others went below decks to find some champagne. The blonde stood and moved to Jo's side, sliding a hand into the crook of the skipper's arm and kissing her cheek softly. "You're a boat owner."

"Holy shit," Jo said, slightly dazed. "I'm a two-boat owner."

Several hours later, Cadie finally managed to persuade Jo to relax. As the realities of Ron's generosity began to sink in, the tall skipper had become increasingly excited by the prospect of running her own yacht charter business. Talk of the possibilities had carried them through the short drive up to Jo's house and a light supper. Now, halfway down a bottle of very good red wine, Cadie could feel Jo's energy levels returning to somewhere near normal.

They were snuggling in the soft leather of the couch. The blonde leaned back against Jo's left shoulder, the taller woman's arm wrapped around her shoulders. They both rested their feet on the coffee table, where the papers Ron's lawyer had given Jo were strewn.

Jo sighed deeply, closing her eyes as she felt Cadie gently kiss the palm of her left hand, triggering a delicious tingling. "Mmm," she purred in pure reaction. "I'm sorry, darling. We've done nothing but talk about the business." She ducked her head and buried her face in the blonde's hair, planting her own tender kiss there.

"It's okay, love," Cadie replied, patting the taller woman's thigh. "It's been quite a week for us both. I was just glad to see you looking happier."

"Tell me what happened with Naomi," Jo said quietly. Cadie leaned forward, placing her wineglass back on the coffee table before turning and snuggling back into the skipper's arms. This time she nuzzled Jo's neck, throwing her left leg over the other woman's long limbs.

"Basically, she told the world's press that not only was I going to give up my business, but that we were going to have a baby just as soon as I could arrange to get myself pregnant," she said simply.

There was a short silence as the impact of her words sunk in.

"I'll say this for her," Jo said eventually. "The woman's got elephant balls." Cadie laughed against her neck and Jo wrapped her arms protectively around the smaller woman, squeezing her gently. "What happened then?"

"You know, I'm not really sure," Cadie replied pensively. "Everyone was kind of stunned for a few seconds, including me. And then it was like a switch flicked over in my head and I decided I wasn't going to let her win this round." She felt Jo's arms tighten around her. "So I took a deep breath and told them all that if I was going to have a big year making babies then I was going to stay in beautiful, restful Australia for another couple of weeks." She grinned as Jo chuckled under her ear.

"Just like that, huh?"

"Yup." Cadie laughed out loud. "It suddenly occurred to me that I could use the media just as well as Naomi could. And there wasn't a thing she could say that wouldn't make her look like a fool."

"So you just waved goodbye and walked away?"

"I kissed her on the cheek first," Cadie said.

That provoked a loud guffaw from the skipper. "Oh that's perfect," Jo said happily once she'd recovered. "How did you get out of there?"

"Jason helped me," Cadie replied. "He got me on to one of those people-mover things and told the guy to get me the hell out."

"Good for him," Jo said. She'd always had the feeling Toby and Jason weren't the yes-men Naomi seemed to think they were. "I bet Naomi was unimpressed."

Cadie snorted. "I almost feel sorry for them all being stuck on that plane with her. I thought she was going to stroke out."

Jo smiled quietly. *Couldn't happen to a bigger bitch.*

"I know what you're thinking," Cadie said softly. "And you're right. But I still feel bad about it."

"Don't," Jo said firmly. "Cadie, I'm incredibly proud of you. Even if you had decided not to come back here, I would still be proud of you."

"Why?" came a small, suddenly uncertain voice. Jo cuddled her even closer.

"Because you were brave enough to take responsibility for your own happiness and to let Naomi worry about her own stuff, for once."

"I guess so."

"Honey, I know so. You did the right thing for you, and that's a big part of the battle." There was a comfortable silence while they both just enjoyed the other's presence. Then Jo spoke up again. "So what did you do after you left her?"

"Went to a hotel and waited for my luggage to catch up with me. I tried calling you but you had your cell phone switched off." She lifted her head and looked at Jo. "Actually I tried to call you for three days with the same result."

"M'sorry, angel," Jo replied. "I assumed you were in transit or in Chicago, and I didn't much feel like talking with anybody else. The whole world and his dog were trying to contact me once the news about Ron filtered through. And then I was kept all kinds of busy trying to arrange things."

Cadie reached up and kissed her softly, nibbling gently along Jo's bottom lip. "It's okay," she said finally, trying to think through the haze of low-burning desire. "I was just worried about you."

A lazy, sexy smile was her answer and Cadie felt a subtle shift in the mood of the tall woman wrapped around her. Jo moved carefully, sliding herself around and cradling the blonde, lowering them both back onto the sofa.

"No need to worry about me, sweetheart," Jo burred in her ear, sending chills down Cadie's spine. The blonde slid one hand around Jo's waist, using the other to brush dark bangs away from the skipper's face, stroking her cheek slowly with a thumb.

"It was a good kind of worry," Cadie whispered, her mouth just millimeters from Jo's. "It was a 'knowing I'd soon be in your arms' kind of worry."

"Oh, really?" Jo rumbled, kissing her way slowly along the line of Cadie's jaw, forcing a low groan from the smaller woman. Her right hand slid down the blonde's left thigh, teasing and tantalizing the soft skin she found along the way. "You're very sure of yourself, aren't you, Miss Jones?"

Cadie gasped, arching under Jo's touch. She found herself moving, her hips undulating of their own accord against the taller woman's. She finally found her voice.

"The one thing I've been sure of over the last few days," she said huskily, "is that with you, I was safe." She kissed the corner of Jo's mouth softly, moaning as the dark woman deepened the contact quickly with the tip of a warm, insistent tongue.

Soon they were lost in the kiss, their bodies moving together in an unconscious, slow rhythm. Legs tangled and thighs pressed against heated centers. Jo felt sensation building low in her belly and forced herself to pull away from the kiss. "God, Cadie," she growled. "Let's go to bed and get comfortable."

"Yes," the blonde replied breathlessly. "I want you so much, Jo."

Quickly they disentangled themselves and Jo stood, offering Cadie a hand up. "Want to grab the wine?" she suggested. "I'll go kick Mephy out of the bed."

Cadie grinned and nodded her agreement. She watched as Jo quickly walked into her bedroom.

If I ever get back use of my legs, I'll follow her. Wow. Cadie giggled nervously to herself as she bent down to pick up the wine bottle and two glasses. *Did Naomi ever make me feel this way?* A shiver of anticipation wriggled down her spine as she made her way to the bedroom.

Jo was working her way around the edges of the room, lighting candles as she went. She had always loved candlelight and now, more than ever, she wanted the atmosphere to be just right. As she lit the last few Cadie wandered in and they smiled quietly at each other.

"You're nervous," Cadie stated softly. Jo nodded, biting her bottom lip uncertainly. "Don't be," the blonde whispered. "I've never felt so right about anything in my entire life." She placed the bottle and glasses down on the bedside table and watched as Jo walked around the bed to join her.

The tall woman slid her arms around Cadie's waist, pulling

her close. "I just want this to be perfect," Jo whispered, ducking her head for another tender kiss.

"It already is," Cadie replied when they broke off. She slid her hands up Jo's stomach, curling her fingers around the smooth fabric of the skipper's silk shirt, and tugging it out of the waistband of her pants. Starting with the bottom button, she began undoing the fastenings, working her way up until she could slide her hands across the velvet skin of Jo's stomach. Cadie slipped the shirt off Jo's shoulders, then leaned forward to kiss gently along the lacy edge of the taller woman's bra.

Jo groaned. The sight and feel of the gorgeous blonde's face nuzzling her cleavage made her weak at the knees. She reached around and tugged at Cadie's t-shirt, determined to have the American's skin against her. Cadie stopped kissing the swell of Jo's breast long enough to allow her to drag the shirt over her head, but then resumed her task. Her hands caressed up Jo's back until they encountered the bra's clip, which she promptly and deftly released.

Cadie backed off a little, watching the bra drop away slowly to reveal Jo's full, exquisite breasts. She couldn't help but groan at the sight, and she stepped forward again, gently cupping one before kissing the proud nipple and sucking it tenderly into her mouth.

Jo's knees buckled as the warm, wet softness curled around her breast, and she cried out even as Cadie's arms quickly wrapped around her in support. The blonde moved them so the bed was against the back of Jo's knees and they dropped together, Cadie still suckling. Jo pulled her down on top of her and wrapped her tighter. "Oh, God, Arcadia, what are you doing to me?" Jo murmured, overwhelmed by the aching tug as Cadie alternated between one breast and the other, teasing with kisses and nibbles.

"Loving you," the blonde mumbled.

Jo reached down and took the younger woman's face in her hands, gently pulling her up. "Come here, so I can kiss you," she urged and Cadie quickly complied, sliding herself up the long, supple body beneath her. They kissed deeply, Jo taking the opportunity to undo the front-fastening of the blonde's bra, slipping her hand quickly under the fabric till she found a hard nub pressing against her palm. She caught it between her thumb and forefinger and squeezed gently, but relentlessly.

Cadie tore her mouth away and cried out as she arched, pushing herself up on her hands. Jo smiled at the intensity of the blonde's reaction, adoring the expression on the American's face as she teased and tweaked and rolled her nipple. Soon they were kissing again. Cadie's hand frantically worked on Jo's belt buckle, flicked it aside and slid the zipper down. Urgently, almost roughly, she wiggled her hand under the layers of fabric, marveling at the strong bands of muscle twitching under her fingers. Soon she was stroking through soft curls, then strongly cupping Jo's heat.

"Ohhh." Jo arched upward into the pressure from Cadie's fingers. She wanted more, so much more, but the blonde withdrew. Jo's eyes flickered open. "No, don't stop," she beseeched, but Cadie was standing next to the bed, fumbling with the fastening of her own jeans.

"I can't stand it anymore, Jo," Cadie muttered. "I have to be naked with you." She pushed down her jeans and panties, stepping out of them as Jo hurried to remove the rest of her own clothes.

Soon—finally—nothing separated them and both women reveled in the feel of skin on skin. Urgency, tempered by weeks of curiosity and desire, made them explore, tease, and tantalize each other until there was nowhere to go but forward. They traveled the contours and folds of each other's bodies with hands and mouths.

"Jossandra," Cadie murmured.

"Yes, my love," Jo replied, her mouth close to Cadie's ear, her low growl pulling an invisible chain attached to the blonde's center.

"Mmm," she responded. "Touch me, please, Jo-Jo. I need you to touch me."

Jo pulled back a little, looking deep into green eyes darkened by desire. She smiled slowly, trying to contain the nervous butterflies jangling in her stomach. She slid her hand under Cadie's shoulders, cradling the blonde close. Her right hand began a meandering journey down Cadie's midline, teasing her belly button, circling the points of her hipbones. Finally her fingertips came to rest at the edge of the blonde's curls.

By now Cadie's hips were moving of their own accord, and it was all Jo could do to stop herself plunging ahead. Instead she ducked her head and captured the blonde's nipple between her teeth, biting down gently. Cadie keened her response, arching again under her. Jo felt the blonde's hand on her wrist, pushing and urging her further. This time the dark-haired woman didn't resist, sliding her fingers through damp curls until she felt herself dipping into warm, moist folds, an exquisite sensation that threatened to tip her over the edge.

"Mmm, you are so wet, sweetheart," she whispered against Cadie's mouth. Her fingers found and teased the blonde's swollen nub, each flicker causing Cadie's hips to jerk.

"God, Jo, don't stop, please, don't stop," Cadie panted, riding the growing tide of sensation welling up between her legs. She slid an arm around Jo's waist and pulled her closer.

"Oh, I'm not going to stop, baby," Jo promised. She let her fingers dance over the sensitive bundle of nerves, then teased Cadie's entrance before returning, knowing instinctively what would drive the blonde to the brink. Cadie rocked against her, eyes closed, her breath coming fast and shallow between moans. Jo's own desire raged and she fought to keep control, wanting instead to concentrate on giving her partner pleasure. *I want this to be perfect for you, my angel.*

"Yes, Jo, please," Cadie almost yelped as she felt Jo's fingertips dip a little further inside her. "Please, baby, I want you inside me."

Jo groaned and slid her thigh between Cadie's, pressing her hand tighter against the blonde's wetness. She waited, reading Cadie's movements and then took her chance, plunging deep inside her with two long, strong fingers, her thumb resuming its teasing motions against her clitoris.

"Ohhh, Jo," Cadie sighed, pressing herself hard against the dark-haired woman's fingers.

"Yes, darling," Jo crooned, her own climax threatening as Cadie's frantic movements under her pushed her wetness rhythmically against the blonde's thigh. "Yes, sweetheart, come for me."

Cadie's consciousness was focused solely on the feel of the woman above her, around her and inside her. She suckled and nuzzled Jo's neck, no longer aware of her own body's movements, instead entranced by the building ache that seemed to flow like fire from Jo's fingertips. *Just...got...to...let...it...go,* her mind insisted.

She realized with a jolt that Jo was just as close as she was, the taller woman sliding wetly against her thigh even as her fingers continued to thrust inside Cadie. Jo voiced her passion in low moans close to Cadie's ear and suddenly the blonde was right on the brink.

"Jo-Jo, baby, come with me. Come with me, darling."

Jo answered with a groan that coursed through Cadie, tripping her over the edge. The dam broke and she was awash with pure sensation that blossomed deep in her guts and spread in waves that opened her wide.

Jo waited until she felt Cadie's climax rip through her and

then, a half-second later, she plummeted over the edge after her. They rocked and slid and convulsed together, their cries mingling and spurring each other on until, finally, inexorably, their movements slowed.   They were nose-to-nose, breathless, sweaty, and wide-eyed at their mutual experience.

"Wow," Jo whispered, searching the hooded green eyes below her. "Have you ever..."

Cadie shook her head weakly, bathing in the glow of the dazed blue orbs gazing into hers.   "Never," she said, trying to catch her breath, still feeling the throbbing deep inside her. *Oh no, Naomi never made me feel like this.* "Have you?"

"No."   Jo collapsed onto her and the blonde carefully wrapped her arms around the skipper, pulling her close and cuddling softly against her.

"Wow," she whispered.

Jo felt a month's worth of tension rush to the surface on the heels of her physical release. Safe in Cadie's arms, she was powerless to stop the sudden, silent sobs from wracking her body. She buried her face against Cadie's neck and held on for dear life.

"It's okay, sweetheart," Cadie soothed, stroking the older woman's silky hair as she held her close. "Let it out, baby, just let it out."   She felt Jo take a long, ragged breath and then, finally, she let loose, giving voice to her tears. "That's it, angel," Cadie crooned.

After a few minutes, Jo's breath came less roughly, and she slid to one side. Cadie reached out and brushed away the last of the tears. "Thank you," Jo whispered.

"For what?" Cadie kissed the end of her nose softly.

"I'm not sure," Jo replied uncertainly, caressing the blonde's stomach as they lay side by side.

"You've never felt safe enough to cry in another woman's arms before, have you, Jo-Jo?"

Jo shook her head mutely, emotion closing her throat suddenly. Cadie saw the helpless look cross Jo's face and she pulled her close again. "You're always safe with me, darling," she said.

"God, you are beautiful," Jo murmured as she leaned on an elbow, gazing down at Cadie, whose blonde locks spilled across the pillow. She traced the flush that rose on the American's skin with a fingertip, watching the goose bumps rising behind it.

Cadie's own fingers were busy, tracing lazy circles around Jo's breast, closing in on her nipple, and then moving out again. Slowly they began moving against each other once more, legs entwined, Jo half-pinning the smaller woman under her.

"So are you, my love," Cadie replied, entranced by the soft

blush that adorned Jo's angular cheeks. She wrapped her arms around the taller woman and pushed up, rolling them both over until she leaned over Jo. Then she began leaving a fiery trail of kisses between her breasts, teasing soft skin with her tongue as she slid down the long body under her.

"Where do you think you're going?" Jo growled softly.

Cadie lifted her head long enough to gaze frankly at her lover. "I want to taste you, darling," she whispered honestly.

"Ohhhhhh myyyyy," Jo responded as a shot of pure lust surged through her at the blonde's words. Cadie slid lower, trailing her tongue over skin suddenly covered in goose bumps. "Ohhh, it's going to be a long night," Jo murmured happily.

An evil chuckle was the blonde's only verbal response.

"Paul, relax will you? You're making me nervous just looking at you." Jo watched the tall crewman pacing the confined space of the *Seawolf's* cockpit like a caged lion. "I don't know what you're so tense about, anyway. We're in the middle of the ocean, and the bride's already on board. She's not gonna stand you up, mate."

"That's not the point, Skipper," Paul growled as he passed her for the millionth time in the last 10 minutes. "This is a big deal. This is for life, you know? Life." He paused and looked her in the eye for emphasis on the last word.

Jo couldn't help giggling. "Oh come on, Paulie. You can't tell me you're having doubts about this? You adore Jen. We all know. Hell, some of us have known it for months. Come to think of it, you were probably the last to know. But I know you, mate. And I've never seen you happier since you proposed to her." She watched as he resumed his pacing. "Snap out of it."

He stopped in his tracks and turned on his heel to face her. "I know, I know. I'm sorry, Skipper. I'm just nervous, is all."

Jo beamed at him and shrugged. "What's to be nervous about, mate?" she reassured him. "Take a look around." She gestured at their surroundings. "It's a gorgeous day. The boat is packed full of your best friends. We're in the middle of Heart Reef. And any minute now, Jen is going to come up that companionway looking stunning. What more could you ask for?"

He nodded. "You're right. I know you're right," he said. "Thanks, Skip."

"Hey, that's what a best man is for, right?" She grinned at the big man. "Go talk to Marilyn." She pushed him in the direction of Airlie Beach's resident eccentric and marriage celebrant, who was communing with nature near the stern. "Make sure she hasn't lost the vows."

"Jesus, you don't think she's—" He caught sight of Jo's face and realized he was being teased. "I'll get you for that, Skipper."

Below decks Cadie was putting the final touches on Jenny's bridal bouquet. Much to her surprise the *Seawolf* hostess had asked her to be her only attendant for the ceremony, a gesture Cadie very much appreciated.

I feel very at home here already, she thought with a smile as she handed the finished bouquet to Jenny. *And these two good people have been a big part of that.* A quick trip to the dress shops of Airlie had turned up a simple but gorgeous summer dress in just the right shade to complement Jenny's bridal outfit. It also happened to set off the green of Cadie's eyes, and all in all she was pleased with the effect.

Living in this kind of weather all year round is going to suit me just fine. She gave herself a quick appraisal in the main cabin's mirror, noting her healthy tan. *Beat's the hell out of winter in the Midwest, that's for sure.*

She turned as Jenny came out of the tiny bathroom. "Ready?" Cadie grinned at the brunette.

"As I'll ever be," Jenny replied, smiling. "Come on, let's go get me hitched, before the big dope changes his mind. He's been fretting for days."

Cadie laughed. "I think he was hoping you wouldn't notice."

Jenny snorted. "The man's been going to the bathroom every three hours for the past four days. It's been kind of hard not to notice." They both giggled. "Let's go put him out of his misery, shall we?"

Cadie walked out ahead of the bride, keying the stereo with the quiet background music Jenny and Paul had selected for the ceremony.

Jo hurriedly moved the nervous groom into position as she heard the music begin. The small crowd of friends and family who had been milling about the *Seawolf's* deck gathered around and she took up her position to Paul's right. The marriage celebrant stood at the stern facing forward.

Cadie came up on deck and Jo, who hadn't yet seen her new outfit, took a deep breath, and drank in the sight of the lovely blonde. The American caught the skipper's eye as she walked to Paul's left and smiled shyly, reading Jo's rapt expression accurately.

With all due respect to Jenny, Jo thought, *I know who the most beautiful woman here today is—and she's mine.* She slowly became aware that she had the silliest of grins on her face. *And I'm sure that everyone here knows that I think so.*

Cadie laughed quietly at the dumbstruck expression on her lover's face as she stood waiting for Jenny to take her place beside Paul. *Damn, she looks wonderful,* Cadie mused as she took in Jo's stylish grey silk pantsuit that nicely complemented Paul's suit. *She certainly knows how to dress.* She tried hard to refocus as Marilyn started proceedings.

"We are gathered here today to celebrate the love of Jenny and Paul," the celebrant began.

I wish we could do this, Jo thought, keeping her eyes firmly locked on Cadie's. She let the celebrant's words flow over her, concentrating instead on feeling the connection between herself and the beautiful blonde across the way. *I know we can do the commitment ceremony thing any time we want to, but...* Green eyes smiled back at her. *Twelve years with Naomi is a long time. She wouldn't want to tie herself down to someone else so soon after that.* Jo recognized her cue and handed Paul the tiny box containing the wedding rings. *Would she?*

Cadie watched as Jo waited for Paul to take both rings out of the box and then tucked the small velvet container back into her pocket. *Would she ever want go through a ceremony like this with me? We haven't talked much about her past girlfriends.* She blinked a couple of times at the thought. *We haven't talked about it at all. I don't really know how she feels about this sort of commitment.* She listened as Jenny and Paul exchanged their vows. *I know there isn't anyone else I want to spend my life with. But I'm not sure she wants that.* Jenny slid the ring on Paul's finger and Cadie smiled. *Does she?*

"And now Jenny and Paul have a rather unusual request to make of you all," the marriage celebrant said. The bride and groom turned to face the guests and Jo and Cadie did the same, exchanging smiling glances. "You are all here today because you are cherished friends and family of these two. Are you willing to offer them both friendship, love, care, and support as they make their way through life together?"

There was barely a pause before the resounding response came from all on board. "We do!"

Jo couldn't take her eyes off Cadie as the ceremony ended and her heart melted as she realized the blonde was having the same problem. Jenny and Paul wandered off to be congratulated by the rest of the guests and the two lovers clasped hands as they met behind them.

"You look stunning," Cadie whispered as Jo leaned down to

kiss her on the cheek.

"And you take my breath away," Jo replied softly, wishing they could be alone. Both took a few seconds to absorb the warmth between them.

"So what's the plan?" Cadie asked.

"Well, we party on here while we sail to Hayman Island, where we drop Paul and Jen off at the resort." She grinned. "And then Rosa and Roberto have invited us to dinner at their place." She indicated the gregarious Italian couple who were laughing with Paul and Jenny further forward. She leaned in and whispered conspiratorially. "I think they want to meet my new girl-friend."

"Oh, Lord," Cadie sighed. "Rosa's already met me, remember?" She winced, recalling that ugly night.

"Mhmm, but this time she wants to meet you as *la parte della famiglia*—part of the family," Jo replied with a reassuring smile.

"Oh, Lord."

Cadie couldn't believe how much food there was on the table. She and Jo were the Palmieri's only guests but... *There has to be enough here to feed 20 people,* the blonde wondered, awestruck. *I didn't even know there were this many kinds of pasta.*

"Honey," a sexy, low whisper came close to her ear. "Don't look so scared. It's only spaghetti."

Cadie giggled, but whispered back. "Tell me that when I've exploded and they're scraping me off the walls."

Jo laughed and slid her hand to Cadie's knee and squeezed reassuringly. "S'all right, sweetheart," she said. "I'll make sure Rosa doesn't stuff you beyond your limits." She grinned.

"Gee, thanks," Cadie sighed. Just then Rosa and Roberto came back into the room, each carrying another enormous platter of food. "Good grief," Cadie whispered, eyes widening. Jo sniggered.

"Here we are, here we are," Rosa exclaimed, putting her dish down on one of the few remaining clear spots on the overloaded table. "Come, come, Arcadia, help yourself, please." She began spooning indiscriminate tablespoons of pasta and sauce onto Cadie's plate.

"Wow, Mrs Palmieri, this is an amazing spread," Cadie said, smiling at the woman.

"Ah, ah, ah, *mia piccola principessa,*" said Rosa, wagging a finger at the American admonishingly. "I have already told you, you must call me Rosa. Everybody, they call me Rosa." She walked behind Jo's chair, ruffling the tall skipper's hair as she went. "Even this one."

"I'll try to remember, Rosa, thank you," Cadie said graciously.

Further conversation was made impossible by the tumultuous arrival of Rosa's youngest, 12-year-old Sophie, dragging her older brother Tony by the hand. "See, I told you they were here, Tony," the youngster squealed in delight, letting the young man's hand go and leaping onto Jo's lap.

The skipper happily absorbed the impact. "Hello, possum, how are you?" she asked as she tickled the squirming girl.

"I'm good." Big brown eyes took in Cadie's presence. "Aren't ya gonna introduce me, Jo-Jo?" she asked cheekily, grinning.

"Yes, brat, I am, if you give me half a chance. Sophie, this is Cadie Jones. Cadie, this little monster is Sophie Palmieri."

"Nice to meet you, Sophie," Cadie said, extending a hand which the girl shook enthusiastically.

"So you must be Jo's new girlfriend, huh?" she asked bluntly.

Jo rolled her eyes and slapped her forehead at the youngster's precociousness.

"Yes, yes I am," Cadie said, grinning back at the pre-teen.

"That's cool," Sophie replied calmly. "You must be pretty special though. She's never brought anybody here for dinner before."

"Is that right?" Cadie looked at her lover, who was blushing deeply, and smiled softly.

"Go, troublemaker," Jo said gruffly as she slapped Sophie on the backside and sent her giggling on her way.

The rest of the Palmieri family settled into their places around the table but before they could begin eating Rosa had them all hold hands for grace. Cadie slid her right hand into Jo's and felt Roberto's larger, rougher hand take her left. The surprised look on Jo's face told her that it wasn't usual for Rosa to say a formal blessing before meals.

"We must thank *Il Padre* before we eat," Rosa insisted, smiling at her guests. Everyone bowed their head and the matriarch led the prayers. "We thank you, Father, for the food on our table and the love of our family, both of our blood and of our choosing." Cadie felt Jo squeeze her hand and she smiled. "We thank you also for the life of Ron Cheswick, for the many blessings he brought to us while he was here." She paused as they all reflected on the week's events. "And finally, Father, we thank you for the new joy we see in *bella* Jossandra's eyes." This time it was Jo's turn to feel Cadie's reassuring squeeze. "You have seen fit to find a way to bring Arcadia into her life and we know it means only good things for them both. Amen." An echo came around the table.

Cadie opened her eyes to a circle of wide smiles that she readily returned. Jo was speechless and more than a little tearful at Rosa's gesture. Fortunately, the Italian didn't expect too much of her in response.

"Don't look so stunned, little one," she pronounced, reaching up with both hands and patting the tall woman's cheeks. "You know we have always wanted the best for you, Jo-Jo. Why would you be so surprised that we give thanks when our prayers are answered?" She beamed at the dark-haired woman.

"Thank you, Rosa," Cadie said quietly. "Thank you, all of you."

Roberto squeezed her hand. "You are *familia* now," he said. "Come on, everybody, we eat now. Enough talk."

Jo laughed and turned to look at Cadie, who brushed away a tear from her lover's cheek with a soft fingertip.

"I'm just a big mushball, aren't I?" Jo asked huskily.

"It's all right, sweetheart, your secret is safe with us," Cadie said solemnly, resisting the urge to tweak the embarrassed woman any further. But her twinkling green eyes gave her away.

"Oh shut up," Jo replied softly as she leaned in to steal a kiss.

"Ewww, mushy stuff. Make them stop, mama," a disgusted voice came from the other side of the table.

"Hush, Sophia," her mother admonished. "One day very soon you will realize that—how do you say it in English, Jo-Jo? *L'amore fa il mondo va rotondo.*"

Jo laughed and leaned towards Sophie. "Love makes the world go round, kiddo."

"Ewww, gross."

Cadie didn't have to do much convincing to persuade Jo to take a midnight stroll along the beach with her before they went back to the *Seawolf.* The evening had been full of fun and laughter and for the first time in weeks she felt fully relaxed and happy. She tucked herself into the crook of Jo's arm as they wandered barefoot along the Hayman Island beach. Away to their left the lights of the resort twinkled and above them the moon, approaching full once again, bathed everything in liquid silver.

Jo was silent but Cadie sensed the tall woman was content just to be together.

"You do realize we're going to save an incredible amount of money over the next few weeks," Cadie said finally.

There was a pause while her lover thought about the incongruousness of that statement.

"Okay, I'll bite," Jo said finally. "Why is that?"

"Because I for one won't need to eat for about a month," Cadie said with a grin. She patted her stomach. "God, I feel like a tubby little Buddha."

Jo kissed the top of her head and laughed at the thought. "S'funny, because you look like a gorgeous, sexy woman," she said softly.

"Ohhh, you are such a sweet talker," Cadie replied, standing on her toes to reach up and plant a kiss on Jo's cheek. "It was a lovely day, Jo-Jo. Thank you."

"For what?"

"For including me in everything. The wedding. Rosa and her family. It's been wonderful."

Jo was a little perplexed and she stopped walking, pulling Cadie around to face her. She tipped the blonde's chin up slightly with her fingertips. "Arcadia," she said gently. "You are a part of me. Somehow I knew that from the moment we met. I couldn't *not* include you in everything if my life depended on it." She gazed down into silvered green eyes. "Is that what you want, my love?" She found herself holding her breath.

"It was a beautiful ceremony today, wasn't it?" Cadie asked after a brief pause. Jo nodded silently. "I kept wondering all through it, if that was the kind of commitment you would want to make to us, one day." She saw Jo's eyes, almost black in the moonlight, widen. "Because I think it's what I want," the blonde whispered. "I just wasn't sure...I mean, we've never talked about...that kind of thing..."

Jo grinned. "When have we had the chance? Talk about your whirlwind romance."

They both laughed softly.

Jo traced Cadie's lips delicately with the pad of her thumb. "Angel, I have never in my life felt about anyone the way I feel about you." She wrapped her other arm around the blonde's waist, just wanting the feel of the compact body against her. "When I was in Sydney..." She paused, reluctant to let her mind go back there. "Women were afraid of me. I was the Dark Avenger, y'know?" She shook her head ruefully and she felt Cadie's arms slide around her reassuringly. "And when I came up here I just kept everyone at arm's length. Emotionally, at least."

Cadie chuckled at the woman's blush, just discernable in the moonlight. "It's okay, sweetheart," she said softly. "I'd pretty much figured out you were no virgin."

Jo snorted. "But then you came along," she continued. "And I didn't want to keep you at arm's length. Not ever. Not in any way at all." Cadie grinned up at her. "During the wedding I was wondering if it was way too early to be asking you to marry me." Jo swallowed hard.

"Are you proposing, Jo-Jo?" the blonde whispered, desperate to be sure she was understood properly.

Jo nodded. "I love you, Cadie. I know you were with Naomi for a long time, and that you've only been away from her for less than a week. But I can't think of any better way to tell you how I feel, than to ask you to spend the rest of your life with me."

Cadie's heart melted at the simplicity of the tall woman's words. She stretched up and captured Jo's soft lips in a deep, passion-filled kiss that escalated quickly until the skipper took them both down into the warm sand. Jo cradled her as they let the desire ebb a little into a gentle undercurrent.

"Jossandra," Cadie whispered close to her lover's ear, "it doesn't matter how long I was with Naomi. It doesn't matter how long I've been away from her. None of that mattered from the moment I saw you. It just took until Sydney Airport for me to realize it." She felt Jo smile. "Yes, my love, I will marry you."

Jo buried her face into the soft skin of Cadie's neck, speechless with happiness. Cadie smiled up at the moon over Jo's shoulder, feeling more contentment than she had a right to, she was sure. "I adore you, Jo-Jo," she said quietly. She felt the skipper pull away just enough that they could look into each other's eyes.

"And I adore you, Arcadia," came the reply. "Now and forever."

"Now and forever," the blonde confirmed.

They were content to lie sleepily entangled in the sand for several minutes, just listening to the rush and retreat of the small waves against the beach.

"There are a lot of loose ends, baby," Jo murmured finally against Cadie's neck.

"Mhmm, that there are," the blonde agreed. "Not the least of which is figuring out what we have to do so that I can stay here permanently."

"Are you sure that's what you want to do?" Jo asked, shifting so she was resting on one elbow. "We could go live back in the States."

Cadie smiled and shook her head. "Sweetheart, you just inherited your dream business. Don't try and tell me you want to give that up, because I know better." Jo grinned down at her, recognizing it for the truth. "My business is the mobile one," Cadie continued. "All I need is a phone and a laptop and I've already got those."

"What about your family, and all your stuff back in Chicago?"

"Well, Mom and Dad will understand. They've already heard a lot about you," the blonde said, brushing a stray lock of ebony hair off Jo's face as she thought about the phone calls she'd had with her mother over the past several days. "By the way, Mom called this morning while you were getting Paul organized."

"Yeah?" Jo kissed the corner of her mouth softly.

"Mhmm," Cadie replied languidly, happily noting the wave of tingles spreading through her as Jo's hands explored. "A van full of my stuff arrived on her doorstep yesterday."

Jo paused and met the blonde's eyes steadily. "Wow," she said grimly. "Fast work."

"Mhmm. The senator doesn't waste much time when she's pissed."

Jo sighed, a frown creasing her brow. Cadie reached up and smoothed it away with a gentle fingertip.

"Darling, don't worry about it. We have two months before my visa runs out. That's plenty of time to work out all these details. After all, look what we've done in just one month." They both laughed softly, and she slid a hand around the back of Jo's neck, tugging her down for another long kiss. "Right now, all I want is you."

Jo groaned. "Your wish is my command, princess," she murmured.

Several heated minutes later, it was Cadie who came up for air first. "Jo-Jo," she gasped.

"Mmm?"

"This beach is very romantic, but if you're going to continue to touch me there..." She caressed the back of Jo's intrepid hand gently and felt her lover grin against her neck. "Then take me back to the *Seawolf* first. Sand in that particular spot doesn't really appeal."

A low rumbling chuckle close to her ear sent sexy chills down the American's spine but before she could make the most of it, Jo was on her feet and offering her a hand up. They walked hand-in-hand back along the beach towards the Hayman Island marina.

"Would you like to go sailing tomorrow?" Jo asked.

"Mmm, yes please," Cadie replied. "I wish we could take Mephisto with us, Jo. He hasn't seen much of us this week."

"We can," Jo said matter-of-factly.

Cadie stopped in her tracks. "Really? On the boat?"

Jo nodded, grinning at the blonde's surprised expression. "Sure. I take him sailing with me a lot. He comes from a long line of ship's cats. The only reason he doesn't come on every cruise on the *Seawolf* is because there's always one guest who's allergic." She kissed Cadie quickly and pulled her along the beach again. "He's an old hand."

"Cool. So we could pick him up in the morning?"

"Yup."

Silence reigned again for a few more seconds.

"Hey," Cadie said suddenly. "First one back to the boat gets to be on top." She raised a playful eyebrow.

"Oooo, you're on," Jo purred, with a lopsided, sexy grin.

Cadie crouched into a starting position.

"On your mark," she said. "Get set..." The blonde set off at a sprint, pounding along the damp, hard sand near the waterline. "Go," she yelled over her shoulder at the stationery skipper left in her wake.

Jo chuckled. "I don't know what the future's going to bring, Cadie Jones, but with you I know it's never going to be dull," she muttered, grinning as she pushed herself off, long legs chasing after the woman of her dreams.

Cate Swannell is a journalist and writer living on the east coast of Australia with her boycat Siggy and her Dell. Her home on the web can be found at www.kotb.net. *Heart's Passage* is her first novel, though not, she hopes, her last.

Printed in the United States
1294500003B/127-129

9 781932 300093